To Malcolm.
I hope that you
this as much as , - ,
writing it.
John Holt. 22/7/2012

A Killing In The City

by

John Holt

ISBN   1475071280

EAN   978-1475071283

'A Killing In The City' is published by Night Publishing who can be contacted at: http://www.nightpublishing.com.

The story that follows is totally fictitious. All places and persons included in the story are totally imaginary, and any similarity to actual persons, alive or dead, is totally coincidental and unintentional. Although many of the places mentioned in the story do actually exist, they have been changed as necessary to serve the needs of this story.

'To make a killing in the City' is a phrase often used within the financial world to indicate making a large profit on investments, or through dealings on the stock market - the bigger the profit, the bigger the killing.

However, Tom Kendall, a private detective on holiday in London, has a different kind of killing in mind when he hears about the death of one of his fellow passengers who travelled with him on the plane from Miami.

It was suicide, apparently, a simple overdose of prescribed tablets. Kendall immediately offers his help to Scotland Yard and is shocked when he is told his services will not be required. They can manage perfectly well without him, thank you.

This is the fourth story to feature Tom Kendall. Once again his ever-loyal secretary, Mollie, ably assists him in his fight against crime.

Chapter One

John Wyndham Collier

The City of London is often referred to as the Square Mile, or just simply The City. Almost two thousand years old, The City is the historic core of London, the central hub around which the modern conurbation grew. It is now a major business and financial centre, ranking on a par with New York City as one of the leading centres of global finance. At its heart is the Bank of England, the controller, and keeper, of the Nation's finances for almost three hundred years. A hundred yards, or so, further to the north is located the second of The City's great financial institutions, the London Stock Exchange, where everyday fortunes are made, or lost, at the whim of world affairs, and the market traders.

Almost opposite the Stock Exchange, at the junction of Threadneedle Street, and Bishopsgate, is the third of The City's major buildings, the Travers Morgan Building, known locally quite simply as The Tower.

* * *

Constructed in the late nineteen eighties, The Tower is a glass and steel structure that rises some twenty-two storeys high. It is home to Travers Morgan PLC, one of the world's leading investment companies. Travers Morgan was founded at the turn of the century, by John Travers, and Clifford Morgan. At that time it was mainly involved in transportation, notably shipping and the railway. Benefiting from the First World War, it had grown into a huge conglomeration of companies encompassing banking, insurance, shipping and trade.

* * *

Seated in his large plush office, located up on the tenth floor was John Wyndham Collier, the head of Travers Morgan. This was to be an important day for John Wyndham Collier. He was expecting some visitors. *Not that the visitors themselves were particularly important.* They were merely incidental, nothing more than necessary players in the forthcoming main event that was soon to unfold.

For the tenth time in as many minutes Collier glanced at the clock on the wall. He smiled and took a deep breath. *This was going to be a big day,* he thought, *a very big day indeed.*

He started to tap the desk with his fingers, the drumming gradually becoming louder, and louder, faster and faster. Patience was a virtue Collier did not possess. Impatient as ever, he was anxious to get on. Time was money, and he had no desire to waste either commodity.

* * *

John Wyndham Collier was a big man, big in every sense of the word. Six feet four tall, and weighing a little over fourteen stone, he controlled this vast financial empire that had a presence in every part of the globe. He wielded power with an iron fist. Nobody crossed Collier, not if they had any sense, that is. Nobody disagreed with him. Nobody argued with him, and nobody ever questioned his judgement. Nobody dared. Not if they wanted to keep their job. What he said went.

He was a self-made man who had worked his way up to the higher echelons of power. He was now head of this financial giant. He owned fifty-one percent of the shares, and was the Chief Executive Officer and Chairman of the Board. Nothing happened in the company without his knowledge, and his agreement.

Of course he hadn't done it entirely alone. He had made good use of several other people over the years. Not that they had any knowledge of what was happening of course, or had actually given their consent. No not at all, far from it. Indeed they hadn't actually suspected a thing. In fact, the vast majority of them didn't even know of his existence. If they had known what was happening they would almost certainly have objected. Many of them had lost their life savings because of Collier, not that they knew of his involvement.

Always the opportunist, Collier had merely taken advantage of various situations that had occurred. And why not, he asked. If a few people were just too gullible, or too stupid, was that his fault? No, it wasn't. So they couldn't think for themselves, was that his problem? *Was he his brother's keeper?* No, he wasn't. If a few people got hurt, or trodden on, along the way, well it was just unfortunate, wasn't it? So be it. It was just one of those things, *one of those things that could not be helped. What did it matter anyway? Did anyone really care?* Collier very much doubted it. Besides he wasn't really worried whether they cared or not. In fact he wasn't worried at all. So he had made a few enemies along the way, *more than a few.* But what did that compare with the power he now possessed. *You couldn't cook an omelette without cracking a few eggs,* could you?

If you don't want to get burnt, stay out of the kitchen. That was one of Collier's favourite sayings. He had got burnt, once, many years ago. He had vowed then and there it would never happen again.

* * *

Collier's office clearly showed the trappings of power, wealth, and success. To one side was a large mahogany desk. On the desk were a number of buff-coloured files and several papers neatly piled on one side. On the wall opposite was a large mahogany cabinet, which took up most of the wall space. On the shelves was row after row of leather bound books. Amongst them were a number of extremely valuable and very rare first editions. Interspersed amongst the books were several large ornaments. Included were a number of vases, and a group of porcelain figurines. The end section of the cabinet contained a selection of drinks. To one side of the cabinet were two leather armchairs, and a low mahogany table. On the adjacent wall were a number of filing cabinets and another small bookcase containing a number of ring binders. Next to the filing cabinets was a large leather sofa.

On three of the walls were a number of original oil paintings, including a Renoir, and a Degas. Not that Collier was an art connoisseur, because he wasn't. He knew nothing about art, and cared even less. All that he knew was the possible monetary value a work of art might have. That was all that mattered as far as he was concerned. Those three paintings were investments, nothing more. So too were the first editions and the porcelain figurines that lined the shelves of the bookcase. *Whatever artistic qualities they possessed were of no interest whatsoever.*

* * *

Collier suddenly stood up and pushed his huge leather swivel chair back hard from his desk. It struck the wall with a loud thud. Collier was breathing heavily. He slowly walked over to the window, and peered out, down to the ground below. It wasn't the most scenic view ever but it did give a commanding view of the main car park area located at the rear of the building. From here he could see every coming or going. He looked over to the far side. The allocated parking space was still vacant. Not that he was surprised. He looked over at the wall clock. *Two thirty-five.* His visitors were not due for almost another hour yet. He looked back at the parking space. *That's where Graham Nicholas Baxter will park*, he murmured.

He turned back towards his desk. Of course he hadn't really thought to see Baxter's car. Not just then at any rate. Not that Baxter would be late, that much was certain. He would certainly be on time. *In fact he would probably arrive a little early if anything*, Collier thought. Baxter could not afford to miss this meeting.

He looked back at the clock. Suddenly he was strangely nervous. No, he wasn't nervous exactly, apprehensive maybe, unsure. Whatever it was, Collier did not like the feeling. He felt vulnerable somehow. *Suppose Baxter had decided not to come after all. Suppose he had decided to make a fight of it instead. Perhaps he wouldn't just take it lying down. That was unthinkable, impossible. Even Baxter wasn't that stupid. How could he possibly make a fight of it?* Collier shook his head. Impossible it may be, unthinkable perhaps, and yet he was still strangely uneasy. *Suppose everything hadn't been covered. Suppose something had been missed. Something he had overlooked somehow. Had he missed a loophole somewhere, a possible way out for Baxter?* He looked over at his desk. There was the document awaiting Baxter's signature. Collier had spent weeks preparing it. He had gone through it over and over. Nothing had been overlooked. There was no loophole. He had checked every word, every letter. He knew every line, every full stop, and every comma. Nothing had been left to chance. He had checked everything. Then he had double-checked, and then he had checked again. He had missed nothing. He started to relax and smile once again. *Baxter would be there, make no mistake. He had no real choice did he?*

Collier looked at the clock once again. *Two-forty.* He sat down. For the twentieth time he started to move things around on his desk. First he moved the telephone into the middle of the desk. Then the computer keyboard was pushed to one side, to make room for the intercom. Then the telephone would be moved once again, and then the intercom returned to its original position. He was becoming increasingly impatient. He glanced at the wall clock once again. Collier hated sitting around waiting. Once he had a course of action in his mind, he just wanted to get on with it, to get it over and done with. He had been planning for this day for a long time now. Long enough, he thought. He just wanted to get on with it now.

He started to tap his fingers on the desk once more, drumming faster and faster, louder and louder. Then he started to move things around once again. An old sepia photograph of a young lady, in a gold frame was moved from one side to the other. He stopped and looked at the photograph for a few moments. He shook his head and raised his hand to his cheek. *It was of his mother. Not that he remembered her. She had died when he was no more than two years old.* He raised his hand to his cheek once again and brushed away a tear. No, the tear wasn't for his mother. The tear came as he remembered how his father had been after her death. How he had beaten, and humiliated the young John Wyndham for poor results at school.

* * *

"Must do better, boy," his father would say. It was never John, or son. It

8

was always 'boy'. "You're not trying, boy." Sometimes his father said nothing at all and simply glared. That was even worse for the young boy, the complete silence, to be ignored, as though he never actually existed.

"There are two types of people," his father would say. "There are those who succeed and those who don't. There is no point in coming second. Remember it's not the taking part that counts. What matters is the winning."

* * *

John Wyndham Collier took those words to heart and lived by that rule from that time on. He stared at the photograph for a few moments longer. He sighed deeply and reached for the frame. Slowly he laid it face down on to the desk. He shook his head and started to nervously tap the buttons on the intercom. Accidentally he pressed the call button. Instantly he pressed the cancel button.

He was too late. Immediately there came an answering call. "Did you want something, sir?" a voice asked. It was his secretary.

"No, nothing," he replied sharply. There was no hint of an apology. He started to replace the handset, and then suddenly changed his mind.

"Is the room ready?" he asked.

"Everything is ready, sir," Joyce replied. "There's nothing to worry about."

Collier grunted, and replaced the handset. He shook his head. "Nothing to worry about," he repeated. *What did she know about it anyway?* Then he started to smile. Really though, she was right. *There was nothing to worry about, was there?* He had thought of everything. Every eventuality had been covered. Every contingency had been allowed for. Every possibility had been taken into account. There would be no surprises. No slip-ups. Nothing could, or would, go wrong.

He stood up once again. As he did so, he pushed his diary to one side. *Too hard.* The diary slid over the edge of the desk and fell to the floor. He sighed and slowly walked around to the front of the desk. The diary was lying open. Collier bent down and picked it up. As he did so he glanced at the entry on the open page. *Six months ago!* Had it really been six months? He nodded slowly. *Six months almost to the day.* That's when his opportunity had come, at last. That's when he was able, finally, to put his plans into operation.

* * *

It wasn't exactly on a par with the great Wall Street Crash of 1929, but on that particular Monday morning, almost six months ago, it had come pretty close. Stock Markets had crashed all around the Globe, losing ten percent of their value in one day. It had started on the Hang Seng with heavy trading on oil and the dollar. This was quickly followed on the Nikkei, and the Malaysian markets. The value of the dollar had plummeted to an all-time low. The effects had then quickly spread, with major panic selling, leading to even greater falls.

The exact cause of the fall was uncertain. High interest rates was put forward as a possible cause; increased levels of borrowing was another possibility. There was no one particular reason however, nothing that could be readily identified, nothing that you could put your finger on. All of the financial experts were agreed, however, on one thing – the market slump was only short term. It was only a temporary glitch and of no major concern. *It would not last*, said Her Majesty's Treasury. *A temporary setback only*, said The Governor of the Bank of England, *it would all be over in a few short weeks*.

This was a view that was echoed in the money markets around the world. "*We have seen this kind of thing before*," said the United States Federal Reserve. "*Don't read too much into it*," pronounced the Editor of the Wall Street Journal. "*It doesn't mean anything. The markets will bounce back, stronger than ever. Just mark my words.*"

But the Markets did not bounce back. They continued to fall unchecked. Share prices went into free-fall. The dollar continued to lose value. The Financial Times, and the Confederation of British Industries called for a substantial cut in interest rates. The Markets still continued to fall. The United States Treasury injected massive amounts into the economy, but to no effect. The Markets still fell. The World Bank called for a massive rise in interest rates to stimulate investment. The Markets still fell. By the end of the second week share values had fallen by twenty-four percent.

* * *

Credit crunch was one of the buzzwords going around at the time. There was, of course, a long official, complicated definition of what that meant, but simply put it meant that the banks had just pulled the plug and had stopped loaning money. Furthermore, any money they had loaned they wanted back, and they wanted it there and then. Furthermore there would be no further loans. *And why would they suddenly stop loaning?* Because, in recent years, there had just been too much credit and too many people were now failing to keep up the payments. Huge losses resulted. The banks were no longer prepared to take the risk. Added to that were depressed share values and high interest rates. It was as simple as that. Any first year economics student would have known exactly what was happening, immediately. They would have done something about it long before. A cap on loans might have helped. More stringent requirements on borrowers, or perhaps re-negotiated loan terms might have had an effect. Or improved collateral possibly, or better security. In any event, they would have done something long ago.

The so-called experts had, however, taken considerably longer to see it coming, and they were still taken by surprise. All right, so it was unforeseen. All right no one could have forecast it, but eventually they came to realise the worst. *The economy was in meltdown.* So now what? What should be done about it? What was the best course of action? What was the best way out of the trouble? Cut public spending, was the judgement of one group. *No*, said another, *not at all, quite the opposite in fact. You have to spend your way out of a recession, and boost the economy. Spend, spend, spend. Nonsense*, said a third group. *Cut interest rates*, was their advice. *A massive cash injection was required*, was the counsel of a fourth group. *Increase public borrowing*, suggested a fifth. Whilst another group advocated wide scale investment, although where the finance was to come from was something of a mystery.

The only thing that the experts could actually agree on was that something had to be done, and done quickly. Although what that something was no one was prepared to say. *More to the point, no one actually knew.*

Chapter Two

It's An Ill Wind

The financial experts didn't know what to do. In fact no one seemed to know, that is, except for John Wyndham Collier. He had seen it coming. And he had made his plans. He was ready for it. *He knew exactly what to do.* Not that he could stop it, of course. Nor, indeed, did he want to stop it. At least not right now. That would not have suited his purpose at all. As far as he was concerned the situation could go on for as long as it liked. He knew how to make the best of the situation and how to take advantage of it. And he did so, to the full.

"*It's an ill wind that blows nobody any good,*" he whispered. Then he shook his head. Not true, because in this case that wind was making him money, and lots of it. As shares prices started to fall, Collier started buying up stock in other companies, *other rival companies, especially The Baxter Corporation.* Fairly soon he had acquired large blocks. In fact, he now had a controlling interest in most of them.

* * *

Was it really only six months ago? He shook his head in disbelief, and slowly placed the diary back on to the desk. Six months, and still there was no consensus of opinion. Still no overall strategy had been put into operation. Oh there had been talks of course. Seemingly endless discussions had taken place. Both the International Monetary Fund, and the World Bank had produced wordy documents on the subject, but no firm universal proposals had, as yet, been put forward. The United States Treasury, and the European Union had produced dozens of reports, but they were only assessments of the situation at that particular time. Forecast after meaningless forecast were issued, only for the figures to be proved wrong, and requiring amendment at a later date.

So much for the so-called experts, Collier thought with disgust. Six months on and the recession was far from over. In fact, if anything, it had got much worse. The economy was now in deep recession. That was now official, finally. Everyone had suspected it for weeks and weeks, but now it had actually been formally confirmed. It was now Global, and affected every major economy in the World. The blame was placed fairly and squarely upon the far eastern markets. They, in turn, had blamed the western economy. Interest rates were cut to their lowest levels since records had begun. It made no difference. It was too little, and far too late. Two more major banks had ceased to exist overnight, bringing the total worldwide to fifty-three. Two other major banks were to receive massive bailouts from the Government. Many more were in a precarious position, teetering on the brink of closure. Companies were going out of business at the rate of one hundred and twenty-four per day.

Bankruptcies and redundancies were becoming commonplace. Shop after shop had closed down, office after office, factory after factory. Unemployment levels were now at a height not seen since the late nineteen fifties. Government borrowing had tripled, with even higher rates predicted. Massive cuts in public spending were announced, together with increased taxes. Still there was no sign of any major change to the situation, and still there was no consensus with regard to a long term solution.

* * *

Amidst all of the doom and gloom, there was, however, one company that stood out like a shining beacon. An example of what good management could achieve. That was Travers Morgan. Whilst every other company was showing record losses, in the past quarter Travers Morgan's profits had soared to a massive twenty-six billion, up by seven percent on the previous quarter. A substantial part of that profit had been set aside to finance an acquisition long planned for by John Wyndham Collier. It had been six years since the idea had first come into his mind. Opposition to his plan had originally been fierce, and widespread. It was far too risky said one. *It would be far too expensive* said another. *What was to be gained?* asked a third. Collier had stuck to his guns however, and would not back down. *Yes, it would be risky, and expensive, but the potential profits would be enormous. Besides he had an old score to settle. One other thing*, Collier told his opponents, *if you don't like the idea, leave.*

Gradually he began to gain support, one way or another. Opposition faded away, and he began to finalise his plan. That plan would now, at last, be put into operation. The Baxter Corporation acquisition was to go ahead. The papers were due to be signed that very afternoon.

* * *

Collier sat back down. He reached over and picked up one of the files lying at the side of the desk. On the front cover there was a small white label. Written across the centre was a single word, Baxter. He opened it and started to flick through the pages. When he had found the section he wanted, he began to read. He read quite slowly taking in every word, even though he knew it almost by heart.

The Baxter Corporation had been established in the early spring of 1858, by Baxter's great grandfather, Thaddeus Jonah Baxter. Originally it was nothing more than a simple loan company, a glorified moneylender offering loans at extortionate rates of interest. The Company had then started to offer mortgages. Gradually the company had built up encompassing a range of financial services regarding property, transport, export and import, trade, shipping and insurance. Then a little over ten years ago it had started to deal in Futures. That is when Collier had joined the firm.

Collier looked up and shook his head. For a while things had been good, he remembered, very good. The business had built up significantly and he was doing nicely, as they say. He gradually worked his way up until he became a Section Head. Then came that little bit of trouble. It was all over something very vague, a large sum of money had gone missing or something of the kind. Then the accusations of insider trading had started. Fraud was mentioned. Then the rumours began and quickly spread. But that was all they were, rumours, nothing but rumours, malicious accusations, hearsay. It was nothing more than circumstantial evidence. Finally there was the official enquiry. It could prove nothing of course, but still the rumours continued. Then there was a second enquiry. It was never proved, and no money was ever recovered, but it had left a nasty taste in the mouth.

He shook his head and tapped the file. It was all there. There were copies of the official reports, the newspaper cuttings and the findings of the enquiry. Still there had been no proof, no conclusive evidence. There had been nothing definite. Nonetheless it had been politely suggested that it might be best, for all concerned, if Collier actually sought a position elsewhere. *Collier had been forced to resign. Naturally he would be adequately compensated.*

* * *

Collier smiled and shook his head again. *That had been old man Baxter's suggestion. Oh certainly he had received compensation, the equivalent of eight weeks salary.* And naturally there had been no possibility of a reference. *That was also Baxter's decision. "I'm sure that you understand?" he had said.*

Collier threw the file back down. *Oh yes he understood right enough.*

He looked at the clock once again. *Two forty-three.* He shook his head. Time seemed to be going so slowly. He hated waiting, wasting time. He needed to be doing something. *Anything as long as it made a profit.* He started to drum his fingers on the desk once again. Then he pushed the file away angrily. It slid along the desk, stopping just a few inches from the edge.

Collier turned to the large dark blue, leather bound diary lying close by. He opened it to where the blue marker ribbon indicated the entries for that day. The entry simply read "Baxter 3.30 pm." It was underlined in red. He flipped the diary closed.

Lying in the middle of the desk was an old fashion leather blotter pad. The blotter paper was pristine and unused. On top of the pad was a flip top notebook. It was lying open. Written on the open page was the date, together with a heading, "Things to be done." Underneath was just one word – *Baxter*. Collier looked at the word for a few moments. He started to laugh and then drew a thick line through the name, and closed the notebook.

Beyond the notebook was an internal intercom. Close by was the telephone and a fax machine. Next to the telephone was a combined walnut pen tray and desk tidy. There was an array of pens and pencils, neatly lined up, together with a number of rulers. In front of the desk tidy was a heavy glass paperweight, and a stainless steel letter opener. To the left side of the desk was a desktop computer. Visible on the screen were two words 'Travers Morgan'. The words continually flew across the screen. Backwards, forwards, up and down, side to side. The computer keyboard had been carelessly pushed to one side. The computer mouse lay dangling over the edge of the desk. For a few moments Collier sat motionless, staring at the keyboard. Suddenly he angrily swept his hand across the desk sending both the keyboard, and the mouse crashing to the ground.

There was a single tap on the office door. Then it opened and a young lady peered into the room. "I heard a noise," she said. "Is everything all right?"

Collier looked over at the door. "Everything is fine," he replied. "Just tell me when they arrive. Now get out."

The young lady did not need to be told twice.

* * *

Next door to Collier's office was the Board Room where the meeting was actually scheduled to take place. Graham Nicholas Baxter would be there, together with his second in command, a Scot by the name of Andrew Kelt. He would also be accompanied by his full legal team. His accountant would be there, together with the Company Treasurer. His solicitor would be there. His Secretary would be there, together with three or four other hangers on. *His so-called advisors.* Collier smiled. Not that they would be of much help to Baxter, not today.

Collier, on the other hand, would be there quite alone. He didn't need anyone else. He could manage this one quite easily alone. He had looked forward to this day for a very long time. This was to be his day. No one else would be with him. The Baxter team would be there in force, to discuss in details the terms and conditions. But there would be no discussion. The terms had already been decided in his mind. He had already made all of the decisions. The Conditions had already been established. He had set them. They were cast in stone. There was no room for manoeuvre. No possibility to change them. All that Baxter had to do was to simply sign the documents.

Collier checked the clock once again. *Three twenty-five.* He stood up and started to pace the floor. Then he walked over to the window again, and looked down into the car park. He smiled. There was the car, and there was old man Baxter just getting out. As he continued to watch, Baxter suddenly looked up. Collier just stared at him, unsmiling.

* * *

Five minutes later, the buzzer on the intercom suddenly sounded. "They are here, sir," Joyce announced.

Collier looked across at the wall clock. "Right on time," he said. *They were punctual at least.* He sighed. He had been waiting six years for this day to come. They could easily wait another fifteen minutes. "Thank you, Joyce," he said. "Show them into the Board Room, will you. Tell them that I'll be right there."

"Should I take in coffee?" she asked.

Collier smiled. *After he had finished with him old man Baxter would want something a lot stronger than coffee.* Collier shook his head. "That won't be necessary, Joyce," he replied. He replaced the receiver.

He slowly opened the desk drawer and took out a photograph in a silver frame. He placed it on to the desk and stared at it for a moment. It was of two men at a formal dinner at the House of Commons. One was a much younger John Wyndham Collier, perhaps no more than twenty-five or thirty years old. The other was a man in his late forties. 'Graham Nicholas Baxter. Chairman and Chief Executive of the Baxter Corporation'.

The photograph had been taken almost ten years ago. *Ten years,* Collier whispered. How time had flown. Collier had worked for Baxter back then. That is until he had been fired. Well, he hadn't exactly been fired, but as good as. Collier shook his head and started to laugh. *He had been requested to submit his resignation.* Oh sure it had all been nice and polite, but at the end of the day he had lost his job. In other words he had been sacked.

Things would be different now, Collier thought. Today the tables would, finally, be turned. *What was that phrase?* he murmured. It was something about revenge. "Ah yes," he whispered. He started to laugh as he remembered. *Revenge is sweet.* For the past five or six years Collier had been buying up stock in the Baxter Corporation, especially when the markets had been low, as they had been for the past six months. He now owned fifty-one percent of the Company.

He continued to stare at the photograph for a few moments and then turned to the newspaper lying to one side. He glanced at the headline. 'Scott Lawrence Announce Losses of Thirty Billion'. He looked up and shook his head. The third largest financial organisation in America was in trouble. *How long before they go to the wall.* He started to smile. What was that, he murmured. *Was that the third, or fourth, of my competitors.* He thought for a few moments, counting out on his fingers. He nodded. It was the third, the third of his rivals who had been in trouble, the third company that had finally been forced to close down.

How terrible, he whispered, trying to suppress the laughter, *how positively dreadful.* He could hold the laughter back no more. He quickly flipped through the pages to the business section. He slowly scanned the share prices. Every so often he would beam widely as he noticed the share price of a competitor falling. "Ah, here it is," he murmured. "The Baxter Corporation." He started to tap the page. "Today's low, £5.22. That's down sixty pence on the day." He punched the buttons of a small calculator. "That's two-twenty on the week." He punched the buttons once more. "A little over fourteen percent." He shook his head, and started to laugh. "Fourteen percent," he repeated. "Fourteen percent down. In just over seven days."

Of the several hundred companies listed, only a handful had shown an improvement on the day. Travers Morgan was one of them. Up by six percent already and there was still another two hours trading before the London markets were due to close.

The intercom buzzer suddenly sounded. "Sorry to disturb you, sir," a voice said. "Mr Baxter was wondering how much longer you would be, sir."

Collier looked at the wall clock once again. Not quite fifteen minutes had passed. He started to laugh. "Was he indeed?" he replied. Then he shook his head. "Tell Mr Baxter that I shall be there as soon as I can." He replaced the handset, and looked at the wall clock once again. "Another fifteen minutes should do it," he whispered. He returned to the newspaper that he was reading.

* * *

As he entered the Boardroom, some twenty minutes later, there was a broad smile on his face. He was looking forward to this meeting immensely. He was really going to enjoy it. Why, he hadn't had so much fun in a long, long time.

17

* * *

Two days later the FTSE 100 had fallen another eighty-six points. Against the general trend, the price of Travers Morgan shares went up by twenty percent to an all time high of £12-56 per share. Shares in The Baxter Corporation had gained sixteen percent.

Chapter Three

Tom Kendall – Private Detective

A little over three thousand miles away, Tom Kendall, Private Detective, was slowly making his way to his office in North Miami Beach. He knew very little about Stocks and Shares, or the Credit Crunch, or bank bailouts, and he cared even less. The Government's debt of four trillion dollars, or whatever the sum was, give or take a billion or two, didn't bother him too much either. After all, it was only money, wasn't it? Besides it was far too nice a day to worry about such mundane things. The sun was shining brightly and there wasn't a cloud in the sky, and soon he would be going on a well-deserved holiday, his first holiday since he couldn't remember when. No, he wasn't the least bit worried. *Besides the recession was all but over, wasn't it?* The economic crisis was finished. The economy was now well on the way to recovery. At least that's what some of the so-called experts were saying.

"Share values climb," announced The Wall Street Journal. The Dow Jones had made its largest gain in five years. "The worst is over," said the Federal Reserve. "We can look forward to healthy growth from now on," said the Treasury. Kendall smiled. *Healthy growth for the bankers no doubt*, he thought.

But Kendall wasn't impressed by all of this talk about recovery. He had heard it all before and he took it with a very large pinch of salt. He couldn't actually say that he felt any different anyway. *What was so different about today anyway*, he wondered. *Compared to yesterday that is, or the day before, or the day before that.* Besides weren't some of the experts actually saying that far from the situation improving, it was actually getting worse? So who was right and who was wrong?

Kendall had no idea who was right or wrong. He suspected that they didn't know either. They were beginning to sound like a bunch of school kids bickering amongst themselves. One thing Kendall did know, however, was that he hadn't actually noticed any change, except it now cost more to run his car and the prices at the supermarket were higher. He didn't feel any better off. As far as he could tell there had been no great improvement to his circumstances. *No great sudden influx of wealth.* In fact, it was quite the opposite. On top of everything else they were talking about increasing taxes. No, he certainly didn't feel any great improvement. The only group who would benefit from any so-called growth would be the bankers anyway, he reasoned. *The bankers, and all of the other financial hangers on and high flyers.* He shook his head, the very ones who had caused the economic collapse in the first place. Their enormous salaries would be safe. They would still get their huge bonuses. *Oh you didn't need to worry about them.* That was certain.

Not that he was really that bothered anyway, not if the truth were known. Besides there was nothing he could do about it anyway, was there? At the end of the day it didn't make a great deal of difference to him, either way. He still had to make a living and he still had to pay his taxes. If he were in financial trouble there would be no Government bailout for him, would there? No one was going to give him a hand-out. As far as they were concerned, if he got into financial difficulties, that was his problem. He had no one to blame but himself. He could just close up the office and go to the wall. He shook his head. No one would care. *The only person who was going to be concerned about his welfare was himself. Oh and Mollie, and maybe his mother.* But that was it.

As it happened, however, he had no such worries. He was doing okay, thank you very much. After years of struggling, the Kendall Detective Agency was, at last, beginning to do all right. Mind you, it was with no thanks to the Government, and certainly no thanks to the banks. When he had needed a small loan a few years ago he had been turned down flat. *Too much of a risk,* they had said, *insufficient collateral.* He shook his head. They had been of no help whatsoever. The success of his business had been all his own-doing. He had worked hard and business had been good. Now he was planning on a little reward for his labours. Oh, and those of his secretary, Mollie. He was planning a little holiday for them both. And it couldn't come soon enough.

* * *

It was still quite early as Kendall came along the corridor leading towards his office. It was located right at the end of the corridor, right next door to *Alexia Fashions*. Kendall smiled as he stopped close to their door. He could not remember ever seeing anyone going in, or coming out, of that office. He moved closer to the door and listened. There was nothing. Not a sound. *How on earth did they survive?* he wondered. In recent months there had been no end of small businesses going to the wall, and closing down. In fact there were several vacant units right here, in the complex. Why only last month *Office Support Services*, at the other end of the corridor, had ceased trading, and that software company, *EasyPC*, on the floor above had gone three or four months ago. Quite a clever name, he thought. *EasyPC*. He shook his head. They hadn't lasted long though. A few short months and that was that. And yet *Alexia Fashions* were still there. They were still going strong, apparently. *How? Why?* He shook his head. He didn't know.

They must be doing something right, he murmured, or something illegal. Maybe the office was just a front, an accommodation address only. Kendall shook his head and smiled mischievously. *Perhaps they were into money laundering*, he thought jokingly. He bent down and tried to peer through the keyhole. The window blinds had obviously been closed over, and the office was in complete darkness.

He stood up and shook his head. *Perhaps they have actually closed down, and just left their sign up*, he murmured. He shrugged his shoulders, and continued on his way towards his own office. There it was, just a few short yards further on. *Tom Kendall, Private Detective* emblazoned proudly across the door in dark blue. That had been Mollie's idea. He had wanted the colour to be bright red. *Blue is more sophisticated, she had said. More refined. It indicates authority, and gives confidence.* So blue it was. What did he know anyway? One colour was as good as any other wasn't it? Blue, red, sky blue pink, what difference? Except yellow, he wasn't fond of yellow. Apart from that any colour would have done in his view, but there it was, dark blue. Although he had to admit that she was right, and it did look quite impressive. *Not that he would ever admit that to Mollie of course.*

As he approached the door he could hear his telephone ringing inside. It was still early. *Who could be calling at this hour?* he wondered. Somebody was desperate to get in touch with him. *An important case, that was obvious.* He shook his head. He hoped that they could wait until after he returned from the holiday. He rushed towards the door fumbling for the key in his pocket. As he reached the door he clumsily pulled the key from his pocket, dropping it on to the ground, and sending it sliding along the passageway. Inside the office the telephone was still ringing.

"I'm coming," Kendall yelled. The telephone continued to ring. "I'm coming," he yelled even louder. Whether or not he actually expected the person on the other end to hear him is unclear. The telephone continued to ring.

Kendall bent down trying to find the key. It was nowhere to be seen. *How could it just disappear like that?* Admittedly it wasn't a huge item, but it was certainly big enough to be seen. *So why couldn't he see it?* He was mumbling angrily to himself. The telephone was still ringing. "I'm coming," he yelled out once more. *There should be a way of automatically opening a door*, he thought, *without the need for a silly old key. Some kind of a detector would work. Or maybe a sensor or a push button of some kind. Or maybe even voice recognition.* That sounded good, Kendall thought. He liked that idea. He shrugged, and heaved a sigh. *Abracadabra*, he muttered. *Open sesame.* He shrugged once again. *Hey, look it's me.* He tried all three options in quick succession. *Open up, now*, he cried out in sheer desperation. The door remained stubbornly closed. *So much for voice recognition*, he murmured. *Perhaps the door didn't understand English. Perhaps it was a foreign door.*

Either way, voice recognition had proved to be an abject failure. He shook his head. So there appeared to be no other way of opening that door. *Oh no, instead he had to use a key. How ridiculous*, he muttered to himself. *How stupid. How primitive. A small piece of metal with a serrated edge, how old fashioned is that. This was the twenty-first century after all. They had been using keys for a thousand years or more*, he thought. *Have we not advanced at all? Are we still living in the Dark Ages? We can land men on the Moon; we can split the atom; we can traverse the ocean floor. We can do all kinds of marvellous things. But can we unlock a simple door without the use of a key? No, apparently we can't!*

The telephone was still ringing inside the office. *Where was that wretched key*, he muttered, getting more and more annoyed. *They will give up soon*, he thought. *They'll go somewhere else. Probably that agency a few blocks away. What was their name?* He couldn't think of it. *Walker*, he suddenly announced to no one in particular. *That was the name, Walker. Peter Walker.* He shook his head. *Or was it Paul?* A few moments went by. *Patrick. It was Patrick Walker.* He shook his head once again. *It was actually Patrick Watson.* Inside the office the telephone continued to ring. *Who cares what the name was anyway*, he murmured angrily. He just had to open that door, answer the telephone, and the problem would be over. He tried the voice recognition idea once more. *If you don't open right now I'll rip your hinges right off.* The door was obviously not intimidated in any way, and remained closed.

Suddenly Kendall saw it, the key. It was glinting in the sunlight that was streaming through the nearby window. *Ha!* He cried loudly, *ha, there you are!* At last, there it was just underneath the radiator. He reached forward and retrieved it, followed by a great black spider whose web he had just disturbed. Kendall shivered slightly. He hated spiders.

He hurried back to the door, the key held firmly in his hand. He was gratified to note that the telephone was still ringing. He put the key into the lock, and turned it. There was a low click. He turned the handle and pushed. The door slowly opened. He rushed in and slipped on the carpet, crashing into the side of the desk, and hitting his knee hard on the corner. The telephone was still ringing. He struggled to his feet, and picked up the handset. "Kendall Detective Agency," he said, breathing hard. "How can I help you?"

"Will it really be warm over there?" a voice asked.

"I beg your pardon," Kendall replied. "Who is this?"

"I said will it really be warm over there?" a voice repeated, slower this time. It was Mollie, his secretary. "After all it is England we are

22

going to."

Kendall sighed, gently rubbing his knee. "It's June, for crying out loud. It's the height of summer over there" he replied, slightly exasperated. *All right so it wouldn't be quite like Florida sunshine, but even so.* "It'll be warm enough, I assure you." She hung up. Kendall sighed once again. He shook his head. It was only the tenth time that she had asked that same stupid question.

* * *

It was a little over a month ago that Kendall had suddenly announced his plans for a holiday. It was just after finishing the Dawson case. Kendall started to smile as he recalled what had happened on that final day.

Peter Dawson had asked him, "What plans do you have for the future?"

Kendall had slowly nodded his head. "A holiday, I think," he had announced. He couldn't think why he had said that. He shook his head. *Where did that come from*, he murmured, as he looked around the room trying to see who had said it. *All right, who was it? Who said that? Own up.* Nobody came forward. Clearly he must have said it, as unlikely as that seemed. *What had he done? A holiday? Just what had he been thinking of?* Truth is, of course, he hadn't been thinking of anything. Clearly he hadn't been thinking at all, period. Although, after some further consideration, he had to admit that it had, after all, been a pretty good idea.

It was really quite exciting. It would be good to get away from it all, a complete change. Rest and relaxation, that's what it was about. He shrugged his shoulders and sighed. *He had done it this time, and in front of witnesses.* There was no getting out of it, not now. There was no way back. Okay, so he had said it, and that was that. There was nothing he could do about it. *Well, he could just say that he never meant it. He was just joking. But if Mollie realised that he wasn't being serious, she would tear him apart.* No, he had said it and he was stuck with the consequences. That was that. Anyway, it wasn't such a bad idea, was it? In fact it was rather a good idea. He started to laugh as he remembered the look on Mollie's face. She couldn't believe her ears.

"I've never been to Europe," he had continued. "I think we'll go to England." He smiled at Mollie, and nodded once again. "Yes, that's what we'll do," he continued. Mollie and I will have a few weeks in England."

"England," Mollie repeated, her eyes wide open.

"And maybe Ireland," Kendall murmured. "I'm sure I've Irish blood in me somewhere."

Mollie shook her head. She knew better. *It wasn't blood that he had in his veins. It was 100% Scotch.*

* * *

Kendall had been a private detective for nearly eleven years. Much of that time he had operated further up north, in Virginia. The last eight months or so had been right here in Sunny Isles, North Miami. In all of those eleven years he had never had a holiday. Not what you would call a real holiday, a proper holiday. There had been the odd day here and there, a weekend away maybe, but never a real long break. And he had never ever been abroad. *Well, there was just that one time when he had crossed over the border into Canada to see Niagara Falls.* He had been there for a whole day and a half to be exact. When was that, he wondered. Over twenty years ago, he suddenly realised, in 1989 to be exact. And that was that. Apart from that trip he had never been any further than Boston. Why he hadn't even seen Washington. He was hardly the seasoned traveller was he? Apart from anything else he could never afford it before.

He was determined that this coming year would be different. He was determined that he would have a really great holiday this year. This year he and Mollie were going to Europe, simple as that. Okay so the decision had been made, all he had to do now was to make the actual arrangements. No problem.

* * *

Mollie had been so excited when Kendall had first mentioned the holiday. For a while she had said nothing. Not entirely believing what she had heard. She knew Kendall's strange sense of humour. *He was only joking, wasn't he? He wasn't really being serious, was he? He didn't really mean it.* But then, slowly she began to realise that he wasn't joking. He was being serious. Gradually it began to sink in. Gradually she began to realise exactly what Kendall had said. "A holiday," she said, over and over. "A holiday." She looked at Kendall, half afraid to say too much just in case it shattered the illusion. "A holiday," she repeated once more. "Do you really mean it?"

Kendall nodded. *Yes he really meant it.* "I wouldn't say it if I didn't mean it, would I?" he replied indignantly. "I'm not in the habit of lying."

Mollie smiled. Lying? Maybe not, but Kendall was not averse to kidding. She sighed and shook her head. "No, I suppose not," she replied slowly.

"A holiday is what I said and a holiday is exactly what I meant," he had replied.

"Where?" Mollie had asked. "Where shall we go?"

24

Kendall had smiled and shrugged. "I already told you. England," he replied quite simply.

England, she murmured. *She couldn't believe it. She must be dreaming. She had to be. Any minute now she would wake up.* "When?" she asked, clapping her hands together and jumping up and down like a young schoolgirl. "When are we going?"

Kendall smiled once again, and thought for a few moments. *When? That's a good question.* He wondered how long it would take to make the necessary arrangements, especially getting a passport. "Let's say three months time, shall we," he replied, hoping that would give him sufficient time. "Well three or four anyway."

"Three months," Mollie repeated slowly. "Three months. I'll need to do a few things before we go." *There was so much to do and so little time to do it in.* Firstly she had to see about her passport. She had never had one before, and hadn't a clue on how to get one. What else, she murmured. Well, she needed to pack didn't she, and to get her hair done. *Must make an appointment*, she murmured. *A day or two before they were due to go would be fine. And most importantly, she had to buy some new clothes.* "There are a million and one things to do," she said. "I don't know where to start." Then she smiled and nodded. "I know where," she said to herself. "I have to go shopping."

A holiday, she thought becoming more and more excited. *No more of those silly crimes to solve, no more of those nasty murders, no more boring detective work, no more mysteries to unravel. This was to be a real holiday. She was going to England. Shopping. London. More shopping. Piccadilly, Oxford Street, Regent Street, Knightsbridge. Harrods. And still more shopping.* She could hardly wait. Her hands were shaking with excitement. She shook her head. This was not really happening was it? *She was dreaming wasn't she? But if it was a dream, it was such a lovely one she did not want to ever wake up.*

* * *

Ever since the day Kendall had mentioned the trip, she had been busy getting ready. For the past three weeks she had been busily packing and unpacking, and then repacking, and then unpacking again. *Decisions, decisions, it was all so difficult trying to decide what to take.* "I shall certainly need a new outfit, or two," she had said. "And a dress or three."

Kendall couldn't understand why she would need so much. *It was a holiday she was going on, or was she actually planning on immigrating?* She was packing enough clothes for a dozen people, not just one. *We aren't going for good you know. We will only be away for a short time*, he murmured. "We are coming back," he said. She obviously wasn't listening. "You will exceed your baggage allowance if you're not careful," he said.

Mollie looked at him and glared. "We will be away for four whole weeks," she said. "I need to wear something, don't I?" Kendall had to admit that yes she had to wear something, but she was taking enough for a lifetime.

"You just don't understand, do you?" she had said. "I'll need clothes for the daytime and then I shall need something to wear for the evenings." She paused for a moment. "Then I'll need something to wear to the theatre." She paused once again and looked at him. "We are going to the theatre, aren't we?"

"Oh yes, certainly," Kendall mumbled quickly.

"Well there you are then," Mollie continued. "It all adds up."

Kendall couldn't quite see what it was that added up. He didn't understand why separate outfits were necessary for different times of the day. What was wrong with wearing the same clothes all day long? He couldn't understand all of the fuss that she was making. He shook his head. He himself was quite the opposite. He knew exactly what to pack. His needs were much simpler. He would take only the bare essentials. If it meant wearing the same shirt, or the same suit, more than once, so be it. It didn't matter to him. *Who would care anyway? Who would know, apart from Mollie that is?* No one would even notice.

He did not need weeks to pack and unpack, like Mollie. He would just throw a few things into a bag. Done and dusted. There was plenty of time. He wasn't going to worry about it until a day or two before the flight. In fact he would probably leave everything until the very last minute. *The day before they were actually due to travel probably. Why rush?* he thought, *what was the point? Act in haste, repent at leisure that was the saying. How much time do you need anyway? Thirty minutes that was all that he would require. Well, all right, forty-five perhaps. Okay, okay, certainly no more than an hour, an hour and half tops.*

* * *

Kendall smiled and shook his head as he slowly placed the handset back on to the cradle. He looked at it for a few moments. Then he smiled. *Mollie was certainly looking forward to this trip*, he murmured. She was so excited, like a child with a new toy. He tapped the handset a few times, and shrugged his shoulders. It was good to see her looking so happy. These past few years she had worked hard. He knew that he would never have managed without her, that was cert and sure. *Not that he would ever admit that to her.* He started to laugh. *He would never live that one down.* She really deserved this break though. There was no question about that.

Then he suddenly sighed, and a frown quickly spread across his face, as he realised something. Something that was quite important. That day, you know the day that he had mentioned, *the day before they were actually due to travel. That day! The day that he would do his packing. Well that day was actually the following day.

Their flight was due to leave in a little over thirty-eight hours time. He hadn't started to pack as yet. If the truth were known he hadn't even given any thought as to what he might need on the trip.

Would it really be warm enough? After all it was England. Perhaps it would rain after all. They had a lot of rain in England, he thought. And cold winds. He shook his head. He hated the rain but, worse still, he hated the cold. *What should he pack? Did he need an overcoat? What about a raincoat? Should he take a sweater? What about a scarf? Or gloves? Precisely what did one wear to the theatre these days anyway? How many shirts would he need? After all they were going for four whole weeks. He had to wear something didn't he?*

He was now beginning to panic ever so slightly.

* * *

Packing was only one of his problems. He suddenly thought of one or two more. *Where were the tickets? Where had he put the passports? And what about the Insurance policy?* He quickly opened the desk drawer, and started to look through. He shook his head. They weren't there. He stood up and walked over to the bureau in the far corner of the room. He opened it and began to search. A few minutes later he shook his head once again. *They were not there either*, he murmured. *Where on earth could they be?* He was sure that he had put them somewhere safe. Somewhere he would be sure to find them easily. *But where?* He slowly glanced around the office. There was no obvious place as far as he could see. Then he noticed the filing cabinets. *Maybe he had filed them.* He nodded. *That's it he had filed them*, he thought thankfully. Then he suddenly sighed, worried once again. *If he had filed them, what were they filed under? T for Tickets, I for Insurance, or D for Documents.* He shook his head. He was getting nowhere, fast.

Twenty minutes later he concluded that they had not, in fact, been placed in the filing cabinets, under T, I or D. Furthermore they were not filed under P for Papers, or H for Holiday, or even E for England. In fact they had not been filed under any of the letters of the alphabet, *including L for Lost. So where were they?*

All of his holiday plans were slowly beginning to evaporate. *Mollie was going to kill him.*

Chapter Four

England Here We Come

Kendall started to nervously drum his fingers on the desk. *What on earth could he say to Mollie? What possible excuse would he have?* He shook his head. He had been looking forward to the holiday, but now it was becoming a fading memory. The telephone suddenly rang. *If that's Mollie again, asking that same stupid question, I shall scream*, Kendall thought, becoming more and more agitated. *More to the point there was to be nothing said about missing tickets, not yet anyway.* He couldn't face that, not right now. He gave a deep sigh. *Maybe they would turn up anyway, he murmured.*

He lunged for the telephone, and picked up the receiver. "What now," he yelled. "If you ask about the ...."

"Kendall, is that you?" a voice asked. "Are you okay?"

Kendall shook his head. *It wasn't Mollie.* "Who is this?" he asked.

There was the sound of laughter. "What do you mean, who is this?" the voice said. "It's me."

"Me," Kendall repeated as though in a daze.

"Yes," said the voice. "Me. Devaney, your friendly neighbourhood cop, remember."

It was Detective Inspector Terrence Devaney of the Miami Police Department.

Kendall heaved a sigh. "Oh, it's you," he said. "I thought it was..."

"Kendall you haven't by any chance been drinking, have you?" Devaney asked. "It's a little early for that, isn't it? Even for you."

Kendall sighed once again. "No, I haven't been drinking," he replied wearily, wishing that he had been.

"Glad to hear it," came the response.

"All right, so what do you want, Devaney?" Kendall asked. Quite often Devaney had passed on some detective work to Kendall. *Maybe he had something of the sort now*, Kendall thought. "I'm a very busy man and I don't have time for gossiping with you all day. I've things to do you know, people to see, deals to make, places to go. Busy, busy. Can't stop."

"There's gratitude for you," said Devaney, sounding hurt. "I'm sorry for bothering you. I'm completely devastated that I should be so thoughtless. I am mortified for causing you such stress. Excuse me for breathing." There was a short pause. "I only rang to wish you a safe and pleasant trip. That's all. I mean please forgive the intrusion. Please

28

accept my deepest sincere apologies. What was I thinking of to disturb you in this way, Your Eminence."

Kendall suddenly felt very small and utterly ashamed of himself. *There was no need for rudeness, was there? It didn't hurt to be civil, did it? It didn't cost anything. My friend is ringing merely to wish me a safe trip and what do I do?* Kendall sighed a third time, and took a deep breath. *What do I do? I basically accuse him of wasting my time. That's what I do, my precious time.* He shook his head, and then he coughed a few times to clear his throat. *I really should not be so selfish, thinking of myself the whole time.*

"Well, er. I mean what can I say? That's really very good of you, Devaney," he said. "Very thoughtful, I'm sure. Much appreciated."

"Hey. What are friends for?" Devaney replied. "It is today that you go, isn't it?"

Kendall shook his head. "No, it's actually tomorrow. We are due to take off at ten forty-five tomorrow night."

"Tomorrow, did you say?" replied Devaney. "How very fortunate."

"Fortunate," repeated Kendall, puzzled.

"You wouldn't care to do a small surveillance job this evening, would you? Be a great help to me. Shouldn't take more than four or five hours. You'll be finished by two or three in the morning, no later than four anyway. Guaranteed."

Kendall shook his head once again. "You're kidding, right?"

Devaney started laughing. "Sure I'm kidding," he replied. "Did you really think I would do such a thing."

"Well," Kendall said slowly. "The thought had crossed my mind."

"I'm shocked," said Devaney, sounding anything but. There was a short pause. "Incidentally, did you hear about Lockhart and Day? Lockhart got ten years, Day got seven."

Lockhart and Day were two local men who had recently been on trial charged with counterfeiting. Their arrest had been largely due to evidence that had been obtained by Kendall.

"Is that all?" asked Kendall surprised. *Ten years for counterfeiting.*

"Ten years," repeated Devaney. "They'll be out on the street again in five, you'll see."

Kendall shook his head in disbelief. "Who says crime doesn't pay."

"Well, it certainly doesn't pay me, that's for sure," said Devaney. "Not that well that is." There was a pause. "By the way, talking about crime paying, did you hear about the jewel robbery this morning?"

Kendall hadn't heard anything that morning, except for Mollie asking stupid questions about clothes and the weather in England. "No, not a thing," he replied, trying to sound interested, "what happened?"

"Eatons, you know the jewellers on Collins. Corner of Collins and Eighth Avenue," Devaney replied.

Kendall knew where Eatons was located. He didn't need a geography lesson. *He just wanted Devaney to get on with whatever it was, and get it over and done with. And quickly, please, preferably while he was still in his prime.* He looked at the wall clock and sighed. Time was marching on. He had a lot to do. He really wanted to get on. He still had to find those tickets, and the money. "So what about it?" he asked, still trying to sound interested.

"Well it was broken into during the early hours this morning," Devaney explained. "About three o'clock."

Kendall sighed once more. *Three o'clock or four o'clock. What difference?* "You can skip the starter course," he said. Let's just get to the main dish shall we."

"The main dish," Devaney repeated, sounding puzzled.

"If you don't mind," said Kendall. "It would be appreciated.

"Oh yes, sure," replied Devaney. "I get it. The main dish." He paused for a moment. "That's funny, very funny."

"Devaney," Kendall said slowly and deliberately.

"I'm getting there, don't rush me," Devaney replied. "The current estimate is that they got away with fifteen million dollars worth of the finest uncut diamonds you ever did see."

Kendall let out a low whistle. He had to admit that the news was, after all, mildly of interest. "Not bad for a morning's work," he said.

"Not bad at all," Devaney agreed. "Now all I have to do is catch them."

"Shouldn't be a problem to you, should it? Miami's greatest detective bar none," Kendall said. "Of course you could wait till I get back, if you like. Then I'll catch them for you."

Devaney laughed. "Sure, I might just do that," he replied. "You have a good holiday, Kendall, and don't you spare a thought about me, will you? Don't you concern yourself one little bit, will you? I wouldn't want you worrying. We'll try to muddle on without you. It'll be tough, I know, but bye." He hung up.

Kendall nodded. *He certainly wouldn't spare Devaney a thought*, he whispered. *Not for a single moment. Not for a second. Not for a millisecond.* He was going on a holiday, wasn't he, and the last thing he wanted was to think about Devaney, and crime, and nasty things like that. He replaced the receiver and patted it firmly into place. "Just who was that anyway?" he whispered. "And what did they want?" He continued to stare at the telephone for a few moments, and smiled. *Must have been a wrong number*, he murmured. *Or perhaps it had been one of those annoying calls telling me that I've won something.* Either way it wasn't something that was going to cause him any further concern.

He nodded his head and sighed. *Now what was I doing before I was so rudely interrupted?* He suddenly started to panic as he remembered exactly what he had been doing. "The tickets," he announced loudly, hoping maybe that they would hear him and suddenly make an appearance. *They didn't.* He shook his head and sighed deeply. "I was looking for the tickets," he mumbled. "And the passport and the insurance policies." He paused for a moment. "And the money," he suddenly exclaimed. "Where did I put them? They must be somewhere."

"The safe," he suddenly announced, feeling quite pleased with himself. "That's it. I put everything into the safe." He stood up and walked over to the safe in the corner of the room. *Obvious place really,* he murmured, wondering why he hadn't thought of it earlier. He slowly turned the handle, first one way and then the other. There was a low click and the safe door opened. Kendall bent down and looked inside. It was completely empty.

"Where are those stupid tickets?" he said, shaking his head. "What did I do with them?" More to the point how could he explain it all to Mollie when he told her that the holiday plans were being scrapped. *Sorry, Mollie, I seem to have mislaid the tickets. Oh, and the money, and the passports.* There was nothing he could do about it, there would be no trip to England, as simple as that. He slowly shook his head. *She would understand, wouldn't she? She wouldn't really mind, would she? Pigs fly, don't they?*

* * *

Kendall need not have worried. The tickets were quite safe. So were the passports, and the insurance documents, and the English currency. Mollie had seen to that. When the holiday plans had first been mentioned she had purchased a special leather wallet in which to keep them. At first she could hardly believe that they were going on holiday. It was only a dream, and sooner or later she would wake up to reality. In fact she had thought that it was one of Kendall's little jokes, *one of his incredibly poor jokes.* But then the more the documents began to accumulate the more she began to think that maybe, *just maybe,* they were going after all. First to arrive was the confirmation of the hotel booking. Shortly afterwards came the insurance documents. Then a short while ago, the airline tickets had arrived.

It wasn't a joke after all. She felt bad that she had ever doubted Kendall, *although in truth, not that bad. It wasn't a dream after all. It was real. She was really going on holiday. She was actually going to England. The slowly growing collection of documents proved it.*

* * *

Kendall really liked the idea of travel. Visiting new places, experiencing new things, meeting new people and learning about their customs. Oh yes, he liked the idea of travel all right. However, he just wasn't too keen on the actual travelling itself, *that little irritating inconvenience that occurred just between leaving home and actually arriving at your destination.* Kendall believed that if you could just close your eyes, snap your fingers and then open them and there you were at your destination, that would be just perfect. That would have suited him right down to the ground. It would have been ideal. But it wasn't like that was it? *Far from it. In reality it was more like an obstacle course with every imaginable difficulty to test a person's nerve and stamina.*

Firstly, there is the trip to the airport. That always seemed to be at an inconvenient time, usually in the middle of the rush hour, or at some unearthly hour in the middle of the night. *And was it absolutely essential for everyone to be travelling on the same day? And going in the same direction, at exactly the same time?* In relative terms this part of the journey always seemed to take the longest in terms of the distance actually travelled. Not only did this part of the journey take an excessive amount of time, it also demanded a certain degree of skill. Skill required in carefully manoeuvring around the seemingly endless road works, and avoiding the usual array of accidents and breakdowns. Not only that, but to make matters worse was the certain knowledge that it all had to be done again on the return trip home.

At last, after what seems like an eternity, the airport terminal eventually comes into sight. A little over two hours before take-off.

* * *

"You stay there with the luggage," Kendall said to Mollie as he got out of the taxi. "I'll get a cart. I won't be long"

With that he quickly walked into the terminal. He sighed as he saw the mass of people milling around. It seemed that everyone was travelling that day. *Not all on his aircraft*, he hoped. He walked across the concourse to one of the cart ranks. It was empty. There was not a cart to be seen.

"You could try over on the other side," somebody suggested helpfully. "There were a lot there earlier today."

Kendall thanked them and made his way over to the other side of the concourse, only to see somebody taking the last of the carts. "There might be a few over by the departures gate," an airline steward suggested as she passed by.

Kendall sighed. He checked his watch. It was now one hour forty-six minutes before take-off. He sighed once again and ran to the departure area. There they were, he murmured, a short row of carts, *a very short row*. Quickly he grabbed one, and started to make his way back to the drop-off point where Mollie was waiting. Wouldn't you know it, he murmured, *I had to pick the one with the wobbly wheel*. He stopped, and turned around. He would change it for a better one. *Assuming there was one*. A minute or two later he was back at the cart rank. It was now completely empty. He shrugged. *It didn't really matter, they probably all had wobbly wheels anyway*, he murmured. *They were deliberately made that way*. He checked his watch once again. One hour forty-two minutes before take-off.

He hurried towards the drop-off point, or at least as quickly as the defective cart would allow him. For some strange reason the cart obviously did not want to go to the Drop-Off point. It had plans of its own and kept veering off in a completely different direction. Kendall would not be beaten, and persevered. *He would not allow a rusting wire cage on wheels to get the better of him*. Ten minutes later, both Kendall and the cart arrived where Mollie was patiently waiting.

"Where have you been?" she asked as she saw him approaching. "I thought that you had gone without me." She paused and glared at him. "We haven't long you know."

Kendall sighed and shook his head. "Oh I just stopped off for a coffee, and a double cheeseburger and fries, you know. Then I thought I'd do a bit of shopping, last minute stuff you know." he replied. He shook his head, and sighed. "Where do you think I've been?"

Mollie shrugged. "We better hurry," she said, ignoring his little tantrum. "We only have an hour and forty-five minutes before take-off. And we haven't checked in yet."

Kendall checked his watch once again. "One hour thirty-five minutes," he corrected her. He quickly loaded the luggage on to the cart and started towards the check in counter. The cart, of course, wanted to go in a totally different direction altogether.

Mollie noticed the wobbly wheel. "Why didn't you get a better cart," she asked. "This one's broken."

"I like this one," Kendall retorted angrily.

* * *

A few minutes later Kendall found himself at the end of a very long queue checking in on flight 332 to London Heathrow. One hour and thirty-two minutes to go before take-off. Kendall heaved a sigh and yawned. *A drink would have gone down well right at that moment*, he thought. He slowly glanced around. There wasn't a bar in sight.

Ten minutes later there had been no movement. Suddenly there came an announcement. "American Airlines regret to announce that flight 332 has been delayed by one hour."

* * *

Twenty minutes later the queue started to move slowly forward. Suddenly Kendall could hear raised voices further down the line. He moved slightly to his right, hoping to see what was happening. He looked along the line of people. Ten yards ahead he could see a smartly dressed middle-aged man talking to an airline official. Talking was probably a bad choice of word. A better word would have been arguing. Kendall strained to hear what was being said. As far as he could make out the man was complaining bitterly about something - *the delay probably.*

Kendall shrugged, turned away and moved back into line. *What was the point in getting all worked up like that?* There was absolutely nothing you could do about it. There was a delay, and that was that. The aircraft would take off when the airline was good and ready – and not a moment before. He shrugged once again, and heaved a sigh. *There's no point getting upset over things like that,* he murmured. *Give yourself an ulcer, or worse. Worse things happen at sea.* He checked his watch. Then he shook his head and heaved another sigh. Wish they would get a move on, though, he murmured. As soon as he got the chance he was going to make a formal complaint to the airline, the airport, the FAA, and maybe even his local Congressman. *Somehow he didn't think the President would be that interested. After all he did have one or two other things to worry about, like the national debt, and bank bailouts, didn't he?* Kendall nodded. He would leave it at the Congressman.

Almost one hour later Kendall arrived at the head of the queue. "Tickets, please," the clerk said mechanically.

Kendall placed the tickets on to the counter top. "What was the hold-up?" he asked.

The clerk looked up. "Hold-up?" he repeated. "What hold-up?"

Kendall took a deep breath and cleared his throat, trying hard to control his temper. "I've been in the queue for over an hour," he said, trying to remain calm. "That's the hold-up I'm talking about."

"Oh that," said the clerk matter-of-factly. He shook his head. "That was nothing, you should have been here yesterday." He paused and shook his head, "Now that really was a hold-up."

Kendall sighed. "I'm not too bothered about yesterday, strangely enough," he replied slowly. "I was wondering what had caused today's little delay."

The clerk shook his head. "That was nothing," he replied, turning back to the monitor screen.

"What caused this nothing?" Kendall asked, beginning to breathe

34

hard. Hoping against hope that maybe, just maybe, he might get a meaningful reply.

The clerk looked up. "It was only a security alert," he replied dismissively for the two hundred and nineteenth time. "Happens all the time." He opened the tickets and glanced at his screen. "False alarm every time." He pressed a few buttons on his keypad. He nodded imperceptibly. He looked at Kendall for a moment and started to smile. "If you thought that delay was bad, just wait till you go into the Departure area." He looked back at his screen. "Right," he suddenly announced. "Passports," he continued. Kendall handed over the passports and waited whilst they were scrutinised, and were then handed back. There was a short pause. "Please place your luggage on the conveyor."

Mollie placed her cases as instructed. "Five kilos overweight," the clerk announced imperiously. "There'll be a surcharge of twenty-five dollars."

Kendall sighed and shook his head. He looked at Mollie. He knew it. He had told her. *"You are taking far too much luggage. You'll be over the limit."* That's what he had said.

Did she listen to him? No, of course she didn't. Not for a single moment. "I need everything I've packed," she had insisted. "I wouldn't be taking it if it wasn't required, would I?" She paused for a moment, and glared at him. "I can't possibly leave anything behind, and that's final."

Kendall wearily took his wallet out of his pocket. He withdrew two ten-dollar bills, and a five, and handed them to the clerk. The clerk nodded and pressed a button. Mollie's cases started to slowly travel along the belt, disappearing at the far end. Kendall sighed a third time and placed his cases on to the conveyor.

"They're okay," the clerk said looking up and smiling. "In fact you could have taken at least another four or five kilos. No trouble at all." He looked up. "You could have taken the young lady's excess in your case. You could have saved yourself that twenty-five dollars."

For a brief moment Kendall wondered if there was a rebate for being underweight. The clerk shook his head. "Too late now, I'm afraid," he murmured. *Clearly there was to be no rebate.*

The clerk pressed the button once again and the cases started on their journey. The clerk stamped the tickets and handed them back to Kendall "Boarding at Gate 42," he said. "Take off is at twenty-three fifty." He looked at Kendall. "That's ten minutes to midnight," he explained.

Really, Kendall thought, as he thanked the clerk for the tickets, and checked his watch. There was a little over an hour before they were due to take off. *Time for a coffee, and a snack*, thought Kendall. *Time to look in the shops*, thought Mollie.

* * *

Almost thirty minutes later they had made their way through passport control and were now in the departure area with just less than thirty-five minutes before they were due to take-off.

"Sorry to say that there's no time for shopping," said Kendall. "What a shame."

Mollie shrugged and smiled. "No time for a snack," she replied. "What a shame."

* * *

Twenty minutes later came the announcement. "American Airlines flight 332 to London Heathrow is now boarding at Gate 42."

Kendall stood up first. "Time to go," he said, as he held his hand out to help Mollie up.

She stood up, surprised by this unexpected act of chivalry. She smiled and took hold of it. "Thank you, kind sir," she said. Kendall didn't hear. He had already let her hand go and was shuffling forward. He sighed as he saw the crowd of people waiting. He just could not believe it.

"It's hard to imagine that they will all get on to one little old plane, isn't it?" a voice close by suddenly announced.

Kendall looked up. It was the irate man who had been arguing with the airline official. He looked a lot happier now, Kendall thought, the argument all forgotten.

"Sorry, what did you say?" asked Kendall.

The man smiled. "Nothing really," he replied. "It's just that no matter how many times I fly, it never fails to amaze me exactly how many people one of those things will hold." He pointed out of the window, to the Boeing 747 that was being prepared for take-off.

"Oh," said Kendall. "That's the little old plane," he said. "I know what you mean. Kendall paused for a moment. "You know I was fortunate to get a ticket," he continued. "I was quite late booking the flight."

The man nodded and smiled. "I've learned to book as early as possible," he said. "Especially if you want a particular seat." He paused. "I like the window seat," he explained. "You're nicely tucked away, you know. No constant interruptions with the trolley going up and down, or people wanting to get past to go to the bathroom. I hate all of that."

Kendall nodded. He had never thought about it before but it made sense.

"I booked this almost six weeks ago," the man continued. He

36

shrugged and shook his head. "And even then there weren't too many seats available. But I got my window seat, no problem. Seat number G6." He started to laugh as he looked around at his fellow passengers. "London is obviously a very popular place."

"Oh yes, I imagine it is," said Kendall. "Right." He too started to laugh, although exactly what was so funny he wasn't absolutely sure.

* * *

Ten minutes later Kendall was on the aircraft waiting patiently to take his seat. He was blissfully unaware of the heated argument that was taking place at that very moment at Gate 42 in the departure lounge. Two men were insisting that they should be allowed through the gate onto Flight 332.

"*It is imperative that we are on that plane*," said one.

"*A matter of life and death*," the other explained.

The airline official was equally insistent. He was very sorry but there was nothing he could do about it. It was too late; the gate was now closed. The plane was ready for take-off. There were regulations and there could be no exceptions. The argument was going nowhere.

"I really must insist," the official continued. "I must ask you to leave." There was a pause. "Or I will be forced to call security."

"Come on, let's go," said the first man to his companion.

The second man, stocky and built like a wrestler, would not budge. The first man started to pull him away. "Come on, Doyle. Leave it," he said. "Let's go."

Reluctantly the second man turned and started to walk away.

There was the sudden noise of a telephone ringing. The first man reached into his pocket and took out his mobile phone. He looked at the screen and sighed. He knew who the caller would be. "Randall speaking," he said quite simply.

"Where are you?" a voice demanded to know.

Randall shook his head once again. He looked at his companion and mouthed the words, "It's Jones."

The second man took a deep breath. "What does he want?" he whispered.

Randall shook his head and glared. "What do you think he wants?" he called back. "Just a courtesy call to enquire about your health possibly or maybe it's to invite you to tea." His companion took another deep breath but said nothing. *Neither suggestion seemed likely*

"We're in the Departure lounge, Mr Jones" Randall replied nervously. "They won't let us through on to the plane."

"Won't let you through?" the voice repeated. "Why not?"

"We were late. Traffic," Randall explained. "You know how it is."

The voice at the other end wasn't interested in excuses. "No, I'm afraid that I don't know how it is," he said. "You must tell me about it sometime." There was a short pause. "Did you see him?" he demanded to know.

Randall sighed and looked at his companion. The other man simply shrugged his shoulders and looked away. Randall sighed once again. *This was going badly, very badly indeed.* He cleared his throat. "Yes, we saw him." He paused. "We picked him up outside the house as you instructed, but ..."

"But? But what?" the voice demanded to know.

Randall shook his head, and started to hyperventilate. "We lost him on the freeway," he replied nervously.

"I didn't quite hear you, Randall," said the voice. "Say again."

Randall coughed nervously. "I said that we ... we lost him somewhere on the freeway."

There was a long silence. "You lost him on the freeway," Jones repeated. "Did I hear you correctly?"

"There was an accident, and ...."

"So you couldn't even do a simple job like tailing him for me," Jones interrupted. "You don't even know if he made it to the airport, do you?" There was another long silence. "In other words you have no idea where he is right now, do you?"

Randall shook his head slowly. "No," he replied simply.

"When's the next flight?" Jones suddenly demanded to know.

Randall looked at his companion and shook his head. He looked over at the Departures board located a few yards away. "There's another flight at just after three, I think."

"Be on it and bring the stuff with you," the voice instructed. "I'll see you both at the hotel. Call me when you get in." The line went dead.

Randall continued to stare at his phone for a few moments. He then looked at his companion once again. "At least Oliver got on board," he said slowly, as though that made everything all right..

"Was he angry?" his companion asked.

"What do you think?" Randall replied irritably. "Was he angry?" There was a short pause. "Of course he wasn't angry. He was just missing your ugly face, stupid, that's all."

* * *

"I'm sorry, sir," the hostess said. "We are now preparing for take-off. All mobile phones must be switched off, I'm afraid. It's airline regulations, you understand."

The man looked up and smiled at her. "No problem," he replied. "I've just finished." He nodded his head. "Last minute stuff, you know." She smiled at him and then continued along the aisle. He watched her for a few moments. He switched off the phone and placed it into his holdall. He placed the bag into the overhead locker. As he did so he glanced towards the front of the aircraft. "There he is," he murmured. "There's my man. Just waiting to take his seat right now."

Standing in the middle of the aisle was a smartly dressed middle-aged man. He was glancing over to his left side looking for his seat. Slowly he started to shuffle forward as the queue started to move. He stopped just behind where Kendall was waiting to take his seat.

"Excuse me," he said, as he drew near. "I believe that is my seat."

Chapter Five

Robert Andrews

Kendall either didn't hear the voice behind him or he chose to ignore it. Either way he made no response but continued to wait patiently for Mollie to move into the window seat. Although why she wanted that particular position so badly he couldn't understand. *What did she expect to see anyway?* he wondered. He shook his head. For the next seven or eight hours, all she would see was three thousand miles of dark, black, ocean, *assuming, of course, that she stayed awake, that is.* And even then she wouldn't see anything unless the thick cloud lifted.

"Would you kindly take your seats as quickly as possible," said the stewardess as she walked along the aisle.

Certainly I would, thought Kendall. *I would be absolutely delighted to take my seat. If only I could. It might have slipped your notice that the entire population of Florida is trying to get past,* he murmured. And furthermore before he could actually take his seat he still needed to put his hand luggage away into the overhead compartment. Every time he tried, more and more people pushed past him trying to get to their seats. Now he had no chance. Now there was a man standing very close at the back of him mumbling something about a seat.

"Excuse me," the voice repeated. I believe that is my seat."

Kendall looked around. He was surprised to see who it was. "I'm sorry, did you say something?" he asked.

The man gave a sigh. "I said that I believe that is my seat," he replied. "That one," he continued, pointing to the window seat, where Mollie was busy making herself comfortable. "That's my seat. G6, yes."

Kendall was no expert in this kind of thing but it certainly looked like G6. "It certainly is G6," he replied. "No question about that."

"Could I get there, please?" the man said.

Mollie looked up and glared at him. She then turned away, settled deeper into the seat and closed her eyes.

Kendall raised his eyebrows and shrugged his shoulders.

"Obviously not," the man murmured. He paused for a moment and sighed. "Not to worry. This seat is as good as any other, I suppose," he said pointing to the aisle seat.

Kendall looked at Mollie. She couldn't be asleep already he thought. *It just wasn't possible.* He turned back to face the man. "It beats standing, anyway," he said. "I'll be out of your way very soon. I just need to put this bag away." He held the bag up.

The man smiled. "I'll do it," he said grabbing hold of the bag and stuffing it on to the shelf above his head.

Kendall thanked him and moved in to the centre seat. He made himself comfortable and quickly scanned through the safety leaflet. A moment or two later he was engrossed in the in-flight magazine. An article about trekking in the Himalayas.

Meanwhile the middle-aged man placed his own bag into the overhead compartment. As he did so he thought that he noticed somebody near the back of the aircraft. Somebody, who seemed to be watching him very closely. He started to breathe hard and sweat began to spread across his forehead.

Kendall was suddenly startled by the sound of heavy breathing. He looked up at his travelling companion. The man looked odd somehow. He seemed to be staring at something. Kendall was puzzled. "Are you all right?" he asked.

The man quickly turned away and looked down at Kendall. "Oh yes, yes, sure," he said quickly. "I'm fine." He looked back along the plane. There was no sign of the person. He shook his head. Perhaps he hadn't seen anyone after all. Perhaps it was just his imagination. He was becoming paranoid. He shook his head once again. He had actually thought that he was being followed right from the time he had left home that afternoon. He was certain that there had been two men watching him. In fact he had been convinced that they had been watching him for several days. He shook his head a third time. *Ridiculous*, he murmured. *He must have been mistaken.* He looked back at Kendall. "I just thought that I saw someone I knew, that's all." He shook his head. "Must have been a mistake."

"Right," he said, unconvinced. It was obviously no mistake, he thought. *He had seen someone, and it was pretty obvious that it was someone who was not entirely welcome. He had looked almost scared.* "I do that all the time," Kendall continued. "See people I think I know, I mean." He shook his head. "I don't know why. There's probably a perfectly good reason for it, I suppose. Maybe it's a feeling that you think you know more people than you really do." He paused for a moment, and then started to smile. "Or maybe it's some kind of inferiority thing, some kind of a desire to know more people than you really do." He shook his head once again. "Hey, what do I know. It's all a bit too deep for me." He turned back to the in-flight magazine that he had been reading.

The man didn't know either. More importantly he didn't really care. He looked back along the aircraft. The person that he thought he had seen was no longer visible. He shook his head. *Perhaps he hadn't seen anything after all. Perhaps he had simply been mistaken.* As his companion had just pointed out, maybe it was some kind of inferiority thing. But then again perhaps it wasn't. Perhaps he had actually seen

41

someone. He looked down at Kendall, who was still engrossed in the magazine. The man reached into the overhead locker and pulled out his bag. He opened the bag and took out a small buff envelope. He looked at Kendall once again. He was still reading the magazine. Suddenly he heard a noise. He looked down and saw a young boy watching him closely.

"Sit down, Ryan," a voice called out. The boy glared at the man and then turned away. The man waited a few more moments and then placed the envelope into the side panel of Kendall's bag, pushing it down as far as he could. He closed his bag and sat down. He looked at Kendall, and gave a deep sigh. "At last," he murmured. "Only two hours late. Take-off I mean, only two hours. Not bad I suppose in relative terms."

Kendall looked up. "I guess so," he replied. "By the way, what was all of that disturbance at the check-in?" he asked.

The man smiled and put his head to one side. He sighed. "You noticed?" he said. "Sorry about that."

"Yes, I noticed," Kendall replied. "So what was it all about?"

The man shrugged. "Oh it was nothing really. There was a query about the ticket or something." He paused. "By the way the name is Andrews," he said holding out his hand.

Kendall took hold of the proffered hand and shook it warmly. "Kendall. Tom Kendall," he replied. "And over there, that's Mollie."

"Pleased to meet you, Tom," Andrews replied. He looked over at the still sleeping Mollie. "And you, Miss Mollie," he said.

Kendall looked at him and smiled. "So," he said, "you were going to tell me."

"Oh yes," said Andrews. "The disturbance. It was nothing really. It was all very trivial, and tedious. It seems that the clerk had merely misread the number on my ticket and it wasn't recognised by the computer. That's all."

Kendall sighed. Somehow he found it difficult to believe that it was that simple. Andrews had seemed quite agitated about something. And then the look on his face just now when he thought that he had seen someone. *Were the two things connected in some way?* Kendall shook his head. *Probably not*, he decided. *It's probably not that important anyway.* "That's computers for you," he said trying to sound knowledgeable about such things.

"Well, to be fair, it wasn't really the computer's fault, it was the clerk," Andrews replied. "I'm afraid I got a little angry. It's not like me, but I really lost it this time."

Kendall smiled. He was exactly like that himself, normally quite placid, easygoing, but with a temper when pushed. "At least we are all on board now, so let's hope for a safe trip."

"Absolutely," Andrews replied. He looked over at Mollie. She was still sound asleep, or at least she appeared to be. He shook his head. *Amazing*, he murmured. He slowly glanced around down the aisle. There was no sign of the person that had been watching him. He shrugged. He knew that the person that he had seen hadn't gone away. He was still on the plane, and he was following him.

* * *

Suddenly there was the sound of a loud buzzer. Then a voice could be heard. "Please take your seats," the voice instructed. "Fasten your seat belts and make sure that your trays are in the upright position. We have been cleared for take-off. We are number three in the queue."

"Not long now," Andrews said to Kendall.

Kendall nodded. He checked his seat belt and took a deep breath. "Here we go," he replied, suddenly wishing that he was somewhere else. Anywhere else. He shook his head. *He should have taken that Caribbean cruise after all or maybe the train journey through the Rockies, but it was too late now, far too late.* He closed the in-flight magazine and placed it back inside the compartment at the back of the seat in front of him. He looked at Andrews and gave a deep sigh.

Andrews smiled. "It'll be all right, you'll see," he said reassuringly. "Don't worry." He checked his seat belt, and gave another quick glance towards the back of the aircraft.

Kendall gripped the seat armrests tightly. He casually glanced out of the window. The plane was now beginning to taxi down the runway. His heart started beating fast and he started to sweat. He began to have difficulty in breathing and then his hands began to shake. He looked around at his fellow passengers. *They didn't seem to be having any similar problems. It seemed to be just him. Perhaps he was more sensitive than the rest.*

Andrews smiled once again. "Flying is still the safest way to travel," he said. "Statistically speaking, that is." Kendall was far from convinced.

Then there came the roar of the aircraft's engines as it slowly began to build up speed and made its way down the runway. The engine noise became louder and louder, mingling with the noise of the wheels bumping along the runway. *Any moment now*, Kendall thought. He looked over towards the door and wondered briefly if he still had time to get off. *Unlikely*, he decided, as he saw the land flashing past his window. He looked down at his hands. His knuckles were pure white. Suddenly the plane shuddered and there was a loud thumping noise.

"That's the undercarriage being retracted," Andrews told him helpfully. "There's nothing to worry about. We're airborne."

Kendall looked at his companion. "Is that right?" he said, trying hard to sound interested, but failing miserably.

"Oh yes," said Andrews. "If you look out of the window you'll see." He paused for a moment. Kendall strained to see out of the window but could see nothing. "I told you there's nothing to be worried about. I fly all the time," Andrews continued. "Seven or eight times a year. There's really nothing to it."

"Really," Kendall replied, sounding anything but enthusiastic. He wasn't feeling too good. He reached up to the panel above him and turned on the air conditioning. There was a sudden rush of air on to his face, and he began to feel a little better. He took a deep breath and glanced over at Mollie. She was sound asleep, and totally oblivious to what was happening. He looked around at his companion, who was looking at him, and shook his head. "I don't know how she does it," he muttered.

Andrews shrugged. "One of those things, I suppose. Anyway, how are you feeling?" he asked. "All right now?"

"Oh I'm fine now," Kendall replied. "Absolutely fine. It's only take-offs and landings that I have a problem with. Oh and that little bit in between."

Andrews started to laugh. "You'll be fine," he said. "I've done this trip dozens of times. I've never had a problem."

Kendall believed everything his companion had said but it made not the slightest bit of difference. He closed his eyes hoping that somehow that would stop the panic that was building up. It didn't.

His fellow passenger didn't even notice and continued talking. "Mainly to Europe, London mostly," he was saying. "South America, and Tokyo of course." He paused for a moment. "By the way I'm an accountant," he said. "I work for Travers Morgan, the Merchant bankers, you know. You've probably heard of them." Kendall would have been forced to admit that he hadn't heard of them. He probably wouldn't have cared either. However, he was fast asleep.

* * *

Kendall was awoken by the sound of an approaching trolley. As he looked up he saw his fellow traveller looking at him. "All right now?" he asked. "Fancy something to eat?"

Kendall glanced at Mollie sitting next to him. She was still sound asleep. He shrugged. *So much for the window seat*, he murmured. He checked his watch. They had been flying for almost three hours and she had slept the whole time. He turned back to face his companion. "Oh yes," he said, "I feel much better now."

"That's good to hear," Andrews said. "It really isn't that bad after all."

"Guess not," said Kendall. "Now what did you say about something to eat?"

* * *

A few minutes later the meal trays had been dispensed and the trolley had moved further down the aircraft. Andrews watched for a few moments wondering if he might have seen the mystery person once again. There was no sign. He turned back to face Kendall. "So what line are you in then, Tom?" he asked. Then he quickly raised his hand. "No, don't tell me. Let me guess." He paused for a moment. "Insurance," he suddenly announced. "You're an insurance salesman."

"No, I'm afraid not," Kendall replied shaking his head. "I'm actually a…"

Andrews raised his hand once again. "No, no. Don't tell me," he said quickly. He thought for a few moments. "Banking," he said knowingly. "You look like a banker to me."

Kendall shook his head again. "I wouldn't mind getting their bonuses. But no I'm not a banker," he said. "I'm a private detective. And sleeping beauty here is my secretary. Well she's my partner actually." He paused for a moment. "My business partner."

Andrews nodded his head. "A private detective. That sounds interesting," he said. "Are you going to Europe on business." He paused. "I mean, do you have a case to investigate? A missing husband perhaps?" He paused for a moment and smiled. Then he shook his head. "Or are you going over for a holiday?"

Kendall smiled. "We are going on holiday," he said becoming slightly more relaxed and looking round at Mollie.

"Oh that sounds exciting," Andrews replied. "So what's the plan?"

"First a few weeks in England. London. Then we plan on going over to Ireland," Kendall replied. "Did you know that the name Kendall is Celtic for Ruler of the Valley?"

Andrews shook his head. *No, he didn't know that*. "Really," he replied. "How interesting."

"I think I may have Irish ancestors," Kendall continued. "Anyway a few days in Ireland and then back to England before heading back home."

"Have you been before?" Andrews asked. "To England I mean."

"First time I've ever left the States. Can you believe that?" Kendall replied. "Except for a day trip I took to Niagara about twenty years ago." He paused for a few moments. "What about you?" he asked. "Are you going over for a holiday?"

The man shook his head. "Partly, I hope," he replied. "But it is mainly for business, I'm afraid."

Kendall was now feeling totally relaxed. "That's a shame," he replied.

45

"You say you've done this trip before?"

"Many times," Andrews replied. "But it has always been on business." He shook his head and sighed. "You know I've been to England ... how many times?" He paused and thought for a few moments. "This will be my fifth trip." He shook his head. "No, it's my sixth. Six trips and they have all been on business." He paused once again. "Do you know that in all that time I've never seen Big Ben or Buckingham Palace. Never been down Regents Street. Never fed the pigeons in Trafalgar Square." He shook his head once again. "It'll be different this time, though. This time I intend doing everything. The whole tourist thing, you know. Including the theatre, and I shall be going to see the tennis at Wimbledon. I've got tickets for the men's quarter-finals, you know." He shook his head. "Should be good." He shrugged. "As long as the weather holds, that is. There's nothing worse than Wimbledon in the rain." He shrugged once again. "Not that I've ever done it, that is." He smiled. "I also hope to see some of the country. That's the plan anyway."

Kendall smiled. He tried to imagine Wimbledon in the rain. He shook his head. *It probably wouldn't be too pleasant*, he concluded. *But there again nowhere was that pleasant in the rain, was it? The last game with the Dolphins was dreadful enough before the rain. Then the rains came and the game suddenly got better – it was scrapped.*

"All work and no play makes Jack a dull boy," he said. "That's what they say, I think."

"That's what they say all right. But this time I definitely intend to get a bit of a holiday," Andrews replied. "I have four days booked at a small hotel in Cornwall. I'm really looking forward to it."

"Cornwall," Kendall repeated. "Why Cornwall?"

"My great-great grandfather, on my mother's side, was a Cornish man. Simple as that," Andrews replied. "I intend visiting his village, and maybe finding his cottage. Assuming it's still there, of course. After all, I am talking about at least a hundred and fifty years ago. You never know, I might meet up with some long lost relatives. Or even ones I never knew I had."

"As long as they don't come looking for a loan from you," Kendall replied grinning.

"Right you are," Andrews replied smiling. He paused for a moment. "By the way my name's Bob, not Jack."

Kendall looked puzzled for a moment, and frowned. "Jack," he murmured. Then he recalled what he had said. "Oh yes, I get you," he continued. "Nice to meet you, Bob." He started to laugh. "So you're an accountant, then."

"That's right, an accountant," Andrews replied. "I work for Travers Morgan. You may have heard of them."

Kendall had to admit that he had never heard of them, but he ventured to suggest that they had probably never heard of him either.

Andrews merely frowned, missing the humour completely. 'Travers Morgan is one of the world's major investment companies. Their head office is in the heart of London, not too far from the Bank of England."

"Is that right?" said Kendall, trying to sound impressed.

Once again Andrews frowned. "You may have heard of the dreadful trading figures for the past three months."

Once again Kendall had to admit that he knew absolutely nothing about it. "The Credit Crunch, is that what you mean?" he said

"Well, not exactly, but that's part of it, I suppose."

"It's all to do with Government borrowing and the huge debt," said Kendall. He paused for a moment. "It's a massive figure, something like thirty thousand dollars each man, woman and child. It's something like that anyway." He shook his head. "They needn't look to me for my share because I don't have it."

Andrews smiled. "It actually a lot worse than that but I don't suppose you'll have them knocking on your door," he said. "The debt is only part of it, though. There are many other factors to be considered."

"You mean bank bailouts, that kind of thing," suggested Kendall.

"Well not in our case," Andrews replied. "In fact Travers Morgan made a fairly respectable profit. Completely unexpected and against all of the market trends. Certainly it was a lot lower than expected but it was still a profit. Everyone else, our rivals in particular, made a loss." Andrews shook his head. "No, business hasn't been that bad." He paused for a moment. "That's not the problem."

Kendall looked at his companion. "So," he said. "Go on. What's the problem?"

"Well, putting it simply, I have found a number of apparent discrepancies in the accounts," Andrews replied.

"Do you mean the figures don't add up?" said Kendall.

Now it was Andrews turn to smile. "Precisely," he replied. "The figures don't add up."

Suddenly Kendall sneezed. "Sorry about that," he said quickly. "Hay fever. I suffer from it." He took a couple of deep breaths, exhaling slowly. "It's a real nuisance." He took a tissue from his pocket and wiped his nose. He looked at Andrews. "Where were we? Oh yes. The figures don't add up."

"That's right," said Andrews.

"Perhaps someone got the adding up wrong," Kendall suggested. "You know they just made an error. It happens. I do it all the time. Or maybe they put the decimal point in the wrong place."

"Nothing quite as simple as that, I'm afraid," said Andrews. "It's much worse than that. This was deliberate."

"In other words there's some money gone missing," Kendall said. "Absent without leave, so to speak."

"That's about the size of it," Andrews replied. "In fact there's rather a lot of money gone absent, as you succinctly put it."

Kendall wasn't too sure what succinctly meant but he did not pursue the matter. He shook his head. "So there's no sign of the money anywhere," he said.

Andrews shook his head. "No sign at all."

"How much are we talking about?" Kendall asked. "I mean roughly."

"Oh, let's just say a few million, shall we?" said Andrews. "Give or take."

"All right," replied Kendall. "We'll say a few million." He thought for a few moments. *That means it's a lot more than just a few.* "Ten million?" he asked.

Andrews shook his head. "And the rest," he replied ruefully.

"Maybe someone has just borrowed it," Kendall suggested helpfully. "You know, a loan, just to get them through this difficult time, to tide them over."

"Maybe," Andrews replied, unconvinced. "It's possible I suppose, but not very likely, I'm afraid." He shook his head. "No, whoever took the money, took it deliberately, I'm sure of that. And they have no intention whatsoever of paying it back."

Kendall frowned. "So where is it?" he asked. "I mean it must be somewhere. Stands to reason."

Andrews looked at Kendall for a few moments. "Maybe," he said quite simply.

Kendall sighed. Maybe, he thought. *Maybe? What kind of an answer is that?* He shook his head. "Usually that sort of cash ends up off-shore somewhere. The Bahamas, or the Cayman Islands. Somewhere like that."

Andrews said nothing but simply nodded his head.

"Or perhaps in a numbered bank account in Switzerland," Kendall continued.

"To be honest, Mr Kendall, I think that the money has all been used." Andrews replied. "Already spent. Probably electronically transferred on the Internet buying shares and stock. Not all at once, of course. It would have been gradual, maybe over a few weeks or months. A little here and a little there. That way it's possible no one would even notice, until it was too late that is."

Kendall smiled. *This was all a little over his head.* "Is that really possible?" he asked.

"Perfectly possible," Andrews replied. "A vast amount of stock trading takes place on the internet these days."

"Clever," Kendall replied. "Have you any ideas as to who took the money?"

"Well I have a few ideas," Andrews replied. "Nothing definite as yet, but that's one of the reasons for going over."

"Oh I see," said Kendall. He suddenly sneezed once again. "Oh I am sorry," he said. "This wretched hay fever."

Andrews shook his head. "No need to apologise," he said. "I have a similar problem. It's probably not hay fever actually. Not here. It's more likely to be the air conditioning, I expect."

"Could be, I suppose," Kendall replied, far from convinced. "But I do suffer from hay fever."

"That's most unfortunate but I don't think there'll be any pollen in here, do you?" Andrews said. "It's the air conditioning for sure. I actually suffer from asthma and the air conditioning affects me as well." He reached into his pocket and took out a small spray canister. "I have to take this." He handed it to Kendall. "I don't know if it works for hay fever as well."

Kendall looked at the canister and shook his head. "I've seen this before," he said. "It's really only meant for asthma sufferers." He handed it back. He then reached into his pocket and took out his own spray can. "This is what I use. It's an anti-histamine."

Andrews glanced at it and handed it back to Kendall. "It wouldn't be much use to me."

Kendall replaced the spray into his pocket. "Do you take anything else?" he asked. "Any other medication, I mean."

Andrews frowned, and then he shook his head. "Someone in our London office, the chief executive in fact, suggested that I tried Syanthol. He also suffers from asthma, or so he said. Anyway apparently he had tried it and it had worked fine for him. I tried them for a while but I gave up after four or five weeks. The side effects were dreadful. Headaches, nausea, you name it. So I stopped taking it." He thought for a few moments. "That was about three or four months ago, I think."

"So what about now?" Kendall asked.

Andrews shook his head. "No I don't take any medication now. Not conventional medication, that is," he replied. "Apart from that spray occasionally."

Kendall looked at him. "Not conventional medication," he repeated.

"That's right," Andrews replied. "For the past month or so I've been trying alternative medicines. You know herbal remedies, homeopathy that sort of thing." He reached into his pocket and withdrew a small packet. "I've been taking Echinacea and now I'm trying these." He handed the packet to Kendall. "Bromelain capsules."

Kendall looked at the packet. "Bromelain," he repeated. He shook his head. "What is it?"

Andrews shook his head. "All I know is that it is an enzyme taken from pineapples." He smiled and shrugged his shoulders. "I know it sounds crazy, but .... "

Kendall nodded. *Yes, it did sound crazy but the proof of the pudding was in the eating, wasn't it?* "Do they work?" he asked. "That's the main thing, isn't it?"

"Well it's early days yet," Andrews replied. "But so far they seem to be working fine."

Kendall smiled. "Mollie over there," he pointed to his right. "She would be pleased. She is in to the alternative medicines. She takes Allicin, Garlic, things like that, you know. Charcoal. She swears by them." He paused for a moment and shook his head. "As for me, well I'm still not sure. The jury's still out on that one."

"Well all I can say is don't knock it until you try it," Andrews replied. "I've been taking them for a while now and they seem to be working for me." He paused for a few moments. "I can't be fairer than that."

Kendall looked at his companion. "Suppose not," he said. "Maybe I'll give them a try myself." He tried to stifle a yawn, without success. "In the meantime, if you don't mind, I think I'll get some sleep."

"Good idea," said Andrews. He looked across at Mollie and smiled. She hadn't stirred.

Kendall made himself comfortable. He closed his eyes and within a short time he was sound asleep. Andrews looked at him for a few moments. He then turned around and looked towards the back of the aircraft. There was no sign of the person he thought he had seen earlier. He turned back and settled down. Within a short time he too was fast asleep.

Chapter Six

A Typical Tourist

A little over five hours later the aircraft started its descent. "Ladies and gentlemen, we will shortly be landing at London Heathrow," the stewardess announced. "Would you please make sure that your tray is in the upright position and that your seat belt is secure."

Kendall felt a gentle nudge in his ribs. "We are about to land," his companion said.

Kendall opened his eyes, yawned and stretched. He looked at Andrews. "Well, that was quick." He looked around at Mollie. Amazingly she was still asleep. He shook her. "Mollie, Mollie," he called. "We're here." There was no reaction. He shook her once again, harder this time. "Mollie," he called once again. "We are landing."

Slowly she began to stir. She slowly opened her eyes, and yawned. "Where are we?" she murmured.

"England," Kendall replied. "We are just about to land at Heathrow."

She sat up and looked at him. "Already?" she replied simply. She yawned once again. "I'm so tired," she continued. "I can't wait to get to the hotel and get some sleep."

Kendall shook his head and smiled. "The journey must have been very tiring for you," he said sympathetically. "You'll be able to rest quite soon now."

* * *

There was a sudden loud thumping noise that appeared to come from just below Kendall's seat. Kendall gave a gasp and gripped the arm rests tightly.

Andrews shook his head. "It's only the undercarriage coming down." Kendall looked blank and continued to grip the arms of the seat. His knuckles turned white.

"The wheels," explained Andrews. "It's only the wheels being lowered. There's nothing to worry about."

There was another loud thumping noise, and the plane began shaking violently. Then there came the noise of the engines throttling back. Kendall looked at Andrews.

Andrews smiled and nodded. "There we are, we are down. Safe and sound," he said.

* * *

Thirty minutes later they had collected their luggage and were in the arrivals lounge.

"Well it was good meeting up with you both," said Andrews, offering his hand to Kendall. He looked at Mollie and smiled.

Kendall shook the hand. He had to admit that it hadn't been too bad after all.

"Well that's that, then," Andrews said hesitantly. He looked over towards the exit area. "Ah, there's my friend over there." He waved.

Kendall looked around in the direction Andrews had indicated.

"My transport into town," Andrews explained. "Perhaps I could give you a lift to your hotel."

Kendall shook his head. "That's very kind of you but it really won't be necessary," he replied. "The hotel has arranged for a courtesy car to pick us up. It should be right outside waiting for us."

"That's good," Andrews replied. "The last thing you want after a long flight is a stressful journey trying to find your hotel. You'll be there in no time." He paused for a few moments. "Right, I'd better be on my way then, I suppose, mustn't keep him waiting." He nodded in the direction of his awaiting friend. "I hope that you have a good holiday." He raised his hand and started to walk away. He suddenly stopped and turned. "Incidentally, Tom, I shall be staying at the Carlton Hotel in Mayfair." He paused as he wrote the name and telephone number down onto a sheet of paper. He handed it to Kendall. "I thought that it might be nice if we met up for dinner one night. What do you think?"

Kendall looked at Mollie. She nodded. He turned back to Andrews. "Sounds good to me," he said. He tapped the paper. "I'll call you and we'll fix something up."

"I look forward to the call," said Andrews. "By the way, where are you staying?"

"The Gresham," replied Mollie. "It's in Knightsbridge, I think."

"Nice hotel, I understand, not that I have ever stayed there," Andrews said. He raised his hand and waved. "Look forward to seeing you both soon." He turned and walked away.

* * *

It was raining quite hard when the car arrived at the hotel. "Here we are, sir," the driver announced. "Hotel Gresham."

Kendall stepped out on to the pavement and waited for Mollie. He looked at the hotel entrance. "Not bad," he murmured. "Not bad at all." He turned back and looked at Mollie. "Come on, Mollie, out you come," he said. "We're here."

Mollie got out. "I told you we should have brought an umbrella." She pulled her coat around her, and quickly walked towards the entrance, mumbling to herself as she went.

Kendall watched her and shrugged. "I'll get the bags, then. Don't you worry about me," he called after her.

Mollie obviously wasn't worried, she was already inside the hotel. *She was right, though. They should have brought an umbrella.*

* * *

"Good morning, sir," a voice said as Kendall approached the reception counter. "Can I help you?"

You might get these bags for a start, Kendall murmured, as he let them fall to the floor. "I have a room booked. Two rooms actually. Name of Kendall. Tom Kendall."

The receptionist looked down at his computer monitor and started to press the keys on the pad. "Ah yes, Mr Kendall," he said. "And Miss Adams." He looked at Mollie and smiled. He turned to face Kendall. "Here we are," he continued. "Rooms 623 and 625." He placed two forms on to the counter. "If I could get you both to sign. Just here," he pointed. "And just there at the bottom."

Kendall took the form and signed as requested. Mollie did the same. The receptionist took the forms back and placed them into a folder. "Now, if I could just take a credit card details."

Kendall reached into his pocket and withdrew a wallet. He took out a card and handed it to the clerk. "It's a Mastercard," Kendall said.

"That will be fine," the Clerk said as he placed it into the scanner.

"Here you are, sir," he said a few moments later as he returned the card to Kendall. "All done. If there is anything you need, just ask,"

Kendall smiled. *He would have liked some help with the cases but it didn't look like there would be any.* "What's with this weather?" he asked,

"The rain, you mean?" the receptionist replied. "Oh it's been like this for the past few days. It's Wimbledon, you see."

Kendall shook his head. No he didn't see.

"It always rains for Wimbledon," the receptionist explained. "You should have been here last week, glorious hot sunshine. The forecast isn't that good either. Rain is expected for the next two days and it will be quite cold. It's supposed to get better by the weekend, though. Or so I understand."

"Oh that's good, isn't it, Mollie?" said Kendall.

Mollie said nothing and merely glared at him.

The receptionist placed two keys on to the counter. He slid one towards Kendall and the other towards Mollie. "I hope that you have a pleasant stay. The lift is over to your right," he said. "Sixth floor, and turn to the left. 623 and 625 are at the end of the corridor."

Kendall looked around at the lift and nodded. He picked up the cases and started towards the elevator.

* * *

Five minutes later Kendall was getting settled in his room. The telephone suddenly rang. Kendall reached for the handset. "Kendall Detective Agency ...." he said.

"Kendall, is that you?" a voice asked.

Kendall sighed loudly. "Yes, Devaney," he answered wearily. "What do you want?"

"What do you mean, what do I want?" Devaney replied. "I mean. Is that nice?"

"What is it, Devaney?" Kendall said firmly.

"I was just checking that you had arrived safely. That's all," Devaney replied. "Just a friendly call. You know, hoping that you had a good flight. Things like that."

Kendall sighed once again. "Nice of you to worry, I'm sure," he said. "So what do you want?"

* * *

"So what did he want?" Mollie asked.

Kendall shook his head. "Nothing really," he replied casually picking up a newspaper.

"What did he want?" Mollie repeated.

"It was nothing," Kendall said sighing deeply.

Mollie glared at him. "What did he want?" she repeated once again.

Kendall slowly folded the newspaper and placed it on the side table. "He just wanted to see how we were that's all," he replied. "Nice of him, I thought."

"And ... " said Mollie, raising her eyebrows.

"And?" Kendall repeated.

"What else did he want?" Mollie explained. "He wouldn't just ring enquiring about your health, that's for sure."

"It was nothing, I tell you. He was just checking to see that we had arrived safely, that's all. I mean where's the problem in that?"

"Are you going to tell me what he wanted or not?" Mollie retorted.

"It was nothing, really," Kendall replied. "Just a few simple questions about a case we were involved with, you know. Simple as that. Where's the harm?"

"I knew it," she said. "I just knew it." She shook her head. "This is supposed to be a holiday, remember."

54

"Don't worry so," said Kendall. "It will be a holiday, I promise you. A real holiday." He paused for a moment and took out a guidebook. "Look, starting tomorrow, first thing, the holiday begins. Detective Inspector Terrence Devaney can just take a run and jump."

Mollie started to smile. *That was exactly what she wanted to hear.*

Kendall started to turn the pages of the guidebook. "Tomorrow we'll make a start with Buckingham Palace," he continued. "That will be followed by the Houses of Parliament, and ...."

"Harrods," Mollie suggested helpfully.

"Let me see," said Kendall completely ignoring Mollie. "Trafalgar Square, and ...."

"Regent Street," Mollie said quickly.

"Probably Westminster Abbey," Kendall continued, ignoring her once again. "Then we'll go to the City, The Bank of England. And that should cover day one."

Mollie glared at him. "What about the shopping that you promised me?" she asked.

"Shopping," Kendall repeated. "Oh don't worry, there'll be plenty of time for that," he said as he turned back to the guidebook. "Plenty of time." He looked at her. "Besides, you've brought so much with you, you hardly need to buy anything, do you?"

Mollie started to tap her hands together nervously. "You promised that we would go shopping," she said. "You promised."

Kendall sighed loudly. "And we will, don't worry," he replied. "I said we would go shopping and I meant it." He paused for a few moments. "A promise is a promise," he continued. He looked at her and smiled. "And I always keep my word, don't I?" There was a brief pause as he waited for a response. None came. He shrugged. "Have I ever let you down?"

Mollie remained silent for a few moments. "Well, there was that one time," she started to say, then thought better of it as she noticed the look on his face.. She shook her head slowly. "I suppose not," she replied. "Not exactly anyway."

She wasn't, however, entirely convinced.

* * *

The following day, as Kendall had promised, the holiday began in earnest. It was a beautiful day and the threatened rain had not materialised. The sun was shining and the sky was clear. There was not a cloud to be seen.

With his sunglasses on, and a camera hanging around his neck, Kendall looked every inch the typical tourist as he stepped out of the black cab. He was holding a large guidebook in his hand. He was followed by Mollie who looked as though she had just completed a twenty-mile forced march, which is almost exactly what she had done. Kendall had dragged her everywhere. Buckingham Palace, the Houses of Parliament, Westminster Abbey, Downing Street, Trafalgar Square. And everywhere they had gone Kendall had insisted on having the obligatory photograph. *Just for the record.* "Show the folks back home," he had said. "Especially Devaney."

"I thought you wanted me to take some exercise," Kendall had said when she had started to complain.

She shook her head. Certainly she had wanted him to take some exercise. He needed to lose a few pounds and get fitter. There was no argument there. In fact for some months now he had been out jogging three or four times a week. Generally he was covering five or six miles each time, and he was certainly looking better for it. *Oh yes, she wanted him to take exercise all right, and she was really pleased with his achievements.*

"Well, did you or did you not want me to exercise?" Kendall had asked again.

She glared at him. "Exercise is one thing," she replied. "But an assault course worthy of the Marines is something entirely different."

* * *

Kendall was leaning into the cab window. "So that's three of these," he said as he held up three five-pound notes. "And how many pence did you say?"

"Seventy-five," the driver replied for the tenth time. "Fifteen pounds, seventy-five pence." He peered into Kendall's hand. "Look, it's one of those fifty pence pieces, and ...." he started to shake his head. "No. Not that. That one there, the funny shaped one." He pointed.

Kendall gave up trying and handed over a twenty-pound note. "Keep the change," he said.

"Thanks, governor," the driver responded. He then put the vehicle into gear and slowly pulled away. Kendall watched for a few moments until the taxi was out of sight. "I'll never get the hang of this money," he murmured.

Mollie shook her head, and frowned. "It's simple," she said. "Instead of dollars and cents, they have pounds and pence."

Kendall looked blank.

"There's a hundred cents to a dollar, right" she continued. "And there's a hundred pence to a pound."

Kendall was none the wiser. "So what, a dollar is the same as a pound, is that right?"

Mollie gave a sigh and shook her head. "No," she said simply. "They are not the same. A pound is worth about one dollar fifty cents."

"We should all have the same currency," Kendall said slowly shaking his head. "It would be a whole lot easier."

Mollie shook her head once again. "It's easy," she said. "Even a child can understand." She looked at Kendall and shrugged. "There again, perhaps it would be too complicated for you." She shook her head once again, turned around and started to walk towards the building in front of her. "Where are we anyway?" she asked.

Kendall was still thinking about the currency. He gave a sigh and shook his head. "It's nothing like dollars and cents," he muttered to himself.

Mollie stopped and turned to face him. "I said where exactly are we?"

Kendall looked at her. "Sorry, what did you say?"

"I was merely wondering where we were," she replied. "Out of idle curiosity, you know. I mean it would be nice to know."

"Oh right," said Kendall, and walked over to where she was standing. "This is the Guildhall," he said. He opened his guide book, and started to read aloud from the guidebook. "The Guildhall has been used as a town hall for several hundred years and is still the ceremonial and administrative centre of the City of London, which should not be confused with Greater London, of which it is only a very small part." He looked at Mollie. "Imagine that," he said.

Mollie could not imagine anything. She had no idea what Kendall was talking about. It could have been a foreign language for all she knew. "Fascinating," she murmured.

Kendall ignored the comment, and continued to read from the book. "The term Guildhall refers both to the whole building and to its main room which is a medieval style great hall." He slowly closed the book and looked up. "Quite amazing," he mumbled.

"Absolutely mind blowing," said Mollie

Kendall looked at her and sighed deeply. "Come on, let's take a photograph." He took his camera from around his neck and slowly took it out of the case. "Over here." Reluctantly Mollie walked over to where he was indicating. "Stand just over there. No, no, to the right. Back a bit. There, that's perfect." He held the camera up to his eye and then pressed the shutter.

"Would you like a photograph taken?" a voice suddenly called out from behind. Kendall looked around to see a young man holding his hand out. "Would you like a photograph taken?" he repeated. "The two of you I mean Together."

Kendall looked at Mollie. She started to smile and Kendall nodded. "That's very kind of you," he said. He handed the camera to the stranger. "You look through there and just press that button," he explained. "The large silver one. That's it."

The young man knew exactly what to do. "Fine," he replied. "No problem. Now stand over there, that's it. Now close together, and hold it. Closer. Now smile. You're not going to a funeral, you know." He pressed the button. "Lovely," he murmured. "That's great." He handed the camera back to Kendall. "On holiday, then?" he asked.

"Yes, we are," Kendall replied.

The passerby started to smile. "You're American, aren't you? I can always tell. Whereabouts are you from, then?"

"Florida," Mollie replied.

"Florida," the young man repeated. "I have a cousin in Florida. Maybe you know her. Catherine Barr. She's been over there for four or five years now."

Kendall smiled. "What was that name again?" he asked.

"Catherine," the young man replied. "Catherine Barr."

Kendall looked at Mollie and shook his head. He had to admit that sadly he did not know her. *Florida was a big place*, he explained.

"Pity," said the young man. "She lives in Clearwater, I think."

"Clearwater," Kendall repeated. "It's nice there. Have you been there?"

The man shook his head. "One day perhaps," he replied.

"Let's hope so, shall we?" Kendall replied. "I'm sorry that I don't know your cousin. Anyway she probably doesn't know me either."

The young man started to frown. "Oh, right," he replied, not fully understanding what Kendall had just said. "Well anyway, must go," he continued. "You enjoy your stay, won't you?" He gave a sigh. "You have a nice day. That's right, isn't it? That's what you say, correct?"

Kendall smiled. "That's right," he said. "That's what we say."

The man smiled back and then slowly started to walk away. He suddenly stopped and turned around. "Don't miss the London Eye, will you? Or the National Gallery, or ...." He waved and hurried on.

Kendall had already moved away, Mollie trailing a few yards behind. "All right, that just about covers that," he said. "Let's carry on to the next, shall we?" He walked on quickly. A few moments later they arrived at the Mansion House.

"Here we are, the Mansion House," Kendall announced as he opened his guide book once again. He started to read. "The Mansion House was built between 1739 and 1752, in the then fashionable Palladian style, by the City of London architect George Dance the Elder."

"Really," said Mollie. "George Dance the Elder. Are you sure it was the elder? I was absolutely certain that it was the younger."

Kendall said nothing but continued his reading. "The construction was prompted by a wish to put an end to the inconvenient practice of lodging the Lord Mayor in one of the City Halls." Kendall paused for a moment. He shook his head. "I guess he had to live somewhere," he murmured. He looked at the building. "Pretty impressive, don't you think?"

Mollie sighed. All of the buildings were beginning to merge into one. *Once you've seen one old building, you've seen them all,* she murmured.

"What was that, Mollie?" Kendall asked.

"Oh I said, really, how absolutely interesting."

Kendall looked at her. He then looked back at the guide book. "Mansion House is the official residence of the Lord Mayor of the City of London. It is used for some of the City of London's official functions, including an annual dinner hosted by the Lord Mayor."

Mollie stifled a yawn. "Fascinating," she murmured. "I wonder where he does his shopping?"

Kendall looked puzzled. "What was that?"

"Shopping," Mollie repeated. "I merely enquired as to where he did his shopping."

Kendall shook his head, and sighed. He looked around slowly. "Do you see that building over there, the one with all of the columns? That's the Corn Exchange."

"Really," said Mollie. "Who would have thought it?"

Kendall made a face at her. He then turned once again to the guidebook and once again started to read. "The Corn Exchange was erected in 1828 from designs by Mr. Smith, at an expense of £90,000. Imagine that."

Mollie shook her head. She couldn't imagine. More to the point she didn't want to imagine and really wasn't that concerned."

Kendall frowned. *Here he was trying to broaden her education, to instil some culture into her life, and what did she do?* "It is a very fine specimen of the Greek Doric style of architecture," Kendall continued to read. "The wholesale corn trade of the city of London is entirely conducted here; and oats, beans, and all other kinds of grain are sold by sample in this market, which is held ...."

"Blah blah blah," mumbled Mollie, opening and closing her hand mimicking the movement of Kendall's mouth. "We really must go in and buy some corn," she said mockingly. "After all, we have to take some presents back with us. A new bunch of corn would be just lovely." She paused for a moment. "I wonder if they would gift wrap."

Kendall ignored her and had already walked further along the street. "There it is, he said to nobody in particular. "The Bank of England." He turned to his guide book and flipped over the pages. "The Bank of England is, despite its name, the central bank of the whole of the United Kingdom."

"So isn't that the same as England?" Mollie interrupted as she finally caught up with him.

Kendall shook his head. "The United Kingdom is England, Wales and Scotland," he replied.

"Oh," said Mollie quite simply.

"Now, where was I?" Kendall asked. "Before I was interrupted?" He looked at Mollie. "Ah here it is. It was established in 1694 to act as the English Government's banker, and to this day it still acts as the banker for the UK Government."

"Is there anything in that book about shopping?" Mollie asked.

Kendall sighed and continued to read. "The Bank was privately owned and ...."

"Does it have any shops?" Mollie asked.

Kendall shook his head. "No, it doesn't have any shops," he replied angrily.

"Pity," said Mollie.

Kendall shook his head once again. "It's a bank," he said. "Why would it have shops?"

"I just thought, that's all," Mollie explained. "A shop would have been nice. She looked at the building and sighed. Her feet were beginning to ache and she was longing for a drink. "How long are we staying in England?" she asked.

Kendall looked at her. "Sorry, what did you say?"

"I just asked how long we were staying in England, that's all," Mollie replied.

"Oh I see. Four weeks," Kendall answered. "Why?"

"Four weeks," Mollie repeated. "So we really don't need to see everything in just the one day then, do we?"

Kendall sighed and pressed on regardless, without comment. He stopped suddenly outside of a modern steel and glass building. "Travers Morgan," he murmured. He turned to face Mollie. "That's the company that Bob Andrews works for, remember."

"Yes I remember," Mollie replied. "So what about it?"

"Travers Morgan," Kendall repeated.

"Travers Morgan, great," Mollie replied. "That's marvellous, wonderful." She paused for a moment. "Fabulous."

Kendall walked over to the main entrance doors and glanced in at the entrance foyer. It was all marble and glass, and crystal chandeliers. "They must be doing very well," he said. "This must have cost a small fortune." He moved closer to the door. "Bob might be in there. Shall we go in and visit? We'll maybe get a coffee or something."

Mollie looked at him and shook her head. A coffee sounded good but not in there. "Why do you want to go in there?" she asked.

Kendall shrugged his shoulders. "Oh I don't know," he replied.

"Perhaps I could offer them my services, you know." He paused for a moment. "Help them find the missing money. Stuff like that."

Mollie looked at him and glared. "Forget it," she said flatly. "We are on holiday."

"We are on holiday," Kendall repeated. "Of course we are on holiday. Who said that we weren't?" He looked at her. "What about it?"

"Well, I thought that we were going to Regent Street," Mollie replied. "You know, the shops, clothes, presents. Things like that." She turned her head to one side. "And I wouldn't mind a drink and perhaps a spot of lunch."

Kendall looked at her and smiled. "All right," he said. "You win. Let's get a taxi. Regents Street here we come."

Her eyes lit up.

Chapter Seven

Travers Morgan

As Kendall's taxi drove away, up on the tenth floor of the Tower, Robert Andrews sat patiently, waiting to be shown into the office of John Wyndham Collier.

"Mr Collier is at a business meeting, I'm afraid," his secretary had explained. "He won't be too long," the secretary continued. "Is he expecting you?"

Andrews shook his head. *No he wasn't expected.* "I'll wait if it's alright. It's not a problem," said Andrews. He picked up a magazine, and slowly started to turn the pages.

The secretary shook her head wisely. *Nobody, but no one, got in to see her boss without an appointment, but if he wanted to sit there and wait that was up to him. It was no skin off her nose. He could sit there all week if he wanted to. That was his problem.* She looked at the visitor and shook her head once again. "That's fine," she said, and returned to her work.

* * *

"Bob? Bob, is that you?" Collier asked as he walked through the outer door and into the waiting area. "It is you," he continued, a broad smile spreading across his face. "What a surprise. Why didn't you let me know that you were coming?" He held out his hand. "Come on in." He indicated the door of his office. As he reached the doorway he stopped and turned. "No calls," he called to his secretary.

Andrews walked into the middle of the room, followed by Collier. "This is a very nice surprise," Collier said. "Have a seat." He pointed to a chair.

Andrews sat down and slowly looked around the room. "I see you've added a few new paintings," he said.

Collier looked over at the wall. "Just one or two, you know. I never could resist a bargain," he replied. "Now, let me get you a drink." He walked over to the drinks cabinet on the far side of the wall. "Now what was it? Scotch, if I remember correctly?"

"Scotch will be fine," Andrews replied. "No ice."

Collier nodded. "No ice, that's right." A few minutes later the drinks were ready, and he returned to his desk. "Now tell me, Bob, what brings you here?" he asked as he placed a drink in front of his visitor. "Business or pleasure?"

Andrews shook his head and took a drink. He looked up at Collier. "We have a problem," he said. "A serious problem."

Collier shook his head. "Oh come now, it's too nice a day for such doom and gloom," he replied. "How's things over the other side?" he asked casually.

"The other side?" Andrews repeated.

Collier looked at him, and smiled. "Miami," he explained. "How's Charlie, the old rogue?"

"Charlie," repeated Andrews. "He's fine."

"And the cancer?" Collier asked.

Andrews shook his head. "He got the all clear," he said. "He's fine."

Collier nodded his head. "That's good to know. And what about ...?"

"I've been checking the accounts," Andrews interrupted. "We have a big problem."

"So you've been checking," Collier said, smiling. "What about it? What's this big problem?"

"The figures don't tally," Andrews replied as he took another long drink.

Collier looked puzzled. "The figures don't add up. How can that be?" he asked. "I mean, are you sure?"

"Yes, I'm sure," Andrews replied. "I've checked and double-checked."

Collier shook his head. "It's probably something quite simple," he suggested. "An arithmetic error, I expect, who knows. These things happen. Human error, it's easily done." He paused for a moment and finished his drink. "It'll turn out right, you'll see."

Andrews shook his head. "I don't think so, John. Not this time," he replied. "There's definitely something going on, that's for sure."

"Something," repeated Collier. "What do you mean something, Bob?"

"Fraud, I'm sorry to say," Andrews replied.

"Fraud," repeated Collier. "You can't be serious."

"Never more so," Andrews replied. "I wish it weren't so, but everything points to it." He opened his case and took out a bundle of papers. He placed then on the desk and started to shuffle through them. "Let me show you this," he continued. He found the paper that he was looking for and held it up. "The Baxter Corporation acquisition," he announced. "You remember that one, don't you? It was your project all along. Your idea." He paused for a few moments shaking his head. "You really fought hard for that one."

"I remember it very well, Bob," Collier replied. "So what about this fraud you mentioned? Are you serious?"

Andrews looked up from his papers and nodded. "It certainly looks that way," he replied. "I wish I was wrong but I'm afraid there is no doubt."

Collier shook his head. "I can't believe it, Bob," he said. "Go on."

"Right," Andrews said simply. He started to look through the papers once again. "That acquisition cost the company one point two billion pounds. Correct?"

"One point two billion, plus a share option scheme for the employees," said Collier. "The Baxter board insisted on that."

"That's correct, but I thought that it was actually your idea," Andrews replied. He shook his head. "No matter," he continued. "It's not relevant. I'm only concerned with the financial aspect. The merger cost one point two billion, but the accounts show an additional figure of fifty million." He paused and shook his head. "How can that be?"

"I don't know," Collier replied. "You're the accountant. Maybe it's the costs in connection with that share option I mentioned. That would have had some financial implication, I would imagine."

Andrews sighed and shook his head. "Yes, it would, but that's not the answer."

Collier looked at him and sighed. "Why not? I'm no expert in these matters but costs of fifty million sounds about right to me."

Andrews shrugged. "The share option actually cost thirty two million pounds."

"Well there you are, then," said Collier. "Time you add on the legal fees, and the Stock Exchange costs, plus the tax." He paused and smiled. "Everything costs, doesn't it? Everyone wants a piece, especially the Government." He shook his head and sighed. "Anyway before you know it, there's your fifty million."

Andrews said nothing for a few moments and merely shook his head. "What you say is absolutely correct. Everyone wants paying. The only problem is all of those extra costs are all included in the accounts as separate entries."

Collier started to rub the side of his face. "Oh I see," he replied. "So we still have a large sum of money to account for."

"Correct," said Andrews.

"Well, I'm sure there's a perfectly simple explanation for it. As I said just now, a typing error maybe," said Collier. "Not very likely perhaps but it happens."

"Nothing quite as simple as that, I'm afraid," Andrews replied slowly shaking his head.

"Well, what about someone simply adding up the figures incorrectly?" He paused and took a drink. "I don't know, but I'm sure you'll sort it out."

"Oh I'll sort it out all right, have no fear," Andrews replied. "It's obvious to me that something is going on," he said slowly. "And I'm sorry to say that it seems that someone in your section is helping him, or herself, to large sums of money."

Collier looked shocked. "Surely not. One of my people, you say? I can't believe it. I mean, I know them all. They wouldn't be capable of such a thing." He paused for a moment and finished his drink. "Tell me, who is it?"

Andrews shook his head. "I haven't yet reached a decision." He paused for a moment and started to tap his papers. "I just need to check a few things here and then I'll be sure." He paused once again, and looked at Collier. "One thing, though. It is certainly one of three people right here in this building."

"Who?" Collier asked. "Come on now, who do you suspect?"

Andrews shook his head. "Not yet," he replied simply.

"What do you mean, not yet?" Collier asked.

Andrews shook his head. "There are three possibilities," he said. "I can't say anything more because I still need one more piece of information before I know for sure." He paused for a moment. "I'm expecting the last piece of the puzzle in a few days' time."

Collier rubbed his chin and slowly shook his head. "If it's one of my people, I'll find them, and I'll deal with it personally."

"No, John, that's not the way," Andrews replied. "This is fraud. It's illegal." He paused for a moment. "The police will need to take action, I'm afraid."

Collier shook his head and sighed deeply. He looked at Andrews. "Have you mentioned this to anyone else?" he asked casually.

Andrews looked at him for a moment. He had briefly mentioned something to the man on the plane but not in detail. And besides that was a perfect stranger so that didn't really count. Of course Paul Sharp knew all about it. He shook his head. "No," he replied. "I've told no one. And it won't be mentioned to anyone until I know for an absolute certainty who the guilty person is."

Collier shook his head. "You know, Bob, I can't help feeling that you're wrong. You must be mistaken."

Andrews shook his head. "There's no mistake, I'm afraid. None at all."

Collier shrugged. "I'm absolutely sure that you are wrong, Bob. If I were you, I would just forget all about it." He paused. "It really isn't worth worrying about. After all, how long will it take to make it back again? A few days, a week at the most."

Andrews shook his head. "More than a week, I would say."

"All right, more than a week. You're probably right. So let's say a month," Collier said. "Anyway you just forget all about it. Just enjoy your trip over here. Have a holiday and don't worry about a thing." He smiled. "That's what the old expense account is for." He started to laugh. "Let me get you another drink?"

Chapter Eight

The Carlton Hotel

It was a little before eight o'clock when Kendall and Mollie walked into the dining room of the Carlton Hotel. "Good evening, sir. Good evening, madam," the head waiter greeted them. "Can I get you a table?"

Kendall shook his head. "We are actually expecting to meet Mr Andrews," Kendall replied as he looked across into the Dining Room. "Ah, there he is, over by the far corner." He waved. Andrews stood up and waved back.

* * *

It had been Andrews' idea. He had telephoned Kendall earlier that afternoon. "Hi, Tom, it's Bob. Bob Andrews," he said. "Are you by any chance free this evening?"

"Hi, Bob, certainly we are free," Kendall replied. "You sound a bit down. Is anything wrong?"

"Oh, I'm okay," Andrews had said, not very convincingly. "I just thought that you and Mollie could brighten me up a little. Cheer me up, you know."

"No problem," said Kendall. "What did you have in mind?"

"Dinner, here at the hotel," said Andrews.

"Sounds good to me," said Kendall. "What time?"

"Oh, eight o'clock," said Andrews. "Eight-thirty, something like that."

"Eight o'clock will be fine."

"Good," replied Andrews sounding a little brighter. "Now you know how to get here?"

"We'll find it, don't you worry," said Kendall. "See you at eight."

"Look forward to it, Tom," replied Andrews.

* * *

"Good to see you both," said Andrews as they reached his table. "Come on, sit down."

"Are you all right now?" Kendall asked as he sat down.

"Much better for seeing you," Andrews replied. He looked at Mollie. "Mollie, you sit here, please."

Mollie sat down and a moment or two later they were approached by the waiter.

Good evening, madam, good evening, sirs," he said. "Are you ready

66

to order."

Andrews looked up. "I think so," he said as he looked towards his guests. "Mollie?"

Mollie looked at the menu for a few moments. "I'll have the grilled chicken and a Caesar salad," she decided.

"And what kind of potatoes?" the waiter asked.

She shook her head. "No potatoes, thank you." She looked at Andrews. "I have to watch my figure, you know."

"And to start, madam," the waiter continued.

"The prawn cocktail."

The waiter then turned to face Kendall. "And for you, sir?"

Kendall was busily staring across at the adjoining table where a steak had just been delivered. It was covered with onions and mushrooms, and a large portion of fries. *That would suit perfectly*, he thought.

"Sir?" the waiter repeated.

Kendall turned around. "I'll have the same as ...." He suddenly saw Mollie staring at him, slowly shaking her head. "I'll have the grilled chicken as well. No potatoes" he continued sadly. "And the prawn cocktail."

The waiter then turned to face Andrews. "And you, sir?" he said.

Andrews nodded and placed the menu card on to the table. "I will have a sirloin steak, well done, with lashings of onions and mushrooms," he announced. "And some of those sauté potatoes they do so well here." He paused for a moment. "Oh, and some broccoli."

"Thank you." said the waiter, "and for a starter?"

"The paté, I think," Andrews replied.

The waiter collected the menus and walked away.

"It's nice here," said Mollie, slowly looking around.

"Yes, it is. I always stay here when I'm in London," Andrews replied. "How's the Gresham?"

"Oh, it's fine," Kendall replied.

"I've heard that it was pretty good," Andrews replied.

Kendall said nothing. He suddenly looked up, wondering whether it was too late to change his order. He looked at Mollie. "I think I've changed my mind," he said. Mollie looked at him, shook her head and glared. "I think I'll have the tuna, not the chicken."

Mollie started to smile. "He's on a diet," she explained. "He needs to lose a pound or two."

Kendall made a face. *Thanks a bunch*, he murmured. *I needed that like a holo in the head.*

Andrews smiled and nodded knowingly. "So how was your day?" he asked.

"It was pretty good. Hectic, but interesting," Kendall replied. "We went to Buckingham Palace."

"And Trafalgar Square, and the Houses of Parliament, and Westminster Abbey," Mollie added wearily.

Kendall ignored her. "Did you know that it was originally known as Buckingham House and that it had been built for the Duke of Buckingham in 17 something or other."

"1703," Mollie advised.

"Right, 1703," Kendall repeated. "It was George the Fourth who purchased it."

"The Third," Mollie corrected. "It was George the Third."

"Right. George the Third," Kendall agreed. "Anyway, he bought it. But it didn't actually become the official royal palace of the British monarch until the accession of Queen Victoria in 1830 something."

"1837," Mollie said. "It was 1837." Kendall said nothing. Mollie turned towards Andrews. "How was your day?" she asked. "You were going to your office, I think."

Andrews shrugged. "That's right," he said and sighed wearily.

"We almost went there as well," said Kendall. "To your office, I mean."

Andrews looked puzzled.

"We went to the Guildhall, the Bank of England, and we ended up outside Travers Morgan," Mollie explained. "He wanted to go in. I wouldn't let him."

"Very wise, I would say," replied Andrews slowly shaking his head. "You seem to have been very busy today. You've seen so many places, I wonder what you'll do the rest of your holiday."

Mollie looked at Kendall and smiled sweetly. "Oh don't you worry about that," she said. "He'll find somewhere to go."

"I see," said Andrews. "I would say that it was a very wise move not to go into the Travers Morgan building. I only went there because I had to." He shook his head and sighed. "I went to see John Collier, the head of the Company." He sighed once again and took a deep breath. "I went to see him about that missing money. You remember, I told you about it."

Kendall nodded. "Fifty million, if I remember correctly. Give or take."

"That's right. Fifty million."

"Is that dollars?" Kendall asked.

Andrews shook his head. "No," he replied. "That's fifty million pounds." He paused for a moment. "That's about eighty million US dollars."

"That's quite a sum," said Mollie. "So what did he say?"

Andrews shook his head. "He told me that I must have been mistaken and that I should just forget about it." He shook his head again. "Forget about it, just like that. I couldn't believe it."

"Well, that's quite a lot to forget," said Kendall. "So what was your response?"

"I was just stunned," Andrews replied. "I really couldn't believe it." He shook his head. "I know I'm right, there's no mistake. There is a shortfall of almost fifty million, give or take a few pounds." He looked at Kendall. "I just said that I would look at the figures again and I would get back to him in a few days."

"Well, perhaps he was right," Kendall said. "After all, it is only fifty million." He started to laugh. "Just forget about it. Oh, it just slipped my mind. After all, it is only fifty million."

Andrews smiled. "Fifty million out of a total budget of some twenty billion," he said. "You're probably right. Its peanuts and not worth worrying about."

"There you are, then. You should just take it easy and enjoy your holiday," Kendall said. "After all, it's only money."

All three started to laugh loudly much to the annoyance of the other diners.

"So what's on the agenda for tomorrow?" Andrews asked.

"Well, the Tower of London, I think," Kendall replied. He suddenly felt a sharp pain in his leg. He looked at Mollie and smiled. "There again, we might go to Harrods."

"You'll like that," said Andrews looking at Mollie.

"What about you?" asked Kendall.

"Well, I had planned on going down to Cornwall for a few days," Andrews replied. "You remember I told you about my great-great-grandfather?"

Kendall remembered.

"Well, now somebody is coming over from the office to see me, so I shall have to put my trip off for a day or two," Andrews continued. "I don't know who but apparently there are a few things they want to go over with me." He shook his head. "I'm not looking forward to it one bit."

"Why not?" Kendall asked.

Andrews rubbed the side of his face. "Mainly because I don't know who is coming," he replied. "I find that a little worrying. I like to know who it is, and when, and, more importantly, why."

Kendall understood perfectly. He hated strangers calling on him and arranging meetings, and you didn't have a clue as to who it is, or what it was about. "I know the feeling exactly," he replied.

Andrews shrugged. "Anyway, once that is out of the way, things will get a whole lot better," he said. "Then I'll be able to take that trip. Cornwall here I come. Four days rest and relaxation."

"Sounds good to me," said Kendall. "I certainly hope that you have a great time."

"I will," said Andrews. "Don't you worry about that."

Kendall smiled. "This calls for a photograph," he announced. He looked at Mollie. "Have you got the camera, please," he asked, holding his hand out.

She looked puzzled. "The camera," she repeated.

"Yes, the camera," Kendall said. "I put it in your handbag before we left the hotel."

Mollie glared and reached for the bag. She opened it and reached inside. There it was. She took it out of the bag and handed it to Kendall. "Here you are," she said sweetly.

Kendall took the camera and stood up. He moved a short distance away from the table. "There," he announced as he focussed the camera on Andrews and Mollie. "Mollie, move over a bit closer to Bob. There that's better. Now, don't move. Say cheese." He pressed the button. "That's great." He then handed the camera to Mollie. "Now you take one of me and Bob."

* * *

Just over six miles away, in a small hotel on the Bayswater Road, two men sat in a room on the third floor at the rear. The Hotel Regent had been built almost one hundred and fifty years ago. At that time it had been fashionable with the well-to-do in Kensington. In recent times it had been badly neglected and was in need of attention. Substantial repairs were required, together with complete redecoration.

The room was small and dark, and sparsely furnished. The floor carpet was worn and faded. The curtains at the windows were soiled and torn. The glare from the single light in the centre of the room did little to brighten the room. On the table in the corner of the room were the remains of a takeaway pizza and a number of empty beer cans.

There was a knock on the door. "That'll be Jones," said the elder of the two men. "Answer it."

There was a second knock. Then a third. "Answer it," the man repeated. "Quickly."

The younger man stood up and started towards the door. He stood there for a few moments.

"Open the door," the first man yelled impatiently. "Don't keep him waiting."

"Suppose it's not him," said the younger man. "Suppose it's someone else." He paused for a moment. "Suppose it's the police."

The first man shook his head. "Doyle, you really are the stupidest man I ever knew. Why would the police be coming?" Randall replied. He shook his head once again. "Who else could it be, I wonder. The Queen maybe, coming round for tea, or perhaps the President is paying a flying visit and just had to stop by." He shook his head once again.

70

"Open the door," he yelled angrily.

Doyle shrugged his shoulders, took a deep breath, and eventually did has he had been instructed. As he opened the door, it was pushed open violently. In walked Oliver Jones. He looked at Randall still seated at the table. "Took your time, didn't you?" He slammed the door behind him. "Busy, were we?" He walked over to Randall. "Not disturbing you in any way I trust."

Randall got up from the bed quickly but said nothing. He knew better to say nothing when Jones was in one of his moods.

Jones looked at Doyle who was still standing by the door. "All right, Doyle, you can sit down now."

Doyle moved over to the side of the room and sat down.

"So you got here, then," Jones said, turning back to face Randall. "Eventually." There was no reply. "You brought it with you, I hope."

Randall looked up. "We got it," he replied. "You don't have to worry, Mr Jones."

Oliver Jones smiled. "That's good to know, Randall," he said sarcastically. "I feel so much better knowing that you feel that I have nothing to worry about. That is so comforting, so reassuring. It's such a weight off my mind." He shook his head. "So. Where is it?"

Randall looked at Doyle. "Get it, then," he instructed. Doyle stood up quickly and went over to the small chest of drawers. He opened the top drawer. A few moments later he returned to where the others were sitting and placed a small bottle on to the side table, "Here it is," he said nervously.

Jones reached forward and picked up the bottle. "Syanthol 25," he read slowly. He tapped the bottle a few times and then placed it into his jacket pocket. "Right. Now remember, I shall be at his hotel tomorrow afternoon." The other two men simply nodded. Jones looked at Randall. "You telephone at one-fifty." He handed a piece of paper to Randall. "That's the number."

Randall took the paper. He put it into his pocket.

"One-fifty," Jones repeated. "Don't forget."

"I won't forget," said Randall. "You can rely on me."

Jones shook his head. "I hope so, Randall," he replied slowly. "I certainly hope so."

* * *

Oh how Kendall hated shopping. Endlessly wandering from shop to shop, looking at things that you had no intention of buying. Things that you neither needed nor could afford. *What was the point of it?* He would only go into a shop if he had a specific purchase in mind. A shirt, maybe, or perhaps a pair of shoes. He would know exactly what he wanted and precisely where he could get it. He would go directly to the shop, pick up the item, and then head straight back home. No messing around. No delaying. Job done. Simple. No problem.

Mollie, on the other hand, she made a career out of it. With her shopping was a major production of epic proportions. It was an event to be savoured. She would spend the whole day just browsing, going from shop to shop. She would try something on, and then something else. Then maybe she would go back to the first item once again. Often it had been known for her to return to the first shop she had been to hours before. Often, after all the effort, she would actually buy nothing.

* * *

It had been a long, exhausting day. It seemed that they had visited every shop in London, some of them at least twice. Kendall shook his head. He couldn't believe it. She hadn't bought a thing. Oh sure, she had seen lots of things that were *'interesting'*. That meant that she would need to go back again, just to check, you know. *Still, she had enjoyed it, hadn't she?* he murmured. *That was something.* He looked at his watch. Seven-thirty. Another thirty minutes and then he would meet Mollie for dinner, and later a relaxing hour or two in the lounge. A few drinks. Sounded good. He smiled at the thought. "*It will definitely be a steak tonight,*" he thought.

He casually switched on the television. There was a news item regarding yet another international conference that had been arranged to discuss the financial situation. Kendall stood and listened for a few moments. "Agreement was reached today," the newsreader was saying. "Regarding the global economic situation."

"Yes," Kendall murmured. "So what was agreed?"

His question remained unanswered, the newsreader had now gone on to the next item. "The body of a middle-aged man was discovered in a hotel room earlier today. The body was discovered in the Hotel Carlton, situated in the heart of London's Mayfair."

Kendall's ears pricked up at the name of the hotel. He moved closer to the television and turned up the volume. A photograph appeared on the screen. "The body has been identified as Robert Andrews, an American accountant who has recently arrived in this country. It is understood that Mr Andrews died from an overdose of tablets." The picture faded and once more the newsreader was visible. "Scotland Yard would like to hear from anyone with information concerning Mr Andrews' movements since he arrived at Heathrow early on Sunday morning."

Kendall shook his head. He could hardly believe. "Dead", he murmured over and over. He couldn't be dead. *It was impossible.*

Somebody had made a mistake, a dreadful mistake. "An overdose." He shook his head once again. This was crazy. *"We were with him only last night, having dinner."* He lowered the sound on the television, and picked up the telephone. "Room 625 please." The call was answered a few moments late. "Mollie," Kendall asked. "Have you heard the news?"

"I've just seen it on the television," she replied. "I can't believe it."

"No, neither can I," Kendall said. "I'm just about to give Scotland Yard a call. We'll have to go to see them, you know."

"I suppose so," said Mollie, sounding distinctly unenthusiastic. "Let me know." She hung up.

Kendall stared at the receiver for a few moments. Dead, he murmured once again. *An overdose.* He shook his head once again, and dialled a number.

"Reception," he said when his call was answered.. "Can you get me Scotland Yard, please."

* * *

The black cab slowly drew to a halt. "Here we are governor," the driver called out. "New Scotland Yard."

Kendall opened the door and stepped out. Mollie waited a few moments, hoping that he would help her out of the taxi. He didn't. She sighed and stepped out, glaring at him. He never noticed. "That'll be fourteen pounds, eighty-five pence," the driver continued, pointing to the meter.

"Here we go again," mumbled Kendall as he took his wallet from his inside pocket. "Here we are," he announced as he handed the driver a twenty pound note. "Keep the change," he said, almost mechanically.

The driver thanked him and quickly drove off.

Kendall stood on the pavement looking up at the building for a few moments. "So this is Scotland Yard," he said to nobody in particular.

* * *

Scotland Yard – or to be strictly accurate, New Scotland Yard - was home to London's police force, the Metropolitan Police, the oldest force in the world. The building had been constructed at the end of the 1960s, and comprised a long nine storey block, linked to a twenty storey section at the rear.

The buildings, although showing signs of wear and tear, were not a bit like the old red-bricked building that was home to the 32nd Precinct of the New York Police Department where Kendall had worked for almost ten years. The New York building was at least a hundred years old and was affectionately known to the inhabitants, or inmates as

73

Kendall called them, as the Workhouse. Oliver Twist would not have felt out of place in it. Kendall smiled as he remembered it.

* * *

"Are you coming?" a voice called out loudly.

Kendall quickly turned around. "Yes," he stammered. "Yes, be right there." He quickly walked over to where Molly was waiting.

"Now who are we to see?" Mollie asked.

Kendall took a small piece of paper from his pocket. "Inspector William Whittaker, CID, Room 4/24, New Scotland Yard, at nine-thirty," he said. He checked his watch. "Ten minutes to go."

"Come on, then," said Mollie sighing deeply. "Let's get it over and done with, and then we can get back to the shops. She quickly walked over to the main entrance and went in.

Chapter Nine

Detective Inspector Whittaker

The entrance lobby was bright and airy. Over on the far side was a reception counter. As they walked in one of the receptionists looked up. "Can I help you?" he called out.

"Inspector Whittaker," Kendall answered. "Room 4/24."

"Are you expected?" the receptionist asked. Kendall nodded. "Take the lift to the fourth floor. Turn left, it's at the end of the corridor."

Kendall and Mollie started to walk towards the elevators. To one side were a number of security screens. "This way, sir, and you, madam," a police officer called out. "Sorry, but we have to check you first."

They walked over to the officer. "It's just a formality, you understand." The officer looked at Mollie. "Would you care to step over there to the lady officer, please." The officer then turned to face Kendall. "Now, sir," he said. "Have you anything metal on you, sir?" he asked.

"Some coins, my watch, oh and my belt."

"Right, sir, let me have them, then walk through the arch."

Kendall handed over the items and walked through the barrier.

"Thank you, sir, you're clear," the officer said. "Off you go."

Kendall collected his belongings. *It was a bit of an imposition*, he murmured, but that's how it was nowadays. He shrugged. Sign of the times. After 9/11 nothing would ever be the same again. *Better to be safe than sorry*, he thought.

Suddenly there was the sound of an alarm ringing loudly behind him. He turned to see Mollie shaking her head. She was holding something in her hand. "It's my brooch," she said. "Sorry."

* * *

Kendall and Mollie took the elevator and a few moments later found themselves in Room 4/24. "Inspector Whittaker?" Kendall asked as he entered the room.

Opposite the doorway, a police sergeant sat at a desk entering something on to the computer. He looked up. "Is he expecting you?" he asked.

Kendall nodded. "Yes, he is," he replied. "I'm Kendall, I rang last night."

"Oh yes, Mr Kendall," the Sergeant replied. "It's about Mr Andrews, correct?"

"That's right," replied Kendall. "Bob Andrews."

"Inspector Whittaker won't be very long, sir," said the police sergeant. "He's actually with the Commissioner right now." He pointed over to the far corner. "Take a seat."

* * *

Ten minutes later the outer door opened and in came Whittaker. The Sergeant looked up. "Mr Kendall to see you, sir," he said, pointing to where Kendall was seated.

The Inspector looked puzzled. "Kendall?"

"It's about Mr Andrews, sir," the Sergeant explained.

The Inspector thought for a moment and then nodded. "Right you are." He turned to face Kendall. "Come in, then." Inside the office the telephone could be heard ringing.

Kendall and Mollie went into the office. Whittaker followed, kicking the door shut behind him as he carefully balanced a large mug of tea, and a cake in one hand, and a bundle of files in the other. As he reached his desk the telephone was still ringing. Whittaker allowed the files to fall down. Carefully he placed the cake and the mug of tea down onto the desk. As he did so, he started to blow on his fingers. "Hot," he murmured. "Just as I like it." He shook his head and looked at the telephone. "That phone never stops," he said as he reached for the receiver. "No, I said four o'clock, not three-thirty." He shook his head and replaced the handset. "I don't know why I bother sometimes," he murmured. "If I said four o'clock, I meant four. Stands to reason."

He shook his head and glanced at the pile of files on his desk. He walked over to the door, opened it, and called out to his sergeant. "Get me Williams, will you," he instructed. "Now."

He returned to his office and closed the door. The telephone rang once again. Whittaker shook his head and looked at Kendall. "What did I say? Never stops," he said. "Just a second, this won't take too long." He reached for the handset. "Yes, sir," he said. He looked at Kendall, and placed his hand over the handset. "The Commissioner," he whispered. "Yes, sir. Yes. I'll get right on it. Leave it with me."

He put the phone down. "As if I haven't got enough to do," he said. He shook his head. "Head cook and bottle washer, that's me." He took a drink of the hot steaming tea. "Sometimes you would think that I was the only one here."

He looked up and noticed Kendall looking at him. He looked down at the tea and then looked back at Kendall. He shrugged and sighed. "Would you like some?" he asked. "And you, Miss?" Without waiting for a reply, he stood up and went back to the door. He opened the door and peered round. "Sergeant," he called out. "A cup of tea for our guests, if you will. Oh, and another piece of this superb Dundee cake." He closed

76

the door and returned to his desk. "It won't be long," he said as he sat down.

Dundee cake, Kendall murmured. Whatever that was. He shook his head. He would have much preferred a nice chocolate biscuit or two.

"Have a seat," the Inspector called out.

Kendall slowly glanced around the room, looking for a vacant chair. He couldn't see one that wasn't loaded with papers of one kind or another.

"Just move those files off of those," the Inspector said as he pointed to two chairs opposite. "Put them down anywhere on the floor, just over there."

Kendall did as he had been bidden and sat down. Mollie did likewise. A minute or two later there was a knock on the door. "Come," Whittaker called out, without looking up.

The door opened and the Sergeant came in carrying a small silver tray, "The extra tea and cake you requested, sir," he said smiling at Mollie. He turned to face the Inspector. "Williams is in Deptford, sir," he said. "They found the car."

Whittaker looked up. "That's something, then. Keep me posted."

"Will do, sir," said the Sergeant as he left the room.

Whittaker looked at Kendall. "A jewel robbery last night. We've just found the getaway car," he explained. "Now, where was I?" He slowly reached for his cup and picked it up. He took a sip of his tea and a bite of cake. He started to chew slowly. "Now that really is a piece of cake," he said, brushing the crumbs from the front of his shirt. As he did so he looked down at his desk. In front of him was a dark blue file. He opened it and took out a sheet of paper. He laid the sheet of paper down. He suddenly looked up. "Help yourself to the cake. It's really very good," he said. "And don't let your tea get cold."

He turned away and continued to read the paper once again. "Huh, huh," he murmured. He started to rub his chin and turned to face Kendall.

"Now, Mr Kenton, this won't ...."

"Ken-Dall," said Kendall correcting the Inspector. "It's Kendall. Not Kenton."

"I beg your pardon," the Inspector said.

"I said the name is Kendall," Kendall repeated. "Not Kenton."

The Inspector looked puzzled. "That's what I said, isn't it?" he replied, shaking his head. He turned to face Mollie. "And you are Miss Adams. Correct?"

Mollie nodded and smiled.

The Inspector took a drink of his tea and looked at Kendall. "Now, Mr, Ken-Dall, we'll get on, shall we?" he said. "As I was saying, this shouldn't take too long. I mean it's pretty obvious what happened." He shook his head. "An overdose of tablets, simple as that." He paused for a moment. "A sad business all the same," he continued. "A young man like that, in his prime, and taking his own life. Terrible."

"Are you sure that he did kill himself?" Kendall asked.

Whittaker shook his head. "A dreadful thing," he said, ignoring Kendall's question. He sighed. "Whether it was deliberate or not, well that's what we need to find out. Although it does seem very likely that it was, I must say." He looked at Kendall for a few moments, shaking his head slowly.

"Are you sure that he did kill himself?" Kendall asked once again.

"Do have some of that cake," replied Whittaker ignoring the question once again. "I see that you are an American," Whittaker went on. "Over here on holiday then, are you?"

"That's right," Kendall replied. "Just over for a few weeks, you ..."

"Yes, that's nice," Whittaker said. He glanced down at the sheet of paper lying on the desk. "I understand that Mr Andrews was on the same plane as you. Is that right?"

"That's right," said Kendall, as he picked up the cake and took a bite. "We flew in a few days ago."

"So you're a Private detective, eh," Whittaker said, interrupting, as he picked up the sheet of paper.

Kendall looked up. "I'm sorry, did you say something?"

"I said so you're a Private Detective," Whittaker repeated. "That's what's written down here." He tapped the paper that he was holding. "It's all there." He paused for a moment. "That's what it says. You are a Private Detective in Miami." He placed the paper back on to the desk and shook his head. "What's that, then? Some kind of Philip Marlowe, are we?" He shrugged, and looked up at the ceiling. "You know I've seen all of those films. Humphrey Bogart, Robert Mitchum. The lot of them." He started to laugh. "The Big Sleep. The Maltese Falcon. You name it."

Kendall began to wonder what all of this had to do with the death of Bob Andrews. "Inspector, I wonder ..." he started to speak.

"Enjoyable in their own way, I suppose, but it's all fantasy, of course," Whittaker continued. "None of its real, you know." He shrugged once again and looked at Kendall. "I mean there's absolutely no way that they would really solve a crime, is there?" He shook his head. "I mean a real crime, that is, not one of those pretend things on the films." He shrugged his shoulders. "Hollywood. Fiction. That's all it is. Fairy tales. It's all staged. Clever mind you, very clever. And very entertaining, I admit. But I mean ...." He shook his head and started to smile. "Stands to reason," he continued, looking up at the ceiling and leaning back in his chair. "Oh no, I'm talking about a proper crime. You know, real life. Things aren't quite so easy in reality, are they? They are far more complex, more involved." He shrugged his shoulders and sat up straight. He looked at Kendall. "You need a real professional for that. Someone with the knowledge and the experience. The skill. Someone who knows what they are talking about. Someone who can recognise the important things. To sift through the clues and arrive at a logical, well thought out conclusion based upon the facts." He paused for a moment. "It's all to do with deduction, you see," he continued. "Deduction and logic." He paused once again. "All right, I suppose they have their uses. Private detectives, I mean. I'll give you that. Limited, though. Like checking up on a husband who is playing around or an unfaithful wife. That kind of thing. The odd insurance claim. You know. Or maybe a benefit cheat. But not real crimes." He shook his head. "Not a chance."

Kendall was about to retaliate when Mollie kicked him under the table. The Inspector never noticed a thing. "Now, Miss," he said, turning towards Mollie. "What do you do?"

Mollie looked at him stony faced. "I am his ..." She paused. "I am the Company Secretary," she replied haughtily. "I'm his partner."

The Inspector merely nodded, apparently unimpressed. He turned back to the paper that he had been reading. He suddenly let the paper fall to the desk and he started to tap the side of his face. "So Mr Andrews was on the same aircraft as yourself," he repeated

"That's right." said Kendall.

"Um," the Inspector murmured as he scribbled something onto his pad. "Did he seem all right to you? I mean, he wasn't acting strange or anything?"

Kendall shook his head. "Not that I noticed, Inspector. But I can't believe that he ...."

The Inspector looked at Mollie. "Did you notice anything then, Miss?" he asked, interrupting once again.

She shook her head. "No, I didn't, Inspector. I was asleep for most of the flight."

The Inspector looked up at her. He was puzzled. "You were asleep the whole time?" he said. "For what, a seven, eight hour flight?"

Mollie shook her head. "I pretended to be asleep at first."

The Inspector looked even more puzzled. "You pretended to be asleep," he repeated. "Why would you want to do that?" he asked.

"I didn't want to speak to him," she replied.

"You didn't want to speak to who?" the Inspector asked.

"Mr Andrews," Mollie replied. "I didn't want to speak to him."

"You didn't like him, then?" said the Inspector "Why was that?"

"He wanted my seat, you see," Mollie explained.

The Inspector obviously did not see and remained puzzled. "He wanted your seat," he repeated shaking his head. "I don't understand any of this."

"It really is quite simple, Inspector," Kendall interjected. "Mollie had taken the window seat on the aircraft but it was really Andrews' place, you see. And he wanted it back, that's all. It's no big mystery."

The Inspector shook his head and looked at Mollie. "So let's get this straight," he said. "You had taken Mr Andrews seat and then pretended to be asleep when he asked for it back. Is that correct?"

Mollie shook her head. "I didn't know it was his seat."

"Inspector, is all of this really necessary," said Kendall. "I mean I can't see any connection with any of this with Andrews' death."

The Inspector looked at Kendall and shook his head. "Ah well, there you are, you see," he said. "That's the difference between us." He paused. "It's what I said earlier. Proves my point completely. Amateur or professional." He paused once again. "Chalk and cheese. There's just no comparison. Here at Scotland Yard we investigate everything, no matter how trivial it seems." He paused and nodded his head. "Quite often something quite small and trivial, and seemingly unimportant, can lead to quite significant results. You just never know." He paused for a moment. "You should bear that in mind. Keep an open mind," he continued. "You might find that useful in your own small endeavours."

Kendall said nothing. He was far from convinced.

The Inspector turned to face Mollie once again. "So you never actually spoke to Mr Andrews, then," he said.

Mollie thought for a moment. "I did, in the arrivals lounge. After we had landed," she replied. "We were talking about what we were going to do here in England, and we were talking about meeting up one evening for dinner." She looked at Kendall.

"That's right, Inspector," said Kendall. "We were going to meet at his hotel. I was to call him and make the arrangements." He paused and shook his head.

"And did you meet up, then?" the Inspector asked.

"Oh yes, we had a lovely evening at his hotel," said Mollie.

"When was that?" the Inspector asked.

"The day before yesterday, in fact," Mollie replied. "The day before he died. I can't believe it."

"And he seemed alright to you," the Inspector asked.

"That's right," said Mollie.

"Correct," said Kendall. "He was okay."

The Inspector murmured once again and scribbled something else down on to a pad.

Kendall shook his head. "He was fine. In fact we had a long discussion about his plans."

"His plans?" repeated the Inspector.

"He said that he had actually booked a short break at a small hotel, in Cornwall," Kendall explained. "He was really looking forward to it."

"Cornwall," the Inspector repeated.

"Apparently his grand-father, or someone, came from there many years ago," Kendall replied. "I'm not sure who exactly."

"Huh, huh, I see," said the Inspector, as he carried on writing. "So he wasn't worried about anything."

Kendall shook his head. "No he wasn't worried about a thing." He paused for a few moments. "Not worried exactly. But I have to say that he wasn't entirely happy."

"Oh," said the Inspector. "Go on."

"Well I don't exactly know what it was," replied Kendall hesitantly. "But he had to postpone his trip because someone was going to visit him at the hotel. He wasn't exactly looking forward to it."

The Inspector nodded. "That would be Oliver Jones. Something to do with business," he said. "We know all about that. Was there anything else?"

Kendall thought for a few moments then shook his head. "No, I don't think so."

Whittaker looked up puzzled. "You didn't notice anything odd or strange about his actions."

Kendall started to shake his head. "No, nothing odd," he replied. Then he stopped as he remembered the look that he had seen in Andrews' eyes on the plane just before they had taken off. "There was something, though," Kendall continued. "On the plane. I'm not exactly sure what. A look?" He looked at Mollie.

Mollie shook her head. "Don't look at me, I was asleep, remember?" she said. "I never saw anything."

Whittaker shook his head. "A look," he repeated. "What kind of look was that, then?"

Kendall shook his head. "Well it was ... kind of .." He paused hesitant, trying to think of the right words. *How could he describe it?* "Well it was, well, you know."

"Go on, Kendall," Whittaker said. "I'm eagerly waiting. I'm all ears."

"Well it was." Kendall paused once again. He shook his head. *Perhaps it was nothing after all. Perhaps he had just thought there was something.* "Well it was strange, that's all."

Whittaker started to frown. "Strange," he repeated, wondering whether it was worthy of a note in his pad or not. He shook his head. *No, it wasn't.* "Go on. What was so strange?" he asked.

Kendall was beginning to sweat now, and feeling a little foolish. *It was beginning to sound more and more ridiculous, and probably of no importance anyway.* "I'm not exactly sure," he replied simply.

Whittaker was now fast losing his patience. "You're not exactly sure of what?" he asked.

Kendall sighed and started to frown. *Perhaps he shouldn't have even mentioned it but it was too late now.* "Something on the plane," he continued. "He seemed surprised about something he had seen."

"Something he had seen," repeated Whittaker.

"Something," said Kendall. "Or someone."

Whittaker sighed loudly. "Is that it?" he asked. "He saw something, or someone, on the plane." Whittaker shook his head. "So what about it?"

Kendall started to feel even more uncomfortable. *Why had he said that? What did it matter anyway? So he saw something, or thought he did. What possible connection could there be with his death?*

"Well," said Whittaker, getting even more impatient. "I'm still waiting."

Kendall took a deep breath and noisily cleared his throat. "Well it was just the way he looked," he replied.

"Go on," said Whittaker. "I'm listening, although I don't know why."

Kendall shook his head once again. "Well, he just looked startled, that's all. Surprised."

"Startled," repeated Whittaker. "He looked startled." He shook his head. "Surprised. So he saw something. So what. What's your point?"

Kendall shook his head and said nothing.

Whittaker started to tap the desk, and shaking his head. "And that's it," he said frowning.

Kendall had to admit that it wasn't much but it had seemed important at the time,

"What about you, Mr Kendall," said Whittaker. "Did you see anything? I mean anything in particular. Anything that might have worried him."

Kendall looked down and shook his head. "No," he said quite simply. "I saw nothing."

"Sorry, I didn't quite catch that," said the Inspector.

Kendall looked up. "I said I saw nothing."

Whittaker shook his head, and looked at Kendall. "So, Mr Kendall, let me get this straight," he said. "Correct me if I'm wrong." He paused for a few moments. "You didn't see anything. Anything significant that is."

The Inspector then looked at Mollie. "And you, Miss, you were asleep at the time. Or at least you were pretending to be asleep." He shook his head and looked back at Kendall. "You both saw nothing and yet you say that Mr Andrews did see something, or someone." Whittaker paused and shook his head. "And you suggest that the something was in some way connected with his death. Is that about it, sir?"

Kendall suddenly began to feel very uncomfortable and started to fidget in his seat. *It did sound very unlikely.* Mollie reached forward slightly. She placed her hand on his arm and smiled.

Kendall looked at Whittaker. "Well, I'm not exactly sure that there is any connection with the death," he replied. "But I'm sure that he saw something that disturbed him."

"And that's it," said the Inspector.

"That's about it, Inspector," Kendall replied.

"Amazing," said Whittaker and grunted loudly. "Absolutely amazing. Anything else, Mr Kendall? Any other earth shattering bits of information?"

Kendall sadly shook his head.

"So all told we end up with a big fat nothing, is that right?" Kendall said nothing. "Is this a sample of your detective skills, then?" the Inspector continued. "Your powers of deduction." Still Kendall said nothing.

The Inspector sighed. "Well, I suppose it might be enough in those Hollywood movies, or maybe in a book, but it won't do in real life. Not by a long way. In real life I need facts. Evidence. Something definite. Not wild speculation. Here at the Yard we analyse the evidence, you see. Methodical. Scientific, you might say." He paused for a moment. "It's the only sure way," he continued. "We don't deal with guesswork, or some odd feeling, or any such nonsense." He shook his head. "No, sir."

Kendall was beginning to think that he shouldn't have mentioned anything at all. *In fact, he was beginning to wish that he was somewhere else. Anywhere else.* Then he shook his head as he remembered the exact look on Andrews' face. "He looked frightened," he said. "That was it, he looked frightened."

"Frightened," repeated Whittaker. "So here we go again, do we? First it was startled. Then it was surprised, if memory serves. Then we had, let me see. Disturbed. Now it's frightened." There was a short pause. Whittaker started to make a clicking noise with his tongue. "So which is it, then?"

Kendall thought for a few moments. "Frightened," he replied.

"Frightened," repeated Whittaker. "You're sure now? You wouldn't like another choice?"

"Frightened," Kendall repeated.

"All right. Frightened it is then," said the Inspector. "Let's settle for that, shall we?"

Kendall nodded. "That's right, frightened," he replied. "He was nervous about something and he kept looking round."

"Nervous," Whittaker repeated. "I thought we were settled on frightened." He shook his head again. "Which is it, Mr Kendall, frightened or nervous?"

Kendall shook his head. He was really wishing that he hadn't gone down this particular road. "It was both," he said emphatically. "He was frightened, and nervous."

"And that is your professional opinion," said Whittaker. "As a detective, I mean." He shook his head, and sighed. "He looked frightened." He paused for a moment. "Oh, and nervous."

"That's right," said Kendall, beginning to get a little agitated.

Whittaker nodded and started to smile. "Well now, Mr Kendall, not that I have a great deal of experience in this kind of thing, you understand. I mean, on my salary I can't afford to go jetting off everywhere, if you get my drift."

Kendall looked at him, totally unsure of where this was leading.

The Inspector started to grin. "As I say, I have no real experience, but wouldn't you agree that the majority of people look frightened, and nervous, on an aircraft, especially when it is about to take off?" He paused and shook his head once again. "It's quite normal, I would say. Quite a natural reaction." He paused once again. "Wouldn't you agree, Mr Kendall?"

Kendall said nothing but glared at the Inspector, although he had to reluctantly agree that what the Inspector had said did actually make sense. *Perhaps that's all it was. He was nervous about the take-off.*

"Well, that's very helpful, I'm sure, Mr Kendall," the Inspector said, as he looked back at his notepad, took up his pen and started to write. He suddenly stopped and put a line through what he had just written. He looked up at Kendall. "So, did Mr Andrews say anything? I mean did he say why he was coming to England?"

Kendall sighed. "He was talking about his job," he replied. "He was an accountant for one of those big financial companies."

"Travers Morgan, we know that," Whittaker said. "Go on."

"Well I don't know much more," Kendall said. "But it seemed that there was some problems with the accounts, apparently." He paused for a moment and shook his head. "I don't know what the problem was exactly. He had come to sort it all out. That's all I know."

"We know all about it," Whittaker said smugly. "We have spoken to John Wyndham Collier." He paused. "He's the head of Travers Morgan, you know," he explained. "He told us all about it."

"I see," Kendall replied. "Did Collier say why Andrews had to come to England precisely?" he asked

Whittaker looked at him and sighed. "I don't follow you, Kendall," he said.

"All I'm saying is that with the Internet, and emails, why did Andrews need to come over here?" replied Kendall. "Surely he could have dealt with the problem quite easily staying in the States."

"Oh, I see," said Whittaker smiling. "Well I'm not a great Internet man myself. You know what I mean. I think it's not as great as it's been cracked up to be, a lot of hype if you ask me. Then there's all the problems associated with viruses and internet fraud." He paused and shook his head. "Oh it has its uses, I grant you. Buying things, and booking theatre tickets. Things like that." He shrugged. "But it'll never take the place of experience and the personal aspect. I mean, a machine, that's all it is." He paused once again. "No heart, you see. No soul." He shook his head. "No feelings." He sighed. "In this game you need feelings. You need to be hands-on, you know what I mean. Maybe Mr Andrews felt the same."

"Possibly," replied Kendall, sounding very much unconvinced.

Whittaker shook his head. "I don't know for sure," he replied. "But I don't think it's that significant. After all, you know what these business executives are like. High flyers. Big expense accounts. That sort of thing. He probably thought he'd get a trip to Europe courtesy of the firm." He paused, and shook his head. "A free holiday, if you like. You don't get that sort of thing with the Yard. I'm fortunate to get a free lunch occasionally." He sighed. "Even then there's four different forms to fill out in triplicate. Everything has to be accounted for, you see. Up front, out in the open."

Kendall started to grin. He tried hard to imagine Whittaker as a high flyer, living it up on a company expense account. He shook his head and gave up. "So you are suggesting that he arranges for a cheap holiday and then kills himself a day or two after arriving in the UK," he said. "That doesn't make much sense to me."

Whittaker ignored the comment, and started to shuffle the papers on his desk. "Maybe," he said without looking up.

Chapter Ten

An Open And Shut Case

Whittaker shook his head and looked up from his papers. "I grant you that it might sound a little odd, putting it like that," he said. "But it does seem that way to us. Clear as day. Mr Andrews killed himself, simple as that." He shook his head. "Open and shut case, I would say."

Kendall shook his head. "I just can't believe," he said. "It just doesn't make sense."

"Never does, of course," Whittaker said. "Make sense, I mean. You know, I've seen it so many times, but a young man taking his own life. Well I dare say I'll never get over that." He shook his head. "Never."

"According to the news, the body was actually discovered by one of the hotel maids. Is that right?" Kendall asked.

The Inspector looked up. "That's correct. She was cleaning the rooms."

"About three-thirty, I understand," said Kendall.

The Inspector shook his head. "Twenty minutes to four actually," he replied.

"So do we know the actual time of death?" Kendall asked.

The Inspector looked puzzled. "Well, as far as the doctor can tell, the actual time of death is put at between twelve and two o'clock."

"An overdose of tablets, is that right?" Kendall asked.

"That's right," Whittaker replied. "Some prescription tablets that he was taking for something or other."

Kendall looked at the Inspector, and shook his head. "But he wasn't taking any medication," he said. "He told me that on the plane. Apart from the nasal spray that he used for his asthma, and some herbal remedy, he didn't take anything."

"I can't imagine why he told you that, Mr Kendall," the Inspector replied. "We know for a fact that he was taking medication. He must have been lying."

"Lying? Why would he do that?" asked Kendall.

"Oh, there could be any number of reasons," Whittaker replied. "Conversation maybe, you know, just something to say. Perhaps he just didn't want you to know. The point is clearly he was taking the tablets, Mr Kendall. We know that. You see, we found them, at least we found the empty bottle in his room."

"I see," Kendall replied, unsure. *Had Andrews lied to him about the medicine?* He shook his head. *Why would he lie?* "Do you know what type of tablet it was?" he asked.

Whittaker shook his head and shuffled through the papers. He suddenly looked up as he found what he was looking for. "Syanthol, or something or other," he replied. "Yes Syanthol, 25 milligrams."

"Are you sure?" Kendall asked. Whittaker nodded. "Where was it?" Kendall continued.

"The bottle?" Whittaker repeated. "It was there, standing on the bedside cabinet."

"And the cap," Kendall continued. "Where was that?"

Whittaker shook his head. "The cap," he repeated puzzled. "I don't know. It was screwed to the top of the bottle, I imagine. Why do you ask?"

"Was there a patient's name on the bottle?"

Whittaker sighed. "Yes, there was a name. Robert Andrews," he replied. "They were his tablets, remember."

"Was there anything else on the bottle?" Kendall asked.

The Inspector started to frown. "Well there was a number, some kind of patient reference, I think," he replied. "Why do you want to know?"

"What about a date?" Kendall asked, ignoring the Inspector's question.

Whittaker shook his head. "A date?" He paused and sighed. "It was dated five days ago."

"Five days ago. So he must have picked them up in Miami, then," said Kendall. "Is that right?"

Whittaker was fast losing patience. "I imagine so," he replied loudly. He sighed deeply. "The bottle actually came from somewhere called the Bay Shore Pharmacy, Miami. If you must know. So what about it?"

Once again Kendall ignored the Inspector's question. "You checked for fingerprints, I suppose."

"Naturally," the Inspector replied indignantly. "The only fingerprints we found belonged to Andrews. They were all over the bottle, as you would expect."

"What about the bottle cap?" Kendall asked.

Whittaker shook his head. "The cap," he repeated. "You seem to be pre-occupied with the cap. What about the cap?"

Kendall shrugged. "I was just wondering about fingerprints on the cap, that's all."

Whittaker smiled. "Oh I see, still playing detective, are we?" He turned the pages of his file. "Here it is," he said as he reached the spot. He started to read. He shook his head. "There's no specific mention one way or the other," he said.

"What does that mean?" Kendall asked

Whittaker sighed deeply and shook his head. "Well, it means that there was no specific mention, its plain enough," he replied. "Either there weren't any prints, or if there were, they were simply not mentioned." He shook his head. "I can't see the problem anyway. Does it really matter?"

"Maybe, maybe not," replied Kendall. "I would have liked to know, that's all."

The Inspector shook his head. "Well obviously it didn't seem that important to us," he said. "The fact that there is no mention probably means that there weren't any. Satisfied?"

"No prints," said Kendall. "Interesting."

The Inspector wasn't entirely sure what was so interesting. He started to tap the desk. "All right, Kendall, what is it?" he asked.

"I was just wondering about this … this overdose," Kendall replied.

"Go on," said Whittaker.

"I was wondering whether you thought it was an accident or do you think it was deliberate."

"Oh, I see," replied the Inspector. "I think you'll find that it was no accident. No, it was suicide all right. Simple as that."

"Are you sure?" Kendall asked.

Whittaker looked at Kendall, hard. *Was he sure? Was he sure? What a question. How dare he even raise the question.* He shook his head. Of course he was sure. It was so obvious. He shook his head once again. "Of course I'm sure Mr Kendall," he replied. "I don't say things like that without being sure. I'm not one for just talking. When I say something, I mean it."

Kendall sighed. What had he done? *He had asked a simple question, that's all.*

"I mean it's a matter of experience," Whittaker continued. "What we were talking about earlier. It's all to do with training. Intuition. Deduction." He paused for a moment, a huge smile spread across his face. "I'm as sure about this as I'm sure that the sun will rise again tomorrow morning."

Kendall sighed once again. "I only wondered, that's all," he said. I didn't mean to suggest anything."

"There's the difference, you see," said Whittaker, still smiling. "You wonder about things. But I know. I'm one hundred and ten percent sure."

"I meant no offence," Kendall said nervously.

"None taken, I'm sure," said Whittaker. "Now, shall we get on."

Kendall shook his head. He opened his mouth to say something. Suddenly the telephone rang. Whittaker held his hand up. "Here we go again," he said as he reached across the desk and picked up the handset.

"Whittaker," he said simply. "Yes, sir, he's with me right now." Whittaker looked across at Kendall. "That's right." There was a short pause. "Yes. No, I won't be much longer." He looked at Kendall. "Yes.

88

Yes, I know that. All right." He shook his head, and took a breath. "No, sir, that won't be a problem. It's fairly obvious what happened." There was another pause. "Certainly, sir. That will be done, today."

Whittaker replaced the handset. He shook his head and looked at Kendall. "That was the big boss. Upstairs. The Commissioner," he said. "He had a call today." He paused for a few moments. "He wants this one closed quickly. Today."

"Today," Kendall repeated. "Why the rush?"

Whittaker rubbed his chin. "The call came from a certain John Wyndham Collier," he explained. "Apparently Travers Morgan don't want the bad publicity. The scandal attached to this case would be bad for business, so I'm told." He took a breath. "Anyway, they want it done and dusted." He paused for a moments and then nodded "It's not a problem. I mean it's pretty obvious what happened. Andrews had been fiddling the books and he got found out. He killed himself. As I said before, it's an open and shut case. Simple really." He nodded. "Case closed."

Kendall started to tap his fingers together nervously. "Case closed," he repeated slowly. "Case closed?"

"Okay, Kendall, what is it?" Whittaker suddenly asked. "I can see that there's still something bothering you."

"There's several things actually," Kendall replied. "But as a start, I was just wondering if there had been a suicide note, something like that."

"A suicide note," the Inspector repeated.

"There's usually a note with a suicide, right," Kendall replied.

"Oh yes there was a suicide note all right. It was found on the floor by the bed."

"Could I see it?"

"I don't really think that's necessary, do you?" said the Inspector shaking his head.

Kendall shrugged. "Perhaps you're right. I was just curious, that's all," he replied. "I thought that I might learn something. You know, get a bit of insight into the workings of Scotland Yard. Something like that."

Whittaker heaved a sigh. "Okay, where's the harm?" he replied. "You might learn something at that." He reached down and opened the top drawer of his desk and took out a buff coloured folder. He placed the folder on to his desk and opened it. Inside was a sheet of paper. He picked it up and passed it to Kendall. "There it is," he said. "It's crystal clear." He paused for a moment. "Suicide, no question about it."

Kendall took hold of the paper and started to read "To whom it may concern," he read. "They know about the money I have taken. I cannot face the consequences. Forgive me."

Kendall looked up and shook his head. "Strange."

89

"Strange," repeated Whittaker. "What's so strange, Kendall?"

"The note," said Kendall. "It's very formal. I mean, to whom it may concern. And it's not signed."

Whittaker sighed and shook his head. "So it's not signed, what about it? There was only one body, one suicide. It was pretty obvious who wrote the note, I would say."

Kendall shook his head. "So it was him, then. Andrews I mean," he said, as he handed the paper back to Whittaker. "He was the one who was embezzling the company. You're certain of that."

"That's correct," said Whittaker. "He must have been altering the books over a long period, I imagine. Got away with millions probably. He got found out, though, and couldn't face the thought of going to prison, and he just took the easy way out." He paused and placed the paper back into the folder. "Suicide. Just like I said."

Kendall nodded. "I suppose," he replied. He paused for a moment and then shook his head. "This is all wrong, Inspector," he said. "I just can't believe that Andrews took an overdose."

"You don't really, why ever not?" the Inspector asked.

"Taking an overdose of tablets is not a very efficient way of killing yourself for a start," Kendall replied. "There's no guarantee of success. It's too much of a risk, I mean you could do serious damage but still live." He shook his head. "Who in their right mind would want that?"

The Inspector shook his head. "The point is, of course, the majority of people who commit suicide aren't in their right mind, are they?" he said.

Kendall said nothing.

"Now, if there's nothing further," the Inspector said decisively. "This is all very interesting, I'm sure." He paused. "I think that we're about done." He stood up and walked over to the door. "It was suicide, I'm afraid. End of story. As I said before, case closed." He placed his hand on the door handle and turned it. "Thank you very much for coming in, Mr Kendall. Oh and you, Miss Adams, for your invaluable help" he said. "I'm sure that it's very much appreciated."

"Well, if I can help in any way," said Kendall as he stood up and walked to the door.

Whittaker shook his head. "Oh, that won't be necessary, sir," he said. "I think that we can manage perfectly well without you, thank you."

"But I thought ..." Kendall started to say.

"Yes, I'm sure you did," said Whittaker. He shook his head. "We can handle it from here, sir. Scotland Yard has had quite a bit of experience in this kind of thing, you know."

"But surely ..." said Kendall.

"Oldest police force in the world, sir," Whittaker interrupted. "Did you know that?"

"But ..."

"That's all right, sir, Not to worry yourself," Whittaker said. He looked towards Mollie. "Now you just enjoy your holiday. I understand that the weather is supposed to get better in the next day or so. Don't forget to see the Tower of London, and you really must see Buckingham Palace."

"But I thought ..." Kendall started once again.

The Inspector smiled and shook his head. "Yes, of course you did," he replied. "It is really very good of you. Very public spirited, I'm sure, very commendable. It does you credit. Wish there were more like you. Thanks all the same. Much appreciated." He opened the door wide. "Just leave your details with my Sergeant over there." He pointed.

He ushered Kendall and Mollie out of the office, and quickly closed the door.

Chapter Eleven

The Letter

Kendall stood there for a few moments, shaking his head in disbelief. *The man is mad*, he murmured. *Totally insane. How can he possibly think it was suicide?*

"Mr Kendall, sir," a voice called out. "Miss Adams. Over here, please."

Kendall turned around to face the voice. "Over here, sir," the voice continued. "This won't take long."

Kendall looked at the Sergeant and slowly walked towards him, still shaking his head.

Mollie followed behind. "Is he always like that?" she asked pointing backwards towards Whittaker's office.

The Sergeant started to laugh. "Oh, you mustn't mind him, Miss. He don't mean no harm. His bark is much worse than his bite." The Sergeant pointed to a couple of chairs. "Now, if you'll both just sit here. I've a few questions to ask." He opened the top drawer of his desk and took out a pad of forms. "It won't take long. We'll start with you, sir. Now, can we have your full name?"

* * *

As they came out of the building Kendall started to quickly walk away. Mollie was a few yards behind him. She suddenly stopped, and smiled mischievously. "Kendall," she called out loudly. "Just a second."

Kendall stopped and turned around to face her. "Yes," he replied. "What is it?"

He is obviously in a bad mood, Mollie thought. "Don't you want to take a photograph?" she asked sarcastically as she pointed at the building behind her.

Kendall looked at the building and shook his head. "No," he said angrily. "I never want to see this building ever again." He turned around and stormed down the street.

Mollie started to laugh and quickly walked after him. She looked at Kendall and shrugged. "Well that's that, then," she said. "Imagine killing himself like that. Such a nice man as well."

Kendall stopped, turned and looked at her. "What are you mumbling about?" he asked irritably.

"I said imagine him committing suicide like that," Mollie repeated slowly.

Kendall glared at her and shook his head. "How on earth can you say that?"

Mollie looked at Kendall, a frown spreading across her forehead. "Well, that's what he said." She pointed to the building behind her. "Whittaker, I mean. He said that it was suicide."

Kendall shook his head. "Well he is wrong," he said, as he too glanced at the building. He turned to face Mollie. "He is as wrong as he can be. He's an idiot." He looked up at the fourth floor of the building. "Pompous fool," he said vehemently. "How dare he make fun of me like that? Who does he think he is, anyway?" Kendall shook his head. "Case closed," he murmured. "Whittaker might think it's all done and dusted, as he put it, but I still have a lot of unanswered questions. I'm far from satisfied." There was a long pause. "Bob Andrews never committed suicide," Kendall continued. "Andrews was frightened on the plane, I'm sure of that."

"Well, perhaps the Inspector was right. Most people look frightened just before the take off, don't they?" Mollie suggested.

Kendall shook his head. "The Inspector was totally wrong. Bob wasn't frightened about the take-off. There's nothing to be worried about, I fly all the time. That's what he said." Kendall shook his head. "There was something, or someone, on that plane that frightened him. And I'm convinced that someone is connected somehow. I'm convinced that Bob Andrews was murdered. There's no doubt in my mind about that."

Mollie shook her head. "But why would anyone want to murder him?" she asked.

Kendall shook his head. "That's what I need to find out," he replied. "I'll start with Collier and then I'll check on the maid."

Mollie shook her head. "You can't do that, the Inspector said."

Kendall looked at her and grinned. "Bob Andrews was murdered and I aim to find out who did it, and why."

Mollie looked at Kendall for a moment. There was something about the way that he had said he was murdered. Molllie knew exactly what the something was but hated to admit it. But at that moment she knew that their holiday was all over, finished, cancelled.

* * *

Just over two hours later Kendall was back in his hotel room waiting for Mollie, to go to lunch. There was a tap on the door. "Who is it?" he called out.

"It's me," came the reply.

It was Mollie. Kendall got up, went to the door, and opened it. She looked puzzled as she walked into the room. "What's this?" she asked,

93

holding an envelope in the air.

Kendall looked up. "What's what?" he replied.

"This," she said, tapping the envelope.

"Well, I would say that it looks a lot like a letter to me," Kendall replied helpfully. "Whose is it?"

Mollie sighed and turned the envelope over. "It's addressed to Mr Robert Andrews."

Kendall sat up. "Andrews did you say?"

"The very same," Mollie replied.

"Where did you get it?" Kendall asked.

"Strangely enough it was in your holdall," she answered. "In the side pocket."

Kendall stood up and took the envelope from her. "In my holdall, are you sure?"

Mollie nodded. "That's what I said, in your holdall."

"I see," replied Kendall. "And just exactly what were you doing with my holdall?"

"You left it in my room last night, don't you remember?" Mollie explained.

"Yes, I remember," said Kendall. "So what?"

"Well, I was looking for my powder compact," Mollie continued. "I had put it in the bag on the plane."

"Okay," Kendall replied. "Go on."

"As I was looking for it, I found that envelope," she replied. "I wonder how it got there."

Kendall shook his head. "Good question," he said. He started to tap it against the side of his face. "I wonder what's inside."

"I suppose it might be a good idea if you actually opened it," Mollie suggested.

Kendall smiled at her. "Good point," he said. "I might just do that." He carefully opened the envelope. Inside was a single sheet of notepaper. He took it out and started to read. "It's from someone called Paul Sharp," he said. "Apparently he also works for Travers Morgan."

"Fine," Mollie said slightly irritably. "What does he say?"

"It's quite short really," Kendall replied. "Have narrowed it down to two of three possibilities. We can discuss in detail when I see you next week. Paul." He shook his head and looked at the envelope. "Postmarked ten days ago."

"It seems that they were due to meet during the last two or three days, then," said Mollie.

"Maybe even the day that Andrews died," suggested Kendall.

"Maybe," said Mollie. "What do you think it means?"

Kendall looked at her and shook his head slowly. "Why, it's fairly obvious, I would say," he replied. "It is clearly connected with this investigation that Andrews was carrying out. The accounts."

"The missing money, you mean," suggested Mollie.

Kendall sighed deeply. "Yes. I mean the missing money. The alleged fraud. The embezzler," he replied. "Mr Sharp seems to be suggesting that there are only two or three people who it could possibly be."

"Which three?" Mollie asked.

Kendall shook his head. "Regrettably they aren't named, I'm afraid."

"Pity," said Mollie. "Are you going to give the letter to Scotland Yard?"

Kendall thought for a moment. "I expect so." Then he started to frown. "On second thoughts, no, I don't think I will," he continued. "Not after our earlier meeting. They wouldn't want me butting my nose in, would they?" He shook his head. "Oh no, Scotland Yard can manage perfectly well without our help," he continued. "They told me that themselves, so they must be right."

"Inspector Whittaker, you mean," said Mollie.

"That's right," Kendall replied. "I mean Detective Inspector Bill Whittaker." He shook his head once again. "He has it all sewn up, hasn't he? Open and shut case, he said. Thinks he knows it all, does he?" He took a deep breath. "No. I don't think I'll bother them with this. It's probably nothing anyway. Besides, they must be very busy with more important things." He started to tap the envelope. "Now, just let me read this once again."

Mollie looked at him, a frown across her face. She was gradually putting two and two together and coming up with an answer she did not like. "You're not really thinking of investigating it yourself, are you?"

Kendall looked at her. He shook his head. "Of course not," he replied. "How could you even suggest such a thing?"

"Easy," she replied. "I know you, don't you forget."

Kendall raised his hands in the air and shrugged. "I'm shocked," he replied in mock indignation. "All I was going to do was have a brief word with Mr Sharpe."

"But we are on holiday," Mollie said quickly. "Remember."

"Of course I remember," Kendall replied quickly. "Surely you didn't really think I had forgotten." He shook his head. "I'm only going to make a phone call. I mean a simple telephone call. Where's the harm in that? How much of the holiday will that take?"

He shrugged his shoulders, reached for the telephone and started to dial. Mollie looked at him. "Who are you calling?" she asked.

Kendall held up his hand as the call was answered. "Travers Morgan," he said. "Could I speak to Paul Sharp?"

"I'll put you through, sir," came the reply. There was a clicking sound and then the line appeared to go dead. A few moments later the voice returned. "Mr Sharp is not available at present, sir. Would you like to leave a message?"

Kendall gave her his name and the hotel telephone number.

"I'll get him to return your call as soon as possible," the voice said. The line went dead.

Kendall replaced the receiver and shook his head. He sighed and started to tap the table. He couldn't tell you why, but he had the strangest feeling. *Somehow he didn't think he would ever hear from Mr Sharp.*

* * *

Five minutes later the telephone rang. Kendall quickly reached for the handset. "Hello, Kendall speaking," he said quickly. "Is that Paul Sharpe?"

"Hello, Kendall, it's Whittaker at Scotland Yard," a voice said. "I just thought that you might like to know that we have concluded our investigation now. It is clear to us that Mr Andrews died from an overdose of the prescribed tablets that he was taking for his asthma. He suffered from it, you know."

"Yes, I know," Kendall replied. But he was puzzled. What was it Andrews had said on the plane? *I used to take Syanthol but it didn't work, so I stopped taking it. He thought for a few moments. That was about three or four months ago, I think.*

"Syanthol, 25 grams," Whittaker continued. "He was supposed to take one tablet twice a day." There was a slight pause. "It seems like he took the whole bottle. They found massive traces in his blood stream." There was another pause. "A simple overdose but it seems that it was deliberate. I mean, you don't take a whole bottle by accident, do you?"

"It was suicide, then?" said Kendall. "That's the official verdict."

"That's right," said the Inspector. "Suicide, as I suspected in the first place."

"In connection with the missing money, I suppose," suggested Kendall.

"It certainly looks that way," the Inspector replied. There was another long pause. "There'll be an inquest, of course. Just a formality. You will probably be called to give evidence, naturally. It will only be to formally identify Mr Andrews, that's all. Nothing more. I'll let you know when it will be. How long are you planning on being in the UK?"

"Four weeks," Kendall replied. "Then we plan to go over to Ireland for a few days, then back to London, then home."

"Um, sounds good," said Whittaker. "All I have to look forward to is a weekend in Brighton. Still, there you are. Anyway you have been a great help to us. I'll be in touch. It shouldn't be too long. The inquest, I mean. Goodbye." The line went dead.

96

Kendall continued to hold the receiver for a few moments, He shook his head. *An overdose of the prescribed tablets that he was taking*, he murmured. "Suicide," he announced. "That's it, the official Scotland Yard conclusion. Suicide."

* * *

"That's tha,t then," said Mollie. "Suicide. Such a shame, a nice man like that." *Now, at last, they could get back to their holiday*, she thought. "So you'll have to leave it now, won't you? I mean there's no point seeing the maid and everything, is there?"

Kendall shook his head once again. "Mollie," he said. "If you had a health problem and you took tablets regularly, do you think that you could actually take an overdose?"

Mollie looked at him for a moment. "Of course, you could," she replied. "Especially if it was deliberate. I mean suicide." She paused for a few moments. "In fact, if you took tablets regularly it would be the perfect opportunity if you wanted to kill yourself."

Kendall shrugged. That was not the answer he had wanted. *Alright, it was possible, he supposed. Not probable, but grudgingly he had to admit that it was possible.* "I suppose you could be right," he said, agreeing reluctantly. There was a long pause. "The only thing is you couldn't be sure of success. I mean there would be no guarantee that an overdose would actually kill you." He shook his head. "Anyway Andrews didn't take Syanthol 25 or any other type of prescribed tablets." He paused once again. "Remember, he told us that on the plane."

Mollie shook her head. "I was asleep at the time," she said

Kendall paused for a moment. "Well, that's what he told me. He said that he was taking some alternative treatment." He shook his head. "What was it?" He thought for a moment. "It was Brom something or other."

"Bromelain," said Mollie. "It was Bromelain and Echinacea.""

Kendall looked at her surprised. "Oh you heard that, then. I thought that you were asleep."

She shrugged her shoulders. "I must have woken for a short time, and then fell back to sleep again."

"Right," Kendall replied. "Either way he wasn't taking Syanthol, or any other conventional medicine for that matter."

"But according to the Inspector, the tablets came from Bay Shore Pharmacy some days before he came to England."

"So, they came from Miami," said Kendall. "What about it?"

"So he must have been taking them," Mollie said. "I mean, you aren't going to bring over some tablets like that if you didn't intend to use them.

"Maybe," replied Kendall. "But who said that he brought them with him?"

Mollie looked puzzled. "Wasn't his name on the bottle?" she asked.

"So just because his name was on the bottle, he must have brought them with him?" Kendall replied. "Is that what you are suggesting, Mollie?"

Mollie wasn't exactly sure what she was suggesting. "It certainly looks that way to me," she said.

Kendall shook his head and started to frown. *It could look like that, he had to admit, but he didn't believe it, not for a second.* "It's possible, I suppose," he said, unconvinced. "But why would he bring them with him? He hadn't taken them for at least three or four months."

Mollie had no idea why he would want to bring the tablets with him.

Kendall sighed. "Perhaps it was all planned and he bought them with him in order to kill himself," he suggested.

"That's right. It was all planned," Mollie said. "So that proves it. It was suicide."

Kendall shook his head. "Mollie, I'm not being serious."

"Oh," Mollie said. She paused for a moment unsure. "Well perhaps he was going to give them another try. To see if they worked." She shook her head. "I don't really know but it's possible, isn't it?"

"It's possible," Kendall agreed. "But on the other hand, they could have been brought over by someone else."

"Someone else," Mollie repeated. "Like who, for example?"

Kendall thought for a few moments. "Perhaps the unknown someone that Andrews obviously recognised on the plane," he replied. "Perhaps it was him who brought the tablets over."

Mollie shook her head. "Why should they do that?" she asked.

"Well, perhaps it was all part of the plan," Kendall started to explain.

"What plan?" asked Mollie.

"The plan to commit a murder," said Kendall.

Mollie shook her head. "If there was a plan to kill Mr Andrews, why wait until he came to England?" she asked. "Why not kill him in America?"

"That's certainly a good point," Kendall admitted. "I would guess that whoever killed him needed to be sure."

"Sure of what?" asked Mollie.

"They needed to know exactly what Andrews knew," Kendall explained. "They also needed to know if he had told anyone else."

"I suppose you could be right," Mollie said. "But it's also equally possible that Andrews brought them over himself, and committed suicide as Scotland Yard suggested."

"Maybe," said Kendall, unconvinced. He remained silent for a few moments then he suddenly shook his head and sighed loudly. "No, no, there's no maybe about it. They were definitely not his tablets," he announced.

Mollie looked at him. "Well that sounds pretty emphatic," she said. "But I don't know why you are so sure."

"I tell you why, shall I?" replied Kendall.

"I wish you would," said Mollie.

"It's those fingerprints on the bottle," Kendall started to explain.

"Andrews' prints, you mean," Mollie said.

"Correct. His prints were on the bottle, as to be expected. But there were no prints on the cap. That doesn't make sense to me." Kendall paused and looked at Mollie. "Doesn't it seem a little odd to you?"

Mollie shook her head. "The Inspector never thought anything of it, did he?"

Kendall had to admit that he hadn't thought anything about it. He shook his head. "That's the problem," he replied. "The Inspector just didn't think. He's missing something.".

Mollie looked puzzled. "Go on," she said.

"How could you open the bottle cap without leaving prints?" Kendall asked. "It's just not possible."

"Maybe he wore gloves," Mollie suggested helpfully.

"Yes, that's possible, maybe. Unlikely, but possible I suppose," said Kendall. "But maybe someone else opened the bottle and then wiped it clean."

Mollie sighed. "This is all over my head," she said. "I don't know. Why don't you have another word with the Inspector."

"Maybe I will," Kendall said. "I might just do that, but not just yet." He paused for a moment. "I think I'll pay a visit to Travers Morgan first. I need to speak to Paul Sharp and John Wyndham Collier."

"But what about the Inspector?" said Mollie. "He won't like that."

"Well then, we'd better not tell him, had we?" said Kendall.

* * *

Later that evening Kendall made a telephone call.

"Devaney, I want you to do something for me," he said. "A little checking."

"What's going on over there?" Devaney asked.

"Oh nothing much," replied Kendall. "Nothing really. Just a few things I'll like to know. Shouldn't be too much trouble to you."

"All right, Kendall," Devaney replied. "What is it?"

"I want you to do a little checking up on a Bob Andrews," Kendall continued. "He worked for Travers Morgan, located in Bal-Harbour."

"Worked, did you say?" asked Devaney.

"That's right," replied Kendall. "He was murdered a few days ago here in London."

"Go on," said Devaney. "What do you need?"

"Find out who is doctor is," said Kendall.

"Just like that," said Devaney.

"Just like that," repeated Kendall. "It shouldn't be difficult for a great detective like yourself." He paused for a moment, waiting for a response. None came. "All you have to do is find out Andrews' address, then check on the local doctors. Simple."

There was a loud sigh from Devaney. "All right, so I've found his doctor, then what?"

"I want to know what medication he was on, if any," replied Kendall. "Especially Syanthol 25."

"Syanthol 25," repeated Devaney. "What's this all about, Kendall?"

"The other thing," Kendall continued, ignoring Devaney's question. "I need you to check on a prescription that was filled a few days ago at the Bay Shore Pharmacy."

"The Bay Shore Pharmacy," Devaney repeated.

"Yes," said Kendall. "It was filled ten days ago, for Syanthol 25. I want to know who the doctor was and the name of the patient."

Chapter Twelve

Travers Morgan Tower

Shortly before ten o'clock on the following morning, Kendall arrived at the Travers Morgan offices. He had a ten-fifteen appointment to see John Wyndham Collier. As he stepped from the taxi, he never noticed the young man standing on the far corner, watching him closely. Very closely.

* * *

It had been late on the previous afternoon that Kendall had telephoned for an appointment. Mollie had protested vehemently, accusing Kendall of interfering in official police business, but all to no avail. "The Inspector won't like it," she had said over and over. "The case is closed," she reminded him. "You are just wasting your time."

"Maybe you're right," Kendall conceded. "But it's my time, and besides, I'm sure that you would much prefer to go shopping in Knightsbridge without me and my constant moaning tagging along."

She had to admit that Kendall was not wrong. The suggestion sounded very appealing. She was still unhappy about Kendall's plans but she knew that once he had made his mind up, that was it. *Let him get it out of his system*, she thought. *The sooner the better, then they could resume the holiday.*

"All right," she replied. "I'll go shopping but you just be careful about what you say, do you hear?"

"Me," said Kendall. "I'm the soul of discretion. Tact is my middle name. You know me. "

Mollie nodded. "That's what I'm afraid of."

* * *

At ten-fifteen precisely, Kendall was shown into the office of John Wyndham Collier.

"Mr Kendall, do come in," said Collier as Kendall entered the room.

"It's very good of you to see me like this," said Kendall, offering his hand. "At such short notice, I mean."

"It's no problem, Mr Kendall," Collier replied, taking the proffered hand and shaking it. "Please do sit down." There was a pause as he waited for Kendall to make himself comfortable. "Now that's better," Collier continued. "Can I get you anything? Coffee, or perhaps something stronger?"

"Oh, no, thank you," Kendall replied.

"Now what exactly is it that I can do for you?" Collier asked.

If he were to be honest, Kendall wasn't exactly sure himself. Oh yes, he wanted to talk about Bob Andrews, that was true, but that was as far as he had got. "Well, it was about Mr Andrews."

Collier looked down at the desk. "Poor old Bob," he said, shaking his head. He looked up at Kendall. "You're a detective, I understand."

"A private detective," Kendall replied. "How did you know that?"

"A private detective," Collier repeated, ignoring Kendall's question. "And I understand that you were on the same plane as Bob."

"You are very well informed," Kendall said.

"I make it my business to be informed," Collier replied. "You have to be one step ahead all the time. Remember that, Mr Kendall, it may help you in the future."

"I will. Thank you."

"So I understand that you are here on holiday. Is that correct?" Kendall nodded. "Is it your first trip?" Once again Kendall nodded. "How are you enjoying it so far?"

"Yes, yes, and so far it's been interesting," Kendall replied.

Collier looked at him, puzzled.

"Yes we are here on holiday," Kendall commenced explaining. "Yes it is our first trip. And the holiday has been interesting." He paused for a moment. "Hectic but certainly not dull."

"You should pay a visit to the Stock Exchange," Collier suggested. "I'll arrange it for you. if you like."

Kendall wasn't listening. He was looking around the room. He looked back at Collier. "What is it you actually do?" he asked.

Collier was surprised at the question. "Well, I ... Travers Morgan is a major financial company. To make a long story short, we are a Merchant Bank. We deal with banking, insurance investments that kind of thing..."

"So this credit crunch, has that affected you?" Kendall asked.

"Well, naturally. It has had an effect on everyone, hasn't it?" Collier replied. "I'm sure that you must have noticed in your own financial dealings."

Kendall smiled. *Somehow he didn't think his financial situation had any resemblance to the financial situation enjoyed by Mr John Wyndham Collier.* "Oh yes, I guess so," he replied. "What about these bailouts I hear about."

Collier shook his head. "No, we have been fortunate in that regard. We haven't had the need of Government help. Not yet, anyway. Although I have to admit that recently times have been tough."

Kendall glanced around the office once again. Oh yes, he thought, *it certainly looks like times have been tough all right.* "Things can't be that bad, though," he said. "I'm sure that I heard somewhere that your company had paid out huge bonuses a few months ago, if memory serves."

"You are remarkably well informed, Mr Kendall," Collier said. "It was, however, quite some time ago now. In fact, I think we have recently announced the figures for the subsequent quarter."

"I sometimes watch the BBC News on satellite," Kendall replied smiling. "They are usually pretty reliable."

Collier started to smile. "I would have said that you were a Fox man."

Kendall shook his head. "Not necessarily," he replied. There was a brief pause. "What about those bonuses? Quite excessive in the present economic climate, I would have thought."

Collier sighed. "Not really, Mr Kendall," he said. "It's clear that you do not fully understand the financial world. You must remember that you must pay top money if you want top people." Collier suddenly stood up from the desk. He walked over to the side cabinet. He opened it and poured himself a drink. He stopped and turned to face Kendall. "Are you sure that I can't get you anything," he called out.

Kendall looked at the clock on the wall, and shook his head. He would have liked a double scotch on the rocks but it was a little early, even for him. He shook his head. Then he started to smile and shook his head once again. *So it was early. What about it? He was on holiday, wasn't he? If he wanted a drink he would have one.* "I'll have a Scotch on the rocks" he called back.

Collier smiled and prepared the drinks. "A man after my own heart," he called out. A few minutes later he was back in his chair. He handed the glass to Kendall. "Now what were we talking about?" he asked. Then he started to laugh as he remembered. "Salaries, that was it," he said. "Huge pay rises." He raised his glass. "I'll drink to that." He paused for a moment. "Seriously, Mr Kendall, in the world of high finance, you really do not have much of a choice. You simply have to just pay up ..."

"What about Investments?" Kendall interrupted.

"Investments," Collier repeated. "Yes, we deal with investments."

"Stocks and Shares?" Kendall asked.

Collier sighed. "Yes, stocks and shares. That's where the real wealth is to be made. Not oil paintings or jewellery." He looked at the paintings on the wall. "They are nice to look at, of course, and they have value, no doubt about that, but stock is what you need." He nodded. "I've been buying up stock in our competitor companies gradually over the past few months. Buying cheaply, you understand. I now have a major holding in seven of those companies. Not very sporting of me, I grant you. But there you are. That's business for you. All's fair in love and war, they say, don't they?"

"That's what they say," Kendall replied.

"Well that applies equally well to the world of business and high finance," Collier continued. "It's a tough world out there, Mr Kendall." He glanced over at the window. "And you have to be tough to survive." He paused and took a drink. "Power, that's what it's all about."

"Power," Kendall repeated. *He thought of Ian Charles Duncan. He was all about power, wasn't he?* he murmured. *He would even commit murder for it.*

"Did you say something, Mr Kendall?" Collier asked.

Kendall looked up and shook his head. "No. I was just remembering someone I once knew, that's all."

"A friend?" Collier enquired.

Kendall smiled and shook his head. "No, not a friend," he replied. "Far from it."

"Oh," Collier said quite simply. "Anyway, as I was saying. Power, and wealth. They are the key words."

"Maybe, said Kendall. "But all I need is enough to pay the bills and to live comfortably without worry. That's good enough for me."

"Good enough for you maybe, but," Collier replied, shaking his head. He looked around the room. "I need all of this," he continued. "Like I need oxygen to breathe, food to eat. You should invest, Mr Kendall. Remember what I say. Invest. Stocks and shares. Then you really would live comfortably and, as you put it, without worry."

Kendall shrugged. "You could be right," he said, unconvinced. "What can you recommend?"

Collier thought for a few moments. "Well, Mr Kendall, let us say you purchased twenty thousand shares in Rockford Metals today, and sold them on Friday, you should make a profit of about twenty, twenty-two, percent. Something like that, give or take a point or two." He paused and shook his head. "In other words, you should make quite a killing."

Kendall looked puzzled. "A killing," he repeated.

"That's right, a killing," Collier continued. "A killing in the City."

Kendall still looked puzzled.

Collier smiled. "It's a saying," he explained. "To make a killing in the financial world means making a profit on investments or stock. The bigger the profit, the bigger the killing." Then he paused once again and shook his head. "But, you know, somehow, Mr Kendall, I don't think you really came here to talk about investments, did you?"

Kendall smiled and shook his head. *No, he hadn't. He had quite a different kind of killing on his mind ..... the killing of Robert Andrews.* "Right," he said. "Absolutely right, I came to talk about Bob Andrews."

"You said that when you telephoned for an appointment," said Collier. "I was intrigued. That's why I agreed to meet with you."

"It is really much appreciated," said Kendall.

Collier sighed and looked at his visitor for a few moments. "Poor

Bob," he said, almost whispering. "To think that he is no longer with us, I just can't believe it. And to think only an hour or so before he died, he was speaking with my assistant, Oliver. There wasn't a hint of what was to come. It's just dreadful, absolutely dreadful." He paused for a few moments. Then he raised a hand to his face and brushed his cheek lightly. "But forgive me, Mr Kendall, I don't understand. I mean, you didn't know him, did you?"

Kendall shook his head. "Only just met him on the plane," he replied.

Collier looked puzzled. "So what has this got to do with you?"

"Oh not a lot, really, I suppose," Kendall replied. "Not when you get right down to it, that is." He paused. "I'm curious, that's all. One of my faults, I'm afraid. My secretary would say that it was one of many faults. She says I have more faults than she has shoes, and she has a lot of shoes."

"Go on, Mr Kendall," Collier interrupted. "If you don't mind."

"Right." Kendall shrugged. "As I said, we met Mr Andrews on the plane coming over from Miami. He was sitting next to me. In fact, Mollie, she's my secretary, she was actually sitting in his seat."

"Really, how fascinating," said Collier sounding anything but. "Did he say anything about his trip?" he asked. "I mean did he say why he was coming over?"

Kendall shook his head. "Not really. Not in any real detail anyway," he lied. "He merely said that he was an accountant, or something, and that he worked for this company. He said he was coming over on business." He shrugged. "That's all. It was all above my head, you know. And a little boring, I'm sorry to say. You know high finance, that sort of thing." He paused and smiled. "I have enough trouble at the supermarket keeping up with the prices." He started to laugh.

"I know exactly what you mean," Collier said. "I'm the same."

Kendall doubted that very much. He smiled. "It was such a shock to hear that he had died. I mean, suicide. I could hardly believe it."

"It was a shock to us all, Mr Kendall," Collier replied.

"I understand that Mr Andrews had been examining the accounts," said Kendall.

Collier looked surprised. "He told you that? What did he actually say?"

Kendall sighed. "Not a great deal," he replied. "It was all a foreign language to me, I'm afraid, but it seemed that there were certain discrepancies in the accounts. Some errors that needed correcting. That's all."

Collier looked at Kendall and smiled. "Some fifty million little discrepancies actually, give or take," he said. "That's how much could not be accounted for. That's the extent of the problem. Somebody has been stealing money from the Company. Fifty million pounds, to be exact, Mr Kendall."

Kendall suddenly remembered what Andrews had said about his conversation with Collier the day before his death. *"He told me that I must have been mistaken and that I should just forget about it."*

"That is quite a problem, I have to say," Kendall replied. He paused for a moment. "I understand that Andrews had narrowed his investigation down to a handful of possibles. No more than two or three."

Collier looked up. "Did he say who the three were?"

Kendall shook his head. "He never said," he replied. "Never will, now, I'm afraid." He paused for a moment. "Who do you think it might have been? Have you any ideas?"

"Oh, Mr Kendall, I have more than an idea," Collier replied. "I know precisely who it was."

Kendall looked at him, a frown on his forehead. "Go on," he coaxed.

"It's absolutely clear to me," he said. "I'm very much afraid that it was Bob himself. It seems that he may have had his hand in the till. Two hands, in fact, judging by the amount taken."

Kendall shook his head. "I hardly knew the man but it's certainly hard to believe," he said. "I mean he seemed such a good man, not the type. You know what I mean."

"It just goes to show that you can't judge a book by its cover," Collier replied. "I knew him well, or at least I thought I did. I would never have thought that he was capable of such a thing. But there you are."

Kendall nodded. "As you say, there you are," he repeated. "Changing the subject slightly, did he leave a suicide note or anything like that?"

"Oh yes, there was a note," replied Collier. "It was left on the bedside table in the hotel."

"I imagine the police have that note, do they?" asked Kendall.

"Yes, they do, but I made a copy," said Collier.

"You made a copy," Kendall repeated, puzzled. "A little strange, don't you think."

Collier shook his head. "Not really," He paused for a moment. "A little mercenary maybe."

Kendall looked puzzled. "Mercenary?"

Collier nodded his head. "Mr Kendall, there are fifty million pounds missing from the company accounts," he explained. "I need justification and cause, for that loss, for the auditors, my shareholders and, most importantly, Her Majesty's Revenue and Customs officials. They are very strict on things like that." He paused once again and shrugged. "That suicide note provides that justification. The reason the money is missing." He shook his head. "A little heartless maybe, but necessary." He shook his head again. "Of course, it doesn't get the money back. It merely shows why it is missing."

"I see," said Kendall. He paused for a moment, trying to visualise some tax Inspector checking that note. "Could I see it?" he asked.

"Why not?" Collier replied as he opened the top drawer of his desk. "Here it is," he said, handing it to Kendall. "I'm afraid there's nothing unusual about it."

Kendall looked at it for a few minutes. Then he shook his head. "No, you're right, nothing unusual." He shook his head and handed the note back. He looked at Collier and heaved a sigh. "There's something puzzling me, Mr Collier," he continued. "Another of my little faults, I'm afraid. I get a problem and I just can't rest until I get an answer." He shook his head. "Could be something quite trivial, but I just can't settle. You know what I mean?"

Collier looked at him. "What's the problem, Mr Kendall?"

Kendall sighed once again. "Earlier it seemed clear to me that the apparent loss of fifty million was a major problem to you."

"And so it is, Mr Kendall, I assure you," Collier replied. "Absolutely. No question about it."

"That's what I thought," said Kendall. "And yet the other night, when we met with Mr Andrews, he gave a totally different story."

"You met with Bob?" Collier asked, surprised.

"Yes, we went to dinner at his hotel. The night before he died," Kendall replied.

"So, tell me, what did Bob say?" Collier asked.

"It was very strange," Kendall replied. "He said that you and he had discussed the missing money earlier that day."

"That's right, we had," Collier replied. "So go on, what was so strange?"

"Apparently you had told him that he was probably mistaken and that he should just forget about it," Kendall said. "Forget about the money, that is."

Collier frowned and shook his head. "Bob said that?" he said in disbelief. "Just forget it? I'm amazed."

"That's what he said. Just forget it."

Collier shook his head once again and started to smile. "I'm afraid Bob was either joking or you must have simply misunderstood, Mr Kendall," he said. "There was a shortfall of fifty million pounds. That is extremely serious, and cannot, indeed could not, just be forgotten." He paused. "I can't imagine why Bob said that, I really can't. Just look at that suicide note." He pointed to it. "It's all there. Clear as day. Bob actually confesses to taking the money. How can you possibly just ignore it?"

"It all looks pretty conclusive, I must say," Kendall replied. "The only thing is why did he come to England? I mean, all that way just to kill himself. It doesn't make sense, Why not stay at home and commit suicide there."

"Oh, I see," said Collier. "Perhaps I can answer that. You see, I actually instructed him to come to London."

Kendall looked surprised. "You did?" he said. "When was that?"

Now it was Collier's turn to look surprised. He thought for a moment. "It was the day before the flight," he replied. "I had telephoned him and told him that there was a flight leaving Miami the following day and that he was to be on it."

Kendall was puzzled. He remembered what Andrews had said at the airport. "*I've learned to book as early as possible, especially if you want a particular seat. I booked this almost six weeks ago.*"

Kendall shook his head. "Why the urgency?" he asked.

"That's really quite simple, Mr Kendall," Collier replied. "You see, I had found out about his embezzlement. As far as I could see, Bob had deliberately altered certain figures in the accounts. Large unauthorised sums of money had been withdrawn. There had been dozens of transactions over a considerable period of time. There was also evidence of insider dealings on the Stock Market, all highly illegal. Tax records had been altered. Some records had been deliberately destroyed. The evidence was overwhelming. I'm afraid there was no error. Nonetheless, I still could not believe it. You can imagine. I refused to believe it. I wanted to talk to him about it." He looked down at the desk. The suicide note lay in front of him. "Bob simply got found out, or maybe pangs of guilt got too much for him. He just couldn't face the consequences," he continued. "I had hoped that perhaps I could help in some way, but I obviously failed."

Kendall shook his head. "I'm sure that you tried," he said. "You can do no more than that."

Collier looked at Kendall and heaved a sigh.

"Earlier, you mentioned somebody named Oliver," Kendall continued. "You said that he had spoken to Bob that same day, the day he died."

"That's right," Collier replied. "Oliver Jones, my right hand man. He had always been close to Oliver. I thought that he would be able to succeed where I had failed."

"So you sent him to see Bob?" said Kendall.

"That's correct," said Collier. "I had thought, hoped, that maybe Bob would open up a little." He shook his head. "Sadly, he didn't." He gave a deep sigh. "Oh, it's just so terrible. Suicide. I still can't believe it."

"I see," said Kendall. "One thing puzzles me, though."

Collier looked up from the desk. "Yes, Mr Kendall, what is it this time?" he asked.

"I was just wondering why didn't you just go to the police and tell them of your suspicions," Kendall replied. "It seems to me that would have been the sensible thing to do."

"You could well be right, Mr Kendall," Collier replied. "With hindsight perhaps that's what I should have done. Maybe if I had, Bob would still be alive today." He paused and shook his head. "But you must remember that Bob was my friend. I had known him for many years. I needed to see him once more, just to be sure. I didn't really want to involve the police. Not without being one hundred percent sure."

"And are you?" Kendall asked. "Sure, I mean."

"You know, Mr Kendall, I can hardly believe it but sadly it is true. I've known Bob for almost twenty years but really I didn't know him at all," Collier replied. "Bob, my friend, had been stealing from the company over a long period. He had managed to get away with a large sum of money. We aren't exactly sure of the figure yet but it looks like fifty or sixty million. We are still checking." He sighed and shook his head. "I don't really think he meant to steal. I understand that he got into serious difficulties. Gambling debts, you know the sort of thing."

Kendall nodded. *Oh yes, he knew the sort of thing, not that he gambled himself.*

"He had apparently accumulated huge gambling debts," Collier continued. "He knew that he could never repay such sums. He was being threatened, I understand. He needed money, a large sum of money, and he needed it fast. He had no choice. He had to falsify the accounts. He was frightened of being discovered and what that would mean. He could not face the possibility of prison. Regrettably, there was no doubt in my mind, Mr Kendall."

"I can understand that," said Kendall. "It must have been quite a shock to you. I mean you never had the slightest suspicion of anything."

"I never knew," Collier replied, full of remorse. "I never suspected a thing. He covered his actions so well. In a vain attempt to solve his problem he merely, shall we say, borrowed from the company. It was easy for him in his position. You know, all he had to do was alter a figure here, delete a figure there. In fact it was so easy that he continued even after clearing his gambling debts." He shook his head sadly and sighed deeply. "My friend is dead and I hadn't been able to help him. Why hadn't he come to me for help? Why hadn't he told me that he was in trouble?" he asked. "If only he had spoken to me, perhaps I could have helped. We could have worked something out, I'm sure that we could have sorted things out between us. That we could have straightened the whole thing out, you know."

Kendall shook his head. He didn't know. *How did you straighten out a small matter of a missing fifty million pounds sterling.*

Collier took out his handkerchief and brushed a tear from his eye. "If only he had asked for my help." He shook his head. "And then to kill himself. It doesn't bear thinking about. A young man like that. His whole life in front of him." He shook his head once again and looked up at Kendall. "Life is full of if onlys, isn't it? What if." He smiled. "What can you do, Mr Kendall? Nothing."

Kendall had to admit that there was nothing that you could do.

"I did try to warn him in a roundabout way," said Collier. "Maybe that's when he realised that he was suspected. That's when he decided to ... He just couldn't handle it, you see." He shook his head and dabbed his eye once again. "I never dreamed that he would do anything like that. I mean, to kill himself. I should have realised, though. At least I should have thought it was a possibility," he continued. "I blame myself for his death, Mr Kendall. I killed him as though I had held a gun to his head and pulled the trigger. Oh yes, I killed him, Mr Kendall. Of that I am quite certain, and I will live with that knowledge for the rest of my days."

"You mustn't blame yourself, Mr Collier," said Kendall. "You weren't to know what would happen."

"You're right, of course," said Collier. "I wasn't to know but I can't help feeling I could have done something."

"That's the sign of a real friend," Kendall said. "Anyway, you have cleared up another one of my little problems. You know, I hate these little queries I just can't fathom. Now I can see why he came over. That's one out of the way."

"I'm glad that I could help," said Collier.

"What do you think actually happened to the money?" Kendall asked. "Where do think it is? I mean, I don't suppose he spent it all, did he."

"Where's the money? That's a good question," Collier replied. "Who knows? It could be anywhere. After all, one stack of fifty million pounds looks just like any other, you know."

Kendall nodded wisely, as though he knew what a stack of fifty million pounds looked like anyway. "You really have no ideas?" he asked.

Collier thought for a few moments. "Well, as I say, it could be anywhere. Perhaps in an offshore account somewhere. Wherever it is, the chances of recovery are slight, to say the least. In fact, with Bob dead, I would say the chances are totally nil. After all, he would have been the only one who knew."

"Right," replied Kendall. "So what happens, then?An insurance claim, I suppose."

Collier smiled. "Oh, I don't think so," he replied. "It will probably just be written off. Tax deductible. A loss set off against profits. Something like that. We shan't want a big fuss, or a long drawn out investigation. Not good for the image, you know."

"So, it will just be forgotten, then," said Kendall. "Just like Andrews had said."

Collier looked at Kendall for a few moments and slowly nodded his head. "Right you are, Mr Kendall," he replied. "The whole thing will just be forgotten."

"It must be nice to be able to lose so much money and just shrug it aside," said Kendall. "No big deal."

Collier shook his head. "Fifty million isn't that big a deal," he said. "Not compared with the company's total assets. In fact, it's fairly insignificant."

Kendall smiled. "It wouldn't be insignificant in my bank account," he replied. He paused for a few moments. "How did Bob actually die?" he asked.

Collier shook his head and sighed. "I thought the police would have told you that," he said, looking surprised.

"They did," said Kendall. "I would just like to hear it from you. Just another of my little traits, drives my secretary crazy. I always like to check, and double-check, and re-check. It's another of my little obsessions, I suppose."

Collier shook his head. *An obsession, maybe, he thought, but a little unnecessary.* He sighed. "It was an overdose, apparently. Prescription tablets, I understand," he replied. "Of course I knew that he suffered from asthma and was on some medication."

Kendall looked up surprised. "Really? Do you know what tablets they were?"

Collier shook his head. "No, I'm afraid I don't. Something for asthma, that's all I know."

Kendall turned his head to one side. "But you know nothing more about them?"

Collier looked puzzled and shook his head. "I just told you, I know nothing about them at all."

"I'm a little surprised," said Kendall.

"Why?" asked Collier.

Kendall shook his head. "I understood that you also suffered from asthma."

Collier looked puzzled and shook his head. I don't know where you got that from, Mr Kendall, but you are very much mistaken."

Kendall shook his head and frowned. "But I was so sure," he replied.

"No," Collier said shaking his head. "You must be mistaking me for someone else, I'm afraid."

Kendall nodded. Maybe, he murmured. *But Andrews had said something quite different on the plane.* that's all. "I must have misunderstood," he replied. "It wouldn't be the first time that I have made a mistake and I don't suppose that it will be the last."

111

"It's simple enough," said Collier. "I know exactly what you mean. I'm constantly making mistakes."

Kendall nodded and smiled. *Strangely enough, somehow he did not think Collier ever made a mistake.* "So Andrews took the tablets regularly, did he?"

"Every day like clockwork, I understand," replied Collier.

"So he couldn't take an overdose by accident, I suppose," Kendall said.

Collier shook his head. "I wouldn't have thought so," he replied. "He would know exactly what he should and shouldn't take. Taking tablets for so long there would be no error. Oh, he meant to take them, that's for certain. Shame, shame." He shook his head and sighed.

"So it was definitely suicide," said Kendall.

"Looks that way," replied Collier. "We have gone over the whole thing with Scotland Yard. I understand they have completed their investigation. Suicide is the official conclusion." He looked at Kendall. "The matter is, as far as I'm concerned, over and done with."

"You're probably right," said Kendall. "By the way, is Paul Sharp around?"

Collier looked surprised. "Sharp," he repeated. "You know Paul? Why do you want him?"

"Oh, it's nothing really. Nothing important, that is," Kendall replied. "I think we have a mutual friend, that's all." He gave a sigh. "I think he knows one of my relatives. A second cousin or something."

"Oh really," said Collier. "How very interesting."

"I'm not even sure that we have ever met," Kendall said nonchalantly.

Collier shook his head. "I'm afraid to say that he isn't. He is on a business trip. Dubai, and Saudi Arabia."

"Too bad," said Kendall. "I was hoping to meet up with him while I was here."

Collier shook his head. "That's pretty doubtful, I'm afraid," he replied. "He's not due back for three or four weeks, I understand. I imagine that you will be back home by then."

"Maybe," said Kendall. "Maybe not. Anyway, I mustn't delay you any more. I'm sure that you have a lot to do." He stood up. "No, don't get up. I can see my own way out. Thanks for your help. It's very much appreciated."

"No problem, Mr Kendall," Collier replied. "Glad to be of help."

Kendall started to walk towards the door. As he reached the doorway, he stopped and turned. "What was that company you mentioned earlier?"

Collier looked puzzled for a moment and shook his head. Suddenly he remembered. "Oh, you mean Rockford Metals." He took a sheet of blank paper and wrote the name down. "Here you are," he said, as he handed the paper to Kendall. "Let me know if you want anything arranged."

Kendall smiled and nodded. "That's it, Rockford Metals," he replied taking hold of the paper. "I'll let you know." He turned, opened the door and quickly walked out.

* * *

Kendall stood in the corridor for a few moments. He glanced back at the office door. There were a lot of things that Kendall disliked. Shopping was one thing. Being kept waiting was also high on the list. Getting caught in the rain was another. Even worse, he hated cold winds. He wasn't too fond of cold coffee, burnt toast, or Chinese food. He wasn't that keen on modern films. But if there was one thing he positively hated, it was being told a lie. Worst still was being told two lies. He looked towards the door of Collier's office. *In there just a few moments ago he had been told a whole mass of lies. So many that he had lost count.*

What did you call a collection of lies anyway, he wondered? A gaggle? He nodded. *Yes, a gaggle of lies sounded good.*

* * *

As Kendall came out the building, Mollie was standing at the corner, waiting. She waved and started to walk towards him. She suddenly stopped as she saw a young man on the opposite corner. He seemed to be watching Kendall closely. The young man noticed her watching him and slowly walked around the corner.

Mollie shrugged. *It probably meant nothing at all.* She walked over to Kendall. "How did you get on, then?" she asked.

"What are you doing here?" Kendall asked, surprised at seeing her. "I thought you were going shopping."

She shook her head. "I decided not to go," she replied. "Besides, I needed to keep an eye on you. You know you're not safe to be let out on your own." She smiled. "So how did you get on?" she asked once again.

Kendall shook his head. "Okay, I guess." He did not sound convinced. "But why did he lie to me?" Mollie looked puzzled. "Just now, up there," he pointed to the upper windows of the building. "Collier gave me a pack of lies, a whole gaggle of them. Why?"

"What lies?" she asked.

Kendall looked at Mollie. "Andrews told me that Collier suffered from asthma, remember."

Mollie shook her head. She didn't remember. "So?" she replied simply.

"So Collier has just flatly denied it," Kendall replied. "He told me that I must be mistaken."

"Well, perhaps you were," Mollie said. "Mistaken, I mean. It has been known."

Kendall started to frown. *Yes, he had been mistaken several times in the past. He would almost certainly be wrong again in the future. But he wasn't wrong this time.* "I don't think so," he replied indignantly. "I know what Andrews said."

"Well, perhaps Andrews was wrong," Mollie suggested. "Perhaps he was the one who was mistaken."

Kendall shook his head. "Perhaps," he replied, far from convinced. *He knew a lie when he heard one. It came from years of experience. Oh yes, he knew, and he had just heard several. But why, he wondered.* He turned to look at Mollie. "No, he wasn't wrong," he said.

Mollie sighed. "Well, does it really matter?" she said. "I mean, is it important?"

Kendall sighed and shook his head. "Probably not," he replied wearily. "Probably not."

Mollie looked at him. *She heard what he said but she knew differently somehow.* She sighed deeply. "Anything else?" she asked.

Kendall thought for a few moments. "According to Collier he had spoken to Andrews a few days before the flight and instructed him to come over to London," he said.

Mollie shook her head once again. "So, he instructed him," she replied. "What about it?"

Kendall shook his head. "Another lie," he replied. "Andrews told me that he had booked the flight weeks ago."

Mollie sighed. "Perhaps he just said that, who knows?" she replied. She looked at Kendall for a few moments. "Incidentally, it's probably nothing, but I thought I saw someone watching you just now. Over there by the corner." Kendall turned to look. "Oh, he's gone now," she said. "As I said, it's probably nothing. You don't think that Inspector Whittaker is keeping an eye on you, do you?".

"No, I don't think so," said Kendall. "But if he is, he might learn something." He shrugged his shoulders. "Come on, let's go. I could do with some lunch. What do you say?"

Mollie looked at him and smiled. *It sounded like a good idea at that.* "Then, after lunch, you can take me shopping," she said.

Kendall smiled and started to walk away.

Mollie suddenly stopped. "Aren't you going to take a photograph?" she asked.

"What a good idea," said Kendall. "Just stand over there by the entrance."

* * *

It was just before ten minutes to five when the call came through on Kendall's mobile. They were just leaving the John Lewis store in Oxford Street. Kendall was exhausted and was anxious to get back to the hotel. Mollie, on the other hand, looked as fresh as morning dew, and would have been happy to carry on for three or four more hours.

Kendall took the telephone from his pocket and looked at Mollie. "I wonder who that is," he mused.

Mollie shook her head. "If it's Devaney again, just tell him to take a hike," she replied.

"It won't be him," Kendall said. "But if it is him, I'll be sure to send him your regards."

The telephone continued to ringing. "Hello, Kendall speaking."

"Kendall, this is Whittaker," a voice said.

"Oh, good afternoon, Inspector, nice to hear from you," Kendall replied. "What can I do for you?"

"Kendall, I've just had a call from The Commissioner," the Inspector said. "I understand that you have been asking a lot of questions at Travers Morgan."

"Travers Morgan," Kendall repeated. "Well, I just happened to be in the area and I thought …."

"Kendall."

"Mr Collier was really very nice," Kendall continued. "We had a bit of a chat. He said that he hoped that I had a good holiday."

"Kendall!"

"He is going to show me around the Stock Exchange which I thought was very nice of him."

"Kendall," Whittaker interrupted. "Mr Collier has made a formal complaint. He advises that you were asking a lot of questions about Mr Andrews and how he died. Is that correct?"

"Well, maybe one or two," replied Kendall.

"Kendall, I realise that you truly believe that you are being helpful," said the Inspector. "But please leave it to us, you know, the professionals. We are, after all, specially trained, and very experienced in this kind of thing. You just enjoy your holiday. Please. Case closed, remember."

The line went dead.

Kendall looked at the telephone for a few moments. A huge grin spread across his face.

Molly shook her head. "The Inspector?" she asked. "I knew it. He wasn't pleased, was he?"

115

Kendall shook his head. "Oh, he was all right," he replied. "No problem really. He told me to enjoy my holiday."

"But you'll have to stop now, won't you?" Mollie said.

"Maybe," said Kendall wistfully.

Mollie smiled. *Good*, she murmured. "Now that's out of the way, what are our plans for tomorrow?"

"Tomorrow," Kendall repeated. "Well I don't know about you, but I think a spot of lunch at the Gresham Hotel might be a good idea."

Chapter Thirteen

The Gresham Hotel

It was a little before eleven forty-five when Kendall walked into the entrance lobby of the Gresham Hotel. Over on the far side was the reception counter. He started to make his way across the marble floor towards it.

There were a few people sitting in the lobby, drinking coffee. To his left, a young couple sat talking animatedly. Opposite, an elderly man lay asleep. Two men walked in behind him and stopped to speak to the doorman. They were noisily seeking directions to the dining room. Kendall gave them a momentary glance and continued on his way. No one took any notice of him as he passed by, except for one young man seated on the far side. He slowly lowered his newspaper a fraction and for the briefest of moments. He glanced over towards Kendall and then went back to his reading. Kendall didn't notice a thing and continued on his way.

As he approached the counter, he noticed that the young lady on duty had also been on the night that he and Mollie had met with Andrews. He hoped that she would not recognise him. *It was, of course, extremely unlikely, but there was a possibility*, he thought. He shook his head. There was nothing he could do about it anyway. *So she recognised him, he could always bluff it out and deny all knowledge. She would hardly start a major discussion about it, would she?*

The receptionist was busy with two other people who were just checking in. There appeared to be some problem with the booking. It looked as though it might take some while to sort out. Kendall moved to the end of the counter to wait. He idly glanced at a rack of brochures placed at the corner of the counter. He selected one of the brochures giving details of London attractions. On the front cover was a photograph of The London Eye. He mentally added it to the other places he intended to visit and folded the brochure, placing it in his inside pocket. As he did so, he turned and leaned against the counter. The young couple was still talking excitedly. The man with the newspaper looked as though he had fallen asleep. The two men who had been so noisy had obviously found the dining room.

Suddenly there was a noise over at the entrance. A small group of people had arrived, all talking excitedly. "Tourists," Kendall murmured with some derision. He watched as they walked to the elevator. He turned back to face the reception. The two people booking in had finished their business and had now moved away.

The receptionist looked up as Kendall approached. "Good afternoon, sir, can I help you?" she said. "Did you require a room?"

Kendall shook his head. "Oh no, thank you," he replied. "I'm just making some enquiries about Mr Andrews, the man who died the other day."

"Oh yes," she replied. "Mr Andrews. He was such a nice man, a real gentleman." She shook her head. "But the police have already ..."

Kendall reached into his pocket and withdrew a small wallet. Inside was his old NYPD badge. He opened the wallet, showed her the badge, and then quickly closed it.

Of course, by rights, he should have handed the badge back when he had left the department ten years previously. In truth he had in fact handed a badge in, but he actually had two. Strictly he should have had just the one badge, that was regulation issue. One badge. That badge had actually gone missing, without trace. Kendall had checked everywhere he could think of. It was nowhere to be seen. He had been told to make a formal request for a replacement. Four different forms were required, in triplicate, including a full report as to when the badge had last been seen.

Three weeks later a shining new badge had arrived, together with a stern warning to be careful and not lose that one. Three days later he found the original badge. It had fallen at the back of the passenger seat in his car. For a while he debated whether or not he should hand the new badge back. It would probably mean another four forms, in triplicate, together with an embarrassing explanation as to why it was no longer required. He just couldn't face that. So he decided against it and merely kept both badges.

"I know they have, I'm a detective," he said, not exactly lying. "There are just one or two loose ends to tie up, you know. It shouldn't take too long."

The receptionist watched as he returned the wallet to his pocket. "I suppose it will be all right," she replied. "I'll be glad to help, if I can."

"I'm sure you'll be fine, Jenny is it?" replied Kendall looking at the name tag on her uniform.

"That's right," she replied. She shook her head. "It was so dreadful, and it was so unexpected."

"What do you mean unexpected?" asked Kendall.

"Committing suicide like that," she replied shaking her head. "I mean, why would he do such a thing? He was planning on going to the Café De Paris for dinner that evening. And then, later in the week, he planned on going to the theatre, I understand."

"How do you know that?" Kendall asked.

"Because he had asked me to book a table," she replied.

Kendall started to tap his fingers on the desk. *Suicide didn't seem very likely*, he had to admit. Then he shook his head.

"Of course something could have happened," Jenny continued. "He could have received some kind of upsetting news. Or maybe there was something about his visitor."

Kendall stopped tapping and looked at the young lady. *Oliver Jones*, he murmured. "Visitor," he repeated. "What time was that?"

"About twelve forty-five," she replied.

"How are you so sure about the time?"Kendall asked.

"I had just come on duty," she replied. "I should have been at the desk here by twelve-thirty, but the Manager had delayed me and I didn't get here until about twenty minutes to one. Three or four minutes later the gentleman came in. He asked for Mr Andrews room and I sent him straight up."

"Do you know his name?" Kendall asked.

She shook her head. "Sorry, I didn't think to ask," she replied.

"Could you describe him?" asked Kendall.

She thought for a moment or two. "Well, he was about your height, I think. Maybe a little taller." She paused and stared at Kendall. "Definitely taller, I would say, but much thinner." Kendall quickly drew in his chest. "And certainly younger than you, I would guess." Kendall glared. "That's about all I can think of. I'm sorry, I'm not really good at that sort of thing."

"That's fine," Kendall replied. *More than enough, in fact. Why there couldn't be more than a million or more people that would fit that description. Why apart from the age thing, maybe it could have been him.* "Do you know what time he left?" he asked.

"Mr Andrews rang down at twenty past one. His friend was about to leave and he requested a taxi."

"Mr Andrews rang down," said Kendall. "You're sure?"

"That's right," she replied.

"And did you order the cab. Sorry, I mean taxi?" asked Kendall.

"Oh yes, we called Belmont Taxis," Jenny replied. "They are just around the corner in Belmont Mews." She paused for a moment. "We always use them. They are so quick and reliable." She paused once again. "It's only a very small business, you know."

Kendall didn't know and he really wasn't that interested in a run-down on the business. "Go on," he said. "What happened next?"

The receptionist shrugged her shoulders. "Well nothing happened. I mean, five minutes later the taxi arrived, that's all. It was Terry himself. He runs the business," she explained. "And a few minutes later the gentleman came out of the lift. Twenty-five past one and he was gone."

Kendall started to rub his chin. "Can you tell me anything else?" he asked.

She thought for a few moments. "Not really," she replied. "Oh, Mr

Andrews rang again to make sure that his friend had gone and that was that."

"Andrews rang again," said Kendall puzzled. "What time was that?"

She shook her head. "Sorry, I can't be sure, but it was after his visitor had gone," she replied. "Perhaps ten minutes afterwards, something like that."

Kendall frowned. *This was all wrong. Andrews was still alive at about twenty to two and the visitor had gone.* "Are you sure?" he asked.

"Sure about what?" the young lady replied.

"Sure that it was Mr Andrews that rang," replied Kendall.

She nodded.

"You're absolutely sure?" said Kendall.

"Yes, I'm sure," she replied. "He said this is Mr Andrews in Room 420. Did my friend get his taxi?"

Kendall shook his head. *It couldn't have been Andrews*, he thought. *Andrews was already dead at that point. He had to be.* He shook his head. *Killed by his visitor, I'm sure of that*, he murmured. "How do you know it was Mr Andrews ringing?" he asked.

Jenny looked at him, surprised. "How did I know?" she repeated. "Well it was obviously him, wasn't it? Who else could it have been?"

Kendall sighed. *He was so sure that Andrews had not made that call and yet the evidence said otherwise.* "The phone call," he said. "Could it have been made on a mobile phone?"

"It wasn't a mobile phone," Jenny replied.

"How do you know that?" Kendall asked.

"I know because the call was made on our own internal service," she replied. "We are able to monitor all calls that way. It's for billing purposes, you see. If you need to make an outside call, you have to be put through. The call did not come through on an outside line. It was Mr Andrews all right."

This was making no sense at all to Kendall. His theory, his absolute certainty, was evaporating fast. *Could he be in error? Had he made a mistake? Was Whittaker right after all? Had Andrews really killewas he supposed to be an expert in this kind of thing?d himself? Was it really 'case closed'?*

"How did he sound?" Kendall asked.

"Sound," said Jenny. "I'm not sure that I understand."

"Well, did he sound depressed?" Kendall explained. "Or worried? Or maybe just in a bad mood, anything like that?"

She shook her head. "Oh, I don't think so."

"Did he sound angry?" Kendall asked.

She shook her head once again. "No, not that I noticed. In fact he sounded perfectly normal to me." She paused for a moment. "It was such a shock. Why would he want to kill himself like that?"

Kendall had to admit that he didn't know why. In fact up until ten seconds ago he hadn't actually thought that Andrews had killed himself. *Besides, was he supposed to be an expert in this kind of thing? Why would anyone do such a thing?* "Can you tell me anything else about his visitor?" he asked.

The receptionist thought for a few moments. "No, I'm sorry, I can't," she replied. "It was a busy afternoon and I didn't really pay too much attention, I'm afraid.

Kendall frowned. Her reply was really no more than he had expected. After all, there must have been dozens of people in the hotel that day, why would she pay any attention to one individual?

Kendall shook his head. *This was not going to plan. He had been so sure but obviously he was wrong. It was clear that Andrews had still been alive after his visitor had gone.* Kendall heaved a sigh. *So he was wrong. So what else was new?* "Can you tell me anything else?" he asked.

The receptionist shook her head. Then she suddenly looked up and smiled. "Well there was an odd phone call at about a quarter to two."

"Odd," repeated Kendall. "In what way odd?"

"Well it wasn't exactly odd," the receptionist replied. "Amusing is probably a better word." She started to smile. "It was a foreign sounding gentleman. He wanted to speak to Mr Andrews."

"Foreign," repeated Kendall.

"Eastern European, I would say," she replied. "Perhaps Polish, or maybe even Russian. I'm not really good at accents. They all sound the same to me."

Why would Andrews get a call from an Eastern European, Kendall wondered. "Did you get his name?" he asked.

She shook her head. "That's what was so amusing," she replied. "That's why I remember it so well. He told me his name but I couldn't understand him. So I tried to get him to spell it but he didn't understand me." She paused. "Anyway, I finally put him through."

"And Mr Andrews accepted the call?" asked Kendall.

"Oh yes, he answered," she replied.

Kendall shook his head. "So he was still alive at about one forty-five?"

"Nearer ten to two," she corrected. "By the time I put the call through."

"How are you so sure of that time?" Kendall asked.

"I made a note of it," she replied. "I was trying to write the name down." She paused for a moment and started to shuffle through some papers on the counter. "Here we are," she said, holding up a sheet of paper. "Here's my note. You can see I tried to write down his name but failed. And just there I made a note of the time." She pointed to the bottom right hand corner.

Kendall saw the time. He could not believe it. *Andrews was still alive some twenty minutes after his visitor had gone.* "Where was that taxi company you mentioned?" he asked.

"Belmont Square," she replied. "Turn left outside." She pointed towards the main entrance. "Then take the second on the right. Belmont Square is about a hundred yards down on the left hand side. Belmont Taxis are on the far side of the Square."

Kendall nodded. "Terry, I think you said."

"That's right, Terry. Terry Woods," she replied. "Here, let me write the details down for you." She reached for a sheet of note paper and started to write. When she had finished she handed the paper to Kendall. "There you are."

Kendall took hold of the paper. "That's very good of you," he said. "I might just pay your Mr Woods a call." He carefully folded the paper and placed it into his pocket. "Incidentally, I understand that Mr Andrews was discovered by the maid," he said. "That must have been quite a shock for her."

"That's right," said Jenny. "It was Maria and it was quite a shock to her." She shook her head. "She's only young. Twenty, I think, and a long way from home."

"It's hard for anyone, but at that age. Well I can imagine," Kendall replied. "Whereabouts is she from?"

"Spain," said Jenny. "Somewhere on the east coast, I think."

"Is she here today?" Kendall asked.

Jenny looked across at the notice board behind her. "According to the staff roster, she is in today," she replied. She looked over at the wall clock. "She's probably up on the fourth floor right now."

Kendall paused for a moment. "I think I'll have a word with her," he said. "You have been very helpful, thank you."

Chapter Fourteen

Room 420

Kendall turned around and walked over to the elevator. A few minutes later he arrived on the fourth floor. He slowly walked along the corridor. "Four sixteen," he murmured. "Four eighteen. Here we are, Four twenty."

He stopped and looked at the door. The door was sealed with police tape. Suddenly he heard a noise close by. He looked up and there, at the end of the corridor, he saw just what he was looking for. The maid was slowly making her way along the corridor, cleaning the rooms, and making up the beds.

As far as Kendall could tell, she was just about to enter room four twenty eight. He started to walk towards her. He raised his hand and waved. "I hope that you can help me," he said. "I need to get into room 420."

"That's Mr Andrews' room, isn't it?" she replied.

"That's right. It was Mr Andrews' room." Said Kendall. "I need to get inside. Can you help me?"

She was hesitant and shook her head. "They said that it was to be kept locked."

Kendall slowly reached inside his jacket pocket and took out his New York Police badge. "I'm a detective," he said as he quickly showed her the badge, and just as quickly placed it back inside his pocket. He was gratified to notice that she had barely looked at it.

She shook her head and started to rub her hands together nervously. She was unsure. "But the police said the room was to remain closed," she said. "Nobody was to go in."

"Quite right," Kendall said. "Quite right, nobody is to go in there, except a police officer." He moved closer to her. "What's your name?" he asked.

"My name," she repeated.

"Yes," Kendall said gently.

"It's Maria, sir," she replied. "Maria Ortega."

Kendall smiled and shook his head. "Maria, really" he replied. "I don't believe it. That was my mother's name," he lied as he raised his hand up to his face and brushed away a tear. He moved even closer to her. "You know, you look a lot like her in a strange way."

"Really?" she replied.

"Oh yes, very much so," said Kendall as he brushed another tear from his cheek. "You have the same hair, same eyes, the same nose.

123

You even have her smile." He paused and took a deep breath. "She was about your height," he continued. "Oh yes, you really are so like her. She was Spanish, you know."

"Really," said Maria. "I am Spanish."

"No. You're Spanish, just imagine that," said Kendall acting surprised. "I wonder if you came from the same area in Spain."

Maria smiled shyly. "Oh I come from Campello, a small village not far from Alicante."

"Alicante," Kendall repeated. "I don't believe it. What a small world it is. That is where my mother came from."

Maria started to smile. "It is a beautiful city, no," she replied.

"Oh yes, a very beautiful city," Kendall said.

"The Esplanade," Maria said wistfully.

"Oh absolutely, the Esplanade," Kendall replied, wondering what it was exactly.

"And the Castille," Maria continued.

"Of course the Castille," Kendall said wondering what a Castille was exactly. "This has been so nice, really nice," he said. "Seeing you and talking to you like this. I just wish I had more time. But sadly I must get on. I must get back to the office. This investigation you know." He shook his head. "There's such a lot still to do."

Maria looked up at him, and smiled. "It has been a real pleasure to meet with you," she said.

"Now about the room, I really need to see inside."

She slowly shook her head. "But they said that the door was to remain closed. No one was to be let in."

"That's absolutely right, and you are correct not to let anyone in," said Kendall, placing a hand gently on to her arm. "But that's the public, they mean. The public mustn't go in but that doesn't apply to me, Maria." He put his hand up to his cheek and brushed away yet another tear. "You know I do like that name. Maria. My mother would have liked you." He paused for a moment. "It doesn't mean me," he continued. "I'm a detective. Besides I was here before. You must have seen me. I just left something behind. It's very important. You'll help me, won't you?"

She was still hesitant. "Oh, I'm sorry," she replied. "I didn't know. You don't look like a detective."

Kendall sighed. *He wondered what a detective was actually supposed to look like.* He shook his head. *It really wasn't worth worrying about.* "Many people have said that," he said. "Now about the room?"

She nodded as she reached for the keys. "I suppose it will be alright," she said hesitantly. He turned and walked to the room. She followed a short distance behind.

"I'll only need a few minutes," Kendall said.

Still unsure, she reluctantly agreed. "You must not be long," she said. "Five minutes, no more. I lose my job."

Kendall shook his head. "Oh no, not long, a second or two. Lightning, that's what they call me. I'll be in and out before you know it."

"Were you on duty that day?" Kendall asked as they walked towards the room. "The day Mr Andrews died."

She looked down and sighed. "Oh yes," she replied. "I was right here, on this floor. I actually found him."

"You found him," he said, trying to sound surprised. "That must have been terrible for you, such a shock."

She looked down and merely nodded.

"I understand that Mr Andrews had a visitor that day," Kendall continued. "Is that correct?"

She nodded once again.

"Did you see him arrive?" Kendall asked.

She shook her head. "Oh no," she replied. "He was already in the room when I came on duty."

Kendall started to rub his chin. "How do you know?" he asked.

"I heard him talking," she replied. "Quite loudly at times. In fact it sounded quite angry."

"Angry," Kendall repeated. "Did you hear what they were saying?"

She shook her head. "No, I couldn't hear," she replied. "It wasn't very clear and I couldn't really make anything out. They were speaking very fast and sometimes I cannot understand."

Kendall frowned. "I don't suppose you heard the man's name, did you?" She shook her head. *Thought not.* Kendall smiled.

"Did you see the man again," Kendall asked. "I mean, when he was leaving."

"Oh yes, I saw him then," she said. "He was walking very quickly. My trolley was in the way. He was angry and he pushed it out of the way. He was shouting at me." She looked down at the ground and shook her head. "He was so angry about it. He made such a fuss. The trolley was only slightly blocking his way. He could have easily got through. He was shouting and threatening to report me to the manager." She paused. "I didn't really deserve that, did I?"

Kendall had to admit that she did not deserve that. "What time was that?" he asked.

"Oh, it was just after twenty-five past one," she replied.

Kendall looked puzzled. "How do you know that?" he asked.

"I had just come on duty after my lunch break, sir," she replied. "I get from twelve-thirty until one-fifteen. I had just started on my second room. Each room takes ten or fifteen minutes."

"But you never saw Mr Andrews again, alive, I mean."

She looked puzzled. "Oh yes, I did," she replied. "He was standing at the doorway to his room watching his visitor leave," she replied.

"You actually saw Mr Andrews," said Kendall. "Are you sure about that?"

She nodded. "Oh yes, it was him all right. He had heard the noise, with the trolley and everything. He came out to see what was happening."

"Did he say anything?" Kendall asked.

"Yes, he told his friend to stop making such a fuss and to stop bullying me," she replied.

So it was definite, Andrews was still alive. Kendall shook his head. *He hadn't been murdered. It was suicide.* He looked at Maria. "You must have been happy that he helped you."

"Oh yes," Maria replied. "He was such a nice man."

Kendall shrugged. "And that was the last you saw of the other man right?"

"No," she said, shaking her head. "I saw him again when he came back."

Kendall looked puzzled once again. "He came back? Are you sure?"

"Oh yes, sir," she replied.

"When was that?" Kendall asked. "Do you remember?"

She shook her head. "Well, I don't really know the time exactly, but it was about half an hour later," she replied. "I was just finishing room four twelve. As I was coming out, I saw him going back into four twenty."

Kendall shook his head. "Did he see you?" he asked.

She shook her head. "Oh no. I must have been in the room when he passed by," she said. "He must have come up the back stairs."

"The back stairs," repeated Kendall. "How do you know that?"

"If he had used the lift or the main stairs he would have had to go past me, and my trolley would have been in the way once again. He would have been angry once again." She shook her head. "I never saw him, so he must have used the back stairs. We are not allowed to use the back stairs. No one should use them."

"Oh, why not?" Kendall asked.

"They are to be kept clear and used only in case of a fire," she explained.

"Can you tell me anything else about the man?" Kendall asked.

"As I passed by Mr Andrews room, I could hear his voice," she replied. "He was talking to Mr Andrews."

"What was he saying?" asked Kendall.

She shook her head. "He never said much," she replied. "But I did hear Mr Andrews. He was very surprised to see the man. He wondered if the man had forgotten something." She shook her head. "I couldn't understand what the other man said."

"Anything else?" Kendall asked.

She shook her head. "I don't think so."

"Did you see him leave the second time?" Kendall asked.

She shook her head once again. "No, I didn't," she replied. "I carried on with my work. I suppose I finished at about two o'clock, then I went up to the next floor."

"And as far as you know, he hadn't left by then," Kendall asked.

She shook her head once again. "I don't think so, but I suppose I could have missed him when I was inside one of the rooms."

"Maybe," replied Kendall. "But you certainly did not see or hear him leave."

"No," she replied simply.

Kendall remained silent for a moment. He was puzzled. *Why did the visitor return? Why did he use the back stairs? Who was the foreign sounding gentleman?* He shook his head. He turned towards Maria.

"When you found Mr Andrews, did you happen to see a pair of gloves in the room," he asked. "By the bed or perhaps on the floor."

She thought for a few moments, and then shook her head. "Gloves, Senor" she said. "No, sir, I saw no gloves."

Kendall sighed and looked at her. "No gloves, okay" He smiled. "Did you notice the bottle of tablets?"

"Oh yes, sir," she said. "It was on the table by the side of the bed." She smiled. "Here is the room, sir," she said as he opened the door, and went in.

Kendall followed. He slowly made his way over to the bed. Instantly he noticed a strange odour. Try as he might, he could not identify it. "What is that dreadful smell?" he asked.

Maria sniffed the air for a few moments. "I don't know," she replied. "It might be one of the cleaning materials that we use."

"Maybe," replied Kendall. "But it's more like Menthol, or maybe peppermint." Kendall looked at Maria. "You have been very helpful to me," he said. He opened his wallet, took out a ten pound note and handed it to her. "Thank you so much."

She took the note and placed in inside her tunic. "Gracias," she said, smiling.

Kendall then took out his notepad. He tore off a sheet and started to write something. When he had finished, he handed the paper to Maria. "If you think of anything else," he said. "You can reach me there." He pointed to the sheet of paper. "Call me any time."

She took hold of the paper and smiled.

"Okay, you can go now," Kendall said as he ushered her to the still open doorway.

She smiled, turned and walked out of the room. Kendall watched as she walked to the end of the corridor and disappeared around the corner. He went back into the room, closing the door behind him. *Now,* he murmured, *let's see what we can see.*

* * *

Twenty minutes later Kendall had found precisely nothing. Of course he wasn't exactly sure of what he was looking for. The bed where Andrews was found had been stripped completely. The bedside table where the tablets had been found was bare. All of Andrews possessions had been removed.

Kendall sighed and shook his head. Nothing, he murmured. He started towards the door. The door suddenly opened. A young man came in. He was visibly shaking and obviously nervous. "What are you doing in here?" he asked. "Who let you in?" He paused for a moment looking at Kendall. He was suddenly unsure. As far as he was aware, the police had finished in the room. So no unauthorised visitors should have been there. He shook his head once again. You shouldn't be here," he announced as he stared at Kendall. "You must leave now."

"No problem, I'm just going," Kendall said.

"If you do not leave now, I will be forced to contact security," the young man continued, trying to sound in control.

"I'm going," Kendall repeated as he continued moving towards the door. The young man opened his mouth to speak. Kendall raised his hand and shook his head. "I'm going," he said as he quickly walked past the man, out into the corridor. He stopped and turned. He raised his hand and waved. He then hurried along the corridor and took the staircase down to the lobby. He smiled at the receptionist as he passed by, and hurried to the exit.

As he came out of the hotel he never noticed the young man walking a few yards behind him.

* * *

Ten minutes later, Kendall arrived at Belmont Square. And there, on the far side, he could just make out Belmont Taxis. A few minutes later he was standing outside of the office. In front there were two taxis parked, the drivers close by talking. One of them looked up as he saw Kendall approaching. "Did you require a taxi?" he asked.

Kendall walked up to the man and shook his head. "Oh no, thanks," he replied. "Is Terry around?"

"Terry," the second man replied. "He's in the office over there." He pointed towards the door. "I'll get him for you." He moved to the door, opened it and peered in. "Terry," he called. "Someone to see you."

"Tell him I'll be right out," a voice replied.

The man closed the door and walked back to where Kendall was waiting. "He won't be long," he said. Kendall thanked him.

Suddenly the window to the office opened and a head peered through. "Dave, pick up at 14 Onslow Square," someone called out. "To go to Heathrow."

The first man nodded. "On my way." He got into his car, switched on and drove away.

"You wanted to see me," a voice called out behind Kendall.

Kendall turned to face the voice. "Mr Woods?" he asked. "Terry Woods?"

"That's right," he replied. "I'm Woods."

"My name's Kendall. I'm a detective. The receptionist at the Gresham Hotel said that you might be able to help me."

Woods eyes lit up. "Which one?" he asked.

Kendall started to smile. "The pretty one," he replied.

Woods nodded and smiled back. "That'll be Jenny," he said. He paused for a moment. "Come into the office and you can tell me what this is all about."

A few minutes later the two men walked into the office. Seated at the desk in the corner of the room was a young lady busy entering details on to a computer. "Susan," he said pointing to her. "Dave's wife. She's the Company Secretary."

She looked up and smiled. "All that means is I do everything around here," she said..

Woods looked at Kendall for a few moments. "She's right, you know." He smiled at her, then looked back at Kendall. "Now. what can I do for you?"

"You picked up a fare at the hotel the other day," he paused. "Wednesday to be precise, at about one twenty five."

Woods thought for a moment or two. Before he could answer the telephone rang. He reached across the desk and picked up the handset, "Belmont Taxis" he said quickly. "Ten minutes," he said and put the telephone down. He opened the window and peered out. "Jack, pick up at 65 Belgrave Street. To go to Victoria Station." He closed the window and looked at Kendall. "Sorry about that."

Kendall shook his head. Oh, don't apologise, he said. " Business is pretty good, I understand."

Woods smiled. "I'm glad to say that, yes, business is pretty good. I could do with some more drivers." He paused and looked at the office. "But I could do with larger premises as well. And that costs money." He heaved a sigh. "Anyway I'm sure that you haven't come to talk about my business, have you?"

"That's right," said Kendall.

"You mentioned a pick up at the hotel," said Woods.

"Correct again," said Kendall.

129

"I remember him," Woods continued. "A real odd one."

"Odd one," Kendall repeated. "What do you mean?"

Terry smiled and shook his head. "Well, it was strange. I picked him up right enough. He asked for an address in the City somewhere." He paused for a moment. "Leadenhall Street, number 434." He smiled. He suddenly shook his head. "It was really strange."

"Strange," repeated Kendall. "What was so strange?"

"434 Leadenhall Street," explained Woods. "There's no such address. Leadenhall Street stops at 268." He smiled. "Not that it matters. We never got there anyway."

"You never got there," Kendall repeated. "Why not?"

Woods shook his head. "We had gone no more than two or three hundred yards when he suddenly tells me to stop. I pull over, he hands me two ten pound notes, and gets out."

"He got out," repeated Kendall, puzzled.

"That's right," said Woods. "He got out and started to walk back in the direction we had just come." Woods shook his head. "I guessed that he had forgotten something at the hotel."

Kendall shook his head. *That made no sense at all.* "If he had, why didn't he get you to drive him back?"

"Just what I thought myself," said Woods. "I haven't a clue. I said he was a strange one, didn't I?"

The phone rang once again. "56 Cutler Street," he said. "Going to City Airport." He paused and looked at Kendall. "I'll be there in fifteen minutes." He put the phone down. "Sorry, Kendall, I have to go."

Kendall stood up. "You have been most helpful."

Woods smiled. "No problem," he said. "But I really have to run now. Duty calls."

Kendall watched as Woods got into his vehicle and drove away. He smiled and looked at Susan. "Looks like it's all down to you," he said.

She looked up. "So what else is new?" she said, smiling.

* * *

It was shortly after five o'clock by the time Kendall arrived back at his hotel. It had been a long exhausting day. But it had also been a productive day. Kendall was now absolutely certain that Andrews had been murdered. He was also certain who the murderer was. *All he had to do now was prove it.*

* * *

"Ah, Mr Kendall," the receptionist said as he saw Kendall approaching. "There is a telephone call for you. You can take it over there." He pointed to the booth over on the far side of the lobby.

"A phone call, did you say?" said Kendall.

"Yes sir. This very moment," replied the receptionist. "Cubicle 4," he said.

Kendall turned and started to make his way over to the booths. *Who could this be?* he wondered. "Devaney," he murmured. "Why can't he leave me alone?" Then he shook his head. *No it's more likely to be Mollie*, he thought. *Yes, it would be Mollie. She's got delayed at the shops and she'll be late back for dinner. What was with shopping? What was the attraction?* He shook his head. Then he looked at his watch. *Five-ten.*

"Cubicle 4, the man said," he whispered as he reached the booths. He entered the cubicle and picked up the receiver. "Hello, Mollie," he said. "Where are you?"

"Kendall," a voice answered. "This is Whittaker."

"Ah, Inspector," Kendall said. "It's very nice to hear from you again."

"Kendall you've been at it again, haven't you?" the Inspector said. "This time at the Gresham Hotel."

"The Gresham?" repeated Kendall.

"Don't deny it, Kendall," the Inspector said. "You were seen."

I was seen, murmured Kendall. *Who?* He shook his head. *Who had seen him? Was it the young couple at the reception? Or maybe it was the noisy ones looking for the dining room.* Kendall started to smile and shook his head. *It was the man with the newspaper, the one pretending to be asleep.*

"Well, I was in the neighbourhood," Kendall replied. "I thought a cup of coffee and a cream cake would .... well ...."

"Kendall, I've told you before," the Inspector interrupted. "Leave it alone. Case closed, remember."

"Yes, I remember," said Kendall. "But he came back."

The Inspector was puzzled. "Who came back?" he asked. "What on earth are you talking about?"

"The visitor came back," replied Kendall. "Andrews' visitor left but came back twenty minutes or so afterwards."

"He came back," said the Inspector. "Are you sure?"

"I'm sure," replied Kendall. "Why would he come back?"

There was silence for a few moments. "Well, perhaps he had forgotten something," said the Inspector. "I do it all the time."

Kendall had to admit that it had happened to him time after time. He was always forgetting things. "Perhaps he had," replied Kendall. "But perhaps he came back for another reason."

"Which is?" asked the Inspector.

"I'm sure you already know the answer to that one, Inspector," said Kendall.

131

There was silence once again. "Kendall, come and see me tomorrow," the Inspector replied. "Two-thirty. We'll discuss it then."

The line went dead. A huge grin spread across Kendall's face. *We certainly will*, he murmured.

Chapter Fifteen

Theatre Tickets

"Mr Kendall," a voice called out as Kendall made his way to the dining room later that evening. "Mr Kendall."

Kendall stopped and turned. It was the receptionist. "Sorry to disturb you, sir. There is a young man here who insists on speaking with you."

Kendall looked puzzled as he glanced around him. "Who is he?" he asked.

The receptionist shook his head. "He won't say, sir," he replied. "He will only speak to you."

Kendall heaved a sigh. "Well, what does he want?"

Once again the receptionist shook his head. "He refuses to tell us anything, I'm afraid. He just keeps on insisting. He wants you."

Kendall heaved another sigh. *He hated unknowns like this. Unknown visitors. Unknown reasons. It usually meant trouble.* "All right, where is he?" he asked wearily.

"Mr Kendall," a voice suddenly called out from behind him. "Mr Kendall."

Kendall turned around. A few feet away stood a young boy, no older than seventeen or eighteen. "Yes," said Kendall. "What can I do for you?"

The boy walked up to Kendall. He was carrying an envelope in his hand. "I heard you talking about Mr Andrews with Maria earlier," he replied. "At the hotel."

"That's right, I was there," Kendall replied. He paused for a moment and looked at the boy. "I remember I saw you in the corridor, didn't I? You're one of the bell boys, right?"

The boy nodded.

"I thought that you were familiar," Kendall continued. "Let's go over there and sit down, shall we?" He started to walk over to the far side of the lounge. The boy followed a few steps behind.

"Here we are," said Kendall, as he found a vacant table. "Sit down." The boy sat down. "Now that's better," Kendall continued. "All right now, what's your name?"

"David," the boy replied nervously. "David Mills."

"All right, David," Kendall said. "So what can I do for you?"

The boy held up the envelope. "I wondered what I should do with these?" He handed the envelope to Kendall.

"What is it?" Kendall asked, as he opened the envelope.

"Tickets," the boy replied. "Tickets for the theatre. Tonight."

Kendall looked at the tickets. There were two tickets for the seven-thirty performance at the Coliseum Theatre that evening.

Kendall looked puzzled. "They were for that nice man in room four twenty," the boy explained.

"Mr Andrews, you mean?" asked Kendall. "These tickets were meant for Mr Andrews."

"That's right, sir," the boy replied. "He asked reception to get them for him."

"Do you know when he did that," Kendall asked.

The boy thought for a moment. "It was just twenty-five minutes to one, the day he ..." He shook his head. "The day they found him."

Kendall looked up. "The day they found him dead, do you mean?" he asked. The boy nodded. "At twenty-five to one?" *The day he died. That didn't make sense.*

"That's right," the boy replied.

"How are you so sure of the time?" Kendall asked.

The boy shook his head and grinned. "Easy, sir," he replied. "I should have gone off duty at half past twelve. My lunch break starts then, you see. I get forty-five minutes." He shook his head. "Everyone else gets an hour. I only get forty-five minutes. Because I'm the youngest, I suppose. It's not fair, is it, sir."

Kendall nodded. "No, it's not fair," he agreed. "But carry on. You should have gone to lunch, so what happened?"

The boy shook his head again. "I stood around talking to the others. You know. That's when the call came in." He sighed. "If only I hadn't hung around, I would have missed that call, and I would have got my break."

"The call," Kendall repeated. "What call?"

"The desk got a call, from Mr Andrews," the boy started to explain. "So they called me. Just pop around to the theatre and pick up Mr Andrews' tickets, they said. It won't take long, they said." He shook his head. "Won't take long," he repeated. "It was at least a fifteen minutes' walk to the theatre. Then five minutes to pick up the tickets, then fifteen minutes back again." He paused once again and shook his head. "That's," he started to add, "fifteen and five, that's twenty minutes. Twenty and fifteen. That's thirty five." He shook his head. "Thirty five minutes, and I only get forty-five." He paused once more. "It's not fair, I said. Why me? It's my lunch break, I said." The boy shook his head. "Much they cared. Get round to the theatre, they said, and be quick about it. And don't ask so many questions. I was to pick up two tickets in the Dress Circle, and that was that."

Kendall nodded, and smiled. "So you went for the tickets, then what?" he asked.

The boy shook his head. "I don't understand, sir," he replied.

134

Kendall sighed. "You still have the tickets," he said. "Why didn't you take the tickets up to Mr Andrews' room?"

The boy started to nod his head. "I did, sir. But it was much later. After what was left of my lunch break. He paused for a moment. I got back at about ten past one. I went into the office and reported back on duty. I said that I was just going up to Mr Andrews' room with the tickets. Leave it, said Mr Bennett." He paused. "He's the head porter. Leave it for now, he says. Mr Andrews has got a visitor. So I left it until later." He paused once again. "Must have been near half past two when I finally went up to the room. I knocked and waited, but there was no answer. I knocked again, but still nothing. I thought that he must have gone out. So I decided to try again later."

Kendall nodded. "But we now know that he hadn't gone out, had he?"

"No, sir. He hadn't gone out," said the bell-boy. "He was there all the time. Inside the room."

"He was dead," said Kendall.

The boy nodded. "Yes, sir." he looked down at the floor.

"Do you know who the second ticket was for?" Kendall asked.

The boy shook his head, and smiled. "No, sir, I don't," he replied. "But I can imagine."

Kendall smiled and nodded. "You could be right, David," he said. *Somehow he didn't think Andrews had been planning an evening at the ballet in the company of Oliver Jones or John Wyndham Collier.* "You could well be right." Kendall looked at the tickets once again. They were for that evening. He looked at the young boy and shrugged. *He had missed a lunch break because of those tickets.* "How long have you been at the hotel?" he asked.

The boy shook his head. "Oh, not long, sir," he replied. "It's only three months."

"Do you like it?" Kendall asked.

The boy nodded. "Oh yes, sir," he replied. "I like it fine." He paused for a few moments. "Maria is nice," he continued. "Mr Bennett is a bit strict, though."

"Oh. Mr Bennett, he's the big boss?" Kendall said smiling. The boy nodded. "You don't like him, then."

The boy shook his head and smiled. "He's all right, I suppose," he replied. "He could be worse."

Kendall smiled and nodded. "What about the other bellboys?" he asked.

The boy smiled. "Oh, we have a good laugh," he replied. "They are good fun."

Kendall looked at the boy, then he looked at the envelope. "Have you mentioned this to the police?" he asked.

The boy suddenly looked nervous. "Oh no, sir. I haven't told anyone. I didn't think," he replied. "Should I tell them?"

Kendall shook his head. "Oh no, that's alright. Don't you worry about it," he said. "I'll make sure that they know." He handed the envelope back to the young man. "You keep them, you've earned them," he said. "Go to the show. Take your girlfriend."

The boy smiled shyly and shook his head. "Don't have a girlfriend, sir," he replied.

Kendall shook his head. "I don't believe you," he replied. "You don't have a girlfriend, a good looking lad like yourself."

The boy blushed and shook his head.

"Take your mother, then," suggested Kendall. "I'm sure that she will enjoy it."

The boy smiled and nodded. "Thank you, sir," he said, standing up.

"Off you go, then," Kendall said.

The boy smiled. "Goodbye, sir," he said. He then turned and walked away.

Kendall watched as the boy disappeared from view. *Perhaps he should have taken the tickets himself. Perhaps he should have taken Mollie to the theatre as a treat.* He shook his head. *No, that would not be right. The boy should have them and that was that.*

* * *

"So he had tickets for the theatre," said Mollie. "So what about it? I wouldn't mind having some myself. I would love to dress up and go out for the evening. The ballet perhaps, or a musical would be nice."

Kendall sighed. *He knew that he should have kept those tickets. He just knew it.* He shook his head. *He shouldn't have said anything. He should have just kept quiet about it.*

"So what about the tickets?" Mollie said. "I mean are you going to tell me, or what?"

Kendall shook his head. "The truth is I don't really know," he replied. "It may be nothing at all."

"Are you going to explain it, or aren't you?" Mollie said.

Kendall shook his head. "All I know is he purchased the tickets and then an hour or so later he kills himself." He sighed loudly. "It doesn't make sense to me."

Mollie shook her head. "Well, are you going to tell Inspector Whittaker about it?" she asked. "I mean you are going to see him again, aren't you?"

Kendall looked at her and nodded. "Oh yes, I'm going to see Whittaker," he replied. "In fact I have an appointment for half past two tomorrow." He smiled and shook his head. "But I think I'll keep quiet about the tickets," he continued. "At least, for the time-being, that is."

Mollie nodded. *Why he needed to wait was a mystery to her, but then there were lots of things about Kendall that she didn't understand. Oh well, it was his problem, she murmured. Let him get on with it.*

"Talking about theatre tickets," she said casually. "I wouldn't mind seeing a West End show. 'Mamma Mia' sounds good."

Kendall shook his head. *I knew I should have kept quiet*, he murmured. He looked at Mollie and smiled. "I'm sorry, Mollie," he said. "I should have realised." He paused for a moment. "I have been totally insensitive and uncaring," he continued. "Naturally all of this detective stuff must be really getting you down."

Mollie looked at him and shook her head. *Suddenly, for some strange reason, she was beginning to feel guilty. Perhaps she shouldn't have complained.* "Oh come on, it's not that bad," she said.

Kendall shook his head. He raised his hand to his eye. "No, no. You're right. It is bad," he replied. After all we are supposed to be on holiday."

Mollie sighed and shook her head. She placed her hand on Kendall's arm. "It wasn't your fault that Mr Andrews died."

"No, it wasn't," said Kendall barely audible. "But even so, a night at the theatre might be just what we need. A little relaxation. It could be fun. Just what the doctor ordered in fact." He smiled.

Mollie nodded, smiling as she patted his arm.

"I'll see if I can get tickets for 'The Mousetrap'," he said.

"'The Mousetrap'," Mollie repeated. "What's that about?"

Kendall shrugged his shoulders. "It's a play by Agatha Christie," he replied. "It's actually a murder mystery."

Mollie glared at him, and pinched his arm hard. "If you don't get tickets for 'Mamma Mia'," she said angrily, "there'll be another murder around here."

Chapter Sixteen

New Scotland Yard

"Here we are. New Scotland Yard," the taxi driver called out in a gruff voice. "That'll be fifteen pounds, forty-six pence."

Kendall stepped out of the taxi and looked at the man. "How much?" he asked.

"Fifteen pounds, forty-six pence," the man repeated.

"But it was only fourteen pounds, eighty-five the other day," replied Kendall.

The driver shook his head. "Inflation," he said, holding his hand out for payment. "It's the Credit Crunch, you know." Kendall heaved a sigh, and shook his head. He started to count out the money. He took out a twenty pound note. "Here you are," Kendall said.

Mollie quickly leaned forward and took the note out of Kendall's hand. "Leave it to me," she said. She opened her purse and started to count out the money into the driver's hand. "There you are," she announced triumphantly. "Fifteen pounds and eighty-five pence exactly." She looked at Kendall. "It's so simple," she said, rubbing her hands together.

Kendall looked at her and sighed. "I was getting there," he said. "I just needed a few more minutes. I would have got it."

Mollie looked at him and shook her head. "Right," she said. "And I might become President one day." She started to walk towards the main entrance door.

Kendall remained at the cab for a few moments, shaking his head. The driver looked at him. "You know, she might just do it," he said.

Kendall looked at him and shook his head. "I hope not," he said. He handed over a five pound note. "Here's a tip for you."

"Thank you, governor," the driver said as he looked over at where Mollie was standing waiting. "And I've a little tip for you, sir."

"Tip," repeated Kendall. "What tip?"

"Never argue with a lady, sir," the driver replied. "Goodbye, sir." He waved casually, checked his mirror and pulled out from the kerb.

Kendall watched until the taxi was out of sight and then rushed over to the entrance door where Mollie was still waiting.

"So here we are again," said Kendall. "I had hoped that I would never see this place again."

Mollie looked at him and smiled. She took his arm, and pulled him towards the entrance. "Come on," she said. "It's not that bad, is it?"

Kendall nodded. "Worse," he replied.

"Now," Mollie said. "You're not going to let that old fossil up there get to you, are you?"

Kendall started to laugh. "Mollie," he said, "that is no way to talk about Detective Inspector Bill Whittaker. Besides, it's going to be a whole lot different today. Come on, let's get it over and done with."

* * *

A few minutes later they were shown into Whittaker's office. Whittaker stood up as they came into the room. "Ah, Miss Adams," he said, smiling at Mollie. "I'm so pleased to see you again. Do come in. Sit down." He pointed to a chair. Then he turned to face Kendall. "Well, Kendall, I really did not expect to see you again quite so soon."

Kendall smiled and shook his head. "Nor me, Inspector, but I thought...."

Whittaker shook his head and sighed deeply. "This has got to stop, you know, Kendall," he said. "It cannot go on."

Kendall looked stunned. "But I thought ..."

"We have spoken about this before, haven't we?" Whittaker continued. "I told you to stop this little investigation of yours." He shook his head again. "First it was speaking to Collier. Now you've been making a nuisance of yourself at the hotel."

Kendall was shocked. "Nuisance," he repeated in utter disbelief. "I only asked a few simple questions. I mean ..."

"Kendall, as far as Scotland Yard is concerned, this case is over, finished, closed. I told you that. Mr Andrews committed suicide and that is that." He looked at Mollie. "I'm sure that you understand, Miss," he said, and smiled. Mollie simply nodded her head. "Please tell Mr Kendall here, would you? He doesn't seem to grasp it."

Kendall glared at Mollie. He then looked back at the Inspector. "So what about the visitor?"

"What about him?" said Whittaker.

"He came back," explained Kendall. "The maid told me. She said that he came back a short time after leaving."

"So he came back," said the Inspector. "So what? He simply forgot something, that's all." He shrugged. "I do it all the time."

Kendall nodded. *He had to admit that he also forgot things. Often in fact. But this was different.* "Inspector," he said, "it wasn't just the fact that he came back."

The Inspector shook his head and looked at Mollie. "Go on," he said. "Although why I'm listening I'll never know."

Kendall gave a sigh. "He came up the back stairs," he explained. "He did not want to be seen. Why not?"

The Inspector shook his head. "You don't know that he didn't want to

139

be seen," he said.

"Why the back stairs?" Kendall retorted.

The Inspector nodded. "Any number of reasons," he replied. "Perhaps he just wanted to surprise Mr Andrews. Who knows?"

Kendall shook his head. "What about the taxi driver?"

Whittaker looked blank. "Taxi driver?" he repeated.

Kendall nodded. "Yes. Belmont Taxis," he said. "They picked him up at the hotel, but then, a short while after, he stopped the cab, got out, and started to walk back towards the hotel."

Whittaker shook his head. "I have to say, Kendall, you don't give up, do you?" He looked at Mollie. "Is he always like this?"

Mollie smiled and simply nodded.

"All right, so he went back to the hotel," the Inspector said. "It's not exactly against the law, is it?"

Kendall had to admit that the Inspector was right but there were still several unanswered questions. "Alright, so it's not illegal," Kendall agreed. "But you must admit that it's a little odd."

The Inspector shook his head. "Maybe, but I can't see that it's of any particular significance. If I arrested everyone that I saw acting a little odd, the prisons would be bursting at the seams."

Kendall sighed loudly. *This was not going well.* "What about the theatre tickets?" he asked.

The Inspector looked puzzled once again. "Theatre tickets," he repeated. "What theatre tickets?"

"Andrews purchased two tickets for the theatre, for last night," Kendall explained. "Hardly the actions of a man getting ready to kill himself, would you say?"

The Inspector thought for a few moments. "Maybe," he admitted reluctantly. "How do you know about the tickets anyway?"

Kendall smiled. *At last, I'm getting somewhere*, he thought. "The bell-boy told me," he replied. "He had actually been sent to collect them from the theatre."

"Where are they now?" the Inspector asked.

"I told the bell boy to keep them," Kendall replied.

Whittaker sighed. "So he had tickets for some play or other," he said. "What about it?"

Kendall shook his head. "Well, it certainly seems odd to me, but there I'm only a private detective," he replied. "What do I know?"

"Odd, maybe, I grant you," said the Inspector. "Of course it could depend on when he purchased them. Couldn't it? I mean was it before or after his visitor had arrived?"

Kendall looked at Mollie and shook his head. He turned back to the Inspector. "It was before," he replied. "But I don't think ..."

"So before he realised that his crime had been discovered, then," the

Inspector said. "Clearly he bought the tickets because he thought he was safe." The Inspector shook his head. "But of course he wasn't, was he?"

Kendall looked down at the floor and simply nodded.

The Inspector looked at him for a few moments and then nodded his head slowly. "All right, Kendall," he said. "I don't know why. Must be my generous nature, I suppose. Anyway, I'll speak to the maid and that taxi company. What was the name again?"

Kendall looked up, a smile beginning to form. "Belmont Taxis," he replied. "They are in Belmont Square, just around the corner from the hotel. Terry Woods is the boss."

Whittaker nodded. "Belmont," he repeated. "Alright, I'll have a word with them, not that I expect anything."

"And the bell boy," Kendall said quickly. "You'll have a word with him. About the theatre tickets?"

Whittaker sighed and nodded. "All right, I'll speak to him as well. Although why I'm doing it, I'll never know," he said. "What's his name?"

Kendall smiled. "David," he replied. "David Mills. He's a bright young man, you'll ..."

"I'm sure that I will," Whittaker interrupted. "Now, was there anything else?"

"Well, there is one other thing," said Kendall.

"I thought there might be," replied Whittaker wearily. He glanced at his watch and sighed loudly. "I do have rather a lot to do, Kendall."

Kendall nodded. "I appreciate that, Inspector, but this won't take long. Promise."

Whittaker shook his head. *How many times had he heard that before*? "Go on," he said.

Kendall nodded. "Well, it's about the tablets. Well, the bottle, really," he said. "Last time we spoke we were discussing the bottle, the bottle the tablets were in, do you remember?"

The Inspector sighed. "The tablets, how could I forget," he replied. He sighed and nodded. "Yes, I remember them very well. What about them?"

"Well you said that there were finger prints on the bottle," Kendall continued. "Andrews' prints, correct?"

The Inspector nodded once again. He needed this like a hole in the head. "Yes. They were his prints. So?"

"But there were no prints on the cap," said Kendall. "If I remember correctly."

The Inspector shook his head. "The report made no mention of prints on the cap, to be exact," he said, trying not to lose his temper. "As far as we know there were no prints on the cap."

"What about teeth marks?" Kendall asked without looking up.

Mollie looked up surprised. "Teeth marks," she repeated. "Teeth marks?"

"That's right," said Kendall. "I said teeth marks."

The Inspector looked at him as though he was from Mars. "Teeth marks?" he repeated. "What do you mean teeth marks?"

Kendall looked up and smiled. "Well if Andrews didn't open the bottle with his hands, he must have used his teeth."

The Inspector started to smile. "Oh I see, still playing detective, are we?" Kendall smiled. "I really wish you would just leave it alone." The Inspector shook his head. "You couldn't open it with your teeth if you tried. It's one of those child proof caps, you know," he said. "Childproof, and probably private detective proof as well, I shouldn't wonder." Kendall gave a short nervous laugh. "You know the type. The ones that you have to press down and turn at the same time."

Kendall looked disappointed. "I thought I was onto something there." He shook his head. "So he must have used his hands, then," he continued. "But there were no prints, were there?" He sighed. "How could that be, I wonder?"

The Inspector smiled and shrugged. "Simple," he replied. "He must have worn gloves."

Mollie looked at the Inspector and smiled. "One glove," she corrected. "He must have worn one glove."

The Inspector looked puzzled once again. "One glove," he repeated. "Why only one glove?"

Now it was Kendall who looked smug. "There were prints on the bottle, right?" The Inspector nodded. "If he had worn gloves on both hands the prints would have been smudged or not be visible at all."

The Inspector nodded. "Well then, he wore one glove only," he said. "So what's your point?

Kendall shook his head and sighed deeply. "Let's get this straight, can we?" He paused for a moment. "This guy, Bob Andrews, is down, way down. Totally depressed about something."

"Not about something," Whittaker interrupted. "He knew that his crime had been discovered. He was facing a long time locked up in prison."

Kendall nodded. "Right," he said. "So he was worried about going to prison. Not an appealing prospect. As I said, he was down. As low as you can get. He has reached the end of his rope. He's had enough."

So have I, thought the Inspector. "Yes, yes. I get the picture. He has had enough," said the Inspector. "Can you just get to the point?"

Kendall shook his head. "Life isn't worth living He's going to commit suicide."

"Yes that's right," said the Inspector.

"He cannot face the consequences of his actions, the note said,"

Kendall continued. "He plans to take an overdose of tablets, to end it all. To take the easy way out. I think that's the phrase."

"Right," said the Inspector. *He was beginning to know just how Andrews must have felt.* "Get on with it, Kendall, I do have other things to do you know."

"Of course you do, Inspector, and I appreciate your time. I'll be as quick as I can." Kendall took a deep breath. "Anyway, as I was saying. He plans to commit suicide. So what does he do? He gets his bottle of tablets. He leaves his fingerprints all over the bottle. But then he decides to put on gloves. I should say one glove, to unscrew the cap. He unscrews the cap. He takes the tablets. And then he carefully replaces the cap, still wearing his glove, and places the bottle neatly on to the side table. He then removes the single glove and places it somewhere." He paused for a moment. "We don't know where. He then lays down. Thirty minutes later, or thereabouts, he is dead."

Kendall shrugged and shook his head. "It's possible, I suppose, but not very likely, I would say." He paused for a moment. "What do you think, Mollie?"

Mollie nodded her head slowly. She looked at Kendall, then she looked at the Inspector. "I would say that it was most unlikely," she replied.

The Inspector shook his head. "All right, Kendall, you've made a good point, I grant you. I'll check on it."

Kendall nodded his head. *Praise indeed.* "Thank you, Inspector," he said. "I have one other question regarding the fingerprints."

"What about them?" asked Whittaker.

"Which hand were they from?" Kendall replied.

"Which hand," the Inspector repeated. He shook his head. "The right hand. I think." He paused for a few moments. "Yes. It was the right hand."

Kendall started to frown. "Andrews was right handed, wasn't he?" he asked.

The Inspector thought for a moment, and nodded. "That's right," he said. "Why?"

"Oh nothing," said Kendall. "I was just thinking, that's all."

"All right, Kendall," said the Inspector wearily. "Out with it."

Kendall frowned. Then he shook his head. "Andrews never opened that bottle," he said. "In fact there were no tablets. That bottle was empty when it was brought into his room. Andrews never took those tablets."

The Inspector shook his head. "He never took them," he repeated. He opened the top drawer of his desk and took out a blue coloured folder. "So how do you account for this," he said, as he placed it on to his desk. "It's the doctor's report." He started to tap the folder.

143

"According to that report, they found huge traces of Syanthol in his blood stream." He slid the report across the desk towards Kendall. "There's the report. Take a look."

Kendall shook his head. *That's right*, he murmured. "You're right," he replied. "So they did." *And yet Kendall was certain that the jar had been empty from the very beginning*. He looked at the Inspector and started to rub his chin. He suddenly looked down at the open file. He reached forward and picked up a photograph. "This is Andrews, isn't it?"

The Inspector started to frown. *Here we go again*, he thought. "Yes, that's Andrews, in the hotel room. That's how we found him."

Kendall tapped the photograph. "What's that mark?" he asked. "That red spot on his arm?"

Whittaker took the photograph from Kendall's hand. "Red spot," he repeated. "What red spot?"

"There on the arm," Kendall replied.

Whittaker shook his head. "That mark," he said pointing to a small red indentation. "I don't know. A scratch or something. It's nothing significant." He placed the photograph back into the file and stood up. "Kendall," he said slowly. "I'm sure that you mean well, and perhaps you really want to help. It really is very much appreciated, but please can we put an end to it." He looked at the report. "That report shows quite clearly that Andrews died from an overdose."

"Would you mind if I had a copy of that?" said Kendall, pointing to the folder.

The Inspector looked at the folder. "Why would you want a copy of this?" he asked.

Kendall looked at Whittaker for a few moments and then smiled. "I just thought that it might finally convince me that I was wrong and that you were right," he replied.

The Inspector smiled and then he shook his head. "It might almost be worth it for that reason alone," he said. "No. I'm sorry but I just couldn't agree to that."

"Thought not," said Kendall. "It was just an idea." He paused for a few moments. "I don't suppose you would agree to me paying the doctor a visit?"

"Kendall you keep away from him," the Inspector replied, quickly closing the folder. "You don't go anywhere near him, do you understand?"

"Just a visit," said Kendall.

The Inspector shook his head. "No, Kendall," he said. "I'll say this once more. It was suicide and that's that. I'm sorry, but we really must leave it at that. All right?"

Somehow Kendall thought that the meeting was over. "All right," he replied. He stood up and smiled. "I won't take any more of your valuable time, Inspector, I'm sure that you have a lot to do." He looked at Mollie. "How about a little shopping?" he said.

She looked at him, smiled and stood up. She turned to face the Inspector and held out her hand. "It was lovely to see you again, Inspector," she said. "Goodbye."

"Oh goodbye, Miss Adams," the Inspector replied.

Mollie started to walk towards the door. Kendall followed a few paces behind her. He suddenly stopped and turned. He raised his hand and waved. "Goodbye, Inspector," he said. "Thank you for your assistance. He then turned around and walked out of the room.

* * *

As they came out of Whittake's office, Kendall was whispering to himself over and over. "Lennox, 249 Harley Street. Lennox 249 Harley Street."

"Did you say something?" Mollie asked.

Kendall shook his head. "Say something," he repeated. "Oh no. I was just thinking aloud."

"Oh," Mollie replied as they stood in the corridor waiting for the lift. "I thought that you weren't going to mention anything about those tickets."

"Well I wasn't going to," Kendall replied.

"What changed your mind?" Mollie asked.

Kendall nodded his head slowly. "You know, I just couldn't resist it."

Mollie smiled. "So where are we going shopping, then?" she asked, as the elevator arrived.

Kendall smiled. "You can go tomorrow," he replied. "I think I'll have a check-up. I'm feeling a little under the weather, you know."

Mollie looked at him, puzzled. "A check-up," she said. "There's nothing wrong with you."

Kendall looked at her and sighed. "How can you say that?" he replied. "I'm not feeling at all well. It's probably something to do with the water."

Mollie looked at him and shook her head. "It's more likely something to do with Doctor Lennox, at 249 Harley Street, if you ask me."

Kendall looked puzzled. "Doctor Lennox?" he replied. "Who is Doctor Lennox?"

"Kendall I saw the report as well as you, don't forget," she replied. "His name was on the top sheet."

"Was it?" said Kendall innocently. "I never noticed."

"I hope that you aren't planning on going to see him," Mollie said. "The Inspector would not be pleased."

"Mollie, how can you possibly suggest such a thing?" Kendall said. "As if I would."

Chapter Seventeen

Harley Street

Kendall slowly placed the receiver back down on to the cradle. "I'm going to the doctors tomorrow," he announced. "I have an appointment for eleven-fifteen."

Mollie looked at him and shook her head. "So you are going, then?" she said. "What about the Inspector? You know what he said. You weren't to go anywhere near Doctor Lennox, remember."

Kendall shook his head. "He'll never know," he replied. "I mean, I shan't tell him, and you won't tell him. So where's the problem?"

Mollie was far from convinced. "And what about our so-called holiday?" she asked.

"Well, how about you going off to the shops?" Kendall suggested. "You'll like that."

Mollie thought for a moment. She knew when she was beaten. But maybe, just maybe, she could salvage something. "All right," she said. "I'll go shopping. Regents Street, I think." She paused once again for a few moments. "I shall need some money, though. Lots of money."

"That's blackmail," said Kendall.

Mollie smiled and nodded her head. "You could say that," she replied.

"Okay," said Kendall smiling. "Agreed. And I'll see you for lunch. How's that?"

Mollie nodded. "Fine," she replied. "One o'clock, at Liberty's. In their restaurant."

* * *

It was just after eleven o'clock when Kendall's taxi arrived outside number 249 Harley Street. Kendall stepped out on to the pavement. He looked up at the building. It was a large red-brick four-storey Victorian building. According to a small plaque attached to the wall, the building had originally provided the fashionable London residence for the well-to-do. It had been constructed in the mid-eighteen hundreds by Adam Stanley Mortimer, a wealthy merchant with the East India Company. For the past sixty years it had been consulting rooms for a number of doctors.

"That will be four pounds, sixty-five pence, please, sir," the driver said, leaning towards the window.

No matter how hard he tried, Kendall just could not master British

146

currency. Of course, to be absolutely honest, he hadn't really tried that much. *What's the point?* he would say. *Another few weeks and I'll be back home and dealing in dollars and cents once more.*

He handed over a five pound note and told the driver to "Keep the change." The driver thanked him and drove off. A short distance away another taxi came to a halt, and a young man got out. He looked over in Kendall's direction for a few moments. He then crossed the street and went into one of the buildings opposite.

Kendall continued to stare at the building for a few moments. It was all very ornate, with elaborate stonework around the window and door arches. *Obviously at one time an area of opulence and wealth*, he thought. By way of confirmation he suddenly noticed a small blue plaque close to a second floor window which advised that George Bernard Shaw had once lived there. *Imagine that*, he murmured. *George Bernard Shaw*. Kendall nodded and smiled. He really must get a photograph or two when he had finished, just to show Mollie.

He nodded once again and then walked over to the entrance door and stopped. On the side wall there were a number of brass plaques. "Doctor Tony Robinson," he read. "Osteopath." The next one was for a certain Mister Mushin, an Optologist. Whatever that was, Kendall wondered. He quickly glanced at the next one, and the next after that. There it was, the one he was looking for. "Doctor Henry Lennox, FRCS, FRCP, Physician and Surgeon."

* * *

Kendall had telephoned for an appointment the previous evening. "Have you been here before?" the receptionist asked. Kendall explained that he had not been there before. Indeed this was his first trip to England.

"Oh, you're an American," she replied, as though that explained everything. "Have you been recommended to Doctor Lennox?"

"Oh yes," Kendall replied, not being entirely honest. He was, however, mindful of the fact that the doctor's name and address had been on that report that Inspector Whittaker had shown him. "I actually got his name from Inspector Whittaker at Scotland Yard," he said, telling the absolute truth.

"Can I tell the doctor what seems to be the problem?" the receptionist asked.

Kendall paused for a few moments. "I am a detective," he started to explain. "Tell Doctor Lennox that I want to see him about the death of Dob Androwc."

There was silence for a few moments and then the sound of papers being shuffled. Then there was a clicking sound. "I can fit you in at eleven-fifteen, tomorrow morning," the receptionist suddenly announced.

* * *

Kendall opened the door and entered into a large hallway. Just in front of him was a sign indicating that the Reception area was to the left. He walked over to the doorway, knocked and went in. As he did so a young lady looked up. "It's Mr Kendall, isn't it?" she said. "Right on time."

Kendall nodded and smiled at her. "I'm Kendall," he replied.

"Do sit down, Mr Kendall," she said indicating a settee over at the far wall. "Doctor Lennox will see you shortly."

Kendall walked over and sat down. Sitting opposite was an elderly lady and a young man. That was all. "Business not so good, then," he said.

The receptionist looked up. "I'm sorry, did you say something?"

Kendall smiled. "I merely said that business wasn't obviously that good." He indicated the two other people who were waiting.

The receptionist nodded. "Oh yes, I see," she said. She smiled and quickly returned to her work.

Kendall shrugged his shoulders. *That had gone down well*, he thought. *Like a ton of bricks*. He stood up and picked up a magazine from the small pile sitting on the table in the middle of the room. "'Home and Garden'," he murmured. He returned to his seat and started to read.

* * *

"Mr Kendall," the receptionist suddenly called out. "Mr Kendall."

Kendall looked up, startled. He shook his head and yawned. He looked around. The room was empty. "Mr Kendall," she called again. "The doctor will see you now. I'm sorry it has been so long."

Kendall shook his head once again and rubbed his eyes. He looked at his watch. It was ten minutes to twelve. He heaved a sigh. He had promised to meet Mollie for lunch at one o'clock at Liberty's Department Store in Regent Street. That did not leave him much time.

"You can go right in," the receptionist continued as she pointed towards the door to her left.

Kendall stood up and started towards the door. "Thank you," he said. He smiled. "Was I asleep?" he asked.

The receptionist smiled back and simply nodded.

Kendall took a deep breath, walked over to the door and knocked loudly.

"Come in," a voice called out.

Kendall opened the door and peered into the room. "Doctor

148

Lennox?" he asked.

"I'm Doctor Lennox," the man replied, with a slight accent. "Come in and sit down."

Lennox was a tall man in his mid to late fifties. He had long dark grey curly hair and a beard to match. As he stood up, Kendall could see that he had a slight stoop. "Sit there, please, Mr Kendall," he said.

Kendall tried to place the accent. "Australian, right?" he said. Lennox looked puzzled. "The accent," Kendall explained. "Australian, right?"

"Oh, I see," Lennox replied. He shook his head. "South African, actually."

Kendall nodded but said nothing.

"Now, Mr Kendall. I understand that you wish to speak about the unfortunate death of Mr Andrews," Lennox said. "Is that right?"

Kendall nodded. "If you've no strong objection."

"Was he a friend of yours?" Lennox asked. "Or perhaps a relative?"

Kendall shook his head. "Oh no," he replied. "He was just a fellow American. We met on the plane coming over, that's all."

Lennox heaved a sigh. "Oh really." He paused for a few moments. "Well I really don't know about this, you know." He paused once again, hesitant. "I'm not sure. After all, it is most unusual, Mr Kendall. I mean, the police have already looked at the case and made their minds up." He paused once again and shook his head. "As far as I am aware the case is closed. Finished." Then he looked up at Kendall. "I understand that you are a detective. Is that right?"

Kendall nodded. "A private detective," he corrected.

"Um," Lennox muttered to himself.

Kendall looked at Lennox and sensed a possible change of attitude. "Of course, before that I was actually a police officer," he continued quickly.

"So you were a police officer," Lennox replied. He smiled and then shook his head. "But naturally, not in England, I imagine?"

Kendall shook his head. "Oh no, not in England," he replied. "I spent ten years with the NYPD."

Lennox looked puzzled once again. "NYPD," he repeated.

"The New York Police Department," Kendall explained. "NYPD."

Lennox nodded. "Yes, I see." He was still unsure. He heaved a sigh and then shook his head. "I'm sorry, Mr Kendall, but I don't really think...."

Kendall smiled. "I actually got your details from Detective Inspector Whittaker at Scotland Yard," he said, nodding his head. "He knows that I'm here."

Kendall hated being lied to, but when it came to it, and it was necessary, he was fairly adept at lying himself. He, of course, put it down to years of mixing with liars, cheats and low down crooks. *A certain amount was bound to rub off, wasn't it?* Besides, it was only a little lie, and if Whittaker was half the detective he thought he was, then he would know for certain that Kendall would be there. So it was all right, wasn't it?

"Really," the Doctor replied. "So you know Inspector Whittaker." He nodded. "He's a good man. I've known him for many years. More than I care to remember, actually." Then he nodded slowly. "Well, if it's alright with him, I suppose, under those circumstances it will be alright," he said. "So, Mr Kendall, what was it that you actually wanted to discuss?".

Kendall nodded and smiled. "Thank you, Doctor," he said. "I appreciate this very much." He paused for a moment. "I understand that the cause of death was an overdose of Syanthol 25. Is that correct?"

The doctor smiled and shook his head. "To be strictly accurate, the actual cause of death was kidney failure as a result of the overdose."

"Kidney failure," Kendall repeated.

The doctor nodded. "That's right," he said. "The kidneys just could not handle the drug overload, simple as that." He paused for a moment. "You see one of the functions of the kidneys is to remove waste products. Material the body doesn't need." He paused once again. "Clever things, the kidneys, they allow so much and then they put on a stop. Enough is enough they say." He shook his head. "They just could not cope with the excessive amount of the drug."

Kendall nodded. "So they just gave up working, is that right? Downed tools."

"As you say, they just gave up," the doctor replied.

Kendall nodded. "So precisely how dangerous are the tablets?" he asked.

"Syanbthol 25?" the doctor asked.

Kendall nodded.

"Mr Kendall, I'm sure that you are aware that all medicines carry some risk of unwanted side effects," the doctor replied. "Some are quite mild and of little effect. Others however are more severe and potentially more serious."

Kendall nodded. "Yes, I'm aware of that," he replied. "It's exactly the same with the medication that I take for hay fever."

The doctor nodded. "There you are."

"But what about Syanthol?" Kendall asked once again.

The doctor nodded. "Syanthol has been around for several years now. It is considered to be a very effective treatment for asthma and similar breathing problems," Lennox replied. "It is generally considered to be a safe drug and normally harmless."

"What about the dosage?" Kendall asked. "I mean, I imagine that there could be a problem if you took too many."

Lennox smiled and nodded. "Certainly there could be a problem. As there would be with any drug," he said. "The recommended dose is no more than two tablets per day. If you took four tablets, six, or even eight, there would be no major problems. A slight headache maybe. Take ten, twelve or fourteen, you would start to feel ill. Nauseous. Aches in the limbs. That kind of thing."

"How many would it take to kill you?" Kendall asked.

The doctor shook his head. "That's hard to say," he replied. "How long is a piece of string? It would depend on all sorts of things. Your physical make up. Your height, weight that sort of thing. Your general health. Were you taking other medication."

"Just a ball park figure will do, Doctor," said Kendall. "I only want an indication."

The doctor nodded. "Well, I would guess thirty might be enough. Thirty-five." He paused. "For someone like Mr Andrews, let us say forty."

"Forty," Kendall repeated. "So it wouldn't exactly be an efficient way of committing suicide, then."

The doctor shook his head. "If you mean that death would not be guaranteed, then you are right," he said. "Certainly just taking a handful of tablets would not be enough."

Kendall nodded. "So how many tablets did Mr Andrews take?" he asked.

"As far as I could tell there was the equivalent of approximately sixty tablets in Mr Andrews' blood stream." He paused for a moment. "It's all very sad." He shook his head.

Kendall nodded. "It certainly is, Doctor," he replied. "Doctor would you know how many tablets there would have been in the bottle?" he asked.

"In Mr Andrews bottle, you mean?" the Doctor replied shaking his head. "No, Mr Kendall, I'm afraid not."

Kendall looked disappointed. "You have no idea at all?" he asked.

The Doctor nodded. "The prescribed dose was one tablet twice a day. Assuming the bottle contained four weeks supply, which is quite normal, there would have been twenty-eight times two tablets per day. That equals fifty-six tablets in the bottle. That is fifty-six, when it was first purchased." He paused for a moment. "I understand that the tablets were obtained several days before Mr Andrews' death." There was another pause. "Let us assume therefore that he had been taking two tablets per day for, shall we say, four days. Then there would have been approximately forty eight tablets left."

"Forty-eight," repeated Kendall sounding puzzled. "But you just said that there was the equivalent of approximately sixty tablets in his blood stream."

The Doctor nodded. "That is correct. In my opinion he took the whole bottle," he replied. He smiled and shook his head. "Of course it is possible that he hadn't taken any tablets on the previous days. Naturally I have no way of knowing."

Kendall nodded. "Would it surprise you if I told you that Mr Andrews had not taken Syanthol, or any other tablet, for at least three months?"

Lennox looked at Kendall. "It would surprise me very much," he replied.

"Well, that is precisely what he told me," Kendall explained. "Apparently there were side effects, so he stopped taking them."

The doctor started to tap his hands together. He looked at Kendall. "Do you happen to know what actual side-effect it was?"

Kendall shook his head. "No, I'm afraid not," he replied.

"Curious," said the doctor. "Syanthol was certainly found in his blood stream, large quantities in fact." He shook his head. "How would that be possible if he didn't actually take the tablets?"

"Doctor would it be possible to inject Syanthol into the bloodstream?" Kendall asked.

The doctor thought for a few moments and then slowly nodded his head. "It's possible, I suppose, although not normal, I would say." He began tapping his hands together once again. "You would have to crush the tablets into a very fine powder. Then you would need to dilute the powder in a substance such as a saline solution perhaps." He nodded his head. "As I say, it's possible, but hardly likely."

Kendall smiled and nodded his head. "Doctor, in your report you make reference to a small red mark on one of Andrews' arms. I think it was paragraph 6.5 of your report."

"The one on his right arm, you mean?" Lennox asked.

Kendall nodded.

Lennox shook his head. "That was nothing," he said. "A very small red puncture mark on the skin, nothing of any significance. An insect bite perhaps."

"Oh, is that all," Kendall said sounding disappointed. "I thought that it might have been the mark of a hypodermic needle, or something like that."

The doctor looked surprised and shook his head. "Oh no," he replied. "Nothing of the kind." Then suddenly he shook his head and a frown spread across his forehead. "Just a moment," he said.

He stood up and walked over to a filing cabinet in the far corner of the room. He opened it. He took out a file and returned to his desk. He placed the file on the desk and sat down. "This is the Andrews case," he said as he opened the file. He withdrew a number of papers and started to shuffle through them. "I shan't be long," he murmured.

A moment or two later he found what he was looking for. It was a photograph showing somebody's right arm. Just at the inside bend of the elbow was a small red spot. The doctor looked at it closely. Then he picked up a magnifying glass and examined it once more. Then he slowly placed the magnifying glass on to the desk. For a moment or two he sat quite still staring across the room. All of the time stroking his beard, and muttering to himself. He suddenly stopped, and turned to face Kendall. He started to nod his head. "You know, Mr Kendall," he said slowly. "It could be the mark from a needle." He paused and shook his head. "But why? Was Mr Andrews a diabetic?"

Kendall looked at him and shook his head. "Not as far as I know, Doctor," he replied. "He suffered from asthma, but not diabetes."

"Ah, I see," said the Doctor, as he carefully stacked the papers together.

"Doctor, you said that the mark could be from a needle, correct?" The doctor nodded. "Is it possible that is how the drug entered his blood stream?"

The doctor looked back at the photograph. He then turned to face Kendall and simply nodded his head.

"Thank you, Doctor," Kendall said, as he stood up. "I won't take up any more of your time. You have been extremely helpful." He turned around and walked towards the door. As he did so he checked his watch. It was twelve forty-five. He had fifteen minutes to get to Regents Street.

He shook his head. *Not a chance*, he murmured. He didn't even have time to take a photograph of the building, he thought sadly.

153

Chapter Eighteen

So Many Pieces

It was twenty past one by the time Kendall arrived for his lunch appointment. Mollie wasn't there. *Had she been and gone? He was late, so she had decided not to wait?* Kendall shook his head. *He was only a few minutes late, after all. Alright, it was twenty minutes. Well, he had been late before, hadn't he? Much later. She was well used to that.*

Should he ring her? He shook his head. *Why not?* He murmured. He took out his cell phone and dialled her number. "The number is unavailable," a mechanical voice announced. "Would you like to leave a message?" As he had suspected, she didn't have it switched on. He shook his head. *She never had it switched on.* Perhaps he should go back to the hotel. He shook his head. *That would be foolish.* There was no guarantee that she would be there. *Besides, I'm here now*, he thought, *so I might as well get some lunch.* He smiled. Without Mollie being around, he could order what he liked. He wasn't restricted in any way. He wouldn't have her watching and shaking her head. *Don't have that. That's bad for you. Too much salt. Remember the calories. Too much saturated fat.*

He started to smile. *So strictly, she was right. A lot of the food was bad for you but he did enjoy a thick juicy steak, or a beefburger, and fries.* I mean it couldn't hurt occasionally, could it?

He picked up the menu. Then he looked around at his neighbouring diners. The person at the next table had a very nice looking hamburger with all of the trimmings. Onions, tomatoes, cheese. *That's for me*, he decided.

He looked around. "Waiter," he called out, holding up the menu.

The waiter hurried over. "Yes, sir, what can I get you?"

Kendall looked at the waiter then he looked across to the nearby table. "One of those," he said. "With all of the trimmings."

The waiter nodded. "Certainly, sir," he said.

Suddenly there was loud noise from the entrance door. Kendall looked around. It was Mollie, loaded with parcels. She saw him and waved. He smiled at her.

The hamburger, he murmured. How would he explain that. *It was a mistake. The waiter obviously misunderstood; I was assured that it was vegetarian; I never ordered that, take it back.* He shook his head. She would never be taken in by any of those. He shook his head. He had no choice. He had to just own up. *Yes, I ordered it. Besides, what about it?*

He shook his head once again. Perhaps he would leave out the second comment. Wise decision.

* * *

"Sorry I'm late," she said as she placed the parcels on to an empty seat. She sat down. She opened her handbag and took out her cell phone. "I better just check this," she said as she switched it on. "Oh, I've a message," she said. "I wonder who that's from," she mused as she looked at Kendall.

Kendall shook his head. "You weren't here," he said sheepishly. "I wondered where you were, that's all"

She started to grin. She switched off the phone and placed it back into her bag. "John Lewis is such an enormous store. I lost all track of time," she said.

She picked up the menu. "Have you ordered yet?" she asked. "I'm absolutely famished," she continued not waiting for a reply. "Shopping really takes it out of you."

She studied the menu for a few minutes. "The Meditteranean Bake sounds good to me," she said, closing the menu. As she did so she noticed the man at the neighbouring table. She smiled and looked at Kendall. "I suppose you were going to order one of those."

Kendall looked puzzled. "One of what?" he asked.

"A hamburger," she replied. "One of those." She pointed.

"Why, I hadn't even noticed," Kendall replied.

At that moment the waiter arrived with Kendall's order. Mollie looked at it and shook her head. "Hadn't even noticed, I think you said."

Kendall smiled. "Well, maybe I had taken a little peek."

She shook her head. "On your own head be it," she said. Then she looked at the waiter. "I'll have the Mediterranean Bake, thank you."

She handed the menu to the waiter. The waiter nodded and walked away.

Mollie looked at Kendall. She sighed. "How is it, then?" she asked. "The hamburger, I mean."

Kendall looked up. "The burger, you mean," he replied. "Oh, it's okay, I suppose." Mollie never noticed the gleam in his eye, or if she did, she never mentioned it.

* * *

"So, how was your day," she asked.

Kendall nodded and gave a sigh. "Not too bad, I suppose," he said. "According to the doctor, Andrews took the whole bottle of tablets, all fifty-six of them. I found that interesting."

Mollie looked puzzled. "What's so interesting about that?" she asked.

Kendall shook his head. "There were fifty-six tablets in the bottle originally."

"So," said Mollie, still puzzled.

"The date on the bottle was five days before Andrews died," Kendall started to explain.

"So," said Mollie once again.

Kendall heaved a sigh. "If Andrews had actually been taking the tablets, as we are supposed to believe, he would have taken two tablets each day, therefore on the day he died there would have been only forty-eight tablets left."

Mollie shook her head. "At the risk of repeating myself, so what about it?"

"According to Doctor Lennox, there was the equivalent of approximately sixty tablets in Andrews' bloodstream. Therefore he must have taken the whole bottle in one go." He paused for a few moments, waiting for a reaction. There wasn't any. He shook his head. "So clearly he hadn't been taking the tablets on the previous days."

Mollie thought for a few moments. "He could have had a second bottle, couldn't he?" she said. "I mean one that he was almost finished with."

It was not the answer that Kendall had wanted to hear. He shook his head and sighed loudly. "There was no other bottle," he said emphatically. "He never took the tablets. He hadn't been taking them for several months."

Mollie shrugged. "Maybe," she said simply. "I still don't understand your point. Anyway, what else did the doctor say?"

Kendall started to smile. "Well, he agreed that maybe the red mark could have been from a needle."

"The red mark on Andrews arm, you mean?" Mollie asked.

"That's right, the very same," Kendall confirmed. "Could be, he said. He wasn't very definite though."

Mollie looked puzzled. "Well what did he say?" she asked.

Kendall shook his head. "He wondered if Andrews had been diabetic." He paused for a moment. "I mean, we are talking about one small pinpoint. I mean, if Andrews had been a diabetic, the mark would have been much more pronounced."

Mollie nodded. "Because the injection would have been on a regular basis, you mean."

"That's right," replied Kendall. "He would have injected himself at least every day. Maybe more, I don't know. This mark is obviously a one-off."

"So what did the doctor say about that?" asked Mollie.

Kendall shook his head. "We never even discussed it," he said. "It's only just occurred to me now." He shook his head. "Wish I'd thought of

156

that before."

Mollie looked down and sighed. "It might have helped," she suggested. "So, all in all, not so good, then."

Kendall shook his head. "As you say, not so good." He paused. "At least not as conclusive as I would have liked. He did at least agree that it was possible, that's something, I suppose."

Mollie sighed and shrugged her shoulders. "Well, maybe it was nothing anyway," she said. "Nothing significant, I mean. Maybe the doctor was right. Perhaps he was a diabetic. Perhaps he did inject himself."

Kendall shook his head. "Perhaps," he replied unconvinced. "But Andrews told me that he suffered from asthma. There wasn't a word about diabetes."

"Well, perhaps he just never mentioned it, that's all," Mollie suggested. "Perhaps he didn't like to say. Some people are like that."

Kendall sighed and shook his head. "That doesn't make sense," He said. "He didn't mind talking about his asthma but he couldn't bring himself to mention diabetes. Why not?" He shook his head again. "I am convinced that someone injected Andrews with that Syanthol and that is what killed him."

Mollie put her hand on Kendall's arm, and smiled. "I don't know," she said gently. "Scotland Yard think it was suicide. So does the doctor. Maybe they're right. Anyway, we are on holiday, remember?" She shrugged and smiled. "Eat your burger."

He looked at her and nodded his head. "Maybe you are right," he said. "Maybe Whittaker and Lennox are correct." He gave a little cough. "After all, they are the experts. They should know. Maybe I am wrong. Perhaps I should just forget all about it." He looked at Mollie and smiled. "That's it," he continued. "I should just forget all about it."

Mollie heard the words but somehow she knew that he did not mean them. He had no intention of just forgetting. Once he had something in his mind, there was no stopping him.

"I'm sure that's right," she said as she started to tap his arm gently. "It's for the best, really, you'll see."

Kendall smiled. "Anyway," he said. "Looking at all of your parcels, it seems that you had a better day than me."

She started to laugh. "I don't know about better, but certainly it was more expensive."

* * *

Shortly after arriving back at the hotel, there was a knock on the room door. "Message for you, Mr Kendall," the young bell-boy announced. He saluted smartly and handed over a small white Probably one of those celebrity magazines that she was so fond ofenvelope.

Kendall took hold of the envelope. He thanked the boy and handed over a five pound note. The boy smiled, saluted once again, turned and walked away.

Kendall closed the door and looked at the envelope for a moment. "I wonder what this is," he murmured.

"Why don't you open it?" suggested Mollie without looking up from her magazine.

Kendall glared at her. "I was just about to," he replied. He opened the envelope. Inside was a single sheet of paper. "It's from Devaney," he announced. He started to read. ".... the prescription was actually made out by a Doctor Felix Stannard, located somewhere over on Bay Shore Drive," Devaney wrote. "However Andrews' doctor is Doctor James Chamberlain, on Sunset."

"How very interesting," said Kendall, tapping the paper.

"According to Doctor Chamberlain's records, Andrews hasn't been taking any kind of a drug for the past four months," Devaney continued. "The name on the prescription was Jones, Oliver Jones."

Kendall started to smile. "I knew it," he said looking at Mollie. "I told you that he wasn't taking any medicine, didn't I?" There was no reply from Mollie.

Kendall looked at Mollie and frowned. "I said Andrews wasn't taking any drugs, didn't I?" Still there was no answer. He walked closer to where she was sitting. She was reading something. Kendall heaved a sigh. *Probably one of those celebrity magazines that she was so fond of*, he thought.

"What's so interesting?" he asked.

She looked up. "Sorry, did you say something?"

"I asked what was so interesting?" he repeated.

"Oh," she said. "Su do ku," she replied simply and then returned to her magazine,.

"Su do what," Kendall said. "What's that, then? Some kind of Chinese food?"

She shook her head and glared at him. "You just wouldn't understand," she replied. "It is a puzzle. A superior brain training device, which is way over your head."

Kendall nodded. "Oh really," he replied, shrugging his shoulders. "Whatever."

"Perhaps you would care to try it?" she said as she offered him the magazine.

Kendall glanced at the outstretched page. He shook his head. "I really can't be bothered with such games," he said. "I have far more important things to occupy my brain, thank you."

"Like what?" Mollie asked.

Kendall smiled. "Like for example whether or not Andrews did really kill himself." He paused. "I just can't get it out of my mind. It just won't go away." He paused once again. "I've got so many pieces to this puzzle now. I just need to put the whole thing together."

Mollie grinned at him. "Are you sure that the pieces are going to fit?" she asked.

He grinned back and nodded. "Oh, they'll fit alright," he replied. "Don't you worry about that. They'll fit, even if I have to squash them together."

Mollie shook her head. "Isn't that cheating?" she asked.

Kendall looked at her. "Maybe," he said. "But if the means justifies the end, then so be it."

Mollie had no idea what Kendall meant by that statement. Furthermore, she had a suspicion that neither did Kendall. She shook her head. "Anyway, I thought that you were going to just forget all about it," she said. "That's what you said.

Kendall nodded. "I did say, didn't I?" he replied. "But you didn't really believe me, did you?"

Mollie heaved a sigh. "Well, I had hoped," she murmured. "Have you ever thought that maybe, just maybe, Scotland Yard are right," she said. "It was suicide after all."

Kendall shook his head. "Scotland Yard are wrong," he said. "Simple as that. They are wrong."

"How can you be so sure?" Mollie asked.

Kendall nodded. "Alright, I'll tell you," he said. He held up one finger. "Number one, if he committed suicide like they say, why did he go to all the trouble of coming to England?"

"What do you mean?" Mollie asked.

Kendall frowned. "Why come here?" he asked. "If you are going to kill yourself, why not do it in Florida? Why England? Why take the time and trouble to fly three thousand miles. Why not just stay at home and do it, that's what I say."

Mollie thought for a moment. "Maybe he committed suicide because of something that happened after he had arrived here," she suggested.

Kendall looked at her. "In two days? I mean, since arriving at Heathrow, that's all it was, two days."

"Well something could have happened during that time," Mollie replied. "It's possible."

"Something to cause him to kill himself," Kendall said disbelievingly.

"Well, it's possible," Mollie repeated

Kendall shook his head and looked down at the ground. He looked back up at Mollie and frowned. *He hated to admit it but she was actually making some good points.* "I suppose," he replied. "Possibly. But what?"

Mollie shook her head. "I don't know," she replied. "But maybe something happened when he went to that company, Travers Morgan. He saw that Collier character, didn't he?"

Kendall nodded. "That's right."

Mollie thought for a few moments. "Well maybe they discussed the missing money and Collier accused Andrews."

"Maybe," Kendall replied. "But I still don't think he committed suicide."

"Well, you haven't convinced me yet," said Mollie. "I still think it's possible."

Kendall shook his head and sighed loudly. Suddenly he nodded. "Alright, here's something," he said.

"Go on," said Mollie. "I'm listening."

Kendall looked at her, and smiled. "The missing money, the alleged fraud," he said. "He told me all about it on the plane."

"So," said Mollie.

"Andrews told me that although he didn't know who had taken the money, he did have a few ideas," Kendall explained. "Nothing definite, but that was one of the reasons for making the trip."

Mollie looked puzzled. "What's your point?" she asked.

Kendall shook his head. "My point?" he repeated. "My point is why would he say that if he was the guilty party himself?"

Mollie sighed. "He could have just said that to throw suspicion from himself."

Kendall sighed and shook his head. "That makes no sense at all," he replied. "Why say anything at all? I mean, I was a perfect stranger. He didn't need to say anything at all."

"Oh, I see," said Mollie, not fully seeing at all.

"And another thing," Kendall continued. "I mean, why make arrangements to see a show, and then actually kill yourself later?"

"What do you mean?" Mollie asked.

"Would you make arrangements to go to the theatre a day or two later if you were planning on committing suicide," Kendall asked.

Mollie nodded. "I suppose not, but you have to admit that people do strange things," she replied. "They don't always act in a logical way."

Kendall sighed deeply and shook his head. "Maybe so," he replied. "But it still makes no sense, not to me. I just cannot believe that he killed himself."

Mollie looked at Kendall for a few moments. "Well, I'm still far from convinced," she said. "Scotland Yard are certain that it was suicide. What about the suicide note?"

Kendall shook his head. "What about this message from Devaney?" He held the piece of paper in the air. "It wasn't even Andrews' doctor who wrote out the prescription for the tablets."

"Well, I grant you that is odd," Mollie said. "But if it wasn't suicide, what was it?"

"Do you really need to ask that question?" Kendall said.

Mollie shook her head. "So you are saying that it was murder," she said.

Kendall nodded. "That's what I'm saying."

"So who murdered him?" Mollie asked.

Kendall thought for a few moments. "He had a visitor, didn't he?" he said. "The afternoon he died." Mollie nodded. "Apparently, he left the hotel at about twenty five past one, according to the receptionist," Kendall continued.

"Andrews was still alive then, wasn't he?" said Mollie.

"That's right, he was," replied Kendall. "But the visitor certainly made sure that everyone knew that he was leaving."

"The argument with the maid," Mollie suggested.

"That's right," said Kendall. "The argument with the maid."

"But he came back later, according to the maid," said Mollie.

Kendall nodded. "Yes, he came back. About half an hour later," he said. "She saw him come up the back staircase. Nobody else saw him, and he never knew that he had been seen."

"That was deliberate," suggested Mollie.

Kendall nodded once again. "As you say, that was deliberate. It was all part of the plan," he replied. "I think Andrews was murdered by that visitor."

Mollie looked at Kendall for a few moments. "Do we know who that visitor was?" she asked.

Kendall started to smile and slowly nodded his head. What was it that Collier had actually said? "*Oliver Jones, my right hand man. He had always been close to Oliver. I thought that he would be able to succeed where I had failed.*"

161

Chapter Nineteen

A Police Warning

"Oh yes," Kendall said. "We know who it was. It was Oliver Jones. Collier actually told me that."

Suddenly the telephone rang. Kendall picked up the receiver. "Kendall Detective Age ..." He stopped as he realised what he was saying. "Tom Kendall speaking."

"Kendall," a gruff voice said. It was Detective Inspector Whittaker.

"Ah Inspector, it's good to hear from you as always," Kendall said. "What can I do for you?"

"Kendall, I hear that despite my instructions, you have been asking Doctor Lennox a lot of questions," Whittaker said. "I have asked you before to leave it to us, remember." There was a short pause, and a deep audible sigh. "Firstly it was Travers Morgan. Then you visited the hotel, and now this."

"I only asked a few simple questions," Kendall protested. "Where's the harm in that?"

"Kendall, that's enough. A few simple questions indeed," replied the Inspector. "I am getting a whole string of complaints about you. They are all here, piling up on my desk. There are complaints from Travers Morgan. There are complaints from the hotel and now there are complaints from Doctor Lennox." He paused for a moment. "Just exactly what do you think you're playing at? I mean you can't just go round asking a lot of questions as you please. It is obvious that you aren't prepared to co-operate." He paused once again. "And, by the way, a New York Police badge has no jurisdiction in the UK. You can't go round displaying it as though it were official. It has to stop, Kendall. If you use it again you will be arrested."

"No jurisdiction, really," repeated Kendall feigning surprise. "I had no idea."

"Kendall, as much as we appreciate all of the help given to us by our American cousins, we really can manage without any further outside assistance," said the Inspector. "I'll ask once more. Just leave it alone. Forget all about it. Please."

Kendall shook his head. "Inspector, I am truly sorry, but I am convinced that Bob Andrews was murdered, and I ..."

"Stop it, Kendall," Whittaker said angrily. "Stop right there. Andrews committed suicide, of that there is absolutely no doubt. It was suicide. Just accept it."

Kendall shook his head once again. "Why would he commit

suicide?" he asked. "It doesn't make any sense."

Whittaker shook his head. "Why I am even bothering to listen to you, I'll never know," he said wearily. "Go on. What doesn't make sense?"

Kendall said nothing for a moment or two. Then he shook his head. *It wasn't suicide. It couldn't have been suicide.* After all, he had spoken to Andrews. He knew exactly what Andrews had been planning. "I'm sorry Inspector but you're wrong. It wasn't suicide," he said. "I spoke to Andrews on the plane, remember? He was really looking forward to this trip. He never had a care in the world."

It was now Whittaker's turn to sigh. He shook his head. "Clearly you must have been mistaken," he replied. "He must have had numerous worries. That missing money must have weighed heavily on his mind. Added to that he had been found out. Collier knew all about it. He couldn't face the consequences and that's why he killed himself. Simple."

"An overdose of Syanthol," said Kendall. "Is that it?"

"That's right," said Whittaker. "A simple overdose of Syanthol."

Kendall started to frown. "Well, I think simple overdose is far from correct," he said. "According to Doctor Lennox, there was the equivalent of approximately sixty tablets in Andrews' bloodstream."

The Inspector sighed. "Alright, so it wasn't a simple overdose," he said. "It was a little more complex. It was still an overdose."

"Doctor Lennox calculates that there were only fifty-six tablets in the bottle to start with," said Kendall.

"Go on," said the Inspector wearily. "I'm sure there's a point to all of this, somewhere."

"There is, Inspector, I assure you," said Kendall.

"Get on with it, then," said Whittaker. "I really haven't got all day, contrary to popular belief."

"Inspector, I know how busy you are, believe me," Kendall replied. "But don't you find it a little strange?"

The Inspector was puzzled. "Don't I find what a little strange?" he asked.

Kendall took a deep breath. "If Andrews had been taking the prescribed dose of two tablets per day, as you believe, then there would have been no more than forty-seven or forty-eight tablets left by the time he is alleged to have killed himself, and not sixty as the doctor stated."

Whittaker paused for a moment as he made a quick calculation. He nodded his head. "Clever, Kendall, I must admit," he replied. "That's very clever. But it's not conclusive, you see."

"Maybe not," said Kendall. "But it is a possibility, wouldn't you say."

"Maybe, I grant you," said the Inspector. "It's certainly possible, but not very likely in my opinion." He paused for a moment. "It's obvious to me that Andrews must have had another bottle of tablets. One that was almost finished that's all. Or maybe he hadn't taken any on the previous few days for one reason or another. In all probability all fifty-six tablets were still there, in the bottle. He just took the whole lot in one go. Or maybe forty-seven tablets was enough to do the job anyway. Who knows?"

Kendall shook his head. "Doctor Lennox knows," he said. "According to him there was the equivalent of approximately sixty tablets in Andrews' bloodstream. Not forty-seven, or fifty-six even."

Whittaker shook his head. "You can't be that precise," he said. "He can't be that precise."

"Doctor Lennox sounded pretty definite to me," said Kendall.

Whittaker sighed. "Alright, then," he said. "So there must have been a second bottle."

Kendall said nothing for a few moments. "When you searched his room after his death, did you find another bottle?" he asked.

Whittaker shook his head. "No, we didn't," he replied. "But that doesn't mean anything. There still could have been another bottle somewhere."

"If there had been another bottle, when do you think he used it last?" Kendall asked. "I mean, your best guess."

The Inspector shook his head. "I haven't a clue," he replied. "What does it matter anyway?"

Kendall shook his head. "Well I'm guessing, but I would think that if there had been another bottle, and I did say if, he would probably have finished it the day before he died," he replied.

"How do you arrive at that conclusion, Kendall?" Whittaker asked.

"Well, firstly, we have to assume that he was taking the tablets diligently, you know two every day," said Kendall. "Is that a fair assumption?"

"Go on, Kendall," said Whittaker.

"Next we have to assume that the empty bottle found on the bedside table had not actually been used, and contained the whole fifty-six tablets," Kendall continued. "If he had in fact had another bottle, and he was in fact taking the tablets correctly on a regular basis, that's the day he would have finished the bottle."

"Well then, the empty bottle would almost definitely have been removed by the maid on the day that he died," said Whittaker. "At the time that she discovered his body."

Kendall smiled. "I don't think so, Inspector," he replied. "The maid told me about the empty bottle standing on the bedside cabinet. She said nothing about any other bottle." Kendall shook his head. "There was no other bottle, Inspector."

The Inspector shrugged his shoulders. "So there was no other bottle," he said. "Let's say that you are right, and I'm not convinced. But let's say so for the sake of argument. So what about it?"

Kendall smiled. "If there was no other bottle, then he hadn't taken any tablets for at least four or five days. Is that correct?"

The Inspector said nothing.

"If he was taking the tablets diligently, then why would he not take them on those few days?" The Inspector still said nothing. Kendall shrugged and then shook his head. "No, Inspector," he continued. "He hadn't taken any tablets. But not just for a few days. In fact he hadn't taken any for several months."

The Inspector shook his head. "That's what you say, Kendall," he said. "But you haven't any proof of that, have you?"

"Well I suppose you could check with his doctor over in Florida," Kendall suggested. "You might learn something useful."

The Inspector shook his head once again. "I could do, but you see I don't need to check anything."

"Andrews' doctor is Doctor James Chamberlain," Kendall said. "He has an office in a very nice part of town. If you checked with him you will find out that Andrews hadn't been taking any kind of a drug for the past three or four months."

"How do you know that?" the Inspector asked.

"Oh, I got a friend in the Miami Police department to run a check," Kendall explained. "That's what he came up with. I thought it was interesting."

"You make a few good points, I admit, but you've not yet said anything to make me change my opinion," said the Inspector. "It was suicide. Let's leave it at that, shall we?"

"No, I'm sorry Inspector, but I can't go along with you," said Kendall. "Did you know that Andrews was planning all kinds of things on this trip? He was going to see a bit of the country. A few days in Cornwall."

The Inspector smiled. "We know all about that, Kendall," he said. "You told me, don't you remember?" he paused for a few moments. "He also had tickets for Wimbledon, did you know that? The Men's Quarter Finals."

"Why would he plan all of that, and then kill himself," asked Kendall. "It's just plain stupid."

"Simple," replied Whittaker. "He thought he was safe, that's all. Then he just got found out and couldn't face the consequences, so he killed himself."

Kendall shook his head and heaved a sigh. "No, I just can't accept that. It just doesn't add up."

"All right Kendall that'll do. It makes perfect sense to me," said the Inspector. "Anyway I've finished. I've had my say. Remember, Kendall, no more questions, all right. You just enjoy your holiday and leave all of this nasty crime stuff to us. Agreed."

"I wish I could see it your way, Inspector, but I can't," replied Kendall.

"Kendall," the Inspector said firmly. "Take my word for it. As sure as eggs is eggs, it was suicide. Case closed. Finished."

Kendall nodded. "I hear what you say, Inspector," he said. "But I think you're wrong and I'm going to prove it. Goodbye, Inspector."

"Kendall," the Inspector called out. "Kendall ...."

Kendall shook his head and hung up.

* * *

"That was Whittaker," said Kendall, placing the receiver back on to the cradle. "Apparently he has had some complaints about me." He shook his head. "Can you imagine. Complaints. About me."

Mollie looked at him. "Yes," she replied. "It's difficult, I know, but I can actually imagine such a thing, strange though that may seem. So what was he saying exactly?"

"Oh, just the usual, you know," Kendall replied. "Leave it alone, case closed. Keep out. Not wanted. You know the kind of thing."

She nodded. "Yes, I know," she replied. "You'll have to stop now though, won't you?"

Kendall shrugged. "I suppose so," he murmured. He did not sound too convincing. He smiled and looked at Mollie. "Do you remember the Richard Dawson case?" he asked. Mollie nodded. "Well, they tried to stop me investigating that one as well, didn't they?"

Mollie nodded once again. "Yes, they did," she replied. "But this is totally different. On that case it was Clark trying to stop you. The one who actually committed the crime. In this case it's Scotland Yard telling you to leave it alone. They can handle it perfectly well without you, I'm sure. After all, they are the oldest police force in the world."

Kendall shook his head slowly. "The circumstances might be totally different, I grant you," he said. "But they were wrong about Dawson. He had been murdered, hadn't he? Well they are wrong about Andrews as well."

Mollie shook her head. "You have to stop," she said. "You've no choice. Not this time. You've been warned."

Kendall smiled. "Don't worry so," he said "After all, what's the worst they can do? Deport me." He shook his head. "We're going home in three weeks anyway." He looked at Mollie and slowly shook his head. "Andrews was murdered, I'm absolutely sure of that. The Inspector knows it as well, I'm sure. He just won't admit it."

Mollie shook her head. She knew when she was beaten. "So what are you going to do?" she asked.

Kendall put his hands together and started to slowly nod his head.

166

"Well I actually think another visit to John Wyndham Collier might be interesting."

Chapter Twenty

Back At Travers Morgan

At first Collier had been reluctant to meet with Kendall for a second time. He was, after all, a very busy man. Furthermore he didn't really think that there was anything more to discuss.

"I think we covered everything on our first meeting, didn't we, Mr Kendall?" he had said. "I really don't see the need, do you?"

"Maybe not," Kendall replied. "The only thing is I don't actually believe that Bob Andrews committed suicide."

There was silence for a few moments. "You don't," said Collier. "So what else do you think, Mr Kendall?"

Kendall started to laugh. "Well, you know, you might think this fantasy but I actually think that he was murdered."

Once again there was a long silence. Kendall actually thought that he had been cut off. Suddenly, there was a crackling sound and then Collier was back on line. "Come along at three o'clock this afternoon," he said. "We'll talk about it then."

* * *

It was ten minutes to three when Kendall had arrived at Collier's office. As he entered the room the receptionist looked up. "Mr Kendall?" she asked. "Please take a seat." She casually pointed to a chair. She smiled. "Mr Collier has someone with him at present," she said. "He won't be too long."

Kendall smiled at her. "That's alright," he said. "I'm early." He sat down and selected a magazine from the nearby coffee table.

He started to flick through the pages. As he did so, the door to Collier's office suddenly opened. A young man came out. Kendall watched him for a moment as he walked over to the secretary. He bent down and said something to her. She looked up and smiled. He smiled back and then quickly walked out of the lobby area. There was something strangely familiar about him, Kendall thought. Then it suddenly occurred to him what it was.

That description, the one from the hotel reception. He thought for a moment or two. "*Well he was about your height, I think. Maybe a little taller. Much thinner, though.*" It fitted the young man exactly. Kendall shrugged. *So what*, he murmured. *That description fitted thousands of young men. Why should it be this particular young man?* Kendall shook his head. *Probably nothing more than a co-incidence.* Kendall shook his

168

head once again. He was not a great believer in coincidence.

"Mr Kendall," a voice suddenly called out.

Kendall looked up. The young girl at the reception desk smiled. "Mr Collier will see you now," she said. She looked at the door to her left. "You can go right in."

Kendall returned the magazine he had been reading on to the low table next to his chair. He casually glanced at his watch. *Twenty past three*, he murmured. He sighed and shrugged. *It wasn't too bad, though*, he thought. *In fact it could have been much worse. He could have refused to see me at all.*

Kendall stood up and walked towards the door. He stopped at the door, turned, looked at the young girl and smiled. She smiled back and nodded. He tapped on the door, opened it, and entered the room.

As the door opened, Collier looked up. "Do come in, Mr Kendall," he said. "I'm sorry to have kept you waiting so long. Have a seat."

Kendall sat down. "It's good of you to see me," he said. "I mean at such short notice."

Collier shook his head. "Kendall, I really didn't expect to see you again," he said. "I imagine that this is still unofficial."

Kendall nodded. "That's right, Mr Collier," he replied. "Just one or two questions ..."

"Just snooping around, are you?" said Collier interrupting. "I'm sorry to put it that way but that is what you detectives do, isn't it? Snooping, I mean. Nosing into other people's business?"

Kendall nodded and smiled. "I'm sorry you feel that way, Mr Collier," he replied. "Is that why you made the complaints about me?"

"Complaints," repeated Collier. He shook his head. "That's not exactly the word I would have used."

"Well it's certainly the word that Inspector Whittaker used," said Kendall.

Collier shook his head. "I merely made a formal approach to him, that's all," he explained. "After all, the police had investigated the whole matter. As far as they were concerned it was over and done with, and then you came along asking a lot of questions."

Kendall looked puzzled. "In those circumstances I'm rather surprised that you agreed to see me again," he said.

Collier shook his head. "You know, Kendall, I only agreed to see you the first time as a mark of respect. After all, you had been on the plane with Bob," he said. "It just seemed right at the time. But now I'm not too sure that there is any point in further discussion." He paused for a moment then shrugged. "So what is it this time?" he asked. "You said something about Bob being murdered."

Kendall nodded. "It's just a theory I have, Mr Collier. I'll get to it later," he said. "But in the meantime I just have one or two things to clear up, you know. A couple of things that don't quite add up."

Collier shook his head. "Kendall I really don't know what you are talking about, so if you could just be a little clearer."

Kendall nodded. "I understand that Andrews came to see you the day before he died."

Collier nodded. "That's right, he did. I had asked him to come."

"Can you tell me why?" asked Kendall.

"Well I really don't see that it is any of your concern, Mr Kendall, but it was about the missing money," Collier replied. "It was him. I just confronted him."

"What do you mean, it was him?" asked Kendall.

Collier smiled. "It was him," he repeated. "He had taken the money."

"What did he say?" asked Kendall.

Collier shook his head. "What could he say? He had been found out, simple as that. Naturally he denied it, but that was to be expected."

"You had proof?" asked Kendall.

Collier nodded. "I had my suspicions for some while," he said. "For a long while I just couldn't prove it. Then, just a few days ago, I got the proof I needed. That's why I instructed him to come over."

"And he never suspected anything," said Kendall.

Collier nodded. "Not a thing."

"So what was the proof?" asked Kendall.

"Mr Kendall, he killed himself, didn't he?" Collier replied. "Proof enough, I would say."

Kendall nodded slowly. "Maybe," he replied. "But there must have been other evidence."

Collier nodded. "Naturally there was other evidence," he replied. "In fact more than enough evidence, I would say."

"Could I see it?" Kendall asked.

Collier shook his head. "I don't think so."

"Any particular reason?" Kendall asked. "I mean, I imagine that you have handed it over to the police."

Collier shook his head and heaved a sigh. "Mr Kendall, this whole business has been difficult for the company, and for me personally," he explained. "Not only was my friend guilty of betrayal, and theft, but he is now dead." He paused for a moment and took a deep breath. "I'm sure that you will appreciate the strain that I have been under."

He paused once again and pointed to a photograph in a silver frame hanging on the wall. It was of two men on a yacht. "That's Bob and myself," Collier said. "Happier times, Mr Kendall." He shook his head once again. "I want nothing more now than to just forget the whole thing. To put it aside and go forward. The evidence will be locked away into the company archives, never to be mentioned again. The whole thing will be quietly forgotten."

"But what about the money?" said Kendall.

Collier shook his head and smiled. "The money is long gone, Mr Kendall. It will never be recovered," he replied. "No, mark my words, it's best just forgotten, for everyone's sake. You understand, I'm sure. There's no point in saying any more about it. It's over and Bob is dead. We can't get him back so there is nothing to be gained in blackening his name any further."

"Yes, of course I understand," Kendall replied. "That's very commendable of you. Very noble."

Collier smiled and shook his head. "Not at all, Mr Kendall," he said. "Bob was my friend, you understand."

Kendall understood perfectly. He nodded. "Of course, this whole thing must have been very distressing for you," he said. "I mean firstly the money disappearing, your friend being accused, and then he kills himself."

Collier nodded. "Very distressing, Mr Kendall," he replied. "Perhaps the worst time of my life."

Kendall nodded. "I can see that, sir," he replied. "The only thing is I'm not actually convinced that there was a suicide."

Collier sighed and shook his head. "No, you're not, are you?" he said. "You believe it was murder, yes?"

Kendall nodded.

"Kendall, don't you think this is all a little unnecessary and, may I say, deeply upsetting," Collier replied. "I mean, the police have investigated the case fully and they have reached their decision. A decision endorsed by the coroner, incidentally. Case closed."

Kendall nodded. "I know, I know. I hear what you say, but what can I do?" He shook his head. "The trouble is I'm stubborn. I'm also a worrier. I can't rest until every little item is cleared up. Then I can say case closed. Put it away. Finished. Done." He started to smile. "It's just me, I suppose. That's how I am."

Collier sighed once again. "Kendall, you know what I think?" Kendall smiled and shook his head. "I think you are nothing more than a nuisance."

Kendall smiled. "You know many people have said that in the past?" he replied.

"You are an irritation," Collier added.

"That has also been said several times in the past," said Kendall shaking his head. "And a lot worse besides, I might add."

"I can imagine, Kendall," said Collier.

Kendall smiled. "Quite often it is deserved, I have to say," he said. "Nonetheless, at the risk of being a bore, there are still a few little points that are baffling me. They are probably nothing significant and probably easily resolved."

"All right, Kendall, you win," Collier said. "Let's get on with it, shall we? I really have a lot to do."

"At our first meeting you mentioned that there had been a suicide note. Do you remember?" asked Kendall. "You had actually taken a copy, for insurance purposes, I think."

Collier nodded. "You have an excellent memory, Mr Kendall. It was indeed for insurance purposes," he replied. "So what about it?"

Kendall remained silent for a few moments. Then he started to frown. He looked up and shook his head. "You know, I still have a problem with that suicide note."

"Go on," said Collier. "What's the problem?"

Kendall looked at Collier. "Well, I have to say that I just cannot believe that it was suicide," he replied. "I think Bob Andrews was murdered."

Collier shook his head and looked down at the desk. He was breathing deeply. "Murdered, you say," he looked up. "I can't believe it, Mr Kendall. You must be mistaken." He paused for a moment. "What does Scotland Yard have to say about it?"

"Nothing," said Kendall in disgust. "They say that it was suicide. And that's an end to it."

Collier sighed. "Well they are probably right, you know," he said. "Maybe we should just leave it at that."

Kendall shook his head. "They are wrong."

"But what about the suicide note?" Collier asked. "Doesn't that show something?"

"Oh yes, the suicide note," said Kendall. "You know anyone could have written that note. Anyone at all, maybe the murderer himself wrote it."

"Why would they do that?" asked Collier.

"That's easy," said Kendall. "To make the murder appear like suicide."

Collier nodded. "Well, that's possible, I suppose," he replied. "But I can't go along with it. Bob just couldn't face the thought of going to prison, simple as that. He killed himself and that's the sad truth. I'm absolutely convinced of that."

"You know, that's another of my problems," said Kendall. "You were so definite, so sure. I was really surprised."

Collier looked puzzled. "Go on, Kendall," he said. "What's your problem?"

"You had known Andrews for many years," Kendall replied. "He was a good friend. You said so yourself just now." He paused and looked over at the photograph on the wall. "That looks like Sanibel," he said.

Collier looked at the photograph and nodded. "That's right," he said. "Three years ago."

Kendall nodded. "Great sailing there, or so I hear." He paused and smiled. "Not that I sail myself, you understand. I prefer solid ground underneath my feet."

"Kendall, if you could just get to the point," said Collier. "As I said, I am a busy man."

Kendall nodded. "Right. Right, so you are. I'll be as quick as I can," he replied. "As I was saying, Andrews was a good friend of yours. And yet you thought him capable of fraud. It didn't seem strange to you? You never doubted his guilt for a moment? I find that incredible, to say the least."

Collier shook his head. "You're not quite right there, Mr Kendall," he said. "Naturally, I was surprised. Extremely surprised. I could hardly believe it. It was so out of character. So unlike the Bob that I knew."

"But you never actually protested his innocence, did you?" said Kendall. "You seemed to have accepted the possibility very quickly."

Collier looked down and started to rub his hands together. "The evidence was just so overwhelming, I'm afraid," he said. "There was no error."

Kendall shook his head. "Mr Collier, Andrews never stole that money," he said. "I know that for a fact now. Mr Andrews never killed himself. And yet you never doubted his guilt for one moment."

Collier looked up. "Now, Mr Kendall, I've heard enough, so unless you have something else, I really must get on."

Kendall shook his head. "Mr Collier, Bob Andrews was murdered. Make no mistake about that," he said slowly. "He was murdered."

Collier shook his head. "Very interesting, I'm sure," he said. "Come back and see me when you have some proof."

Kendall smiled and stood up. "I'll do that, Mr Collier," he said. "If you can be sure of anything, be sure of that."

Chapter Twenty-One

Oliver Jones

Kendall gave a deep sigh. "This is completely crazy," he suddenly announced to nobody in particular. He sat upright and looked at Mollie. "Absolutely crazy."

Mollie looked up from the magazine that she had been reading. "I thought you were asleep," she said.

Kendall looked at her and shook his head. "I wasn't asleep," he replied. "I was merely thinking."

"Right," Mollie said. "Do you always snore when you think?"

"I do not snore," Kendall replied. "The very idea."

"Whatever," said Mollie. "Anyway, what is so crazy?"

"This whole thing," Kendall replied. "This alleged suicide. It just doesn't make sense to me."

Mollie looked at him and smiled. *Here we go again*, she thought. "So go on," she said, trying hard to sound interested. "I'm listening."

Kendall looked at her. "Do you remember how Andrews was on the plane?" he asked.

She looked puzzled. "How he was?" she repeated. "What do you mean?"

Kendall nodded. "There was something about that plane," he said slowly.

Mollie was now even more puzzled. "Something about the plane," she repeated.

"Or someone," said Kendall as he turned to face her. "Something worried him, that was obvious. But what was it?"

Mollie hated it when he was like this. Why couldn't he just say what was on his mind without all of this drawn-out build up. "What do you mean?" she asked.

Kendall shrugged. "You must remember how he looked," he replied. "You must have seen it."

Mollie shook her head. "Saw what?" she asked.

Kendall looked at her. "You must remember." Then he suddenly shook his head. "No, you don't remember, do you? You didn't see anything, did you?" He shook his head. "You were asleep."

She smiled and nodded. "That's right, I was asleep," she replied. "So what did you see?" she asked.

"Well he obviously saw something, or thought he had," Kendall replied. "Something that caused him considerable concern." He paused for a few moments as once again he recalled the look he had seen on

Andrews' face. "I would go so far as to say that he actually looked frightened."

Mollie looked up, startled. "Frightened," she repeated almost in a whisper. "Frightened of what?"

"There was someone on that plane that Andrews did not want to see," Kendall said in a hushed voice. "Someone that scared him. But who was it?"

Mollie shook her head. She looked at Kendall. He was staring across the room. She thought for a few moments. "Well, why not check with the airline?"

Kendall turned to face her but said nothing.

"I mean you could check the passenger list," she continued.

What a good idea, Kendall thought, wishing that he had thought of it himself. He shook his head. "No, I don't think so, not really. I'm mean what would that show?"

Mollie looked disappointed. *She thought that it had been such a good idea*. She shook her head. "It's a long shot, I know," she said. "But there might be a name. Something, who knows." She shook her head once again. *The chances of something meaningful turning up was remote, to say the lea*. "Oh, I don't know. It was just a thought." She shook her head a third time. "Oh, just forget it."

Now it was Kendall's turn to shake his head. "No," he said. "It might be worth a try, I suppose." He paused. "I mean, I don't expect it will show anything but well I'll give it a try. We've nothing to lose, have we? A few hours maybe, but well .... I'll go tomorrow."

* * *

It was just after eleven o'clock when Kendall walked into the Departure area in Terminal five at Heathrow Airport. As he slowly walked through the concourse, he was looking for the American Airlines desk. A security guard at the entrance had given him quite detailed directions. The problem was that they were too detailed and Kendall could not remember them clearly. *Was it over to the left after the Avis car rental, or was it to the right?*

Twenty minutes later Kendall saw the desk that he was looking for. Two people were standing at the desk, deep in conversation with the clerk. It looked as though it would last some time. He looked around and found a seat that allowed him a good sighting of the desk. He sat down to wait. As he did so he glanced at the clock. Ten twenty-seven. He looked at the desk. They were still deep in conversation. There was nothing for him to do but wait.

* * *

He wasn't sure what had woken him. Whether it was the sound of the child calling out or the ball hitting his leg. Whatever it was, he woke with a start, to be confronted by a young boy apologising for hitting him with his ball. Close behind was a young woman, the boy's mother, admonishing the boy and apologising profusely.

"I've told him to be careful, sir," she said over and over again. "He isn't really a bad lad, sir," she continued.

Kendall shook his head. "I'm fine, he said quickly. Don't worry about it. Accidents happen."

The young woman nodded and smiled. "I've told him that he shouldn't play with that ball in here, time and time again." She looked at the boy and shook her hand. "He's a handful, he is, and no mistake." She took hold of the boys hand and dragged him away. "You ever do that again and I'll ...."

Kendall watched until they were out of sight. He then looked at the clock. *Eleven-forty.* He shook his head. He could not believe it. He had been asleep for over an hour. He looked over at the desk. The official was alone. His visitors had gone. Kendall got up and walked towards the desk. The official looked up as he heard Kendall approaching. "Can I help you, sir?" he said.

Kendall nodded and smiled. "I certainly hope so," he replied. "I'm making enquiries about American Airlines flight 332."

The official smiled. "Oh, you need the Arrivals desk, sir" he said. "It's on the second floor. Take the stairs over there." He pointed. "At the top of the stairs, turn to the left, and you'll find it over on the far side." He looked at Kendall. "But it's not due until eight-twenty in the morning," he continued.

Kendall smiled again and shook his head. "It's last Sunday's flight that I'm enquiring about."

The official looked puzzled. "Last Sunday's flight," he repeated. "What is it that you want to know?" he asked.

"Could I see the passenger list, please?" Kendall asked.

The official shook his head. "I'm afraid I can't help you with that, sir," he replied. "Company rules, you understand."

Kendall moved closer to the desk. He glanced all around and took out his NYPD police bade. As he did so he suddenly remembered Whittaker's warning. "*You can't go round displaying it as though it were official. It has to stop, Kendall. If you use it again, you will be arrested.*"

Kendall gave a sigh and shrugged. He didn't mean it, not really. *What did his Sergeant say about him? His bark is worst than his bite.*

He opened the wallet and showed the badge to the official. He then quickly put it back into his pocket. The clerk had barely glanced at it. Kendall quickly glanced around and then placed his head close to that of the official.

"This is extremely important," he whispered. "We are working closely with Scotland Yard on this one." He looked around once again. "This comes directly from the top," he continued. "I can't say any more than that, but I need your co-operation."

The official looked up hesitant. "I don't know, sir," he replied. "It's company rules." He heaved a sigh and then he started to press the keys on the key pad. The monitor screen changed to show a long list of names. "I'm not supposed to divulge this kind of information," he said. "But if you happened to glance at the screen, then that wouldn't be my fault, would it?"

Kendall agreed that it would not, indeed, be his fault. The official nodded and turned the monitor slightly so that Kendall could get a better view. The official then stood up and slowly walked away, and stood at the rear of the area.

Kendall slowly looked down at the screen. He wasn't exactly sure of what he was looking for. It was just a list of names, a long list of names. There were one hundred and ninety-two names in total. There in seats 7A, 7B, and 7C was his own name, and that of Mollie and Robert Andrews. He continued to read down the list. Then he saw it. Allocated to Seat 31D was a name that he had been hearing a lot of late. Oliver Jones.

Kendall pushed the monitor back into its position and looked over at the clerk. "Thank you," he called out. "I'm all done here."

The clerk nodded back and Kendall walked away. So now what, he murmured. *So Oliver Jones was on the plane. What about it? Nothing but a coincidence.* Then he shook his head. *No.* Kendall didn't believe in coincidence, did he? *So Oliver Jones was on the plane. But why did it concern Bob Andrews so much? Why was he so frightened?* Kendall decided that it was time to have a word with Mr Oliver Jones.

* * *

"It's really very good of you to see me, Mr Jones," said Kendall as he was shown into Jones' office. "At such short notice."

Kendall had rung earlier that day to make an appointment. At first Jones had been reluctant. After all, what had it all got to do with him anyway? A perfect stranger. All right, so he had been on the same aircraft as Andrews. So what about it? But then Collier had said to humour him. "Just agree to see him," he had said. "What harm can it do?"

"All right, Mr Kendall," he had said eventually. "Four o'clock this afternoon. Although I can't see what you hope to achieve."

Kendall smiled. "You're probably right," he said. "Probably a total

177

waste of time, I expect. I'm just stubborn that's all. I just go on and on with things. I just can't let them go." He started to laugh. "One of my major failings, I'm afraid," he continued. "According to my friends, it's one of many. Anyway I'm sure that ten minutes of your time will clear up a few little niggles that I have."

* * *

"Ah, Mr Kendall, do come in," said Jones. "Have a seat." He pointed to a chair. Kendall sat down. "Now what can I do for you?" he asked

Kendall looked over to the corner of the room. There was a small drinks cabinet. *A double Scotch sounded good*, he thought. Somehow it did not seem likely that one would be coming his way any time soon.

He smiled and turned to face Jones. "I understand that you were the last person to see Bob Andrews alive," he said.

"Really?" Jones replied. "How do you come to that conclusion?"

Kendall nodded. "You were seen at his hotel shortly before his death," he explained. "Just as you were leaving."

Jones smiled and nodded. "Oh, I see," he replied. "Probably the maid, I expect. We had a bit of an argument, you know. My fault, really. I should have been, well let's say, more tolerant. It was all a bit ridiculous. I just blew my top. Crazy really, I don't know what came over me." He paused for a moment. "Anyway, yes, you are correct, I was at his hotel. We had an appointment that afternoon. You know, business."

"You say you had an appointment?" Kendall asked.

Jones nodded. "That's right," he replied. "It was some details about the Baxter deal, that was all." He paused for a moment. "Routine stuff, really."

Kendall nodded. "Go on," he said.

"Well there's not much more to say," Jones said. "We completed the business pretty quickly. As I say, it was all pretty routine."

"Then what?" asked Kendall.

"Well, let me see," said Jones. "We started to discuss the plans for the evening. We were going out to dinner, Bob and myself."

"Dinner?" repeated Kendall. "You were going out for a meal?"

"That's right," Jones replied. "But he suddenly changed and got very quiet." Jones shook his head. "He was in such a bad mood. Anyway he said that he wouldn't be going out that evening and we should scrub the dinner. Perhaps another time, he said, but he didn't sound convincing."

"So why do you think he cancelled?" asked Kendall.

Jones shook his head. "I don't know what happened," he said. "Perhaps I had said something but I don't think so. He was certainly depressed about something."

"And you don't know what?" Kendall asked.

Jones shook his head once again. "Whatever it was he never said," he replied. "Some news from home perhaps, I don't know. All he said was that he didn't know what to do. I didn't know what it was and I didn't press him." He shook his head and heaved a sigh. "Perhaps I should have. I might have changed things. I mean, perhaps I could have helped. It never dawned on me that he was in financial difficulties. I mean embezzlement never entered my mind. Not Bob. He wasn't the type. And then to commit suicide like that, certainly not. It just doesn't bear thinking about. If only I had tried to do something."

"So when did you leave?" Kendall asked.

Jones nodded. "It was about one twenty-five, one-thirty, something like that," he said. "That's when I lost my temper with the maid. Silly of me. Not like me at all. I just lost it, that's all. Disappointed maybe."

"Disappointed?" repeated Kendall, puzzled.

Jones nodded. "Because Bob had cancelled the dinner maybe," he explained. "I had been looking forward to it. We were good friends, Bob and I. I hadn't seen him for about six months or more." He paused and shook his head. "Anyway, I asked Bob to ring down for a taxi for me, and that was the last time I saw him."

Kendall nodded. "Really," he said. "I understood that you actually returned to the hotel later. Apparently you had forgotten something." Kendall shook his head. "I don't know what."

Jones looked puzzled and shook his head. "Sorry, return did you say?" he replied. "Not me, I'm afraid. I never went back."

Kendall nodded. "My mistake, sorry," he said. "I get a bit mixed up sometimes." He smiled. "By the way, do you know what tablets Andrews was taking?"

Jones looked puzzled. "Tablets?" he repeated shaking his head.

"Yes," said Kendall. "For his asthma."

Jones shook his head. "I've no idea," he replied. "I didn't even know that he had asthma. All I do know is that he took an overdose but I don't know what tablets they were, sorry."

Kendall nodded. *It was no more than he had expected.* "By the way, there's another small thing that just keeps nagging, you know," he said. "It's terrible when it gets like that. I can't do anything until it's cleared up."

"Go on, Mr Kendall," said Jones. "What is it?"

Kendall shrugged. "It's about the plane," he said.

"The plane," repeated Jones obviously, puzzled.

"Yes, the one from Miami," explained Kendall. "The one that Andrews was on."

"Oh that one," said Jones. "You were on it as well I understand."

"That's right, I was," said Kendall. "So how do you know that?"

"Simple, Collier told me, that's all," Jones said. "No mystery."

179

Kendall nodded. "Of course, I should have guessed," he said. "I was actually sitting next to Andrews. Small world."

"As you say, small world indeed," said Jones. "So what about it?"

"I understand that you were also on that flight," said Kendall.

Jones started to nod his head. "That's correct," he replied. "I had been in the States on business, just for a few days."

"I see," said Kendall. "I imagine that you must have seen Andrews during that time."

Jones shook his head. "No, sadly not," he said. "There just wasn't the time, I'm afraid. As I said, I was only there for a few days."

Kendall nodded. "Unfortunate," he said. "I wonder if he had known that you were in the States."

Jones shook his head. "I doubt it," he said. It was only a administrative problem that needed sorting. It didn't involve Bob."

Kendall nodded. "I understand perfectly," he said. Then he paused for a moment. "It's strange though."

Jones looked at Kendall. "Strange," he repeated. "What is so strange?"

Kendall looked at Jones and shook his head. "It's strange that you didn't come over to Andrews, on the plane, I mean. Being colleagues, I would have thought that it would have been quite natural to meet up for a chat."

Jones started to smile. "Oh, I see." He then shook his head. "The strange thing is I never even knew that Bob was on that plane. I only found out a few days ago. Collier told me. Can you believe that?"

Kendall smiled, not entirely sure that he could believe that. "Well that clears that up anyway," he said. "Another one of my little niggles." He nodded. "There's one last thing, Mr Jones."

"Go on," said Jones.

"Collier describes you as his right hand man," Kendall said. "What did he mean by that?"

Jones looked at Kendall and smiled. "Simple," he replied. "He relies on me, that's all. If Collier wants something, I would arrange to get it."

"I see," said Kendall, slowing nodding his head. "And if he wanted something done?"

"Then I do it," replied Jones.

"Anything?" asked Kendall.

"Pretty much," Jones replied smiling. "Only a fool turns Collier down."

"Right," said Kendall. "That's very helpful. Thank you, Mr Jones. Thank you very much." He stood up. "I don't need to delay you any further. I'm sure that you have far more important things to do." He turned and slowly walked towards the door. *Just as I thought*, he murmured.

180

Chapter Twenty Two

Why Would He Lie?

It was almost one o'clock by the time that Kendall arrived back at his hotel. Mollie was waiting for him. "Well, here you are at last," she said as he came into the room. "Are we going to lunch or not?" she asked.

Kendall looked at her and started to frown.

"You said that you would be back by twelve," she continued. She looked at her watch. "It is now ten minutes to one. Where have you been?"

Kendall looked at her and shook his head. "He lied to me," he said quite simply. "He lied, why?" He shook his head. "Why would he do that?"

Mollie looked at him. Suddenly she knew that lunch had been cancelled, or at least postponed, until he had got this particular item, whatever it was, out of his system. "What are you talking about?" she asked. "Who lied to you?"

"Jones," he replied, shaking his head. "Oliver Jones. He lied to me. A whole string of lies."

"Gaggle," Mollie interjected. "It's a gaggle, not a string."

Kendall looked at her and shook his head. "Gaggle?" he repeated.

Mollie smiled and nodded her head. "A gaggle of lies," she explained. "That's what you called it."

Kendall smiled as he remembered. "That's right, I did say that," he said. "Well whatever, Oliver Jones has just come out with a whole gaggle-full." He paused for a moment. "Firstly he said that they had an appointment, him and Andrews." Kendall shook his head. "Andrews told us that he didn't know who he was seeing, remember."

Mollie nodded. She remembered the conversation. "He was actually not looking forward to the meeting," she recalled. "So he was lying, or perhaps he was merely mistaken," she suggested. "Does it matter?"

Kendall looked up at the ceiling and shook his head. "He wasn't mistaken. He knew exactly what he was saying. Why would he lie?"

"I don't know," said Mollie. "You're the detective. You tell me."

"Well I can think of a pretty good reason," said Kendall. "Besides it wasn't the only lie he told. There were several others."

Mollie shook her head. "Go on, do tell." *The sooner this was over, the sooner they could get lunch*, or so she hoped.

Kendall took a deep breath. "All right, here goes. Number two. Jones said that he and Andrews were good friends."

"Well," Mollie said, trying to sound interested.

"Jones said that he didn't even know that Andrews had asthma," Kendall continued. "Doesn't that sound just a bit odd to you?"

Mollie looked puzzled for a moment. "Do you know the entire medical history of your friends?" she asked. "I certainly don't."

Kendall shook his head and glared at Mollie. "I would certainly know whether they had something serious like asthma," he replied.

Mollie wasn't entirely convinced.

"And another thing, he said that they were going out to dinner."

"Who was?" Mollie asked.

Kendall sighed. "Andrews and Oliver," he replied. "Jones said that they were going to dinner that evening."

"So," said Mollie. "They were going to dinner. What's the problem with that?"

"So" Kendall repeated. "So?" He shook his head. *What was the problem?* he suddenly wondered. "Well, he said that Andrews suddenly cancelled it. Why would he do that?"

Mollie shook her head. "Well perhaps Jones had said something to him," she suggested.

"Like what?" asked Kendall.

"Well perhaps he said, Bob, we know all about the money," Mollie replied. "Well, something like that anyway. Andrews panicked and, well, we know the rest, don't we?"

Kendall shook his head. "Jones never said that or anything like it."

"How do you know?" asked Mollie, beginning to wish she hadn't come on this trip after all. It wasn't working out the way she had hoped.

"Jones told me that Andrews seemed depressed, that's all," Kendall replied. "Depressed. He said nothing about the missing money. Besides, if they knew that Andrews had been helping himself to the Company funds, why hadn't Collier said anything days ago, when Andrews went to see him?"

"Well perhaps he had said something," Mollie suggested, hoping that this would soon be over and they could go to lunch. She was beginning to feel quite hungry.

Kendall shook his head once again. "That was days ago," he replied. "Are you seriously suggesting that Collier told Andrews that they knew all about it? Then some days later Andrews books tickets for the theatre and then kills himself."

Mollie smiled. "It doesn't really sound realistic, I have to admit."

"It isn't realistic," said Kendall. "Besides, what was it that Collier had said to Andrews." He paused for a few moments trying to remember.

"Andrews said that Collier had told him he should just forget about it," said Mollie.

Kendall nodded. "That's right," he said. "He did say that." He looked at Mollie and smiled. "And another thing," he continued. "Jones said that he never returned to the hotel that day. Another lie."

"Well maybe he didn't go back," Mollie suggested. "Maybe the maid was mistaken. Or maybe she was lying. Getting her own back because of the argument."

Kendall sighed. "How would she get her own back merely by saying that he had come back?" he asked. "I mean what would be the point?"

Mollie couldn't think of a good reason but she was still sure that she was right. *The maid had been mistaken.*

"What about the taxi driver?" Kendall said. "He told me that Jones had gone back to the hotel."

Mollie shook her head. "No, he said that Jones walked back towards the hotel. That doesn't prove that he did go back."

Kendall shook his head. *He hated to do it but he had to admit that she had made a valid point.* It did not prove that he went back to the hotel. He shook his head again and started to smile. "Oh no, Jones went back to the hotel, I'm sure of that." He shook his head again. "He lied all right. But why? What did he have to hide?"

"I don't know," said Mollie. "Perhaps to give the impression that a perfectly normal evening had been arranged, but then Andrews is depressed about something."

"Depressed enough to commit suicide," said Kendall.

Mollie shook her head. "I don't know," she said. "I suppose …."

She was interrupted by the telephone ringing.

* * *

Kendall shook his head and slowly replaced the receiver. He looked at Mollie. "That was Whittaker," he said. "He's had a call from Collier. Formally complaining about my visit to see Jones."

Mollie looked puzzled. "But Jones would never have agreed to see you without Collier's say-so, would he?"

Kendall thought for a moment and slowly nodded. "You know, that is odd," he said. "You are absolutely right. Collier must have agreed."

"So why the complaint?" Mollie asked.

Why indeed? thought Kendall. He started to tap his hands together, and then heaved a sigh.

"So what else did Whittaker say?" asked Mollie.

"Just the usual," Kendall said. "He told me to keep out of it and leave it to the experts." He paused once again, and started to laugh. "Experts, that's what he said. Experts."

"I suppose you'll have to stop, then," said Mollie. "You've no choice."

Kendall smiled at her. "I suppose you're right."

Mollie smiled. "We're on holiday, don't forget," she said. "And besides, Scotland Yard are pretty good at this kind of thing. I think you can leave it to them."

Kendall looked at her. "Maybe, but they are wrong this time, plain and simple," he said slowly. "He was murdered. There's no doubt in my mind."

It was at that moment that Mollie knew that the holiday was over. Kendall was already back at work. "How do you know that?" she asked

Kendall turned his head and raised his eyebrow. *How do I know?* he murmured. *She dares to ask, how do I know?* He sighed deeply. "I just know, that's all."

Mollie frowned and started to tap. A sure sign that she wasn't prepared to be palmed off by platitudes. *I just know*, was not good enough.

Kendall knew the signs. "All right, all right," he said. "Let's think about it, shall we?" He paused for a few moments. "Andrews told me himself that he had come over on business. He was an accountant and he had been checking the figures." He paused for a moment. "What was it that he actually said?"

Mollie shook her head. "I was asleep, remember."

Kendall smiled. He remembered. "Anyway he told me that he had been checking the books and that he had found a number of apparent discrepancies. Collier actually told me there were some fifty million little discrepancies, give or take. That's how much could not be accounted for. That was the extent of the problem."

Mollie thought for a moment and then nodded. "There you are, then," she said. "That's why Andrews killed himself. He was embezzling from the company." She smiled. "Stealing. Fraud. Altering the books. Call it what you like."

Kendall shook his head. "Someone was altering the books, I agree, but it wasn't Andrews."

Mollie looked puzzled. "Why not him?" she asked.

"If it was him, why come over here and risk being found out?" Kendall asked. "Would you?" Mollie said nothing but continued to look puzzled. "Why not just take the money and run. Hide."

Mollie continued to look puzzled. Kendall shook his head, "He didn't take the money but he knew who did." He paused for a moment. "He didn't kill himself, he was murdered."

"But what about the tablets that he had?" Mollie asked.

Kendall shook his head. "Andrews never brought them with him. Those tablets were brought over to England certainly, but not by Andrews."

"How do you know?" Mollie asked, wishing that this would all suddenly go away and they could get on with their holiday once again. *She hadn't done half the shopping she had planned.*

Kendall looked at her and nodded. "I told you what Devaney said about the prescription," he said. "It wasn't made out by Andrews' doctor."

Mollie sighed as she remembered.

"Do you remember when Andrews was closing the overhead compartment on the plane?" Mollie looked blank. "He had just put my bag away."

Mollie shook her head. "I was asleep," she replied. "Or at least I was pretending to be asleep." She smiled. "So he had put your bag away. Well?"

He was staring down the aisle. "And he saw someone, someone he knew."

"That's right," said Mollie. "It was Oliver Jones."

"Correct, Oliver Jones," repeated Kendall.

"What about it?" asked Mollie.

"Why didn't they speak to each other?" Kendall asked. "Why not meet up on the plane? I mean the whole trip there was nothing. No one came over to him."

"Well, perhaps Mr Andrews knew the person but didn't actually like them," Mollie suggested. "Perhaps the other person did not like Andrews. Perhaps they deliberately avoided each other."

Kendall started to smile. "That's a very good point," he said slowly. Then he shook his head. "Problem is that we know that the other person was Oliver Jones, remember," he said. "And according to him, he and Andrews were good friends."

Mollie shook her head. "Perhaps he lied," she suggested.

Kendall looked at her, and frowned. "Do you really think so?" he asked.

"It certainly seems possible," Mollie replied.

Kendall started to rub his chin. "So Jones lied," he said slowly. "So why would he lie?"

Chapter Twenty-Three

Kendall Takes A Boat Ride

Five minutes later the telephone rang once again. Kendall looked at it for a moment. "If that's Whittaker ringing again, he'll get a piece of my mind," he said.

Mollie shook her head. She looked worried. "No," she said. "Don't say anything. Just agree to keep out of it, that's all." She started to smile. "Just say that he won't hear another word from you."

Kendall shrugged. The telephone continued to ring. "Let it ring," he said angrily. "I've had enough of Scotland Yard for one day." He turned away. The telephone continued to ring.

"Tell him that as far as you are concerned, it's over and done with," Mollie said, almost pleading.

Kendall shook his head. "I'm not answering it, simple as that."

"You must answer it," Mollie said. "It could be anyone."

Kendall shook his head. "Mollie," he said. "Who knows that we are here? No one. It must be Whittaker again."

"You don't know that for sure," she said. The telephone continued to ring. "It might be reception about something."

Kendall sighed and shook his head. He had to admit that it might be reception. Or it could be the travel agent regarding their planned trip to Ireland. It might also be about his surprise booking for the theatre later in the week. *Mollie was right, it could be anyone.* He shook his head. *It was definitely Whittaker,* he murmured. "All right, I'll answer it if you insist." He picked up the receiver. "Kendall here," he said angrily.

"Mr Kendall," a voice said. "You don't know me but I was a friend of Bob Andrews."

Kendall didn't like telephone calls from complete strangers. "Who are you?" he asked.

"Mr Kendall, Bob Andrews never committed suicide," the voice continued. "He was murdered."

"Who are you?" Kendall repeated.

"I understand that you are over here on holiday," the voice said completely disregarding the question. "You might enjoy a boat trip down the Thames to Greenwich. There's one leaving Westminster Pier at three o'clock this afternoon." The line went dead.

Kendall continued to stare at the receiver for a few moments. He then turned and looked at Mollie. "You were right," he said. "It wasn't Whittaker."

She looked puzzled. "So who was it?"

Kendall shook his head. "Someone suggesting we take a little boat ride on the Thames."

"Who?" she asked.

Kendall frowned and shook his head. "I don't know."

Now it was Mollie's turn to frown. She looked at him, her head turned to one side. "You're not going to, are you?" she asked slowly.

"Going to what?" Kendall asked.

She shook her head. "You know what," she replied.

Kendall stared blankly. "The boat ride?" he said innocently.

Mollie nodded. "Yes, the boat ride."

"Well, it's a nice day," Kendall said. "It might be fun."

* * *

As Kendall stood on the pier waiting to board the boat, he wondered where the mysterious caller was. Kendall glanced all around. *Was he here amongst the crowd waiting to board*, he wondered, *or was he already on the boat? Perhaps he hadn't actually arrived yet and was still on his way.* Kendall looked at his watch. There was still ten minutes before they were due to depart. He sighed. *How would he recognize the caller anyway*, he wondered. He had no idea what the person looked like.

Suddenly Kendall began to feel unsure. Perhaps he should have insisted that the caller wore a white carnation as a buttonhole or maybe carried a rolled up newspaper. He looked around once more and shook his head. How did he know that the caller would be coming anyway? Perhaps he never had any intention of coming. Perhaps the boat ride was just a friendly suggestion. Kendall shook his head. He hated calls from strangers, especially when they told you nothing. *He didn't know the person's name. He didn't know what he looked like. And why this trip?*

He shook his head once again. *Why this particular boat anyway? Why not any boat, any day?* He had always said that he would never agree to meet with perfect strangers. Yet here he was. *Gullible, that's what he was.* Kendall heaved a sigh. He looked at his watch once again. *Five more minutes*, he murmured. He continued to look all around him, although exactly what he was looking for was uncertain.

"All aboard, now," came an announcement.

Suddenly Kendall felt someone nudge him hard in the side. He turned. It was Mollie. "Come on," she said. "We're moving."

People started to move slowly forward along the gangplank ready for departure. Kendall was still looking for his mystery caller. *Surely he would have been approached by now*, he thought. He stopped and shook his head. *They just weren't going to come*, he murmured. *A total*

187

misunderstanding on my part, he thought, *nothing more.*

"Keep moving there," a voice called out.

Kendall looked up startled. "Sorry," he called out and quickly moved forward.

A few minutes later everyone was settled on board. There was a loud crackling sound as the public address system came on. "Welcome on board," a voice suddenly announced. "Our trip today downstream to Greenwich Pier should take about an hour. So please make yourselves comfortable, we are just about to leave. We hope that you will have a pleasant trip. Should you have any questions, please ask any member of the staff who will be pleased to help in any way."

There was the sound of an engine revving loudly and then a violent shudder as the boat began to move. As the boat slowly pulled away from Westminster Pier there was the crackling sound once again. "Just before we leave look over to your right. There is the old County Hall. At one time home to the Greater London Council. Now it is a conference centre and hotel."

Kendall raised his camera to his eye, focused for a few moments and then pressed the button.

"Here we go again," Mollie murmured. More sightseeing. Then she suddenly noticed it, peering out of Kendall's pocket. She was beginning to dread seeing it, but there it was, clear as day. *A Pocket Guide To London.* She sighed. She shook her head. She couldn't complain too much though. At least as long as he was doing the tourist thing, he wasn't being a detective.

There was another loud crackling nose. "Next to it you can see the London Eye," the voice continued "Also known as the Millennium Wheel, at a height of 135 metres it is the largest Ferris wheel in Europe."

Kendall took another photograph.

For a short while the only sound that could be heard was the chug chug of the engines. Then suddenly there was more crackling and the voice returned. "Now you can see the Royal Festival Hall."

Kendall quickly turned the pages of his guide book and started to read. "Opened in 1951 as part of the Festival of Britain celebrations." Mollie glared at him. He stopped reading. She would have loved to have grabbed that old guide book and thrown it into the Thames.

"So where is our mystery man?" she asked. "It doesn't look like he has come."

Kendall shook his head. He had no idea where the mystery man had got to. "I don't know," he replied. "I expect he will contact us when it suits him." He paused for a moment. "Of course, he might not even be on the boat," he continued. "We might not actually see him until we get to Greenwich."

Mollie shook her head. And we might not see him at all," she said. "It was probably just a scheme to get you out of the way for a while. Who was it anyway?"

Kendall shook his head. *A scheme to get him out of the way.* The thought had never entered his head. "Perhaps it was Whittaker," he suggested. "To keep me out of trouble."

Mollie shook her head. "It wasn't Whittaker," she replied. "If he wanted you out of the way, he could just arrest you and throw you in a cell." She shook her head once more. "So who was it, then?" she asked.

Kendall shook his head slowly. "I've no idea," he replied.

"You don't know who it is," Mollie said disbelievingly. "It could be anyone."

Kendall nodded in agreement. "I know, I know," he said. "It was foolish of me to agree. I just never thought. That's all. It was just what he said."

"Just exactly what did he say?" asked Mollie.

Kendall looked at her for a few moments. "He said that Bob Andrews never committed suicide," he replied. "He said that he had been murdered."

Mollie shook her head. "And that's it," she said. "We are here just because someone, some complete stranger, said that Andrews had been murdered." She looked up at the sky. "I can't believe it." She looked back at Kendall. "I just can't believe it."

Kendall shrugged his shoulders and smiled. "Hey, he probably won't come anyway, so why are we worrying," he said. "It's a nice day, let's just enjoy the trip."

Mollie nodded and smiled. She could hear the words, but she knew that Kendall was thinking along completely different lines. "Aren't you going to take some more photographs, then," she asked.

Kendall looked at her and nodded. "Why not?" he said. He held up the camera once again. "That's a great shot," he said. "All three in one go. The Royal Festival Hall, the London Eye, and County Hall." He pressed the button. "Great."

* * *

"Shortly we will be passing the Tower of London and Tower Bridge," the guide announced. "The Tower of London is often identified with the White Tower, the original stark square fortress that you can see. It was built by William the Conqueror in 1078. The tower's primary function was as a fortress, a royal palace, and a prison."

"That's probably where Whittaker will put you, I expect," said Mollie.

Kendall looked at the building for a few moments and shrugged.

189

"Could be," he said and smiled.

"Tower Bridge is a combined bascule and suspension bridge." The voice was off once again. "The bridge consists of two towers which are tied together at the upper level by means of two horizontal walkways."

"You know, I don't think anyone is going to come," said Mollie. Kendall said nothing but continued to read from the guidebook.

"Over to the right is HMS Belfast, now permanently moored in the Pool of London," the voice continued. "It is one of Britain's wartime battleships and saw action in the Atlantic Ocean."

"Did you hear what I said?" Mollie said. "I don't think anyone is coming. This was definitely a trick. Nothing more."

Kendall looked up from his guidebook and smiled at her. "And why would anyone play such a trick?" he asked. "What would be the point? What would they gain?"

She sighed and shook her head. "I don't know. You're supposed to be the detective," she replied. "Maybe it was to get you away from the hotel for a few hours." She paused for a moment, and then she started to laugh. "Perhaps it was Whittaker after all."

Kendall smiled and shook his head. "There'll be someone waiting for us at Greenwich, you'll see," he said.

"You might be right," she said. "But I still think it was just a trick, to spite you, or to cause trouble." She shook her head. "I don't know."

* * *

Ten minutes later the Millennium Dome came into view. The boat slowed down and began a wide turn.

"We will soon be arriving at Greenwich," a voice called out. "Please ensure that you take all of your belongings with you. We hope that you enjoyed your trip and hope that you will sail with us again in the future."

Kendall looked at Mollie. Well, here we are," he said. "We'll soon know if I'm right. If there's no one waiting for us, then we have been taken for a ride. Literally."

As the boat pulled alongside Greenwich Pier, Kendall could see someone watching him closely. The boat came to a stop and the passengers started to disembark. Kendall stood back and allowed Mollie to go first. He followed close behind.

"Mr Kendall," a voice called out. Kendall looked round. It was the man who had been watching him. "I'm Paul Sharp," he said. "I believe you want to speak to me."

Chapter Twenty-Four

Paul Sharp

Mollie recognised the young man instantly. He had been the man that had met Andrews at the airport. He was also the man that had been at the corner close to the Travers Morgan building the other day. "I've seen you before, haven't I?" she said "You were outside the Travers Morgan building, weren't you?"

Sharp nodded. "That's right, he said. "You are very observant."

Kendall looked puzzled. "And I'm sure that I've seen you at our hotel." Mollie continued. Once again Sharp nodded. Kendall continued to look puzzled.

"And you were at the doctor's office, weren't you?" Mollie once again

Sharp nodded once again. "Right on all counts," he replied.

Kendall shook his head. "You've been watching us," he said disbelievingly. "But why?"

Sharp nodded his head and smiled. "Bob told me about you when I met him at the airport," Sharp started to explain. "I asked him how his flight had been. He just said fine and told me all about you." He shook his head. "He seemed to think you were all right but I'm afraid I wasn't at all convinced."

"Why not?" asked Kendall.

"Bob was convinced that he was being followed," Sharp replied. "Right from when he left home, back in Florida, he was sure that someone was watching him. He had seen you a few times at the airport and for a while he actually thought that it was you." He paused for a moment. "Then, of course, he saw you on the plane. For a while he wasn't sure what to do. Then he thought he saw someone at the back of the plane."

Kendall nodded "I remember," he replied. "The look on his face. He seemed frightened almost."

Sharp nodded. "He thought that it was Oliver Jones."

Kendall nodded. "It was Jones," he said as he looked at Mollie and smiled. "I checked the passenger list with the airline."

Sharp nodded. "Yes, it was Jones, and suddenly you were all right. But then I saw you at the office the other day." He paused. "The day you went to see Collier. Suspicions arose in my mind. Perhaps you weren't okay after all. I wasn't so certain. I didn't know if you were working for Collier. Or whether I could trust you."

Kendall shook his head. "And can you?" he asked. "Trust us, I mean."

Sharp nodded. "I think so," he said. "In fact I don't really think that I had any real doubts. It was only that trip to Collier's office that threw me."

"So what changed your mind?" asked Kendall.

Sharp started to laugh. "Funnily enough, it was Collier himself."

Mollie looked puzzled. "Go on," she said.

Sharp smiled. "After you left, I went to see Collier. He told me that he had just been visited by a nosy, interfering private detective asking a lot of questions." He paused for a moment and smiled. "Butting his nose in where it wasn't required was what he actually said." Sharp paused once again and shook his head. "I've never seen him so annoyed. He was fuming. So I knew that you couldn't be all bad."

Kendall smiled. "I often have that effect on people," he said. "It's my fatal charm."

Mollie nodded in agreement, then she looked at Sharp. "But why would anyone be following Mr Andrews anyway?" she asked.

"Because of the discrepancy in the accounts," suggested Kendall. "Someone with something to hide."

"That's about right, I would say," said Sharp.

"Incidentally, I thought that you were in Saudi Arabia or somewhere,"Kendall said.

Sharp looked puzzled and shook his head. "Who told you that?"

Kendall shook his head. "Collier," he replied. "He said that you wouldn't be back for two or three weeks."

Sharp shook his head. "It's the first I've heard about it," he replied, and started to smile. "It would seem that tales of my foreign travels are greatly exaggerated. But it's so like Collier. Anyway, how about a drink?" he suggested.

It sounded like a good idea to Kendall and he nodded his agreement. Mollie wasn't quite so sure but suspected that she had no real choice and had to go along. "There's a nice place just along here," he continued as he started to walk away from the pier. "It's by the river. It's a very old place, you might enjoy it." He smiled "Apparently Nelson used to go there."

Mollie wondered who this Nelson character was exactly. *And just because he went there, was that any reason why they should go as well?* And who was this Paul Sharp anyway? She looked at Kendall. He merely smiled back at her.

A few minutes later Sharp stopped. "Here we are," he announced. He looked at the building in front of him. "The Trafalgar Tavern," he continued. "Built in 1807 to commemorate the Battle of Trafalgar." He suddenly paused and looked at Kendall. "I'm sorry," he said. "Have you any idea of what I'm talking about."

Kendall smiled and nodded. Mollie pushed forward. "No," she said quite simply. "None whatsoever."

Sharp started to smile. "Horatio Nelson?" he said quite simply. Mollie shook her head. Sharp sighed and looked at Kendall. "Do you know who I'm talking about?"

Kendall shook his head. "Sorry, I've never heard of him," he replied. "But, there again, he's probably never heard of me either."

Sharp sighed and shook his head. "Not likely," he replied. He's been dead for two hundred years." He started to laugh. "Not to worry," he said and waved his hand in the air. "Shall we go in?" Without waiting for an answer he walked to the door and went in. Kendall and Mollie quickly followed.

Even at the early hour the bar was extremely busy. "Very popular with the students," Sharp explained. "The college is located just around the corner."

Kendall looked at his watch. It was just ten minutes after four. "Obviously College has finished for the day," he said. Sharp did not hear him as he continued to push his way towards the bar. As he did so he glanced around looking for somewhere to sit. "There," he called out pointing towards the window. A small group was just getting ready to leave. "Mollie go and grab that table. I'll get the drinks."

Mollie looked in the direction indicated and started to make her way through. Suddenly she heard Sharp calling to her. "What will you have?" She stopped and turned. "A Martini," she called back. "Dry." She continued heading towards the table, arriving just as the people were leaving. She grabbed three chairs, sat down and waited.

Meanwhile Sharp and Kendall were standing at the bar, waiting to be served. "Is it always like this?" Kendall asked.

Sharp looked at Kendall and then looked around. He smiled and shook his head. "This is a quiet day," he replied. "Sometimes it gets quite busy."

Kendall looked at him and started to laugh.

"Yes, sir," said the barman. "What can I get you?"

Sharp looked at Kendall. "What will it be then?"

"Scotch and a little water," Kendall replied. "Very little."

"What about something to eat?" Sharp asked. Kendall nodded.

"What about a ploughman's?" Sharp suggested.

Kendall shook his head. "A ploughman's?" he repeated.

"Cheese and pickle, and French bread," Sharp explained. He slowly looked around. "There," he said. "See that chap in the corner."

Kendall turned and looked over to the corner. He nodded. "Yes," he said.

"He's having a ploughman's," Sharp explained.

"That looks fine," Kendall said. *He would have preferred a double cheeseburger and French fries, but cheese and pickle would do.*

Sharp placed the order, and a few minutes later he and Kendall were slowly making their way over to where Mollie was waiting.

* * *

"So what do you think?" Sharp asked.

Kendall looked puzzled. "Think," he repeated. "About what?"

Sharp shook his head, and smiled. "Here," he replied. "The pub. And that view." He looked out of the window. Then he turned back to face Kendall. He was no longer smiling. "I understand that you are a private detective, Mr Kendall. Is that correct?"

Kendall nodded. "That's correct," he replied. "Over here on holiday."

Sharp nodded. "How are you enjoying it so far?" he asked.

"Well, apart from trips to Scotland Yard and visits to Travers Morgan, it's great," said Mollie quickly.

Sharp nodded. "I understand that you have been making a lot of enquiries," he said.

Kendall nodded once again but made no response.

"I'm guessing that you saw my letter to Bob. That's why you rang me."

Kendall nodded. "That's correct," he said. "Your letter was found in my shoulder bag. I can only imagine that your friend Bob put it there for a reason."

Sharp took a drink. "A pretty good reason, I would say," he replied. He heaved a sigh and took another drink. "You know there's no way that Bob would kill himself." He shook his head once more. "I've known Bob for almost eight years. He would no more embezzle from the company than fly to the moon."

"It has been known," suggested Kendall.

Sharp shook his head. "Yes, it has," he agreed. "Many a time, I know. But not Bob."

"Why not Bob?" asked Mollie.

Sharp looked at her for a moment. "It's hard to put into words," he replied. "But if you knew." He paused. "If you had known Bob you would know the answer to that. It's all about values. Old-fashioned values and standards." He paused once again. "Bob was well paid, you know. He did a good job and he got a fair reward. That's all he wanted. He was not a greedy man. Oh, he was ambitious, that's for sure. He built up to the position he had and he deserved it. He worked hard for what he got." He shook his head and took a drink. "But he was not greedy. More to the point, he was honest."

Kendall looked at Sharp. "If it's any help, Mr Sharp, we don't think he committed suicide either." He took a drink. "In fact, just like you, we think that he was murdered."

194

Sharp looked at him, and started to smile. "That's good to hear," he said. "My thoughts exactly."

"Incidentally, did you know that Andrews suffered from asthma?" Kendall asked.

Sharp nodded. "Oh yes, I knew," he replied. "He had suffered from it for years, although I understand that lately it hadn't been too bad."

Kendall nodded. "Do you know what medication he was taking?"

"Medication," Sharp repeated, and shook his head. "As far as I was aware he wasn't actually taking anything," he replied. "He hadn't been taking anything for the past few months, I'm sure of that."

"Why are you so sure?" Kendall asked.

"Simple. He told me," Sharp answered. He thought for a few moments. "He said that he was so fed up with taking stuff that a) had nasty side effects, and b), they didn't work anyway." He paused once again. He shook his head. "Poor old Bob," Sharp continued. "He said he wasn't going to bother any more. The tablets were a complete waste of time."

Mollie smiled. "Do you know if he ever tried any alternative medicines?" she asked.

Paul shook his head. "I don't think so," he replied. "But I don't really know."

"When did he tell you all of this about the tablets?" Kendall asked.

"It was earlier this year. The middle of January," Sharp answered. "I was over in Miami for a few days. On business. We met up for a drink. It was then that he told me that he had thrown the tablets out. He would never use them again. That's what he said. He was quite emphatic about that."

"Do you know what tablets they were?" Kendall asked.

Again Sharp shook his head. "Sorry. I've no idea," he replied. "But it was probably one of those long unpronounceable names." He shook his head once again. "Sorry, I can't help. Was it important?"

Kendall shook his head. "No, not really," he replied. "It was just another of those loose ends I wanted to clear up, that's all."

"Sorry, I couldn't help you," Sharp said as he drained his glass.

Kendall stood up. "Let me get you another," he said. "What was it?"

Sharp looked at his empty glass. He looked at Kendall. "That was a pint of Harveys Best Ale," he said, licking his lips.

Kendall smiled. "Harveys Best Ale," he repeated, making it sound almost like a foreign language, which indeed it was to him. He quickly drained his own glass. "Same again for you, Mollie?" She nodded. Kendall turned and made his way over to the bar. It was beginning to get clearer. Many of the students had now gone and it was still too early for the business caller.

Mollie watched as Kendall disappeared into the crowd. She turned towards Sharp. "So exactly who was this Nelson guy?" she asked

* * *

A few minutes later Kendall arrived back at the table carrying a tray of drinks. Sharp and Mollie were deep in conversation. Mollie looked up as Kendall approached. "Mr Sharp ..."

"Paul," Sharp interrupted. "Please call me Paul."

Mollie smiled. "Paul has been explaining a bit more about his work," she said. "It's all high finance. Quite fascinating."

Kendall sat down. "I can imagine," he said. "I've just had a little example of high finance myself." He smiled. "Over there with the barman." He shook his head. "I'll never get used to this currency." Sharp smiled.

Kendall passed the drinks around. "That's yours, Mollie," he said placing a glass in front of her. "And a pint of Harveys best for you." He took a drink. "Now, Paul, about your letter. You said that there were only three possibles who could have altered the accounts."

Sharp nodded. "That letter was written a few days a ago," he replied. He pulled his chair closer to the table and leaned forward. "As far as we could see there were only three. Oliver Jones. Then there's Harry Gale, Collier's Solicitor, and then, of course, there's Collier himself."

"And maybe Bob Andrews himself," suggested Kendall.

Sharp shook his head. "No, not Bob," he said.

Mollie looked at Sharp. "Perhaps all three were in it together," she suggested.

Sharp shook his head. "Collier was certainly not averse to using people for his own purposes, and certainly Gale and Jones worked for him." He paused and shook his head again. "But Collier would never ever take them, or anyone else, on as a full partner. Never ever."

"So which of the three do you think it was?" Kendall asked.

"Well actually I had narrowed it down to just two, Jones and Collier," Sharp replied.

"What about who was it you said?" Kendall paused. "Gale? Harry Gale?"

Sharp nodded. "Harry Gale," he repeated. "A sly one if ever there was," he replied. "For a while it looked a possibility. But I checked up on his share dealings." He shook his head. "He just wasn't in the same league as the other two."

"So who do you think it was?" asked Kendall.

"I'm more and more convinced that it was Collier himself," Sharp replied.

"Any particular reason?" Kendall asked.

Sharp sighed. "Collier is the one with the brains," he replied. "Jones, on the other hand, is, shall we say, a little lacking in that department." He started to smile and then took a drink. "Certainly he could go where Collier went, but he needs to be led."

"Anything else?" Kendall asked.

Sharp nodded. "I've just been doing some checking into Collier's finances," he replied. "Its early days, and it's pretty inconclusive, but there are certain coincidences that seem to crop up every so often."

"Coincidences," Mollie repeated. "Like what?"

Sharp shook his head. "As I say, it is early days, and it may not mean anything at all," he replied. "It might just be coincidental. Nothing more."

Kendall shook his head. "Paul, I don't believe in coincidence," he said. "So just what's on your mind?"

Sharp nodded. "All right, here goes," he replied. "Certain money transfers in the company accounts seem to correspond with financial transactions in Collier's own personal accounts."

Mollie looked puzzled. "Could you explain that a little?" she asked.

Sharp smiled and nodded. "All it means is that where certain payments appear to have come out of the company accounts, a similar sum has suddenly appeared in Collier's bank account," he explained. "They're not exact, you understand, but the amounts and dates are fairly close."

"Fairly close?" repeated Kendall. How close?"

"Well maybe within a few days. A week say," Sharp explained. "The amounts are within a few hundred pounds."

"Just close enough to warrant further investigation?" suggested Kendall.

Sharp nodded. "Exactly," he said. "That's not all, though."

Kendall nodded. "Go on," he said.

"I have also done some checking on the market," Sharp started to explain. "Collier has been buying up a lot of stock, especially in rival companies."

Kendall smiled as he remembered what Collier had told him. *I've been buying up stock in our competitor companies, gradually over the past few months.* Kendall nodded. "That's right," he said. "He actually told me that himself. He had bought a lot of stock and actually had a controlling interest in a number of companies."

Sharpe started to smile. "That's correct," he said. "He now controls seven of his competitors." He paused for a moment. "The thing is, as far as I can see, each block of shares was purchased within a few days of a withdrawal from the company accounts." Then he paused and shook his head. "The only thing, it's a similar story, although not to the same scale, when I looked at Oliver Jones' finances."

Kendall shook his head and started to rub his face. "Who precisely is

Oliver Jones?" he asked.

Sharp started to grin and nodded. He took a drink. "Jones is a nasty piece of work if ever you saw one. If Collier wanted something done, Jones did it. No argument." He paused and nodded. "It certainly looks like Collier is our man but that is only my suspicion. I can't prove it. Not yet. I've some more checking to do when I get back. Then I'll know for sure."

Kendall looked puzzled. "When you get back," he repeated. "Are you going away?"

Sharp nodded his head. "I have a day off tomorrow," he replied. "I'm planning on going down to Sussex to see my parents. I'll be back sometime in the evening." He looked at Kendall and smiled. "You might like to come along," he suggested. "You'll see a bit of the English countryside, you'll love it."

Kendall smiled and nodded. *He would have liked to have joined him.* A trip down the country sounded good. For a brief moment or two he was tempted to invite himself along. Then he suddenly remembered that he had promised to take Mollie to Harrods. He sadly shook his head. The thought of going shopping at Harrods did not appeal to him that much, but he really had no choice, it had to be Harrods. He had promised. Given his word. *And he was nothing if not a man of his word.*

"Sorry, no can do," he replied. He shrugged his shoulders and sighed.

"Pity," said Sharp, shaking his head. "It might have been fun. Perhaps another time."

Kendall nodded. "Perhaps," he replied, far from convinced.

"I'll be leaving at about ten, ten-thirty in the morning," Sharp continued. "I should be back by five, or six. I'll call you tomorrow evening."

Kendall smiled once again. "Have a good trip," he said quite simply.

"I will, don't you worry about that," said Sharp as he checked his watch. "Anyway, I'd better get going, I'm sorry to say." He stood up from the table. "Goodbye, it was nice to meet you both." He turned around and walked away.

Kendall watched Sharp for a few moments. He then looked at Mollie. "There, I told you it wasn't a trick, didn't I?" he said.

She smiled. "No, it wasn't a trick," she agreed. "In fact it was a very pleasant afternoon."

"It was indeed," said Kendall. "Very pleasant."

Mollie suddenly looked puzzled. "One thing, though," she said. "Why did you ask him what tablets Andrews took? I thought you already knew what they were."

Kendall nodded. "You're right, I do know. They were Syanthol," he replied. "Andrews told me."

"Mollie was more puzzled than ever. "Well then?"

Kendall smiled. "I just wanted to be sure that Sharp didn't know," he said.

Mollie was still puzzled. "Why?" she asked. "I still don't understand."

Kendall took a breath. "It's very simple," he said. "The fact that he did not know about them completely clears him from any involvement with the alleged suicide."

Mollie still looked puzzled. "Did you think he might have been involved, then?" she asked.

Kendall looked at Sharp as he reached the exit door. He stopped, turned and waved. Kendall waved back. "To be honest, I had no idea," he said. "But it was, of course, a strong possibility. I just needed to be sure whose side he was on."

Chapter Twenty-Five

A Fatal Accident

It was late in the afternoon by the time Kendall arrived back at his hotel. He was surprised to see Inspector Whittaker sitting in the lobby.

Kendall smiled and walked over to him. "Inspector Whittaker," he said. "What a pleasant surprise."

The Inspector glared at him. "Kendall, you've been at it again, haven't you, despite my warnings."

Kendall looked puzzled. "At it again, Inspector?" he repeated. "I don't know what you mean."

"American Airlines this time, I understand," the Inspector continued. "Making enquiries about a certain flight. Showing the old badge once again, I'm told." He paused for a moment and shook his head. "What exactly do you hope to achieve by all of this?" He opened his notepad. "That airline clerk could be in serious trouble, you know."

Kendall opened his mouth to explain.

"Kendall this isn't one of your silly detective games, you know," the Inspector interrupted. "This is real life."

"Inspector, Oliver Jones was on that plane along with Andrews," Kendall said, as though that explained everything.

Whittaker smiled and nodded wisely. "So he was on the plane," he replied. "Do you think that means anything in particular?"

Kendall shrugged and sighed deeply. "Well, doesn't it mean anything to you?" he asked. "I mean, that name keeps cropping up."

"I think you're exaggerating a bit, Kendall," the Inspector replied. "So he was on the same plane, that's all. There's nothing unusual in that. He had probably been in America on business, I expect. Just happened to be on the same plane back. What about it?"

"Maybe so," said Kendall. "But why didn't he make contact with Andrews on the plane? After all, they were colleagues."

Whittaker shook his head. "How do I know the answer to that?" he said. "Perhaps he didn't realise that Andrews was on the plane. Who knows?"

Kendall sighed and shook his head. "Why was he even in America?" he asked.

"I told you," said the Inspector. "He was probably there on business." Suddenly he started to smile. "Or perhaps he just thought he would get a cheap trip, you know a few days away on company expenses," Whittaker continued. "Just like I said about Andrews, remember?"

Kendall nodded. *He remembered.* "So, he just happened to be on the same plane, is that correct?" Whittaker nodded. "And he just happened to be at Andrews hotel the same afternoon that he was killed."

"The afternoon that he committed suicide, you mean," corrected the Inspector.

Kendall shook his head. "I said killed, Inspector, and that's what I mean."

The Inspector smiled. "You never give up, do you?" Kendall shook his head. "Nothing more than coincidence, in my opinion," he said. "They were colleagues, weren't they? It would be quite natural for them to meet."

Kendall smiled. "Perhaps, but I'm not convinced," he said. "If you knew me, Inspector, you would know that I'm not one for coincidence."

Whittaker looked at Kendall and nodded his head slightly. "All right, I'll tell you what I'll do. I'll check up and have a word with Jones. Does that make you any happier?" he said. "No promises, mind. I'll be in touch. Where will you be tomorrow?"

Kendall thought for a moment and then sighed as he remembered the plan. "Shopping," he said in disgust. "Harrods. I promised Mollie a day at the shops. Should be back by five, I hope."

The Inspector nodded. "Until tomorrow, then," he said.

* * *

The following day Paul Sharp came out of his apartment shortly after ten-thirty. He was much later than he had intended. He had meant to be out by ten at the latest. He shrugged and sighed deeply. It couldn't be helped, could it? He was late and that was that. He would just have to make up for lost time once he was on the motorway. He ran out of the house and quickly down the stairs to the street. He was surprised to see Oliver Jones standing at the corner, by his car.

"Oliver?" he said, puzzled. *Perhaps Collier had changed his mind*, he thought. *Perhaps the Windsor trip had been cancelled*. He shook his head. If it had been cancelled, Collier could just have rung. "What a surprise, Oliver, I didn't expect to see you," Sharp said. "What are you doing here?"

"Morning, Paul," Jones said, ignoring the question completely. "John wanted you to have this file." He handed a thick buff folder to Sharp. "I don't know what it is but it's for the Windsor office." He paused for a moment. "It's very important, apparently," he continued.

Sharp took hold of the file. "Thanks," he said. "I'll be sure that they get it." He opened the car door and threw the file onto the back seat. "Anyone in particular?" he asked as he turned back.

Oliver Jones had already gone.

Sharp heaved a sigh and got into the driver's seat. He really was not looking forward to this trip. He heaved another sigh, as he thought of the conversation that he had with Collier the previous night.

* * *

It had been almost a quarter to ten when the telephone had rung. Sharp had just settled down to watch a film on the television. It was one that he had particularly wanted to see. He looked up at the sound. He glanced over at the clock. The telephone kept ringing. *Who on earth could that be*, he murmured, *at this time of night*. He sighed. He decided to ignore it. The telephone kept on ringing. He looked at the telephone again and sighed a second time. It was probably only one of those irritating calls telling him that he had won something or other, or trying to sell him something. *Where do they get my number from anyway*, he wondered. He looked back at the television screen. The telephone kept ringing. He shook his head. *Why doesn't the Government do something about this kind of thing?* He shook his head once again. Whatever the reason was, it wasn't going to help him, not right now. The phone kept ringing, and ringing. He knew that he was beaten. He knew that he had no choice. Whoever it was just wasn't giving up.

He stood up and went over to the telephone. He picked up the handset. "Hello," he said. "0208 946 2 ..."

"Paul, is that you?" a voice interrupted. It was John Collier. Sharp shook his head. It would have been better if it had been one of those prize draw calls after all. At least he could have just hung up. "Yes, John," he replied, trying not to sound too weary. "What is it?"

"You weren't asleep, were you?" the voice asked. "I never realised it was so late."

"No, I wasn't asleep," Sharp replied, wishing that he had gone out for a drink instead of staying home. He shook his head once again. Collier knew exactly what time it was, to the minute. Sharp shook his head a third time. *To the second.* "I was just watching a film on television, that's all."

"Not that old Robert Mitchum one," Collier asked. "On TCM, is it? What's it called?"

"'Build My Gallows High'," Sharp replied. *That old Robert Mitchum one*, he murmured. *This was a classic. One that he hadn't seen for a long time.* In fact it was such a great film that he had decided to tape it onto video. Sharp looked at the screen. "The very same," he replied. He suddenly glanced down at the video recorder. "*Oh no*," he gasped audibly. He had forgotten to switch it on. "I'm sure that you didn't call to discuss what was on the television," he said. "What did you want, John?"

202

There was silence for a few seconds. "I'm sorry about this but something has come up," Collier replied. "I need you to go to the Windsor office tomorrow."

"You're kidding," Sharp retorted.

There was another short silence. "Sorry, Paul," Collier replied. "This is no joke, I'm afraid."

Now it was Sharp's turn to remain silent for a while. *He could not believe it*. Was he actually asleep and this was a bad dream. He shook himself. He wasn't asleep and it wasn't a dream.

"But, John, it's my day off," he protested.

"I'm sorry, Paul," Collier continued. "I know, but this is important. I wouldn't ask otherwise, you know that."

Sharp wasn't convinced about that but he knew that there was nothing he could do about it. *Windsor, here I come*, he muttered.

"Sorry, Paul, did you say something?" Collier asked.

"No," replied Sharp. "Nothing important."

"Fine," said Collier. "I really am sorry about all this, but I'll make it up to you, you'll see." He paused for a moment or two. "Anyway, have a good trip," Collier continued. "Oh, and enjoy the rest of your film." The line went dead.

Sharp continued to stare at the handset for a moment or two. *So much for my day off*, he murmured.

* * *

So much for my day off, Sharp murmured. Instead he had to go to Windsor. It would take hours to get across town. All right, once he had got onto the M4, then admittedly it would get a little easier, a little less congested, as long as there weren't any roadworks. But the actual journey through London would not be pleasant. He sighed once again. He had no choice. The sooner he got going, the better. At least the weather was good. That was something. The forecast had said rain but there was a clear blue sky with a gentle breeze. He checked his watch. It was ten-forty. If he could get to the M4 by twelve, he would make Windsor by about one. Just in time for lunch at his favourite haunt, the River Tavern down by the Thames. He nodded. *It might not be that bad after all*, he murmured. He was feeling better already. He closed the car door. Secured his seat belt. Checked his mirror, signalled and slowly pulled out from the kerb.

As he had expected, the traffic through London was bad. In fact if anything it was worst than ever. It seemed that the whole of London was heading west. Added to that was the usual helpings of roadworks and accidents.

On paper, the journey was straightforward enough. He needed to

203

take the A41 just to the west of Regents Park, straight through to Marylebone Road. He nodded. *That's where it would all go wrong.* There were roadworks all the way along the route, something to do with renewing the water mains, or something. He smiled and shook his head. As far as he could remember, there was always something being done on that stretch of the road. If it wasn't water mains, it was electricity cables. If it wasn't the cables, it was probably the drains, or maybe a repair, or perhaps resurfacing, you name it.

Once he was on the Marylebone Road he followed it through Edgware Road, then Bayswater, into Westway, and on into Western Avenue. He checked his rear view mirror. There was a black Toyota right behind him. He thought nothing of it. At Hanger Lane he turned south onto the North Circular Road. He never noticed that the black Toyota behind him had also turned south, forty yards behind. Just to the north of Kew he turned west onto the M4, The Great West Road. The black Toyota, now twenty-five yards behind, also turned west.

It was twelve forty-five by the time he got onto the M4. He wouldn't reach Windsor now until one-thirty at the earliest, maybe even two o'clock. He would have to cut lunch short. *Pity, he had been looking forward to that.* He hadn't really wanted to make this trip at all, but lunch by the river was to have been some kind of compensation, A reward, if you like. But even that seemed to be fading away as time continued to pass by. He heaved a sigh. *He should have left earlier, he just knew it.*

He shrugged. At least he had reached the motorway at last. That was something. He could now start to put on some speed. All through London he had crawled along at no more than twenty miles per hour, slower in some areas. Now he could really open up and see how fast he could go. He checked his mirror and pulled out into the middle lane. He checked his speed. Gradually it began building up. Thirty, forty, fifty. He suddenly found himself too close to the car in front and gently applied the brakes. Sharp could see that the road ahead of the car was clear. He started to tap the steering wheel impatiently. "Why don't you move?" he murmured.

The car in front stubbornly refused to speed up. "Come on," he cried out. "Get a move on." There was no response from the driver in front. *So what was their problem*, he wondered. *Perhaps they didn't know how to change into third gear.* He shook his head and glanced at his speedometer. Not quite forty. He looked at the car in front. *Hey, this is a seventy miles per hour limit, don't you know*, he murmured. Obviously the driver was not aware of that fact because the car continued at its present speed.

Sharp shook his head once again, and sighed deeply. His lunch break was getting shorter and shorter. If this carried on, he wouldn't arrive until midnight. Normally Sharp was a tolerant, patient man, but this was all too much. He was already running late, this was only adding to that delay. Sharp started to feel for the horn. Should he press it, he wondered. He was sorely tempted. He shook his head. No. He sighed deeply. He just could not bring himself to do it. "Please get moving, will you?" he pleaded. Nothing happened. He checked his side mirror. The outside lane was still busy. There was no opportunity to overtake, not yet anyway. He slowed down to thirty-five, waiting for a gap to appear in the outside lane. It wasn't long coming. He pulled out, tyres screeching, smoke billowing from the exhaust. His speed started to build once again. Fifty, fifty-five, sixty. His foot was hard to the floor. He changed into fifth gear. The car shot forward. Sixty-five miles per hour.

There was a low muffled sound from underneath the car. The car shuddered. Sharp put his foot hard on the brakes. Nothing happened. The car hit the centre safety rail and bounced back across onto the middle lane. The driver of an articulated lorry following behind had no chance of stopping. The lorry ploughed into Sharp's car at sixty miles per hour. The car spun around, flipped, and rolled over. Then there was another muffled sound as the petrol tank exploded.

Chapter 26

No Word From Sharp

It was just a few minutes before six o'clock by the time that Kendall got back to his room. He was exhausted after his trip to Harrods. *How anyone could possibly say that they enjoyed shopping, he would never know. They just could not be serious. They could not be normal.* He absolutely hated it, now more than ever. He had never seen so many people in one place. Nobody had told him that there was a sale that day. *Such pushing, and shoving, he thought, that would not have looked out of place on the football field.* Just to get to a so-called bargain. He shook his head. Naturally Mollie had enjoyed it and had come back laden.

He shook his head again. He felt terrible. His head was aching and his feet hurt. He slumped into a chair. He glanced at the clock. He had a little over an hour before he was due to meet Mollie for dinner. He reached for the remote control and switched on the television.

"The much anticipated increase in fuel duty, announced by the Chancellor in his Spring budget, comes into effect at six o'clock this evening," the newsreader reported. "The price of petrol has now reached the £6 per gallon figure." There was a slight pause. The reporter looked up and continued. "Traffic on the M4 was severely disrupted earlier today when a Jaguar FX was involved in a collision with an articulated lorry. The driver of the car was pronounced dead at the scene. The lorry driver was taken to Slough General Hospital suffering minor cuts and shock. It is expected that he will be discharged later this evening. It is understood that defective brakes on the sports car were the cause of the crash. A witness reported that they thought they had heard a muffled sound, like a small explosion, a few seconds before the accident. A police spokesperson said that investigations were being carried out to find the cause of the accident."

Kendall shook his head. Dreadful, he murmured, *simply dreadful.*

"Tension mounted on the West Bank today," the newsreader continued. "After a suicide bomber ..."

Suddenly the telephone rang. Kendall looked away from the television and over to the telephone. "That'll be Sharp," he whispered. He stood up and walked over to the television and switched it off. Then he reached for the telephone.

"Hello Paul," he said. "This is Kendall."

"Hi, Kendall," a voice replied. It was not Sharp. It was Detective Inspector Terrence Devaney of the Miami Police Department.

"Devaney," Kendall said. "What do you want?"

"Well there's a nice greeting if ever I heard one," replied Devaney. "What do you want, indeed."

Kendall sighed. "All right, Devaney, all right," he said. "So how are you and what do you want?

There was a slight pause. "Oh, I'm fine," Devaney replied. "I was just wondering how you were, that's all. You know, just checking." There was a slight pause. "How's the holiday?" Devaney continued. "I haven't received my card yet. You know the 'Glad you're not here' one."

Kendall started to smile. "Oh, the holiday is coming along quite nicely, thank you," he replied. "How's it going with you, by the way? Caught those jewel thieves yet?"

There was a long pause. Kendall could hear Devaney clearing his throat and sighing deeply. "Not yet," he replied. "But we are getting closer every minute. It's only a matter of time now."

Kendall nodded. "Of course it is," he replied sarcastically. "The question is how much time."

Devaney sighed once again. "We're getting there," he said. "We are closing in, I tell you. They won't get far, we'll catch them soon enough."

"Right," said Kendall. "But you haven't caught them yet."

Devaney started to cough once again. "Well, not exactly," he replied. "But we are very close."

"That's good to hear," replied Kendall. "Incidentally, how close is close?"

Devaney coughed loudly. "Well ....."

"Go on," coaxed Kendall. "I'm listening."

Devaney grunted loudly. "Well it seems that they might actually be in England," he said quickly.

"England. You're kidding, right?" Kendall repeated. "England?"

"Yes. England," said Devaney.

"How can that be?" Kendall asked. "Do you mean to say that they managed to avoid your steel-like cordon, your iron grip, and escaped the country."

There was a very long pause. "I was just wondering if you might...." said Devaney.

"I'm on holiday," Kendall quickly interrupted.

"Yes, sure, of course you are. I know that." Devaney said. "Don't you think I know that. I just thought that with your connections. Your friends at Scotland Yard, you know."

Kendall sighed. "Go on."

"I've just sent an email to you at the hotel. There are full descriptions and photographs," Devaney explained. "If you could just help, you know."

"Yes, sure," said Kendall. "You know, I just knew that you would never manage without me." He paused for a moment. "It's understandable, of course," he continued smugly.

"Okay, okay," said Devaney. "Will you help or not?" There was a long pause. "Kendall, are you still there? Kendall?"

Kendall sighed. "I'm still here."

"Will you help me or not?" Devaney asked once again. "You owe me one, remember?"

Kendall sighed. *Yes, he did remember.* "I expect so," he replied. "I'll see what I can do. I'll be in touch." He hung up. Somehow, though, he didn't really think he would have much influence with Inspector Whittaker. In fact he didn't think he had any influence with him at all.

* * *

There was a sudden knock on the room door. Kendall looked over and smiled. Perhaps Sharp had decided to call on him instead of telephoning. He stood up, hurried over, and opened the door. Standing in the corridor was one of the young porters. He was holding a large brown envelope.

"This message came for your earlier today, sir," he said as he handed the envelope to Kendall.

Kendall took hold of the envelope and thanked the young man. He started to reach inside his pocket. He wanted to give the lad a tip. *One of those pound coins would do*, Kendall thought. Eventually he pulled out a handful of coins. He started to fumble through, trying to find one, without success. "Take something," he said, holding out his open hand.

The boy sighed. "That's all right, sir," he said, and quickly walked away. Kendall shook his head and returned to his room. He walked over to the small table on the far side of the room and sat down. Carefully he opened the envelope and emptied the contents onto the desk. There were two photographs and a typed sheet describing two men that the Miami Police Department were anxious to meet up with.

Kendall shook his head and started to tap the photographs. *If Devaney thinks that I'm going to spend my holiday searching the country for these two, he is very much mistaken*, he murmured. He shook his head once again and slowly returned the documents into the envelope. He nodded his head. *Yes, he did owe Devaney a favour, that was certain. It wouldn't actually do any harm if he passed the documents over to Whittaker, would it?* he thought. *It might not do any good but it certainly wouldn't do any harm*. He nodded. "Besides, a promise is a promise," he said.

At that moment the telephone rang once again. *This had to be Sharp*, he thought. He picked up the receiver. "Hi Paul," he said.

"Kendall," a voice answered. It was not Paul Sharp.

"Inspector," Kendall replied. "I was just thinking about you."

"I've been trying to get hold of you since five," the Inspector continued. "You said that you would be back by then."

"Sorry about that," Kendall said. "I've only just got back. The crowds were …"

"Forget the crowds," the Inspector interrupted. "I've spoken to Jones, as you suggested."

"And," said Kendall. "What did he have to say?"

"Well, firstly he admits that he was on that plane."

"What did I tell you?" said Kendall enthusiastically.

"Apparently he had been in America for a few days on business," the Inspector continued. "As I had imagined, if you recall."

Kendall had to admit that the Inspector had indeed mentioned something of the kind. "Did he see Andrews on the plane?" he asked.

"No, he didn't," the Inspector replied. "In fact it was a great surprise to him to learn that Andrews had been on the same plane. So nothing significant there, I'm afraid."

Kendall sighed. "What about the hotel?" he asked.

"He was there all right," said the Inspector. "He admits that. He was merely visiting a work colleague who was over here for a few days. There was some business to discuss. There's nothing wrong with that. Perfectly natural, I would say."

"Perhaps," agreed Kendall reluctantly. "Did you ask him why he went back to the hotel?"

"He never went back, Kendall," said the Inspector. "You must be mistaken."

"But the taxi driver," Kendall said. "He told me."

"No, Kendall, you're wrong," replied the Inspector. "What he actually said is that Jones started to walk back in the direction of the hotel." There was a short pause. "That's not the same as he definitely went to the hotel. The driver had to admit that he really didn't know where our Mr Jones did go."

Kendall shook his head. *Once again the Inspector was wrong. Jones went back to the hotel. The maid said so.*

"Have you spoken to the maid?" he asked. "She'll tell you."

"Not yet but I will rest assured," said the Inspector. "I'll let you know what happens. In the meantime, no more amateur sleuthing, please, Mr Kendall." He paused and sighed. "Just leave it to us. We'll get along a lot better, and a lot quicker, that way, I'm sure." The Inspector hung up.

Kendall continued holding the handset for a few moments. He shook his head. *Whittaker was missing the whole point. He just couldn't see it.* He started to tap the handset and then slowly placed it on to the cradle.

He suddenly realised that he hadn't said anything about the two men Devaney wanted to find. It probably didn't matter, Kendall thought.

There was absolutely no way the Inspector would ever find them anyway.

* * *

"Did Paul ring you yet?" Mollie asked as they sat down to dinner later that evening.

Kendall looked at her and shook his head. "No," he replied. "No, he hasn't. There's been no word and I'm getting a little concerned."

Mollie nodded. "He's probably busy, that's all," she said. "He'll probably ring in the morning."

Kendall nodded. "Maybe," he replied. "If he doesn't ring by ten, I'll call his office."

Mollie nodded once again and picked up the menu. "Now, what shall we have this evening?" she said. "I'm famished. Shopping really takes it out of you, you know."

Kendall smiled. *Oh yes, he knew, but if it were that tiring, why do it? Anyway, he certainly needed something to build his strength back.* He looked at the menu and then glanced across at the neighbouring table. He nodded and returned his attention to the menu. The way he was feeling he was tempted, very tempted, to have the steak, well done, with lashings of onions and mushrooms.

Mollie shook her head. "I wouldn't if I were you," she said. "A very bad idea."

Kendall shook his head. *Quite honestly he couldn't care less how bad the idea was. He was determined. Tonight he would put his foot down and stick with it.*

"Tough," he announced. "Steak is what I fancy, and steak is what I shall have."

Mollie sighed deeply. "You know all that oil and fat is bad for you," she said.

Kendall sighed. "Tough," he repeated quite simply.

Mollie shook her head and sighed. "On your own head be it, then," she said. "Don't say I didn't warn you." She returned to studying the menu. "I shall have the grilled chicken, and some broccoli, and a jacket potato." She closed the menu and placed it on the corner of the table. She then looked at Kendall.

Kendall smiled and shook his head. "The steak," Kendall replied. He then looked up and waved over to the waiter.

210

Chapter Twenty-Seven

So It Was Murder

The following day there had still been no word from Sharp. "I'm getting worried," said Kendall. "Do you think anything could have happened to him?" he asked Mollie.

Mollie smiled and shook her head. "Why should anything have happened to him?" she asked. "He'll be in touch, don't worry. He'Car crash on the M4, a Jaguar FX, brakes failed.s probably just busy, that's all."

Kendall shook his head. "I'm sure there's something wrong," he said.

Mollie placed her hand on Kendall's shoulder and smiled. "Why don't you ring him?" she suggested. "He probably hasn't had a chance to call. You'll see."

Kendall nodded. "Maybe," he said. He reached for the telephone and dialled the number.

"Travers Morgan," a voice answered. "Can I help you?"

"Oh yes, please," Kendall replied. "Could you put me through to Mr Sharp? Mr Paul Sharp?"

There was silence for a moment or two. "Hello," said Kendall. "Are you still there?"

"Yes sir," the voice responded. "I'm still here."

"Could I speak to Mr Sharp?" Kendall asked.

There was another pause. "I'm afraid that Mr Sharp is dead, sir," the voice said. "He was killed in a car crash two days ago."

"Car crash," repeated Kendall startled.

"Yes, sir, on the M4," the voice explained. "A few miles east of Windsor."

"Did you say two days ago?" Kendall asked. "That was his day off, wasn't it?"

"Well it was originally, sir," the voice replied. "But there was a change of plan, I'm afraid. Mr Sharp had to make a business trip to our Windsor office. It was arranged at short notice." There was a slight pause. "Can I put you through to someone else?"

Kendall suddenly remembered the news item. *Car crash on the M4, a Jaguar FX, brakes failed.*

* * *

Kendall slowly replaced the handset. "He's dead," he said almost in a whisper. "Paul Sharp is dead."

Mollie looked at him. She shook her head. "What happened?" she asked.

Kendall looked at her and shook his head. "A car crash," he started to explain. "The brakes failed. He's dead, just like that."

Mollie started to cry. "It was an accident," she said.

Kendall looked up and started to frown. "Accident," he repeated. "Maybe, but somehow I just don't think so." He shook his head once again, slowly reached for the telephone, and dialled. "Inspector Whittaker, please," he said when his call was answered.

"Can I tell him who is calling, sir?" the operator asked.

"Kendall. Tom Kendall."

"Will he know what it is about?" the operator asked.

Kendall nodded. "Oh yes," he replied. "He'll know, I'm sure."

The line went dead for a few moments. Then Whittaker came on the line. "Kendall, the very man," he said. "I want a word with you. I've just been speaking with Doctor Lennox."

"Oh well, he can't possibly be complaining, not this time," Kendall replied. "I haven't been to see him again."

"It's nothing like that," Whittaker explained. "He is still talking about your first visit. You know when you were asking about the red mark on Andrews' arm."

"Yes, that's right," said Kendall. "I thought that maybe it was ..."

"You thought that it might have been from a hypodermic needle," Whittaker interrupted.

"That's right, I did," said Kendall. "It looked just like one to me. I believe that Andrews was killed not by an overdose of tablets." He paused for a moment. "There were no tablets, there never were," he continued. "I believe that the drug was injected into his bloodstream and that is what killed him."

Whittaker sighed. "Well, you will be pleased to know that the doctor actually thinks you could be right," he replied. There was a pause and another heavy sigh. "Kendall, this is, shall we say, difficult for me," he continued. "The thing is, I could have been wrong." There was another long pause. "I am now reviewing the case from the very start. I I don't suppose that you could spare some time to discuss it with me, could you? It would be greatly appreciated."

"But I thought you wanted me to stop asking all the questions and to leave it to you," Kendall replied.

"Kendall, are you prepared to help or not?" the Inspector cried out.

Kendall smiled. "Thirty minutes," he said. "I'll be there in thirty minutes."

"Fine," said Whittaker. "I was hoping that you would say something like that."

"That's all right, Inspector," Kendall replied. "I wanted to speak to you about Paul Sharp anyway. That's why I rang."

"Sharp," Whittaker repeated. "The man killed in that M4 crash the other day?"

"That's the one, Inspector," replied Kendall.

"You didn't know him, did you?" the Inspector asked.

"We were out with him only a couple of days ago in a pub in Greenwich," Kendall explained. "So what happened, then?" he asked.

"We don't know exactly," said the Inspector. "But it looks like it was an accident."

Kendall started to frown. "An accident, did you say?" he replied. "A bit of a coincidence, wouldn't you say?"

"Coincidence," Whittaker repeated. "In what way?"

"Well, did you know that Sharp worked for the same company as Bob Andrews," said Kendall. "Travers Morgan."

Whjittaker shrugged his shoulders. "Yes, we know that. What about it?" he asked. "It's purely co-incidence, I can assure you, nothing more."

Kendall shook his head. "Andrews was murdered, Inspector," he replied slowly, and so was Sharp. I'll see you in thirty minutes."

Kendall hung up.

* * *

Thirty-five minutes later Kendall arrived at Scotland Yard. "Good afternoon, Sergeant," he said, as he walked into the office. "Is he in?" he asked as he pointed to the door opposite.

The Sergeant looked up and smiled. "Oh yes, he's in right enough, sir," he replied. "He's in a right good mood today as well. Go right in."

"Ah, Kendall, do come in," said the Inspector, as Kendall entered the room. "Good of you to come. Do sit down." He pointed to a chair. Kendall was surprised to see that it was not laden with a pile of files.

"What about a spot of tea and a toasted tea cake?" the Inspector continued as Kendall sat down. As far as Kendall was concerned the Inspector was speaking a foreign language. The Inspector stood up and walked over to the corner of the room. He plugged in the kettle and switched it on. He then placed a tea bag into two cups. "Do you take sugar?" he asked.

"Yes, yes, please," Kendall answered quickly. *It might kill the taste of the tea*, he thought hopefully.

The Inspector added some sugar to the two cups. "Milk, I imagine," the Inspector called out. "I don't have any cream, sorry."

"Milk will be fine," replied Kendall.

The Inspector added the milk. He then took out a packet of tea cakes from a small cupboard just on his right hand side. He cut two of them in half and placed them onto a small electric grill. "Won't be long,"

213

he called out.

A few moments later the Inspector returned to his desk, carrying a small tray containing the tea and the cakes. "There you are," he said, placing them in front of Kendall. "Now, if you don't enjoy that, then I'll eat my hat."

Kendall glanced over to the side wall where the hat stand was. He looked at the Inspectors homburg. *It did not look particularly appetising*, he thought. At that moment he hoped more than anything else that he would indeed enjoy the tea and cake, "It looks great," he said, hopefully. He picked up the cake and took a bite. Hot melting butter mixed with the crisp cake and the raisins. He started to smile. "What do you call these?" he asked. "They're very good."

"They are called tea cakes," the Inspector replied. "I've a packet or two you can have." He paused for a moment. "What about the tea?"

Kendall took a drink. It wasn't entirely to his liking but it wasn't that bad after all.

"Of course you Americans only drink coffee, don't you?" Whittaker said disdainfully. "Tea drinker myself. Always have been. It's far more civilised."

"Well, it's certainly different," Kendall said quickly.

"An acquired taste," the Inspector suggested.

Kendall nodded. "I have to say that really it's not too bad. I don't think you will need to eat your hat after all."

The Inspector looked over at the hat stand, then he turned back to face Kendall and smiled. "Thank goodness for that," he said and laughed. "I wasn't looking forward to it. Besides, I've only just bought it."

"It looks very smart, I must say," said Kendall.

The Inspector looked back at the hat stand and nodded. He then turned to face Kendall. "Right, I think we better get on, don't you?"

Kendall nodded. "Before we do, Inspector, I wonder if you would take a look at this." Kendall reached into his inside pocket and withdrew a brown envelope. He handed it to the Inspector. Inside were the photographs and descriptions of two men. "The Miami Police are anxious to catch those two. They broke into a jewellery shop a few days ago," Kendall explained. "They are believed to be in England somewhere. You might be able to assist."

Whittaker took the envelope. He opened it and took out the photographs. He looked at them for a few moments. He then put them back inside the envelope and walked over to the door. "I'll see what we can do," he said.

He opened the door. "Sergeant," he called out. "Put out a call nationwide on these two, will you?" He handed the envelope to the Sergeant. "Our American cousins would very much like to speak with them about something or other."

"Right away, sir," said the Sergeant..

The Inspector returned to his desk and sat down. "Now, Mr Kendall, let's get to work, shall we?" He took a sheet of paper out of his drawer and passed it over to Kendall. "That's the doctors report," he said. "After his conversation with you he is now convinced that the drug was actually injected into Andrews' arm, as you suggested. Probably by force, or maybe Andrews was already unconscious. Chloroform, or something like that."

Kendall immediately remembered the strange smell he had noticed in the hotel room. *He had thought that it was menthol or peppermint.* "Chloroform," he repeated. "Makes sense."

The Inspector nodded his head. "That's right," he said. He looked at the empty cup sitting in front of Kendall. "More tea?" he asked.

Kendall thought for a moment. *One cup was probably enough*, he thought. *More than enough.* "Oh, no, thank you," he said. "I'm fine."

The Inspector nodded. "You don't mind if I do?" he said as he stood and walked towards the corner of the room.

"Oh, no, not at all, go right ahead," said Kendall, beginning to feel a little guilty. *Perhaps he should have agreed to a second cup by way of being polite.* He opened his mouth to speak. He had changed his mind. And he would be happy to have a second cup. *Somehow the words would not form in his mouth.*

A few minutes later the Inspector returned to his desk. He was carrying two cups. He put one down in front of Kendall. "Sorry," he murmured. "I just forgot. Leave it if you don't want it."

Kendall smiled. "That's fine, thank you," he said. He took a drink. "It really isn't that bad. It just takes a bit of getting used to, that's all."

The Inspector nodded but said nothing for a moment. "Now to Mr Sharp," the Inspector said. "We've been looking into that car crash." He shook his head. "It's strange, you know," he continued. "Sharp's car had been serviced only a few days before the crash. We found out that new brake pads were fitted all round." He paused for a moment. He placed a sheet of paper down on the desk in front of Kendall. "There you are," he said. "That's the receipt from Motor Maintenance, Maldon Road. Just a few streets away from where Sharp lived." He started to tap on the paper. "New brake pads and brake fluid. Look at the date. Two days before he was killed." He shook his head and raised his eyebrow. "A bit pricey, I'd say."

Kendall shook his head. "Perhaps they were badly fitted," he suggested. *He had experienced poor mechanics in the past. It was not unusual*

Whittaker smiled and shook his head. "We actually thought of that possibility ourselves, strangely enough," he replied. "We had the

215

braking system thoroughly inspected. There were no problems. As far as we could see the pads were in perfect condition. There was nothing."

Kendall nodded. *He had actually expected nothing different.*

"It was actually the brake fluid cable that caused the accident," the Inspector continued.

"Was it damaged?" asked Kendall.

The Inspector shook his head. "Damaged," he repeated. "You could say that. It was literary torn to shreds. It seems that the brakes had been deliberately tamped with. It was a simple explosive device fitted to the brake cable. There was a short length of wire attached to it. The other end of the wire was attached to the speedometer needle. When the needle reached sixty-five, the circuit was completed and the device exploded rupturing the cable." The Inspector paused for a moment and took a drink of tea. He looked at Kendall and smiled. "It seems that you were right after all," he said. "Sharp was murdered."

Kendall was tempted to say, *I told you so*, but refrained. "Clever," said Kendall.

Whittaker sighed. "I agree very clever indeed."

"So do we know who did it?" Kendall asked.

Whittaker shook his head. "I don't know the answer to that, not yet," Whittaker replied. "We are now checking for finger prints."

"It was Oliver Jones," Kendall announced. "I'm sure of it."

"What makes you say that?" the Inspector asked.

Kendall reached into his inside pocket and took out an envelope. He handed it to Whittaker. "That letter was meant for Bob Andrews," he explained. "It was written by Paul Sharp. It might give you a clue."

The Inspector looked puzzled. He took hold of the letter and started to read it slowly. After a few moments he looked at Kendall. "Where did you get this?" he asked.

Kendall shook his head. "It was in my flight bag, on the plane coming over," he replied. He paused for a few moments. "I think Andrews placed it there after he had seen Oliver Jones on the plane. I don't know whether it was done deliberately or whether it was a mistake. Perhaps he thought it was his bag. I don't know."

Whittaker shook his head and smiled. "So you had this letter all the time and you didn't tell me," he said. "I wonder why."

Kendall shook his head. "I only realised I had the letter a couple of days ago," he started to explain.

Whittaker shook his head once again. "But you still kept it to yourself," he said. "Interesting." He started to tap the letter. "All right, let's see what it has to say, shall we?" He started to read the letter once again. After a few moments he looked up at Kendall. "You do realise that withholding evidence is a criminal offence," he said. "I could have you arrested."

. Kendall nodded. "You could," he replied. "But you won't. You wouldn't want me hanging around so long. I mean there'd be the trial, and then the appeal, and the re-trial, and ...."

"All right, you've made your point. We'll overlook it this once," the Inspector hurriedly interrupted. "This letter mentions three people who could have been embezzling from the company."

Kendall nodded. "That's right," he replied. "In Sharp's opinion there were three. He later eliminated Harry Gale. That left Oliver Jones, and Collier himself. Sharp was almost certain that it was Collier. He just wanted to be sure before he said anything, but sadly he was murdered before he could tell me."

"So why did he think it was Collier and not Jones?" the Inspector asked.

"According to Sharp, Jones didn't have the brains for such an operation," said Kendall. "But you also have to remember that Jones did Collier's bidding. So really they were probably both involved."

"Did he actually have any proof?" asked Whittaker.

Kendall shook his head. "I'm not entirely sure," he replied. "I know that he had checked Collier's finances. His bank accounts. Share dealings, that kind of thing."

"And what did he find?" said the Inspector.

"Well it's certainly over my head," said Kendall. "But it seems that there were certain similarities between money leaving the company and money going into Collier's own account."

"I see. I'll get our people checking that right away," Whittaker replied. "Incidentally, why didn't you tell me about this before?"

Kendall looked at the Inspector and turned his head to one side. "Sharp told me that he had some more checking to do before he finally came to a conclusion," he started to explain. "I thought that I would wait until he had got back to me."

Whittaker shook his head. "Sadly that was not to be be, was it?" he said slowly. Then he nodded. "You know, I actually thought there might have been a totally different reason."

Kendall smiled. "Just goes to show how wrong you can be, Inspector."

The Inspector nodded. "It certainly does," he replied. "Although it's possible that had you shown me that letter earlier, things might have been different."

Kendall shook his head and smiled. "You know, Inspector, somehow I don't think it would have made any difference."

The Inspector started to laugh. "You know, you are probably right," he said.

* * *

"So it seems that Paul was murdered as well," said Mollie.

"That's right," said Kendall. "Apparently his brakes were tampered with. It probably happened on the day of his trip, maybe that very morning."

"Or more likely the night before," suggested Mollie.

Kendall sighed. *He hated to admit it but she was right. It was probably more likely.* "Or the night before," he agreed.

Mollie looked at him and smiled. She looked back at the magazine she was reading. She shook her head. "Did you know that John Wyndham Collier is to be made Business Man of the Year at a special dinner later this month."

Kendall shook his head. "Show me that," he replied.

She passed the magazine to Kendall. "It says so right there," she continued to explain. "It's to be held at the Dorchester Hotel."

Kendall took hold of the magazine and started to read. As he did so the telephone rang.

"It looks like you were right once again, Kendall," said a voice. It was Whittaker. "We've been speaking to some of Sharp's neighbours."

"Go on," said Kendall.

"Well it seems that one of them was having trouble sleeping the night before Sharp's death," the Inspector continued.

"I'm listening," said Kendall.

"A Mr Taylor, in flat 4c," the Inspector replied. "Well it seems that he got up. He went to his kitchen to get some hot milk. He thought he heard a noise and looked out of the window." Whittaker paused for a moment. "The window overlooks the entrance to the underground garage," the Inspector continued. "He saw someone walking up the ramp, coming out of the garage."

"Do we know who it was?" asked Kendall.

"Well, judging from the description it sounded very much like our old friend Oliver Jones," Whittaker said. "I'm having him brought in for questioning. I thought you might like to know."

Kendall nodded and smiled. "That is very much appreciated, Inspector," he replied. "Thank you."

"Incidentally, Sharp's flat was broken into last night and searched pretty thoroughly," Whittaker continued. "Probably looking for that letter, I expect."

Kendall was not surprised. "It doesn't surprise me," he said. "Let me know how you get on with Jones."

"Speak to you later, Kendall," said the Inspector. The line went dead.

Kendall stared at the handset for a few moments. Then he looked at Mollie. "We were right," he said smugly. "It was Jones who tampered with the brakes, and it was the night before, just as you had said."

Mollie smiled. She was pleased with herself. "So it was Oliver Jones who carried out both murders then," she said.

"Well, yes and no," Kendall replied.

Mollie looked puzzled. *A nice straightforward answer would have been nice.* "What do you mean?" she asked. "It's either yes or no. It can't be both."

Kendall looked at her and smiled. "Oh, Jones killed them all right," he answered. "There's no question about that. But he was only carrying out instructions from someone else."

There was a long silence. "Someone else," Mollie repeated. "You mean Collier?"

Kendall nodded. "That's right," he replied. "John Wyndham Collier, our man of the year. I wonder how that would go down at the dinner."

"Can you prove it?" Mollie asked.

Kendall shook his head. "No, I can't, not right now," he answered.

"Kendall," Mollie said slowly. "Whatever you do, just be careful."

"All right," Kendall replied. "I'll be careful, don't you worry."

It was clear that Kendall had something in mind. "What are you planning?" Mollie asked.

Kendall looked at her and started to grin. "Time to visit Collier again," he said. "I could offer him our congratulations."

He opened the drawer to the side table and took out the telephone directory. "Now, what was Collier's number?" He started to leaf through. "I need to discuss some investments with him." He continued turning the pages. "Here it is," he suddenly announced, as he wrote the number down. "I'll go this afternoon."

Mollie shook her head. "Suppose he refuses to see you," she said.

Kendall smiled, and nodded his head. "That is a definite possibility," he said.

"Then what will you do?" she asked.

Kendall smiled again. "What will I do?" he repeated. "I'll go anyway."

Chapter Twenty-Eight

Can You Prove It?

It was a little after two o'clock when Kendall arrived at Collier's office. He stood in the corridor for a few moments shaking his head. *What if he isn't in,* he murmured. *I mean he could be out, a big important meeting somewhere perhaps.* Kendall shook his head. *After all, he's not expecting me, is he?* "I should have made an appointment," he announced to no one in particular. "And suppose he refused to see me?" he continued. "What then?"

Kendall looked at the closed door in front of him and slowly reached for the handle. He then stopped and removed his hand. *All right, Kendall,* he murmured. *What exactly is your problem? Are you going in or what? Or are you going to spend the rest of the day admiring the door?*

Kendall continued to stare at door for a moment or two longer. Then he nodded his head. "I'm going in," he said. He reached for the handle, and opened the door.

"Is he in?" he asked as he poked his head around the door.

There was a young lady seated at a desk, busily typing into a computer. She looked up. "Do you mean Mr Collier?" she asked, hardly trying to hide her disgust.

Kendall smiled and nodded his head "That's right," he replied. "Collier. Is he in?" he repeated pointing to the door.

"Mr Collier is in conference," she replied. "He has given strict instructions that he is not to be disturbed."

"Really?" said Kendall, trying to sound impressed. "He'll see me." He started to walk towards the door to Collier's office.

The young lady looked horrified. "Have you an appointment to see Mr Collier?" she asked as she quickly glanced at the diary page that was lying open. There was nothing marked down, not until later that afternoon.

Kendall shook his head. "No, I'm afraid I haven't," he replied. "But not to worry, he won't mind. In fact he'll be pleased to see me, you mark my words." Kendall moved closer to Collier's door.

The young lady stood up and quickly walked over to where Kendall was standing. "I'm sorry," she said. "You can't go in. Not without an appointment."

Kendall shook his head, and smiled. "Really?" he said. "I think you'll find that I can." He quickly opened the door and walked in.

"Good afternoon, Collier," he announced as he entered the room.

Collier looked up. "Kendall, you back again?" he said wearily. "What are you doing here? Barging in like this." He looked over at the young lady who was now standing by the open door. "I thought that I had said I was not to be disturbed."

"I'm sorry, sir," the young lady replied nervously. She looked at Kendall. "I tried to stop him."

Kendall smiled and nodded. "She's right, you know," he said. "She did try to stop me. She made quite a determined effort in fact." He looked at the girl and shrugged. "It's not her fault. I'm just stubborn, I suppose." He paused for a moment and looked at Collier. "I've always been the same," he continued. "Once I make my mind up about something, well there's just no stopping me. I just go on and on." He walked into the middle of the room. "My mother, bless her, always said that one day my stubborn streak would get me into trouble," he continued. "You know, she was right, but who cares."

The girl glared at Kendall. "Should I call security, sir?" she asked.

Kendall shook his head. "I wouldn't, if I were you," he said.

Collier shook his head. "No, Joyce," he said slowly. "That's all right. I'll deal with Mr Kendall myself. That will be all. I'll call if I need you."

The young lady nodded and walked out, closing the door behind her.

Collier shook his head and sighed deeply. "Kendall, seeing that you are here, you might as well sit down."

Kendall smiled and walked over to a chair. "Very kind of you," he said as he sat down. "Very generous in fact." He slowly looked around the room and then turned back to face Collier. "By the way, I understand that congratulations are in order," he said. "Business Man of the Year. Very impressive." Kendall nodded his head. "So what do you get for that? A silver cup? Or perhaps a crystal vase?"

Collier looked at Kendall and started to tap the desk. "Kendall, this is getting to be a bit of a habit, don't you think?" he said. "A nasty aggravating habit."

Kendall looked up shocked. "Oh, I'm sorry you feel like that, Mr Collier," he said. "And all this time I thought you liked me."

Collier shook his head. "I had thought that Scotland Yard was going to put a stop to all of this," he said. "I really must speak to the Commissioner."

"Oh, there's no need for that," Kendall said. "This will be the very last time, I promise you."

"Oh I am sorry to hear that, Mr Kendall," Collier replied. "I have so enjoyed speaking with you."

"Oh, so have I," replied Kendall.

"So what is it this time?" asked Collier.

Kendall smiled, and looked around the room once again. "You know, I do like this room," he said. "And those paintings." He paused for a moment. "What are they? I forget. Renoir was it?" He shook his head. "I'm not very good at that sort of thing."

"Kendall, just get on with it, will you?" Collier said forcefully.

Kendall nodded. "You know, I've actually been doing some checking," he said. "That's what detectives do, you know."

"Some checking?" Collier repeated. "Checking on what?"

"I'm glad you asked that," Kendall said. "I've actually been checking on you."

"About me," said Collier. "I'm flattered. But please do go on."

"You've done very well for yourself, haven't you?" said Kendall. "Worked your way up from virtually nothing to become the boss of a huge organisation in a little over six years."

"It's actually nearer eight, Mr Kendall," Collier corrected. "But close enough."

Kendall nodded. "You are a major shareholder in a number of companies," he continued. "Seven, I think you said at a previous meeting."

"Seven it is," Collier replied. "As I believe I also said before, you have an excellent memory, Mr Kendall."

Kendall nodded. "Seven, right." He paused. "And all rival companies to Travers Morgan."

Collier smiled. "That's right, Mr Kendall," he replied. "Originally they were all competitors. Now I have the controlling share in all of them. So they are no longer rivals."

Kendall smiled. "You could say, no longer a problem," suggested Kendall. Collier said nothing, and merely smiled. "Clever," Kendall continued. "And, unless I'm very much mistaken, most of those shares purchased within the past six or seven months."

"That's right," Collier said. "Exactly the same time that the market was depressed. It's the best time to buy, you know. When the price is low. You can get a real bargain that way."

Kendall nodded. "Makes sense," he said. "Incidentally, it just happens to be exactly the same time that funds started to disappear from the company accounts."

Collier looked surprised. "Really?" he replied. "I never noticed. How clever of you to spot that."

Kendall smiled and shrugged his shoulders. "Coincidence, I expect," he said. He paused for a moment and then nodded. "Originally from Canada, mother French, born in Marseilles, father Canadian, born in Toronto. You worked for a shipping company in Vancouver. Worked your way up." Kendall paused once again. "But for some reason or other you left the company in a bit of a hurry, I understand."

Collier smiled and shook his head. "I got restless, that's all," he replied. "Itchy feet."

222

Kendall smiled. "So the story concerning some kind of bribery was just …"

"Just a story, Mr Kendall, nothing more," said Collier.

Kendall nodded and smiled. "Okay, let's leave it at that, shall we?" Kendall paused for a few moments. "You came over to England ten years ago."

Collier nodded. "It was twelve years, actually, this coming January," he replied. "January 14th, to be precise."

Kendall nodded. "The fourteenth," he repeated. "You quickly got a job with the Baxter Corporation in their Futures Department. You did very well, working your way up to Section Head in a little over three years. Then came that little trouble about some missing money."

Collier smiled. "That's right, Kendall," he replied. "You are extremely thorough. I'm impressed. Two hundred thousand pounds was the sum. It was never found. There was a full enquiry, of course, and I was completely exonerated."

Kendall smiled and nodded. "That's right," he said. "You were indeed, completely cleared. It seems that Fred Harket, your partner, was actually the guilty party." There was a slight pause. "He committed suicide, I understand."

Collier nodded his head slowly. "That was the formal conclusion of the inquest," he replied.

"Correct, Mr Collier," said Kendall. "He was killed by carbon monoxide poisoning. He had connected a rubber tube to the car exhaust."

Collier heaved a sigh. "You seem to have done your homework, Mr Kendall," he said. "Indeed you are remarkably well informed."

"We do try," said Kendall.

"So what's your point, exactly?" Collier asked.

"Point," repeated Kendall. "Point."

"Yes, what's the point of all of this?" Collier asked. "Interesting though it may be."

"Oh I see," replied Kendall. He shook his head. "There's no point, not really. It's just observation. It tells me what kind of a man you are, that's all."

Collier smiled. "Really?" he said. "And you can tell that from just a few short facts."

Kendall nodded. "Oh yes, I know with absolute certainty."

Collier smiled once again and shook his head. "So precisely what kind of a man am I?" he asked.

Kendall smiled. "You answered that question at our very first meeting," he replied. "What was it you said?" He nodded as he remembered. "You said that you needed power, like you needed oxygen to breathe. Food to eat."

"Correct," said Collier. "I did say that. Bravo. You do have an excellent memory."

Kendall smiled. "What else was it that you said?" Kendall continued. "It's a tough world out there and you have to be tough to survive. Power, that's what it's all about."

"Correct, Mr Kendall," Collier replied clapping his hands. "Without power you are nothing." He shook his head and started to grin. "Remember, Mr Kendall, there are only two kinds of people in this world. The leaders and the rest, the has-beens, or the never-were."

"Fred Harket was a has-been, I imagine," Kendall said.

Collier shook his head and smiled. "A never-was."

"I see," said Kendall, nodding his head. "As for yourself, I imagine you need always to be first, the winner. One of the leaders."

""Not one of the leaders, the leader," Collier replied. "As you said, the winner. Remember, there are no prizes for coming second."

Kendall nodded and smiled. "You could be right, I suppose," he said.

"I am right, Mr Kendall," Collier said. "Make no mistake." He paused for a moment waiting for a reaction. There was none. "If you are not a winner then you are nothing. A loser. No one wants to know a loser."

"Isn't playing the game, the taking part, more important than winning?" Kendall asked.

Collier shook his head, and thumped the desk. "Don't you believe it, Mr Kendall," he replied. "Perhaps in story books but not in real life." He shook his head and looked at Kendall. "Look around you." He waved his hand. "There is no point in just playing a game. What matters most is the winning." He paused once again, and sighed. "Anyway, games are purely for children, Mr Kendall. Wouldn't you agree?"

Kendall shook his head. "I find it hard to go along with that," he said. "But, hey, what do I know about it?"

"All right, Mr Kendall. I'm sure you haven't come to discuss my career or the virtues or otherwise of power," Collier said. "So what can I do for you this time?"

Kendall nodded. "You are right, absolutely," he said. "The thing is I still have a lot of problems with this alleged suicide of Mr Andrews."

"I'm sure that Scotland Yard has it well in hand and that perhaps you really should not be concerning yourself," Collier replied. "In fact I thought that the case had been closed." He looked at Kendall, awaiting confirmation. Kendall said nothing. "Very well," Collier continued. "Don't ask me why, but I'll try to help as much as I can."

"That's really very good of you, Mr Collier," said Kendall.

Collier nodded. "All right," he said. "Exactly what are these problems?"

"Well, the first problem relates to the flight from Miami," Kendall said.

Collier looked at him, a frown across his forehead. "The flight?" he

224

repeated. "What about the flight?"

Kendall sat forward in his chair. "At one of our previous meetings, the first one I think, you said that you had actually instructed Andrews to come to London."

"That's right," said Collier. "I told him to catch that flight, the one that you yourself were on, I believe."

"Yes, I was on the same flight," replied Kendall. "And you gave him that instruction on the actual day of the flight, I understand. Is that correct?"

Collier shook his head. "It was actually the night before, if I remember correctly," he replied. "I needed to see him urgently."

Kendall shrugged and held his head to one side. "About the accounts, you mean?" he suggested. "The missing money?"

"That's right, the missing money," said Collier. "Why do you ask?"

Kendall shook his head, and heaved a sigh. "The thing is, Andrews actually told me that he had booked that flight six weeks previously," he replied. He shook his head once again. "You see the problem."

Collier smiled and shook his head. "There's no problem, Mr Kendall," he said. "Obviously he lied to you, as simple as that."

Kendall looked perplexed. "You think so?" he said.

Collier nodded. "It would seem so," he said.

"Why would he do that?" Kendall asked. "To lie to me like that? After all, I was a perfect stranger. It made no difference to me either way."

Collier smiled once again. "I'm afraid I have no idea why he would lie to you," he replied. He slowly shook his head. "Why would he rob the company like he did?"

"Well, you know, Mr Collier, that actually brings me to another little problem I have," said Kendall.

"Go on," coaxed Collier.

Kendall smiled. "You see, I don't actually believe that Mr Andrews did lie," he replied. "Furthermore I don't believe that he, how did you put it, robbed the company either."

Collier shook his head. "How can you say that, Mr Kendall, you're an intelligent man. He committed suicide, didn't he? Killed himself because his crime had been discovered. Proof enough that he robbed the company."

Kendall shook his head slowly. "You know, that's something else I just don't believe," he replied. "Andrews didn't commit suicide. He was murdered."

Collier started to grin. "You said that at our last meeting, didn't you?" he replied.

"You're right, I did say that, Mr Collier," said Kendall. "And you said that I should come back to you when I had the proof."

Collier smiled and nodded. "I did indeed, Mr Kendall," he said. "I did

225

indeed."

Kendall nodded. "That's why I'm here," he said. "To provide you with that proof."

Collier looked puzzled. He looked at Kendall. "So you insist that Bob was murdered, Mr Kendall?"

Kendall nodded.

A frown spread across Collier's forehead. "So who in your opinion killed him?"

Kendall smiled and shook his head. "It's not quite as straightforward as that," he replied. "Oliver Jones actually committed the murder, although he was under orders from someone else."

Collier shook his head. "Oliver, that's absolute nonsense and you know it."

"Oh, it was him all right," said Kendall. "There's no doubt about that. He was at the hotel that afternoon, the afternoon that Andrews died."

"That's right, he was," said Collier. "I sent him there. I told you that myself."

Kendall nodded. "Yes you did, Mr Collier. I think you said that Jones and Andrews were good friends."

"That's right," said Collier. "They had known each other for many years."

Kendall nodded. "You had thought that maybe Andrews might have been spoken about his troubles." He paused for a moment. "Maybe he would open up a little. I think that was the expression you used."

Collier nodded. "That's what I said," he replied. "But my plan didn't work and Oliver left the hotel at about one-thirty and Bob was still alive then."

"Correct, Mr Collier, he did leave at one-thirty, or thereabouts," Kendall agreed. "We have enough evidence to show that."

"Well, there you are," said Collier.

"Not quite, Mr Collier," said Kendall. "You see, he came back about twenty minutes later."

Collier shook his head. "What nonsense is this?" he said.

"We have witnesses," said Kendall. "Firstly we have the taxi driver who picked him up at the hotel, and then we have Maria, the maid at the hotel. Their evidence shows quite clearly that he returned to the hotel."

Collier shrugged his shoulders. "So he returned to the hotel," he replied. "What about it? He probably just forgot something."

Kendall smiled. "Funny that," he said. "That was Scotland Yard's first reaction."

"That settles that, then," said Collier.

Kendall shook his head once again. "Not really," he said. "You see it's not just that he returned to the hotel. It's the fact that he didn't want anyone to know that he had returned."

Collier looked puzzled. "I don't follow you," he said.

"It's simple enough," said Kendall. "He used the back staircase, actually the fire escape, and not the front entrance to the hotel." He looked at Collier for a few moments. "Why do you think he would do that?" he asked.

Collier rubbed his chin. "I really couldn't say, Mr Kendall," he replied. "But I imagine that you will tell me."

"It's really quite simple," said Kendall. "It was then that he killed Bob Andrews."

Collier started to laugh. "Excuse me, Kendall, it just sounds so ludicrous."

Kendall smiled. "I can assure that it is far from ludicrous," he replied. "Jones did kill Andrews, make no mistake about that."

Collier shook his head. "Kendall, this is all very fascinating," he said. "But where exactly is your proof?"

"Depends what you mean by that statement," Kendall replied, shaking his head.

"I would have thought that it was simple enough, Kendall," Collier said. "Can you prove any of what you are saying?"

Kendall shrugged his shoulders. "Now, you know, it really isn't as simple as you might think," he replied. "You see, there's really two things to consider." He held up one finger. "One, can I prove murder? Then there's question number two." He held up a second finger. "Can I prove fraud?"

"Kendall, I'm sure this is quite interesting," said Collier, sounding anything but. "Could you get to the point. I really am a very busy man, you know."

Kendall smiled. "I'm glad that you find it so interesting," he replied. "It actually gets better, you'll see. You see the two things, the murder and the fraud, are so tightly linked. They are really two sides of the same coin. I really only have to prove one side or the other."

"Kendall I have no idea of what you are talking about," Collier said, beginning to get impatient.

Kendall looked at Collier and shook his head. "Really, I thought it was crystal clear," he replied. "What I am saying is if I can prove who the murderer was, then it is obvious who carried out the fraud. Or vice-versa, if I prove who committed the fraud, then I have the murderer. Do you see?"

Collier sighed deeply. "All very fascinating, I'm sure," he said. "But you are doing an awful lot of talking and saying very little."

Kendall nodded. You are absolutely right, Mr Collier," he said. "I tend to talk a lot, especially when I get excited. It's a bad trait I have." He smiled. "One of many, I'm afraid. Something to do with nerves, I think."

"Kendall, just get on with it," Collier said, as he looked at the wall clock. "I have a rather important meeting in forty minutes."

"With Mr Jones if I'm not mistaken?" Kendall replied.

Collier looked surprised. "That's right," he said. "How did you know that?"

Kendall smiled. "I'm a detective, remember," he replied. "Anyway, I digress. Let's look at our problems logically and let us see what we can prove."

"It would be appreciated," said Collier. "Go on, let's hear it."

Kendall shrugged. "Well, let's start with what we do know, shall we?"

"And that is?" said Collier.

"We know that someone has been embezzling from the company," Kendall went on. "You thought that it was Andrews."

Collier nodded. "Yes, I did," he replied.

"Why was that?" Kendall asked. "I mean what put you onto him in the first place?"

"Why?" repeated Collier. He heaved a sigh. "It stands to reason. I mean, just look at his position. Chief Accountant. He was ideally placed and could easily alter the books, adjust the figures. Who would know the difference?"

"Well that's a fair point, I suppose," said Kendall, unconvinced.

"Then, when Bob was found dead, and they said it was suicide," Collier continued, slowly shaking his head, "I naturally thought that poor old Bob had got found out and had taken the easy way out."

Kendall smiled. "They do say that, don't they? Take the easy way out." He shook his head. "It doesn't seem very easy to me."

"Nor me," Collier agreed.

Kendall nodded his head. "And yet you never doubted that it was him, did you?" he said. "Not for a single moment." His gaze went to the photograph that was hanging on the wall. It showed two men on a yacht. "What's that?" he asked. "It looks like a thirty footer to me."

Collier looked at the photograph. "Forty-five, actually," he replied.

Kendall nodded and turned back to Collier. "You know, you were convinced that it was Andrews, your long time friend, right from the start." Kendall paused for a moment and looked at Collier. "I thought that was odd."

Collier shook his head. "Oh no, you're quite wrong. It wasn't quite like that," he said. "I did have other suspects."

"Really," said Kendall. "Like who, for instance?"

Collier hesitated for a few moments. "Well, for a while I thought it was Paul Sharp."

"Paul Sharp," Kendall repeated. "Why him?"

"Oh, there were a number of reasons," Collier answered. "But then the evidence against Bob was just so compelling."

"What evidence?" Kendall asked.

Collier hesitated once again. "I thought that I had already told you that," he replied. "The suicide just confirmed my suspicions."

"There was no evidence, Mr Collier," Kendall replied. "We know without a shadow of a doubt that Bob Andrews did not commit suicide. He was actually murdered. Oh yes, it was an overdose of Syanthol all right, but it was not self-administered." He paused for a moment. "We know for a fact that Andrews had not been taking that particular drug for three or four months. In fact he hadn't been taking any drug."

"How do you know that?" Collier asked.

"We checked with his doctor," said Kendall

"But why would anyone kill Bob?" Collier asked.

"Good question," said Kendall. "As we know, his killing was made to look like suicide. That was to give more credence to the alleged fraud." He paused for a few moments. "As you yourself just said, the suicide just confirmed your suspicions."

Collier nodded. "Correct, I did say that."

"The other important question, of course, relates to the alleged embezzlement itself," Kendall continued.

Collier looked at him puzzled. "I don't understand, Mr Kendall."

Kendall slowly nodded his head. "It's quite simple, really," he said. "If Bob Andrews did not commit suicide, it stands to reason that he was not the embezzler. Furthermore, if it wasn't suicide, we have another little problem."

Collier started to frown. "Problem," he repeated. "You'll need to explain that one."

"No suicide, then why would there be a suicide note?" Kendall replied.

Collier looked at Kendall and shook his head. "I really haven't time for these guessing games, I'm afraid," he replied.

Kendall sighed. "You're right, it is a game, isn't it? Like a jigsaw, trying to get the pieces to fit," he said. "It's quite a puzzle, wouldn't you say? I mean, it's clear to me, in fact it's clear to everyone now, that Andrews was murdered. There was no suicide, there should not have been a suicide note."

Collier shook his head. "I don't know where this is heading, Kendall, but there was a suicide note, the police found it."

Kendall nodded. "That's right," he said. "They found it on the bedside table next to Andrews' body." Kendall paused for a moment. "How do you think it got there?"

"Well I don't really know," Collier replied. "I guess that it was probably left there by the murderer."

Kendall smiled. "What I thought exactly," he replied. "And the last person to see Andrews alive was Oliver Jones."

Collier looked shocked. "So are you saying that Oliver committed the murder?" he asked.

Kendall nodded. "That's right," he said. "That is precisely what I am saying."

"And exactly how did he do it, Mr Kendall?" asked Collier.

"First he rendered Andrews unconscious," Kendall explained. "A simple cloth impregnated with chloroform was all that he would need."

"Go on," said Collier. "I'm listening."

"Then a syringe full of Syanthol was injected into his arm, and a few minutes later he was dead."

Collier thought for a moment. He shook his head. "I don't know. This is all too fantastic."

Kendall shook his head. "Believe me, Mr Collier, it's all true."

"Well, if Oliver committed the murder, then he must have been the embezzler," said Collier.

Kendall smiled. "Close," he replied quite simply.

"Close," repeated Collier, surprised. "Well either he was or he wasn't."

"Did you know about Paul Sharp's letter?" Kendall asked. Then he nodded. "Of course you did." He paused for a moment. "Anyway, in that letter Paul mentioned three possibles." He paused once again. "One of them, Harry Gale, was eliminated," Kendall continued. "That left two people."

"Oh, and who were they?" Collier asked.

"Well one that he actually had in mind was Oliver Jones," Kendall replied.

Collier started to laugh. "So it was Jones," he replied. "Just as I said."

Kendall shook his head. "Not exactly, but let me continue for a little longer," he said. "You see the other person that Paul had in mind was yourself, Mr Collier."

Collier started to laugh. "Me," he replied. "How very amusing."

"Bob Andrews didn't think it amusing," Kendall replied. "That's why he was murdered."

"Here you go again, Kendall," Collier said. "You are speaking a lot and saying nothing." He shook his head. "How do you arrive at that conclusion?"

"We know that Andrews died from Syanthol poisoning," Kendall started to explain. "Correct?"

Collier made no reply but merely nodded.

"You were the only person who knew that he had been taking that particular drug," Kendall continued. "You had actually recommended it to him."

Collier shook his head. "Are you suggesting that no one apart from myself knew about that drug?" he said. "No one."

Kendall rubbed the side of his face and started to smile. "Oh, I imagine other people did know," he said. "People back in Florida perhaps. Members of his family maybe. But no one over here knew. Sharp didn't know. Neither did your friend Oliver Jones. But you knew."

Collier shook his head. "I had no idea what tablets Bob was taking."

"Wrong," Kendall interrupted. "Andrews told me the whole story. You had actually suggested that he take them. And for a while he did take them. But he had a bad reaction, so he stopped."

Collier shook his head. "I tell you, I knew nothing about those tablets."

"That's odd, Mr Collier," said Kendall. "You see Scotland Yard have checked your medical records. And it seems that you do, or at least did, suffer from asthma. It also seems that you did, at one time, take Syanthol 25 tablets, two per day apparently. Interesting, I thought."

"It doesn't prove anything," Collier said.

"Wrong," said Kendall. "It proves that you lied to me. You told me that you never suffered from asthma. Clearly you did." He paused for a moment. "Shall we carry on?" he continued.

Collier shrugged. "Please do, the sooner this is over and done with the better," he replied. "What shall we discuss now?"

Kendall nodded his head and smiled. "Well, I thought that perhaps we could now direct our attention to another murder," he replied. "The murder of Paul Sharp."

Chapter Twenty-Nine

The Murder of Paul Sharp

"Murder, did you say?" said Collier. "You must be mistaken. Paul wasn't murdered. Tragically he died in a car crash."

Kendall nodded. "Yes, you are absolutely right, he did die in a car crash," he said. "The trouble is that his car had been tampered with."

"Tampered with," Collier repeated. "What do you mean?"

"The car had been rigged so that once it got to sixty-five miles per hour there would be a mild explosion," Kendall explained. "That explosion severed the brake cable, causing the car to crash." Kendall shook his head. "I understand that he had been sent out on a trip for the company," he continued. "You sent him, I believe."

Collier nodded. "That's right," he replied. "It was to one of our offices in the south-west, to Windsor, actually."

"To Windsor," repeated Kendall. "A trip that took him onto the M4, I think."

Collier nodded. "That's correct," he said. "Have you been there?"

Kendall smiled and shook his head. "Oh no," he replied. "But we were talking about Mr Sharp."

Collier nodded. "We were indeed," he said. "Do please continue."

Kendall nodded. "Once he got onto the motorway, he put his foot down. His sports car, a Jaguar, I believe, reached sixty in next to no time. Sixty-five was no trouble. Suddenly there was the muffled explosion. The broken brake cable was all too evident." He shook his head. "No, it was no accident. It was deliberate. He had no chance."

"Deliberate, why that's terrible," said Collier. "I had no idea. No one told me." He shook his head. "I just thought that it was a terrible accident." He shook his head once again. "And to think I sent him. I'm responsible. It was my fault. I killed him."

Kendall paused. "Incidentally, why did you tell me that Sharp was in the Middle East somewhere?"

Collier looked puzzled. "I'm sorry, I don't ..."

"Unless I'm mistaken, you told me that he was in Dubai or Saudi Arabia," Kendall continued. "He was right here in England all the time. Why did you lie to me?"

Collier shook his head. "I didn't lie to you," he replied. "I just made a mistake, that's all. I thought that he had gone but then later I realised that his trip was going to be the following week."

Kendall shook his head. "Collier, you are not the type to make mistakes," he said. "Not a simple one like that anyway. No, you deliberately lied to me. For some reason you just didn't want me to meet him."

"Why would I do that?" Collier asked.

"Because of what he knew maybe," Kendall replied. "And that's why he was murdered."

"Go on, Kendall, this is intriguing," said Collier. "Boring but intriguing."

Kendall nodded and started to grin. "I'm sorry you find this less than interesting," he said. "It does actually get better. Once again Jones was the actual murderer. He was seen talking to Paul that morning, the day of the accident, at about ten-thirty."

Collier nodded. "That's right," he said. "There's nothing strange about that. There was a file that I wanted to go up to the Windsor office, that's all. I asked Oliver to give it to Paul to take with him."

Kendall nodded. "That's fine," he said. "The only thing is that Jones had actually been seen the night before." There was a slight pause. "You see, one of Paul's neighbours had apparently seen him coming up from the underground car park where Sharp kept his car. At about three o'clock in the morning."

Collier heaved a loud sigh. "I'm sorry, Kendall, whatever Oliver was, or was not, doing at three in the morning is of no real interest to me," he said wearily. "So someone apparently saw Oliver acting a little oddly, according to you. What does that prove?"

"Oh, nothing really," said Kendall. "Except that obviously Jones likes to visit underground car parks in the middle of the night." He paused and slowly shook his head. "Oh no, you're absolutely right, in itself it proves nothing. However, his fingerprints on the car bonnet do prove something. They prove that he opened the bonnet. Why would he do that?"

Collier shook his head. "I've no idea, I'm afraid, Mr Kendall."

"You don't know," said Kendall. "Let me give you a clue, shall I? You need to open the bonnet to get to the back of the speedometer. And why would he need to do that, I hear you ask." Kendall paused for a moment. "Simple," he continued. "It was to make a connection between the speedometer and the brake cable. You know, despite the damage to the car and the brake cable, that connection to the speedometer was still intact. Quite amazing, really."

Collier shook his head. "Kendall, this is all a little bit technical for me, I'm afraid," he said. "All I know is that you switch on the ignition then put your foot down and the car goes."

Kendall shrugged. "You know that's about the extent of my knowledge as well," he replied. "Obviously Jones knew a whole lot more. He knew what to do to make sure that the car crashed."

Collier shook his head. "Do I understand that you are seriously suggesting that Oliver deliberately killed Paul as well as Bob?" he asked. "I just can't believe it."

"I can assure you that it's all true, I'm afraid," replied Kendall.

"You really don't know people, do you?" Collier said. "I mean, I've known Oliver ten, twelve years. Now you are telling me that he is nothing but a cold-blooded killer." He shook his head and looked down at the floor. "There is no way that I would ever imagine him doing such a thing," he continued. "Are you sure?"

"I'm sure," said Kendall. "I'm also sure of your involvement."

"My involvement?" Collier repeated puzzled. "What exactly has all of this got to do with me?"

"Oh, that's easy to answer," replied Kendall. "You see, the key to this whole mystery lies with you."

"What do you mean by that?" Collier asked.

"Do you remember what we said earlier?" asked Kendall. "We said that this whole thing had actually started with the embezzlement." He paused for a moment and looked back at the photograph on the wall. He heaved a sigh and looked back at Collier. "The stolen money, right," he continued. "That eventually led to Andrews' death, and then Paul Sharp's murder."

"Both murdered by Oliver Jones, according to you," said Collier.

Kendall nodded. "That's right, both murdered by Jones," he replied. "But Jones was working for you. What was it he told me? He relies on me, that's all, that's what he said. If Collier wants something, I would arrange to get it." Kendall smiled, slowing nodding his head. "And if he wanted something done? Then I do it." Kendall looked at Collier "His words," he continued. "Only a fool turns Collier down." He shook his head. "Jones carried out those murders on your instructions."

Collier shook his head and started to laugh. "I really do not know where you are getting this from, but I really have far more important things to attend to."

"It was you, wasn't it, Collier?" said Kendall. "You were the one falsifying the accounts. You stole the money and then you set about blaming Andrews."

"What's this, Kendall, more of your nonsense?" said Collier. "Enough. I think you'd better go now."

Kendall shook his head. "I've been looking into your finances, Mr Collier," he said. "It makes very interesting reading."

Collier looked surprised. "I understood that in this country, a person's bank details were private, and ..."

Kendall quickly raised his hands and shook his head. "Right, absolutely right," he said. "No question about that. Not without a warrant, that is." Collier looked puzzled. Kendall shook his head. "I haven't been anywhere near your bank account. I promise you." He paused. "But your dealings on the Stock Market, well that's an entirely different story. That is a matter of public record. Anyone who has a mind to can look at those details."

"Go on," said Collier. "My dealings on the Stock Market are all perfectly legal, and proper."

"I'm sure they were, Mr Collier," said Kendall. "But what interests me is the money. What happened to it?" He paused for a moment. "I mean, fifty million English pounds went missing. That's about eighty million dollars, unaccounted for. Sums like that don't just vanish into thin air. So where is it, and more importantly, who took it?"

Collier started to smile and shook his head. "I really don't know, but I think you are going to tell me."

"You have been a very busy man, Mr Collier," said Kendall. "You spent a little over thirty million pounds in a little over six months. In fact, just about the same time as the little errors started to occur in the accounts."

Collier smiled. "Coincidence, nothing more," he said.

Kendall hated that word. Coincidence. He shook his head. "Perhaps," he said. "But tell me how did you accumulate all of that cash? I mean thirty million is quite a sum."

Collier shook his head and glared. "Well I can't see that it really is any of your business, but do you remember what I told you when we first met?"

Kendall looked puzzled. "About what?" he asked.

Collier rubbed his chin. "Surely you remember," he said. "About making a killing in the City."

Kendall smiled and nodded as he remembered. "Yes, I remember," he said. "It was something about buying shares at a low price and selling high, and making a big profit."

"Precisely," said Collier nodding his head. "And that is exactly what I did. I sold a block of shares at a high price and, as I said, made a killing."

Kendall smiled and nodded. "That's precisely what I had thought." Then he shook his head. "But then I checked the records, and you know what? There's no record of you selling a block of shares during the time."

Collier shook his head. "You must be mistaken, Kendall," he said.

Kendall shook his head. "There's no mistake," he replied. "You made a killing all right but it wasn't by selling stock."

"Go on, Kendall," said Collier. "This is really fascinating stuff."

"It gets better," Kendall responded. "Those seven companies that you mentioned, well I checked the records at Companies House. That gave me seven names. I then checked all seven companies regarding share dealings over the past twelve months. That gave me all of the

235

information I needed. Dates, amounts, and, interestingly enough, names, it was all there. The dates and amounts correspond fairly closely to the dates and amounts shown as being transferred in the accounts. As for the names, there were two which kept cropping up."

"And they were ..." said Collier.

"Well one was Oliver Jones," Kendall replied. "The other was John Wyndham Collier."

"Of course that doesn't actually prove fraud," Collier said.

Kendall smiled. "Well, you know, I'm not so sure about that," he replied. "A court of law might think differently." He paused for a moment. "Anyway, at least there's enough for the proper authorities to carry out a thorough investigation," he continued. "They are probably better at that sort of thing than I am. I'm sure they will be able to prove it." Kendall started to frown. "Well, anyhow, it's a good start, I think," he said. "In fact, if I have missed something, I expect that Jones could fill in the gaps. He was arrested by the police last night, you know. They picked him up at Heathrow. I understand that he was booked on a flight to Buenos Aires. I'm sure that he will have quite a story to tell,, don't you think?"

Collier shook his head but said nothing.

There was a knock on the door. A few seconds later there was a second knock. The door opened and Joyce came in. "I'm sorry to disturb you, sir," she said. "But there are two gentlemen from Scotland Yard. They would like a word with you."

Kendall looked at Collier and smiled. "Right. I better get going. I've finished anyway," he said. He stood up and started towards the door. "Incidentally, I see that the price for Rockford Metals has gone right down. Just as well I didn't act on your advice. I would have made a thumping great loss." He paused for a moment and then started to laugh. "But, hey, it wouldn't have been as great a loss as yours, not by a long way." He stopped at the open door and turned to face Collier. He raised his right arm and waved. He then went out of the room.

* * *

It was half past five when Kendall arrived back at the hotel. "Where have you been?" asked Mollie. "I expected you back here ages ago."

"Oh, I had a couple of calls to make, that's all," Kendall replied. "Nothing of any great importance."

Mollie sighed. "I suppose you've been in a bar somewhere," she said glaring at him. "It would never occur to you that I would like to go out somewhere, would it?"

Kendall smiled at her and quietly laid an envelope onto the bedside cabinet. "You better get ready," he said. "And be quick about it." He pointed to the envelope.

Mollie looked down at the envelope. "What's that?" she asked.

"We are going to the theatre," Kendall replied. "Unfortunately, I couldn't get tickets for 'The Mousetrap'." He paused for a moment. "So it will have to be 'Mamma Mia', I'm afraid. Hope you don't mind."

Chapter Thirty

The Case Is Closed

"So that's over and done with, at last." said Mollie. "Perhaps now we can get back to our holiday."

"Well, we just have this meeting with Whittaker later today and that is it," Kendall agreed.

Mollie nodded and a huge smile spread across her face. *All of the detective work was finished, there was no more sifting through the clues, no more solving the crime. It was done and dusted.*

"Of course, there will be the trial in a few months' time," said Kendall. "We'll have to come over for that."

Mollie looked puzzled. "Really," she said. "Why?"

Kendall sighed. "Mollie, we will be called as witnesses," he replied. "Naturally we will have to give evidence. The prosecution will need to prove that Andrews did not commit suicide."

Mollie nodded. "So we might get another holiday," she suggested hopefully.

Kendall nodded. "Perhaps it'll make up for this one, what do you think?"

"Let's hope so," Mollie replied. "Incidentally, what happened with Collier?"

"Well, Collier has been charged and is now in custody awaiting trial," replied Kendall. "As you might expect, he has denied all of the charges and insists that Andrews committed suicide."

"What about the death of Paul Sharp?" Mollie asked.

"Oh nothing more than a simple, tragic accident," replied Kendall.

Mollie shook her head. "He can't possibly think anyone will believe that, can he?"

Kendall thought for a few moments. "Well, you would think not, I agree," he replied. "But Collier is the type who thinks what he says goes."

"And up to now that's been pretty much true," said Mollie.

"Pretty much," agreed Kendall. "And even now he believes that he only needs to say something and it will be accepted." Kendall shook his head. "He'll soon learn different."

"So it wasn't suicide after all," Mollie said. "You said that from the very start, and you were right."

Kendall smiled smugly and nodded his head. "Correct. I was right. Naturally," he said. "As always."

Mollie hated it when he was in one of his '*I told you so*' moods. She fell silent for a moment, a puzzled frown on her forehead. She sighed and shook her head. "I still don't understand, though," she said slowly.

"What don't you understand?" Kendall asked.

Mollie shook her head once again. "It was supposed to be a suicide, right?" Kendall nodded. "An overdose of tablets."

Once again Kendall nodded. "So?"

Mollie looked at him. "So what?" she replied.

Kendall sighed. "What don't you understand?" he said. "Are you going to tell me or not? I'm getting old standing here waiting." Mollie looked at him and grinned. "All right, all right," Kendall continued. "I'm getting older, is that better? Now what is it that you don't understand?"

"If it was murder," she said slowly, thinking it out as she went along. "How is it possible to force someone to swallow a handful of tablets? I mean you would resist, right?"

Kendall nodded. "That's a very good question," he replied. "One that stumped me for some while." He nodded. "Not only is it difficult to force tablets down somebody's throat, I think it would actually be absolutely impossible, especially if the person put up a struggle, You would need two or three people to hold them down and then someone else to put the tablets into the mouth." He shook his head. "Even then you still couldn't be certain that they would actually swallow them. No, I have to say that I don't believe that it's possible."

"So how was it done then?" Mollie asked.

"You remember I visited the hotel room shortly after Andrews had died."

Mollie nodded. "The Inspector wasn't pleased was he?"

Kendall sighed. "No, he wasn't," he replied. "Anyway, I told you about that smell that I couldn't recognise." Mollie nodded once again. "I thought that it was menthol, or maybe peppermint. Maria the maid thought that it was some kind of cleansing fluid. Well it was actually Chloroform. It had obviously been used to render Andrews unconscious." Mollie nodded, still not fully understanding. "Then I saw the doctor's report. It mentioned a small red spot on the inside of his right arm, just at the elbow joint. The classic mark of a hypodermic. Once I realised that, the rest was easy. The tablets had not been swallowed at all. They had merely been crushed, mixed with a liquid of some kind, probably saline, and injected straight into his blood stream whilst he was unconscious."

"What about the empty bottle at the side of the bed?" Mollie asked.

"The empty bottle was exactly that, an empty bottle," Kendall replied. "It had been left standing on the bedside cabinet just to give the impression that Andrews had taken them. But of course he hadn't."

"So it was murder, then," said Mollie as she nodded her head. "How were you so sure that it wasn't suicide in the first place?"

Kendall shrugged his shoulders. "There were a number of things I suppose," he replied. "Firstly, taking an overdose of tablets is hardly an efficient way of committing suicide. I mean how many should you take? Some people might need more than others. How would you know how many you required? How long will it take? Minutes, hours, days perhaps." He shook his head. "Not very efficient, I would say, and with no absolute guarantee of success. Secondly, it was said that he had taken an overdose of prescribed tablets, remember?"

Mollie nodded. "That's right," she said. "They were supposed to be tablets that had been prescribed for him by his doctor."

"That's right," said Kendall. "But we know, because he actually told us, that he hadn't been taking any tablets for at least three or four months. And certainly he had not been taking Syanthol."

"So what about that bottle of tablets, where did that come from?" Mollie asked.

"Another good question," replied Kendall. "Where did they come from? One thing we know, and that is they weren't prescribed by Andrews' doctor."

"That's right," said Mollie. "Devaney told us that."

"Correct," said Kendall. "So if Andrews never had them, someone else must have brought them over."

"Oliver Jones," suggested Mollie.

"Possibly," said Kendall. "Oliver Jones was certainly on the plane as well. So it could have been him."

"So the tablets were brought over to give the impression that Andrews had them with him all the time," said Mollie. "Someone just placed the empty bottle on to the table next to the bed, and that was that."

Kendall nodded. "That's the way it looks to me," he said. "But the someone, whoever it was, slipped up."

"Slipped up?" Mollie repeated. "How?"

Kendall smiled. "The fingerprints, remember?"

Mollie sighed and nodded her head. "I remember the fingerprints," she said. "But I didn't really understand the point."

Kendall smiled. "It's really quite simple," he said. "Somebody went to great lengths to make sure that Andrews' fingerprints were on the jar, but they completely forgot all about the cap."

Mollie was still puzzled. "The cap," she repeated. "What about it?"

"According to Whittaker, there were no prints on the cap," Kendall explained. "And yet Andrews apparently emptied the bottle of tablets, swallowed them, then he replaced the cap, and placed the bottle carefully back on to the bedside cabinet."

"That's right," said Mollie.

"Wrong," said Kendall. "Firstly if you had just taken an overdose of

240

tablets I don't really think you would be too concerned about replacing the bottle cap, would you?"

Mollie thought for a moment and then simply nodded her head in agreement.

"And, anyway, if Andrews had done that why were there no prints on the cap?" Kendall asked.

Mollie had to agree that was a good point and one that she could not answer.

"The only fingerprints were Andrews'," Kendall continued. "There were no other prints. That doesn't seem natural to me. What about the pharmacist who prepared the prescription, where are his, or her prints? What about the maid who would almost certainly have moved them has she tidied the room?"

Mollie had to admit that she could not answer any of the points.

Kendall shook his head. "No, those tablets only arrived at the hotel on the day that Andrews died," he said. "They had been brought into the room by the murderer. Not in the jar, though." Kendall shook his head. "The bottle was empty. It always had been. The tablets had already been crushed up and placed inside the hypodermic syringe." He paused for a moment and slowly shook his head. "The bottle, and the cap, had been wiped clear of prints. They then placed Andrews hands onto the bottle so that his prints would show. But only on the bottle, they completely forgot about the cap."

Mollie nodded and smiled.

"And what about those tablets anyway?" Kendall continued. "Those Syanthol? Who actually knew about them?"

"What do you mean?" asked Mollie.

"Andrews told us that he used to take Syanthol, right?" Mollie nodded. "Who else knew that Andrews took them?" Mollie shook her head. "Paul Sharp didn't know," Kendall continued. "And he was Andrews' friend. Even Oliver Jones never knew." He paused for a moment. "The only person who knew was Collier himself," Kendall continued. "He had actually recommended them to Andrews."

"That's right, he did," said Mollie.

"But what he didn't know was that Andrews had stopped taking them months ago," said Kendall. "Oh no, it was obvious to me that it wasn't suicide."

"And yet the Inspector was so sure," said Mollie.

Kendall started to laugh. "He certainly was hard to convince, that's for sure," he said.

"Well, it's all over now," said Mollie. "And you were right."

Kendall nodded. "Yes, it's all over now," he replied. "All over." He shrugged and looked over at the clock. "Look at the time," he announced. "It's later than I thought. We have a little over an hour and a half before we are due to see Whittaker."

Mollie looked at the clock and nodded. "You're right. I'd better get changed, and quickly," she said. "You know how slow I am."

Yes, Kendall knew all right. He said nothing but merely raised an eyebrow. He watched her as she left the room. He then went over to the radio and switched it on.

"... and now for business news," said the newsreader. "Rockford Metals have announced their trading figures for the last quarter. They show a continued fall in pre-tax profits, which are down by a further six percent on the previous quarter. On the strength of the announcements, share prices, which had previously hit an all time low, continued to fall, finishing the day fourteen percent lower."

Kendall heaved a sigh. He looked over towards the brief case lying on the bed. Inside was a share certificate for two hundred shares in Rockford metals. *Why had he ever listened to Collier?* He switched off the radio. *The price was bound to go back up*, he thought. *Sooner or later, wasn't it? It had to.*

* * *

"Ah, Mr Kendall," said a voice. "Good to see you again, sir, and you, Miss."

"It's good to see you, Sergeant," replied Kendall. He looked at the door. "Is he in?" he asked.

The Sergeant nodded. "Go right in, sir," he said. "He's expecting you."

Kendall walked to the door and knocked. He then opened the door and walked in.

"Ah, Kendall," Whittaker called over as he saw Kendall at the doorway. "And Miss Adams, do come in and sit down." He waited for Kendall and Mollie to take a seat. "This is Roger Andrews," he continued, pointing to a young man to his left. "Bob's brother. He arrived yesterday evening."

Kendall looked surprised as he took hold of the hand being held out. "No, Mr Kendall," the visitor said smiling. "We weren't twins, although we were remarkably alike."

"You can certainly say that again," Kendall replied.

"I am actually two years younger," the visitor continued. He paused for a moment. "Strong genes, I suppose." He paused once again and took a bite of cake. "This is really very good," he said looking at the Inspector. "What did you say it was?"

"Dundee cake," Kendall replied, without looking up.

"Oh I am sorry, Kendall," said the Inspector. "Where are my manners? Would you like some tea and some cake?" He did not wait for an answer. "And I'm sure that you wouldn't say no, Miss Adams."

He poured out two cups of tea and cut two slices of the cake. "Here you are," he said as he placed them in front of his guests. There was a long silence. "Mr Andrews would like to thank you for everything, Mr Kendall, as indeed I do," the Inspector continued. "So you were right all along. I just didn't see it." The Inspector shook his head. "I must be getting old or something."

Kendall smiled and shook his head. "No, it's nothing like that, Inspector," he said. "I'm constantly missing things, or forgetting, all the time. I go upstairs, and when I get there, I can't remember why I went there." He started to smiled. "Then I go back down the stairs and then suddenly remember why I went in the first place."

Roger Andrews smiled and nodded. "I'm like that," he said. "I put things away and then can't remember where I put them."

Kendall nodded. "You know, I make notes and then I still can't think why."

"But you persevered, Kendall," said Whittaker. "You knew that you were right and you just carried on."

Mollie nodded. "He's always the same, Inspector," she said. "When he gets something, some idea, firm in his mind, he just won't let go." She looked at Kendall and smiled. "He just goes on and on until he either proves he was right, or he is convinced that he was wrong."

The Inspector nodded. "Like a dog with a bone," he said. "That's what they say. Just won't let it go."

Kendall smiled, although he wasn't really sure that he wanted to be compared with a dog.

"You were a bit like that, Kendall," the Inspector continued. "I warned you off so many times, but you just kept on, over and over."

Kendall smiled. "What would you have done if I had continued being a nuisance?" he asked.

The Inspector shook his head. "I don't really know," he replied. "I suppose I kept hoping that things would be all right and that your holiday would be over, and that would be the end of it."

Kendall nodded. "So you wouldn't have had me locked up or deported," he said. "Or locked in the Tower?"

The Inspector started to smile. "Oh no, nothing like that," he said. "We haven't locked anyone in the Tower for a few hundred years now." He shook his head. "Besides I had started to have second thoughts about you anyway. Perhaps there was something in what you were saying after all."

Kendall looked puzzled. "Oh, when was that?" he asked.

"After you told me about Doctor Lennox and what he had said about the amount of tablets taken," the Inspector replied. "It slowly became clear that Andrews had not been taking the tablets after all."

243

"So what was it that aroused your suspicions anyway, Mr Kendall?" asked Andrews.

Kendall paused for a few moments and sighed. "There were many things, I suppose. But what really got me thinking was the fingerprints."

Andrews looked puzzled. "The fingerprints," he repeated.

"That's right," said Kendall. "You see there were no prints on the bottle cap. There were prints on the bottle, your brother's, but none on the cap. How would he have opened the bottle without leaving prints. You see?"

Andrews nodded but Whittaker shook his head. "Well now, Kendall," he said. "I actually meant to speak to you about that."

Kendall looked puzzled. "Go on," he said.

The Inspector nodded. "Well, I had a long conversation with our fingerprint expert," he continued. "He tells me that due to the nature of the cap, the very rough serrated edge, it's quite possible that there would be no prints. They simply would not register, you see." There was a pause. "We actually tried it on a number of bottle caps, including that bottle. Sure enough there were no prints."

Kendall nodded and smiled. "Is that right?" he said, as he shook his head. "You live and learn, don't you?" He shook his head once again. "I came to the same conclusion a few days ago."

The Inspector smiled and nodded. "Well, I suppose that's the end of that particular piece of evidence, then," he said.

Kendall shook his head. "Not at all," he said. "I am still absolutely convinced that Andrews never actually touched that bottle."

"I agree with you, Kendall," said the Inspector. "But we can't prove it, not now."

"The prints on the bottle were definitely Bob's", said Roger Andrews. "There's no disputing that."

"That's right. They were Bob's fingerprints," said Kendall. "They were actually prints of his right hand, correct?"

Whittaker nodded. "That's correct."

Kendall nodded "So Andrews held the bottle in his right hand. So he must have used his left hand to unscrew the cap."

"Obviously," said the Inspector. "So what's your point?"

"Right," said Kendall. "Now I don't know about you, but opening a bottle with a, what did you call it, Inspector, a child-proof cap?"

The Inspector nodded once again.

"Private Detective-proof as well, I think you said," said Mollie as she looked at Kendall.

The Inspector started to smile. "That's right," he said. "I did say that."

"So you did, Inspector. So you did," Kendall replied. "Difficult enough, then," he said. "I think it would have been almost impossible for Andrews using his left hand."

The Inspector looked puzzled.

"Andrews was actually right-handed, you see," Kendall explained..

The Inspector started to tap his fingers together. "So he was right-handed," he replied. "He could have opened the cap using his left hand. Unusual, I grant you, but perfectly possible."

Kendall shook his head. "I'm not so sure," he replied. "I would imagine that a cap like that would be quite difficult to open. You need to press the cap down and turn it at the same time. You would need quite a bit of control, I would say." There was a pause. "Now, I'm right-handed. That means I have more control in my right hand. Now if I wanted to open that bottle, I would actually hold the bottle with my left hand. Not my right. I would open the cap with my right hand. You see."

Roger Andrews nodded. "That makes sense to me," he replied. "So what actually put you onto Collier?"

Kendall thought for a moment and then smiled. "It was the asthma," he said, nodding his head.

Whittaker looked puzzled. "The asthma," he repeated.

Kendall nodded. "It was at our very first meeting," he started to explain. "I asked him about it. Andrews had told me that Collier suffered from it, you see."

Whittaker shook his head. *He didn't see, not at all.*

"Anyway, when I questioned him about it, Collier said that he didn't suffer from asthma and that I must have been mistaken," Kendall continued. "I knew then, at that moment."

Whittaker shook his head. "I'm sorry, but I don't follow any of this."

Kendall smiled and nodded. "Andrews had told me that Collier suffered from asthma, just like he did."

"Understood," said Whittaker. "So far at least."

"Andrews also told me that Collier had been using a certain tablet to treat the problem and that he had recommended that same tablet to Andrews," Kendall continued. "The tablet was Syanthol."

Whittaker nodded as he began to grasp the significance of what Kendall was saying.

"Collier knew that Andrews was taking Syanthol, or at least he believed that he was," said Kendall. "It had actually been his idea all along. As far as I can tell, Collier was the only one who knew, apart from close family that is." He paused for a moment. "Collier arranged for Oliver Jones to bring a bottle over from the States. It was a simple matter to change the label to show Andrews' name on the label."

The Inspector nodded. "They were actually brought over by a couple of charmers by the name of Doyle and Randall," he said.

Now it was Kendall who looked puzzled. "They worked for Jones," the Inspector explained. "We picked them up at a cheap hotel in the Bayswater Road last night."

Roger Andrews shook his head. "Syanthol," he said slowly. "My brother hadn't taken those tablets for a very long time."

"I know, "Kendall said. "He told me that he hadn't taken any tablets for at least three or four months. I got my friend Devaney, of the Miami Police, to run a check for me. He found out who Andrews' doctor was." He paused for a moment. "Doctor James Chamberlain. Oddly enough he is located just a few blocks from my office, on Sunset. Small world." He paused once again. "He confirmed that totally against his professional advice, Bob had positively refused to take them for at least three or four months."

Roger Andrews smiled and nodded. "Bob wasn't one for taking tablets, anyway," he said. "He said that the side-effects were worse than the complaint."

Mollie smiled and nodded. "I absolutely agree," she said.

"Mollie is into alternative medicines," Kendall explained.

Roger nodded. "Bob was leaning in that direction," he said. "He reckoned that Collier had recommended then deliberately, as some sort of bad joke." He shook his head. "Some joke. Poor old Bob."

"You know you could be right," Kendall said. "Collier did recommend them deliberately. It was all part of his plan." Kendall looked at Roger.

Roger Andrews nodded. "So it was all Collier's idea?" he said.

"That's right," said Kendall. "I think he had actually planned the whole thing some months ago. Of course Collier didn't know that Andrews had stopped taking the tablets. He had no way of knowing. As far as he was concerned, Andrews was still taking them as he had suggested." He paused for a moment and heaved a sigh. "His plan was working perfectly, or so he thought."

Roger Andrews nodded. "I can understand that but I can't see that would be enough to arouse suspicion," he said. "Recommending some tablets is hardly proof."

Kendall looked at Andrews. "Maybe not," he replied. "But there were a number of things." He paused. "For example, let's consider the alleged suicide."

"What about it?" asked the Inspector.

Kendall nodded. "You know Collier never ever expressed any doubts at all that Andrews had killed himself," he replied. "Oh, he expressed some mild surprise. Disbelief even, but only after I pressed him on the matter." Kendall shook his head. "But it was just an act," he continued. "There were no strong protestations, no emphatic denials. You know what I mean." He paused and shook his head. "There was no question in his mind." He looked at Roger Andrews. "He was so quick to accept your brother's guilt. Apparently the evidence was so overwhelming. There was no doubt at all that Andrews had indeed committed suicide." He shook his head once again. "I thought that was strange to say the least."

The Inspector started to frown. "Strange, in what way?" he asked.

"Collier had known Andrews for a long time. They had been friends for many years," Kendall replied. "And yet Collier never said that it was out of character. Stealing money from the company like that. He never expressed any surprise or shock. He never had any doubts. Nothing. In fact he said that he had suspected it for some time," he said. "Why he barely showed any emotion at all. Andrews had killed himself. plain and simple. There was no hint of sympathy. Nothing. It was almost as though he had expected it." He looked at the Inspector and slowly nodded his head. "Hardly the actions of a friend, would you say? I mean, you always think the best of your friends, don't you, no matter what. You need to have more than normal evidence to prove it, and even then you still refuse to believe the worst. Of course sometimes you'll be disappointed and your loyalty is misplaced. Nonetheless you generally stand by your friends until the end. Not so with Collier. He was ready to accept Bob's guilt from the very first. And then, of course, there was the cover up."

"Cover up?" said Roger Andrews.

Kendall nodded. "Collier said that the evidence was not to be made public. It was to be locked away in the company archives and never mentioned. The whole thing was to be quietly forgotten."

"Well at least that shows some regard for a friend," suggested Mollie.

Kendall looked at her and grinned. "There was no evidence," he said. "At least there was no evidence to implicate Andrews. Collier's idea was to simply eliminate any possibility of further investigation that might have led to his exposure."

Roger Andrews shook his head. "One thing that puzzles me," he said.

"Go on," said Kendall.

"I was just wondering why, in the circumstances, Collier agreed to speak with you like that," Andrews said. "I mean, didn't he think it was perhaps risky?"

Kendall shook his head. "Not at all," he replied. "Collier never took risks. Everything he ever did was thought about long and hard. Nothing was left to chance." He shook his head once again. "No, Collier had no choice, he had to speak to me. It was imperative. He knew that I had spoken with Andrews on a number of occasions, once on the plane, and again at his hotel. He needed to know exactly what Andrews had told me. Then all he had to do was discredit him. Make me believe that Andrews had lied."

Whittaker nodded. "A clever man."

"A very clever man," said Kendall. "A man who let his power take over and turn into greed."

247

"One thing, though," said Mollie. "How did Collier know that Mr Andrews was coming over to England anyway?"

Kendall nodded. "That's a very good question," he replied. "Maybe our friends Doyle or Randall can answer that, but I suspect that Bob was being followed. Of course he may have mentioned his plans to Oliver Jones without realising the possible consequences."

"That sounds reasonable to me," the Inspector said.

"What about Paul Sharp?" Mollie asked. "Why was he murdered?"

"To keep him quiet," suggested Roger Andrews.

Mollie shook her head. She was still puzzled. "But we had a long conversation with Paul," she said. "He had told us about the money and his suspicions, and all sorts of things. It would be a little late to kill him after that, wouldn't it?"

Kendall shook his head. "Not necessarily," he said. "Telling us is one thing but giving evidence in a court of law is something else. Collier could not risk Sharpe talking in court. No, he had to be killed."

Mollie nodded. *That made sense*, she thought. "So what about the Eastern European man?" she asked.

The Inspector looked at her and frowned. "What Eastern European?" he asked.

"The one who telephoned the hotel that afternoon," she explained. "He spoke to Andrews."

Kendall shook his head. "There was no Eastern European," he said. "That production was all about making sure that the receptionist remembered the call. It was just a ruse to make us think that Andrews was still alive at that particular time. And it worked. The receptionist remembered it exactly. She had actually made a timed note about it." He shook his head. "I think that you will find that the call came from one of Oliver Jones' associates, our friend Doyle, or Randall."

"But he actually spoke to Mr Andrews," said Mollie.

Kendall shook his head. "No, he didn't. Sadly Bob was already dead by then," he replied. "He actually spoke to Oliver Jones who was still in the room."

Whittakler nodded. "Well, Kendall, I suppose I have to thank you," he said. He smiled. "I hate to admit it but you were a big help."

"Praise indeed coming from you, Inspector," Kendall replied. Mollie kicked him hard in the shin.

There was a knock on the office door. A few moments later the door opened and the Sergeant entered the room. "Sorry to disturb you, sir," he said. "We've just heard some news about those two Americans."

"What about them, Sergeant?" asked the Inspector.

"They have just been picked up at Harwich Docks," the Sergeant replied. "They were boarding a ship bound for Amsterdam."

Whittaker nodded and looked at Kendall. "That's excellent," he said.

"What about the jewels?"

The Sergeant smiled. "They had them with them, sir."

"Good news, Sergeant," said Whittaker, as he turned to face Kendall. "Your friend in Miami will be pleased."

Kendall smiled and nodded. *He will indeed*, he thought. *Very pleased*.

"So, Mr Kendall, your holiday is almost over," said Roger Andrews.

"That's right," said Kendall.

"So what's the plan now?" Whittaker asked.

Kendall thought for a moment. "Well, we have a few days left," he said. "We haven't seen Downing Street yet, or the Houses of Parliament, or the ...."

"We still have plenty of shopping to do," Mollie interrupted.

Kendall nodded and smiled. "She's right, you know."

Whittaker nodded and smiled. "So, Kendall, we'll see you and Miss Adams in a few months, then."

Kendall nodded. "For the trial, you mean?"

Whittaker nodded. "That's right," he said. "We'll let you know when it is." He turned towards Mollie. "Miss Adams," he said. "It was a real pleasure meeting you. You have a good time now, and I look forward to seeing you again."

Mollie stepped forward and planted a gentle kiss on his cheek. Blushing, he then turned to face Kendall. "Kendall, I have to thank you for your help in this matter," he continued. "You'll be glad to hear that I now have a totally different opinion of private detectives."

Kendall smiled. "For the better, I hope."

Whittaker smiled and nodded once again. "For the better," he agreed. He held out his hand. "I have to go to a wretched meeting now, so it's time to say farewell."

Kendall nodded. "See you in a few months, then, Inspector," he said. He and Mollie stood up and started towards the door. He paused for a moment. "What was the name of that cake again, Inspector?" he asked.

Whittaker looked puzzled for a moment, then he started to laugh. "Dundee," he replied. "Dundee Cake."

Kendall nodded. "Dundee," he repeated. He raised a hand and waved, turned and left the room, Mollie a step behind him.

* * *

As they emerged from the main entrance, Kendall suddenly stopped and looked back at the building. "We really must have a photograph taken here," he announced. "It's right and proper. For the record, you know. And, besides, Devaney will just love it."

Mollie, who was standing a short distance away, looked at Kendall for a few moments. "But I thought you said that you didn't ..."

Kendall nodded. "Yes, that's right, I did," he agreed. "But that was then, this is now. It's not such a bad place after all."

Mollie gave a sigh. "Here we go again," she murmured.

Kendall looked at her. "I'm sorry, did you say something?" he asked.

She smiled and slowly walked towards him. "I said why not. We've had photographs taken everywhere else. So why not here."

Kendall nodded. "Over there would be good," he said pointing to the side where the New Scotland Yard sign slowly turned around. "Pity we couldn't get Whittaker as well," Kendall muttered. "Should I give him a call to come down?"

Mollie shook her head.

"You don't think so?" said Kendall.

She shook her head once again. "He's far too busy," she said. "Besides, wasn't he going to some meeting or other?"

Kendall nodded in agreement. "Probably not a good idea after all, never mind" he said. He looked over at Mollie. "That's it. A little to the ..."

"Would you like a photograph of the two of you," a voice called out from behind.

Kendall turned . A young man stood there pointing. "Would you like a photograph of the two of you," he repeated.

Kendall looked at Mollie. "That'll be nice," Mollie replied. "That's very good of you."

Kendall nodded and looked at Mollie. "Do you realise in this entire holiday this will be only the second photograph of the two of us together."

Mollie nodded. *Yes, it would*, she murmured as she thought of what seemed like hundreds that had been taken. "Is that right?" she said. "Wow."

"You remember the other one, don't you?" Kendall asked. "At the Guildhall, if I remember correctly."

How can I possibly forget it, Mollie murmured.

"Did you say something?" Kendall asked.

"I only said how could I possibly forget it."

Kendall nodded. "Oh right." He paused for a moment. "Some people are very kind. It kind of renews your faith in human nature. It's good to know that it's not all bad." He turned towards the young man and handed him the camera. "That's the viewfinder," he said. "You press that button." He paused and smiled. "That one there." He pointed.

The young man nodded. "That's fine, no problem. Now stand over there," he said. Kendall moved over to where Mollie was standing. "Closer, go on. Closer. Put your arm around her. That's better. Now smile." There was a pause. "Hold it. Hold it."

Suddenly the man turned around and ran down the street as fast as he could. Within a few seconds he had disappeared completely, together with Kendall's camera.

Kendall shook his head. "How do you like that?" he said to no one in particular.

Mollie shook her head. "You just can't trust anyone these days," she said, trying hard not to laugh. "Right in front of a police station as well." She looked at Kendall. "We'll have to go shopping now, I'm afraid."

"We will?" replied Kendall puzzled.

"Yes, we will," said Mollie. "After all, you will want to buy another camera, I expect."

OTHER BOOKS BY THE SAME AUTHOR

THE MARINSKI AFFAIR

ISBN-10: 1616670150

The Marinski Affair begins as a dull, mundane case involving a missing husband. Okay, so he is a rich missing husband but he is, nonetheless, still only a missing husband.

However, the case soon develops into one involving robbery, kidnapping, blackmail and murder.

But has there really been a kidnapping? And exactly who is blackmailing whom? Who carried out the robbery? Who committed the murders? And what connection is there with a jewel theft that occurred four years previously? All is not as it seems.

Tom Kendall, private detective, haa the task of solving the mystery. He is usually pretty good at solving puzzles but this one is different somehow. It isn't that he doesn't have any of the pieces. Oh no, he isn't short of clues. It is just that none of the pieces seem to fit together.

EPIDEMIC

ISBN-10: 161667170X

Tom Kendall, a down to earth private detective, is asked to investigate the death of a young newspaper reporter.

The evidence shows quite clearly that it was an accident, a simple, dreadful accident. That is the finding of the coroner and the local police. Furthermore, there were two witnesses. They saw the whole thing.

But was it an accident or was it something more sinister?

Against a backdrop of a viral epidemic slowly spreading from Central America, a simple case soon places Kendall up against one of the largest drug companies in the country.

THE COLLECTORS
by Ron A Sewell

ASIN: B007HEVSDK

Disgraced British soldier and disenchanted mercenary, Petros Kyriades, is one half of an elite pair of soldiers-for-hire known as 'The Collectors'. William ('Bear') Morris, ex-SAS sergeant, is the other half. Their motto is, "If it's there we will find it, and for the right price recover it.'

Accountant Bernie Cohen cannot recall the first ten years of his life. But with the assistance of a psychiatrist, he exposes an undesirable truth. An abandoned house close to Chernobyl holds the mystery of his past, and Bernie hires The Collectors to retrieve something that should have remained hidden.

The Collectors always play the game by their rules – that is until someone or something forces them to rewrite them.

REPRISAL
by Alfie Robins

ASIN: B006C75RJY

Some of the most vibrant and varied crime writing around anywhere is centred on the evocative industrial fishing port of Hull, with its shadowy wind-swept streets, its hard-bitten attitudes, its drugs, its gangsters and yet its underlying humanity that clings like untended weeds amid the cracks of the endemic poverty and the violence.

And Alfie Robins' 'Reprisal' is an outstanding example of the genre, a classic police procedural where you can hear the streets, smell the weather, savour the taciturn banter, and feel the four inch nail being driven into the heads of victims by a vengeful, meticulous and psychotic serial killer.

MRS JONES
by B A Morton

ASIN: B006OEVRBM

A British girl with a secret.
A New York cop with a past.
And a mob that wants revenge.

In the slickest, sneakiest twistiest-turniest hard-boiled crime noir novel to come out in a long time, ruggedly pragmatic but honest cop Detective Tommy Connell picks up an English girl, Mrs Jones, who claims to be the witness to a murder, and promptly falls in love with her.

Well, Mrs Jones, whoever she is, must be very attractive because an awful lot of people seem to want to get their hands on her if they can prise her from Connell's determined grasp, including some prominent representatives of organised crime and the Feds.

Detective Connell definitely has his work cut out here if he wants to end up with the body of Mrs Jones, dead or alive, that's for sure.

All-in-all it's probably safe to say he hasn't a clue what is going on. It is probably equally safe to guess that Mrs Jones does.

Not that 'safe' is quite the right word to use here or, there again, maybe it is.